HELL'S HEART

HELL'S HEART

ALEXIS HALL

TOR PUBLISHING GROUP
NEW YORK

This is a work of fiction. All of the names, characters, organizations, places, and events portrayed in this work are either products of the author's imagination or used fictitiously.

HELL'S HEART

Copyright © 2026 by Alexis Hall

All rights reserved.

A Tor Book
Published by Tom Doherty Associates / Tor Publishing Group
120 Broadway
New York, NY 10271

www.torpublishinggroup.com

Tor® is a registered trademark of Macmillan Publishing Group, LLC.

EU Representative: Macmillan Publishers Ireland Ltd, 1st Floor, The Liffey Trust Centre, 117–126 Sheriff Street Upper, Dublin 1, D01 YC43

The Library of Congress Cataloging-in-Publication Data is available upon request.

ISBN 978-1-250-39495-8 (hardcover)
ISBN 978-1-250-39496-5 (ebook)

The publisher of this book does not authorize the use or reproduction of any part of this book in any manner for the purpose of training artificial intelligence technologies or systems. The publisher of this book expressly reserves this book from the Text and Data Mining exception in accordance with Article 4(3) of the European Union Digital Single Market Directive 2019/790.

Our books may be purchased in bulk for specialty retail/wholesale, literacy, corporate/premium, educational, and subscription box use. Please contact MacmillanSpecialMarkets@macmillan.com.

First Edition: 2026

Printed in the United States of America

10 9 8 7 6 5 4 3 2 1

In token of my admiration for his genius, this book is inscribed to Nathaniel Hawthorne

ETYMOLOGY

I'm not a linguist. I've had enough of the Catechism of Prosperity to know that the word *Leviathan* comes from the Testament so that makes its origins—what? Proto-Exodite?

Something to do with the hundred different languages people spoke in the dark days of Old Earth?

Behemoth is the same. Not *Kraken*, though. Least I don't think so.

EXTRACTS

Collected by a sub-subroutine of a bored neural network.

"And the Father created Great Whales."
—The Testament, first installment

"Ahab, can't you see? The whale is a metaphor!"
—*Crazy Ex-Girlfriend*, S1 E15

"There go the ships; there is that Leviathan whom thou hast made to play therein."
—The Testament, additional materials

"By art is created that great LEVIATHAN called a COMMONWEALTH, or State—(in Latin, CIVITAS), which is but an artificial man."
—Old Earth text on statecraft, author unknown

"Life is an act of consumption, Jupiter. To live is to consume. Now the human beings on your planet are merely a resource waiting to be converted into capital. And this entire enterprise

is just a small part in a vast and beautiful machine defined by evolution, designed to a single purpose: to create profit."
—Balem Abrasax, *Jupiter Ascending*

"Towards thee I roll, thou all-destroying but unconquering whale; to the last I grapple with thee; from hell's heart I stab at thee; for hate's sake I spit my last breath at thee. Sink all coffins and all hearses to one common pool! and since neither can be mine, let me then tow to pieces, while still chasing thee, though tied to thee, thou damned whale!"
—Last words of an Old Earth Leviathan hunter

"How would you describe your generation?"
"Born too late for tall ships, but too soon for star ships."
—*Dinosaur Comics*

HELL'S HEART

Chapter One

Cthonius Linea

Call me . . . call me whatever the fuck you like. Isha. Or Isobel. Io. Imogen. Iris. Ivy. If there's a point to all this—to any of this cacophonous bullshit in my head—it's that I don't think I've ever been sure what the *I* in *I Am* stands for. But it's the only word or name or pronoun that's always been mine. That nobody's tried to take from me. That's always felt right.

I've never been a grounded person. Or a rooted person. It's not that I haven't tried. There've been days when I thought I could settle. When I even thought I could belong somewhere. But then there's always other days when my whole life feels like a prison and my body feels like the jailer and something inside me wants to tear out through my chest or my throat and scream to the stars.

That's when I figure it's time to go voyaging.

It's a choice I make. The other choice would be to walk out of a fucking airlock. To let the Europan winds or the Venusian rains or the beautiful lethal sunlight of Mercury do what they will with me. Not that I've ever been able to afford a trip to Mercury or Venus. I'm not made of money.

Still, one way or another, when I get like that, I have to leave.

The last time I got the sky-lust I'd been on Europa three months and was flat broke. And since that meant I couldn't keep up repayments to the pharma-state of Aphrodite Terra, and *that* meant I was risking getting half my body repossessed, I needed a job, and ideally—for where-my-head-was-at reasons and dodging-the-flesh-bailiffs reasons—I wanted that job to be in the skies.

So I went hunting Leviathans.

Looking back, it was a mistake. I say looking back, but it wasn't even that long ago. Still—fuck me, does it feel like I was young then.

I should have booked on with a merchant ship, but the outer worlds were disaligned and the Europa–Rhea runs were cutting crew to compensate. Besides, I wanted to see something new. To catch a glimpse of the great Jovian beasts whose cerebrospinal fluid powered every ship, lamp, relativistic damper, and oxygen diffuser in the system.

The hunter-barques fly from three ports on the Jovian moons. The largest is Loki Patera, on the banks of the great Ionian magma-lake where the titanomachic and mining industries feed each other in an ever-widening sprawl of steel, sulfur, and spermaceti.

For those of you who aren't technically minded, *spermaceti* is the name we give that cerebrospinal fluid I was talking about, like, two paragraphs ago. You may never have heard of it; you almost certainly never think about it. Especially if you live on one of the core worlds, light-hours away from the monsters it comes from and the people who hunt them. In the business there really are people who call it *sperm* with a straight face. I'm not one of them. Then again I wasn't in the business very long.

In any case, there are two other big hunter-cities out there. Enki Catena, one of the few settlements that sit on the surface of Ganymede instead of luxuriating in its subsurface oceans, is the wealthiest, but real Leviathan hunters look down on it for the same reason the whole Commonwealth looks down on Ganymedians. They've been rich too long to know what's what but not long enough to have any class. No, for me there was only one place to go Leviathaning: Cthonius Linea, first and best and most broken.

I traveled from Harmonia Linea with a crew of ice miners looking to take their earnings offworld. I didn't fancy their chances. Cthonius was a vampire city; half the population was just passing through and the other half lived by sucking the first half dry.

"This time," one was saying as our shuttle rattled over rails that hadn't been repaired in a century, "it'll be different."

"You said that last time," replied another. Both men were old, their skin frost-burned from the mines and their lips cyanotic from years of not quite enough oxygen. "You never made it past Pilgrim's Row."

"This time it'll be different," the first repeated. "Can't do another three years."

In my long and fucky life, I've been many things. A trader, a teacher, a pilot, and a poet. But I've always stayed clear of mine work, ice-mine work especially. I can't stand feeling trapped, so I can't imagine much worse than a life in freezing, flooded tunnels. It's a job for the hardy and the desperate, and I've only ever been one of those things.

"What about you, girl?" the second miner asked me.

I'd not expected him to ask me anything, so I stalled. "What about what about me?"

"Where you headed? Io? Ganymede? Out-of-well?"

"Hunting," I told him. It was short, it was clear, and it was true.

Didn't stop them laughing.

I drew my coat tighter against the chill. "Something funny?"

"Fools and mad folks go to the hunt," a third miner said. The ice had taken his nose and three fingers from his left hand.

"Fools and mad folks go down the mines," I replied.

They laughed again. But with me this time. Which was warming in its own way. I appreciate that I might be coming across a bit of a misanthrope here, what with all the talk of walking out of airlocks and shitting on Ganymedians (*everybody* shits on Ganymedians), but I don't actually hate people. Most people. Most of the time. And maybe if we hadn't been packed like farmed eels in a tin box that would kill us all in seconds if its thermals failed I'd have been friendlier. Hell, maybe I'd have blown one of them just to feel something—sorry, that's the airlock voice again. Anyway, point is it was a short trip and I was in a weird mood and I'd already made up my mind to head out into the sky to try and kill the biggest thing I could possibly kill.

We've all been there, right?

I said goodbye to the miners as the shuttle docked and the antique hydraulics spat us out into the first of Cthonius Linea's 109 habitation domes. There's this ritual I do whenever I arrive in a new place. I stop and I breathe and I take in the scent of it. That's harder on Europa, of course; the atmosphere outside—what little there is of it—is at fifty and this near to the walls the air is so cold you can barely inhale it, much less smell it. But you can't jam this many people this close without there being some kind of savor on the breeze. Cthonius Linea, then, smells of travelers, of the nothing-scent of the ice, of the fried fish hawked by the street food vendors. Under that there's rust and ozone, the signs of a life-support system that's definitely seen better days and probably better decades.

Spermaceti built the city of Cthonius Linea. With Old Earth long out of resources and the transuranics available in the rest of the system cutting it less and less over the centuries, energy had become our number-one problem. That's "our" as in "humanity's." Because let's face it, we're all stuck in this mess together. Well, most of us. The people on the core worlds seem fine, actually, even though energy-crisis-wise they're the ones who need the most on account of it being really hard to maintain a garden full of orchids on a world where the temperatures outside cross seven hundred and it rains acid.

All part of the divine plan I suppose.

Where was I? In case you either skipped history in school or this book gets inexplicably popular thirty years after my death and you're reading it in a totally different cultural context, a few centuries ago we were, as a species, fucked. So the discovery of the Leviathans, right when we needed them most, must have felt like a miracle. Of course the Plutonian Church says it was exactly that. Proof of a benevolent Father who wishes to guide the Worthy to Prosperity. I think the Venusian Church says it's proof that a benevolent Father seeks always to safeguard life, for life is all that is holy. Other cults say different. Whoever's right, a rush of the faithful and the entrepreneurial came to the outer worlds. Merchant-pilgrims in solar ships pushed to the limits of their photoelectric sails.

I sometimes wish I'd been born back then. In the frontier years, before the sky was carved up and tamed. Back when people believed the future would be better than the past instead of worse. The Cthonius I saw when I finally arrived was a shadow of a ruin of what it used to be. In the launch towers of the docklands, water-ships outnumbered hunter-ships by twenty to one. Still, the streets thronged with travelers from across the system—corporates from the inner worlds, indolent Ganymedians, severe scholars from the Golden City on Pluto—and that was enough of a crowd to lose myself in. But I could imagine a time when all those thousands of people, to the last, would have been here for the hunt.

Except those days were gone. Had been since long, long before I got there.

CHAPTER TWO

The Coffin Inn

It was late by local time when I spilled out onto the streets of Cthonius Linea, so I wandered the docklands looking for somewhere to stay. In some ways, I wasn't choosy. Cold, tired, and hungry, I would have taken a blanket in the exhaust port of an ore frigate if the price had been right. And even the blanket would have been optional.

The price, though, wouldn't. Prices never are.

That was part of the reason I passed by the Harpoon. Its intentionally suggestive sign—a supple youth picked out in pink-and-purple neon riding a long, lusty shaft into the night—didn't especially bother me. I've stayed in similar places before and sometimes the blaring music and the promise of getting railed hard for a small extra fee is exactly what I need. But the fact that every part of the sign was still lit, that the people inside seemed happy and free and well-sheltered, suggested that it'd be more than I could afford. Hell, the fact that it had a *roof* suggested it'd be more than I could afford.

I skipped the Swordfish for similar reasons; the atmosphere was less orgiastic and more refined, but I was still wearing my worn environment suit and had exactly one change of clothes with me. Refinement was not something I was able to offer.

The trick would be to move down. Not physically down,

Europa is famously the smoothest body in the system, so there isn't really an up or down except where miners or fishers have cut into its ball-bearing surface. I needed to move socially down. To where the buildings were as old as the colony and the walls had been peeled back to the original titanium then repainted with whatever pigments a desperate local could forage or fabricate. To the kind of place where they don't tell you what organism your meat is coming from and you know you're better off not asking.

My feet worked on their own, taking me to the parts of the city that people with choices avoided. They didn't always work the way I wanted, mind you. Years in the Catechism of Prosperity meant they kept trying to guide me into churches, and on that day at least I wasn't in the mood for religion. Eventually, though, they brought me somewhere more promising.

It was called the Coffin Inn and I hoped that it might be exactly that—a place that would rent me a six-foot-by-two-foot shelf for the night, just stable enough to sleep lying down and just warm enough that I'd wake up with most of my fingers.

As it turned out, it wasn't that. It was something older and homier which, if I'd been in a better mood, I might almost have called "quaint." I made my way inside and found myself in a common room of the old kind, paneled in sheet metal and scattered with human flotsam. A screen on one wall flicked between pictures slightly too fast to make out any one individually. Between them, they made an impression that was almost hypnotic—an advertisement for a soda whose name I kept failing to read would flick into a digital portrait of a star-cutter in flight, then one of the old solar ships, then a fog-shrouded beast of unguessable proportions, then another advertisement, this time for a sleek H_2-burning groundcar that no customer of the Coffin could possibly afford.

I once asked a man I half knew why they did that, why the trade-states tried to sell things to people who would never be able to buy them.

"Aspiration" had been his only answer. And although I hadn't liked to admit it, I'd known what he meant. The trade-states didn't sell products, not really. They sold dreams. They sold hope. And at such *reasonable* prices.

Tearing my eyes away from the ever-cycling screen, I button-holed the landlord.

"No room," he told me at once. "'Less you're inclined to share."

Inclined was a strong word. But I was out of options and he knew it. "Depends who with."

He looked at me in a scrutinizing way that I saw a lot and imagined more. "There's a lady has half a bed spare. Harpooner, mind."

That was actually forty times better than I'd expected. In my experience *if you're inclined to share* means something on the spectrum from "you can sleep in the pit with my guard-crabs" to "I will definitely be wanting to fuck you."

"You setting out into the storms?" the proprietor continued conversationally.

I nodded.

"Then you'll need to get used to close quarters. Not a lot of space on a hunter-barque."

I nodded again. All star-craft were cramped in one way or another. It was a kind of cosmic joke, I think, that trapped in a metal box was the freest I ever felt. As long as it was the right kind of metal box. The kind that went up instead of down and where if you died it'd be amidst the stars, not deep in a freezing pit or buried under water-ice.

Once I'd agreed to share a bed with a complete stranger and paid up-front for the privilege, the landlord told me to take a seat and wait to be called through for supper. That I did, and as I sat I found my eyes being drawn back to the screen on the wall and its rotating images of monsters and merchandise. I would count the seconds before the first ship-picture gave way and the beast in the fog appeared again until I convinced my-self that I could predict its arrival down to the eyeblink.

I'd convinced myself wrong. Somehow it still surprised me every time. Or maybe that's just how it feels now, looking back.

We were called through to the dining hall in little clusters of three or four. The room was small and would almost have been homey if it hadn't been for the lack of underfloor insulation. On a frozen world heat leaves through the soles, and my boots weren't thick enough or powered enough to keep my feet from going numb. The food, though, was more than adequate; the polypous meats of Europa's native sea life grilled and served in a stew alongside dumplings made from some cheap hydroponic grain. It was warming, filling, and cholesterol-rich enough to fuel my endocrine synthesizers, which had been blinking a warning light on my arm for two days.

My companions were a mixed band: a tall Phobosi who I hoped wouldn't start trouble; an impractically dressed Ganymedian dandy whose burgundy morning suit looked wonderful in a dome but would offer no protection at all if a seal failed; a slim, pale woman wearing a trapezoid necklace of shining silver wire sat beside a smaller and if anything even paler man sporting the same iconography.

Something about them caught my eye, an odd mix of commonality and distance. They both wore the bracelets of shell casings that were common amongst Deimosi munitions workers, which was a job I'd done myself when I was much, much younger.

There was also the fact that they were sitting a little aloof from the company, and the part of me that liked to pick scabs and fuck strangers wanted to find out what the hell their deal was.

"Not wanting to be rude," I said, and I genuinely didn't. Although not wanting and not doing were different things. "But do you have some kind of problem with the rest of us?"

"We mean no disrespect," the woman replied, which put us even on disingenuous disclaimers. "Our faith teaches us to avoid the First Devoured where practical."

I should have left it there, but I had to ask. "And those would be . . ."

The man next to her—a man I'd soon come to know better, in some ways at least—gave me an apologetic smile. "Sorry," he said. "Sister Jermyn is a missionary so she's a bit . . . explicit."

Sister Jermyn turned her head just slightly in her companion's direction. "Mr. Marsh, condescending to unbelievers is all very well but your speech strays perilously close to secularism."

"I just meant," Marsh explained, "that since she doesn't know what the First Devoured *are*—"

The Phobosi nudged me. He was a large man with radiation burns up his arms and warsuit interface ports visible at his wrists. Not every Phobosi was a merc, but enough were that it was a safe assumption. "You won't get sense out of these fuckers," he said. "They're Wisdom."

"They're what?" There were literally thousands of tiny peculiar sects out there, I could think of at least half a dozen "Wisdom" cults from Deimos alone.

"Church of Starry Wisdom," he explained. "They think the whole universe was made by a giant space monster and that one day it'll come back and eat everybody except them."

Sister Jermyn raised an eyebrow, and I really tried not to find her attractive. I have this idea in my head that very religious people are good in bed on account of all the repression. It's never been true yet but I can't quite stop checking. "A common misconception. Our faith holds that the Devouring God will consume everything *including* us. But we will be last, and we take solace in that."

Marsh, if I was being honest, didn't look like he took very *much* solace in it.

"They also," the Phobosi added, now sounding actively contemptuous, "think that melanin is a curse from the ancient space monster, which means the whole order-of-getting-eaten thing depends on your skin tone."

"Thus we maintain the purity of our faith, and the purity of our blood," Sister Jermyn confirmed, as if that made total sense.

"In order that we may be the last devoured," Marsh concluded, like an amen. And I recognized a rote quality in his recitation, a quality I'd heard in my own voice so often. One I'd spent half my life hoping nobody else would spot.

"And you really think"—what can I say, I was still in that scab-picking, stranger-fucking mood—"that the fact your skin is a slightly lighter shade of brown than most people's"—I saw Sister Jermyn stiffen, and I'd later learn that Starry Wisdomers *hate* to be reminded that they aren't literally a different color from all other humans—"remotely matters to an all-devouring space god from beyond oblivion?"

To my surprise, Marsh looked genuinely hurt. "You know, it's not polite to mock other people's religions."

After that we moved from theology to safer subjects. And as we talked and ate, I became worryingly aware that Sister Jermyn was the only other woman present, which led to the troubling thought that she'd be the one I was sleeping with. And despite my continued belief that hate sex is the best sex, I really didn't want to share a room with a member of a phenotypically obsessed apocalypse cult if I could possibly avoid it. As subtly as I was able, I beckoned over the landlord. "She isn't the harpooner, is she?" I asked him.

He chuckled. "Lord, no, the harpooner is"—here he grinned wide—"quite a queer sort, if you catch my meaning."

His meaning could have been one of a thousand things. "Maybe throw it harder?"

Crouching down, he brought his lips to my ears and whispered two words: "Old Earth."

It wasn't what I'd expected. Though I'd traveled widely and met or fought or fucked people from all over the system—Proteans, Cereans, even Erisians—I'd never even seen a Terran. The Great Churches bicker constantly, but they all agree that after the Exodus there was nothing left on Earth but cannibals and criminals.

"Where is she now?" I asked.

The landlord shrugged. "Out."

I fixate sometimes. On ideas. On unknowns. On hopes or

goals. And whether he knew it or not, the landlord had given me something sharp to fixate on. Who was this Earther I'd agreed to spend the night with? What business was she out on? How much of what the preachers had taught me about Terran ways was true, and how much did it matter?

As the hours slipped by, as the other guests came and went and I saw all the things my new bunkmate wasn't—the honest local fisherfolk with their eyelashes still frosted, the tourists from the inner worlds who wouldn't last the week—the more pressing those questions became.

I fought my fatigue as long as I could, but by midnight I was done. I'd crossed half the body that day and my mind was beginning to skip like interwell streaming. So I told the landlord that I was chucking it in.

The room in the Coffin was slightly better than its name suggested, a whole ten feet by five feet with a ceiling high enough that I could just about stand. Between the travel and the time, I was too exhausted to worry about an angry Earther coming back and slitting my throat in the night. I took the opportunity to strip off the environment suit I'd been wearing since Harmonia and then I collapsed into sheets that were cold, grimy, and still more comfortable than anything I'd felt in days.

I don't know how long I slept, or how well. I only know I woke up with a knife at my throat.

CHAPTER THREE

The Harpooner

The carbide sting of the blade woke me first. Then the weight of the other woman kneeling astride me. Then the light that shone from every inch of her skin, intricate skeins like maps or blueprints that glowed pale blue and irregular.

"Quis," she demanded. "Quis es."

I didn't know her language, but I knew context. Context, unfortunately, wasn't telling me how to keep the blood in my veins. "Friend," I tried. "Friend."

The electric glow from her markings faded slightly, and she drew her knife just a half inch away from my neck. "Cuius *friend* es?"

Carefully, I raised my hands. "I won't hurt you."

She didn't look like she believed me, but she looked like she understood me, which was all I could really hope for. Keeping her weight mostly on my ribs, she took the weapon far enough away that she could only kill me with it on purpose. Which was about as comforting as a stranger with a knife gets.

"If you let me call the landlord," I offered, "I am sure he can explain."

Landlord she got. Although from the expression on her face I didn't think she liked the man much.

Gingerly, I reached for the intercom and pressed to open the channel.

"What can I do you for?" asked the landlord from the other end with uncalled-for cheeriness.

"The Terran is here," I said quietly, "and she wants to kill me."

"I'm sure she doesn't."

It's probably a legacy of my upbringing that I hadn't expected an Earther to know how a communicator worked, but she spoke into the device as naturally as she spoke to me. *"You,"* she said to the landlord, "explicare mihi."

The line went dead a moment. Then the landlord's voice returned. "The thing is . . ."

I severely doubted this would end well. In fact, I was beginning to worry that I was fucked, and not in the fun way.

"No," the harpooner snapped into the communicator.

"I said it was a double room. I'll give you a discount."

Her markings were glowing again, paler this time. "Pedicabo ego vos et irrumabo."

"No need to be like that. Calm down. Think of it as extra warmth for the night. Gets mighty chilly here on 'Ropa."

The harpooner looked like she was about to stab something, hopefully something not me, but in the end restricted herself to giving a cry of frustrated rage and cutting off the channel.

While I didn't think the landlord had done the best job of smoothing things over, it *did* seem like he'd given us a mutual enemy. The harpooner moved off of me and sat on the edge of the bed, quietly steaming and glaring at me over her shoulder.

"Friend?" she asked.

I nodded.

"That man." Her mouth was set in a grim line. "Fur." Then when it became clear I had no idea what I meant she added, *"Thief."*

I nodded again.

For a moment we stared at each other, and I searched her face for answers. Aside from her markings, which were like nothing I'd ever seen before, she seemed not that different from the hundred other strangers I've met in places like this.

Admittedly, the fact that she was emitting light rather than reflecting it made details rather tricky to pick out, but I could tell that she was shaven-headed, that she had a strong jaw and high cheekbones. Her eyes, lit from above and below with those holographic tattoos, seemed impossibly large and dark and endless. I didn't think I was staring, but something about the way she held my gaze made my skin prickle, made me very conscious, all of a sudden, of the way my tongue felt inside my mouth. I gave up caring how other people saw me long ago, but there, in that moment, I felt so utterly *beheld* that it was almost unbearable.

I told her my name—the name I was using then—and she told me hers. I'm not going to share it with you. Some things are precious. But let's call her Q.

Shuffling to one side, I made room for her to lie next to me. Whatever the landlord might have said, it was not a double room by any real standard and there was no way we could share without getting well into each other's space.

I wasn't entirely complaining. The landlord had been right about the warmth, and I've always had a yearning for touch that nearly matched my yearning for sky. I curled into her arms and closed my eyes. For a woman who'd begun by pressing a knife to my throat, she held me surprisingly gently. But perhaps she thought I was surprisingly gentle for a woman who'd begun by stealing into her bed without asking. Or perhaps she thought I was trash. That was more likely.

When day came and the dome-lights started bleeding in through the windows she was still holding me. And even though she was a complete stranger, I let myself feel safe.

"It's morning," I told her. Because it seemed like I should.

She made a sleepy noise against my shoulder which suggested that, from her perspective, morning could get fucked.

"I need to look for a ship."

The mention of ships stirred her slightly, but only slightly. "*Ships*," she said. "Multae."

"The landlord said you were a harpooner," I tried.

Bleary and disinterested, she waved a hand in the direction of a wicked-looking coilgun. *"Yes,"* she said. *"Harpooner* sum."

There were no two ways about it, this was a massive stroke of luck. My plan for finding work had been to walk the docks until I saw a promising vessel, then see if I could find somebody in a position to offer me a job. In hindsight, it had been an *incredibly shit* plan. And now by chance I'd met a woman who'd already been on the hunt. Who seemed like she might be willing to help me. It was almost enough to make me believe in providence.

Carefully, I rolled over to face her. "Do you—would you look for a ship with me?"

Q's endless eyes met mine. And for a moment I saw something, imagined I saw *her* seeing something. Perhaps it was just the morning light, or the still needing to get out of my head, or the long, weird day I'd had yesterday. Whatever it was, I had an unexplained and powerful urge to kiss her. I resisted for a dozen different reasons. For a start, she'd woken me up with a knife. That's the sort of thing should put a girl off.

I mean, it didn't. But I tried to act like it had.

"We should get breakfast," I said instead. And a part of me regretted it.

We hovered in that space, me not kissing her and her not kissing me either, for moments that stretched out like blown glass, and then she turned away, swung out of bed into the foot or so of space that made up the rest of the room. She touched the biometric seal of her traveling bag and, from within, produced a small rectangular icon. It was black, jet black, and almost mirrored. As she moved her fingers over its surface, I saw symbols dancing across it, and the lines of her markings glowed in sympathy with them.

I had no idea what she was doing. Terrans, I was always told, have little in the way of technology. How, after all, could they develop it without the churches or the vast incorporated conglomerates of the trade-states to guide them? I decided, in the end, that it was a religious matter, and waited for her to finish.

"*Yes,*" she said as the surface of the icon returned to darkness.

"Yes what?"

"*I will sail with you.*"

CHAPTER FOUR

The Hunter's Story

Breakfast in the Coffin was better than I'd expected. It was too low-rent to serve offbody food, which meant it was all ice fish and algae, but they were well prepared and I've eaten a lot worse in my time. Q was diving in with enthusiasm, spearing slices of eel with the knife she'd nearly used to spear me.

The dining hall was filling with skyfarers. Some I recognized from the night before; others had drifted in since. The Starry Wisdomers were there, sitting even farther from the rest of us than they had previously, perhaps not wanting a repeat of the theological debate. Two workers from a Martian rust convoy—easily identifiable by the dust, which gets everywhere—had settled in opposite us and were telling lewd stories about their stopover on Vesta. One or two others I thought might be from the hunter-ships. They looked too worn for merchants, too lean for scavengers, and too lightly armed for pirates.

Curious about what I was getting myself into, I asked this last group if they had any stories. Voiders always do, and this lot turned out to be no exception. The man who was speaking now was, by his accent, Ionian. He was old—eighty if he was a day, even accounting for the hard life of a skyfarer—and as fortune or, if you prefer, the ineffable will of the Father would have it, he was later to be one of my shipmates. I never got to know him that well, and so many years have passed since that I only remember him as the Old Ionian.

A rotten thing, memory.

"Some thirty years ago," he was saying, "when I was just a lad"—okay, maybe he was a bit less than eighty, or maybe *a lad* was a very subjective term—"I shipped aboard a hunter-barque called the Essex, under Captain Pollard."

"Would that be the Essex that they made a very popular streaming show about relatively recently?" asked the Ganymedian, only a little bit superciliously.

"Might be," replied the Old Ionian. "But I wouldn't know. Still, you'll have the tale from me as true as it happened." He took a breath and launched into his story. "For six months we'd been skimming ammonia, playing in the upper atmosphere where the sprites and elveses dance."

At the time I assumed sprites and elveses were some whimsical cloudhunter's superstition, but I eventually learned differently. They're actually the technical terms for a kind of intense electromagnetic discharge you get in the atmosphere of gas giants. Consider this foreshadowing.

"Cautious captains," the Old Ionian went on, "or fresh ones, they like to stay shallow on account of it keeps you in lower gravity, which in turn spares the afterburners when you're leaving the well. But as Pollard was learning to his cost, the shallow skies aren't where you find the best or the richest Leviathans. No, to get those you have to go deep, and after six months—"

"You already said it was six months," the Ganymedian pointed out.

"After six months with nary a spout to be seen, by eye or by scan, the captain decided that we'd be best risking the plunge."

With a storyteller's instinct, he paused, letting us hang a moment as no doubt the Essex had hung before its pilots steered it from the ammonia-ice of the upper reaches to the hydrogen-sulfide depths.

"Down we went," quoth the Old Ionian. "And down and

down to where the winds are so strong they'll strip the flesh from your bones and the clouds are so dense you can chew on them if you take your helmet off. Well, chew on them for the forty seconds you'd live in that heat and that pressure and—"

"And with the wind so strong it'll strip your flesh from your bones," offered the Ganymedian, now openly mocking.

The Old Ionian fixed him with a cold stare. "Fie on ye, thou pamperloin. A fine waste of air-rations you'd be on a hunting voyage."

"Wouldn't go near one." The Ganymedian was giving intense wouldn't-be-caught-dead energy. "A nice safe merchant run for me."

A nice, safe merchant run seemed about the Ganymedian's speed, and probably it *was* the most sensible option (spoilers: given what happened to me and my shipmates it was *definitely* the most sensible option). But hearing him say it, in that moment, I felt such a bile of contempt rise up within me that, if I hadn't been such a giant fucking coward, I'd have called him a prick there and then.

"We had better luck in the deep sky," the Old Ionian went on, apparently deciding that it was better to just ignore the interruptions. "And we took plenty of sperm on that run. But one day, some sixteen hundred klicks out from resupply station kappa-two, we caught a spout the like of which none of us had seen, the like of which I've nary seen since."

The Ganymedian seemed about to say something, but he got cut off.

"A spout that lit up the array, so strong was its pulse, and when we got into visual, we saw an enormous Leviathan. Twice as long as our barque and pure white—"

"Hang on." Now it was the Phobosi interrupting. "Pure white? You're talking about the Möbius Beast."

The Old Ionian nodded. "That I am, friend. That I am."

"One"—the Phobosi held out a finger that I couldn't help noticing was missing a fingertip—"the white Leviathan is a myth, and two"—he held out a second, which was missing the tip and half its length; the pair together looked like they'd been cut through with a single stroke and probably had been—"even if it weren't, nobody ever said it was the beast that wrecked the Essex."

"Perhaps," pitched in the Ganymedian, "they should have hired you as a consultant on the adaptation."

"Tace," said Q to the Ganymedian and the Phobosi both. And while none of us spoke her language we got the sense that it meant *Shut up*.

The Old Ionian gave her a grateful nod. "Glad to see there's some young folk still have manners. But I'll not waste more of the story on this lot, though it's true as I'm sitting here."

At my side, Q stifled a laugh. "Habeoque senectuti magnam gratiam," she mused to nobody in particular, "quae mihi sermonis aviditatem auxit, potionis et cibi sustulit." Then, smiling at some private joke, she rose, placed a hand on my shoulder, and added, "*I will walk. You will walk with me?*"

The Starry Wisdom cultist was already raising her own objections to the hunter's story, and I couldn't personally be fucked to join in with the inevitable rounds of pics-or-it-didn't-happen that would follow. Besides, we had work to look for, so I set my hand over Q's, stood beside her, and let her lead me out into the streets of Cthonius Linea.

CHAPTER FIVE
The City

When I'm in a... a walking-out-of-airlocks mood, I think every city looks the same. Tranquility Settlement, Aphrodite Nine, the Experimental Prototype City on Titan. Each one was built by the same small group of conglomerates, working with the same materials to similar budgets and reporting to the same head offices on the core worlds.

On better days, I look closer and realize that not even the infinite reach of the trade-states can fuck everything up the same way every time. Every body in the system is geologically unique and while a dome is a dome is a dome, an ice sheet—even one buried under layers of atmospheric control and composite lagging—will never feel the same as a desert, or a ring of volcanoes.

And even without the physical differences—even if every rock in space was just a rock in space and not a cloud of solid ammonia or a ball of metallic hydrogen—there'd have been changes. The system has been settled for centuries now, and a hundred or so years of living builds up history, no matter what the shareholders might prefer. In Cthonius Linea, that history was all to do with the Leviathans. And it was a history in layers.

The first layer was industry. The city was built around its docks, and its docks were built around the trade in the bodies of titans. Where other ports were meant to accommodate smaller, more agile vessels—messengers and orbit-to-orbit ships, pure rockets and interwell haulers—the landing towers of Cthonius Linea had been built around hunter-barques. An unwieldy but versatile craft, the hunter-ship needed to operate both through the journey in hard vacuum from moon to planet, and also in the violent atmospheric conditions of Jupiter. Which meant they were part winged, part jet, part rotor; elements of the carrier and of the fighter and of the ancient tall ships of Old Earth all factored into their design. This made them, in my opinion, quite the most beautiful vessels ever created, despite the popular perception that they are, for the most part, complete shit.

Atop the industrial layer sits the layer of *product*. Although spermaceti (if I say it often enough you'll get used to it) is the main target of the hunt, most parts of the Leviathan are valuable. Or at least, valuable enough that people hang on to them. So the visitor to Cthonius Linea sees that the bones of the great beasts (a biologist would say that *bone* is not quite the right word for the creature's endostructure, but I'm not a biologist so I don't care) are worked into every part of the city's architecture. Advertising hoardings are projected onto sheets of white starivory. Street vendors hawk their wares from within gargantuan hollowed-out teeth laser-etched with intricate cosmonautical carvings. Half the dress of half the citizens is fashioned from the beasts' hides—often very processed forms of them, admittedly, because the hides themselves are thick and unsupple.

At last, above the layer of product is the layer of disuse. As the business of hunting moved to other bodies, it became less the province of the individual adventurer and more of the bioindustrial enclaves of the resource-states. The shipyards and refineries and hunters' inns began to close down, with new businesses blooming like rot on their corpses. So now you'll see a casino where once there was a refinery, a scrap-metal dealer where once there was a lively trade in beastbones or, as often as not, nothing at all where once there was a tavern alive with hunters' songs.

I told all this to Q as she walked beside me. She nodded

sagely and added, in her heathenish tongue, "Sic transit gloria mundi." No idea what she meant by it.

We made a strange pair, Q and I, strolling the narrow prefabricated streets of the old quarter and watching out for likely starships. Port cities tended to skew cosmopolitan, but even here it was rare to see a Terran and, being a kind of wandering vagabond from everywhere and nowhere, I wasn't exactly inconspicuous either. Fortunately, I was accustomed to ignoring catcalls and Q seemed truly not to understand them. To me at least it was the silent stares that were more disturbing, the looks that could've been completely in my head or could've meant I was two bad steps and a wrong word away from a gutful of flechettes.

Still, we'd managed to walk for some while unshot when we happened upon the door of a little hunters' chapel. Once the docklands would have been crawling with them. Many of the early hunters had been steeped in the Plutonian faith, offering up their toil to the Father in the hope that he would reward them with his extremely lucrative favor. He never did, as far as I could tell. At least not most people. The Church teaches that those few men who grew wealthy in those early days were definitionally the most holy, and that makes a certain kind of sense. After all, the Father is all-good and all-powerful and he loves us. How fucked up would it be if he let people get rich even if they *weren't* smarter, harder-working, and more moral than everybody else?

I didn't know much about Q's religion, although I assumed it had something to do with the little glass idol she carried. As a result, it was hard for me to explain to her why exactly—despite our having set out in search of a boat and having promised to keep one another company—I felt so compelled to enter the chapel. Honestly, it was hard to explain it to myself. To say that my feelings towards the catechism were complex at that time would be an understatement; there were days when I would swear it was a tissue of lies, there were days when the certainty of its truth gnawed at my chest like rats in my lungs. And there were days—most days, candidly—when I felt both at once. When passing by a chapel made me feel an uneasy yearning for salvation.

So I went inside, letting Q follow me and hoping she would indulge my strange outworlder's ways.

Hunters' chapels are gloomy, desperate places. Sky-hunting is dangerous and half the parishioners in any given church will be grieving or waiting to grieve. In the Plutonian Church, that can be an expensive business. Many a hunter has come home to find their loved ones spent so much on prayers that half their pay has gone before it was even claimed.

And if you want evidence both for the perils that await the hunter-ship and the lengths a hunter's kin will go to in their memory, you need look no further than this. Three of the chapel's five walls were given over to memorial plaques, all that remained of dead souls lost to the Jovian winds. Q and I both—despite our radically different contexts—found ourselves drawn to them at once; she holding her idol up before them for reasons I couldn't understand, me scanning them for names or memories or meanings.

They were all of them small, all of them similar. One, for example, read thus:

SACRED to the MEMORY of JOHN TALBOT. Lost in the eternal storms of JOVE, now with ETERNITY in truth. This memorial is SPONSORED by AXIOM ENERGY DRINK, a product of Coradini Food and Beverages, a wholly owned subsidiary of Aphrodite Pharma State.

Most were shorter still. The Church charges by the character for immortality, and so many more ran along these lines:

S2TM; AO, LB, XH, NN, NN, FR, YK, L, TRC; Others; GBNF

I still wasn't in a safe mood to dwell on death; although I'd committed to seeking my fate amongst the Leviathans rather than beneath the wheels of a groundcar, I could feel within myself that instability I knew to mistrust. Not quite sure how to tell Q any of this, I placed my hand on her shoulder and whispered to her that I needed to stay, that I needed to do something. And before she could ask me what, I took up my place at the rear of the congregation and, heart clenching in my throat, waited for the sermon to start.

Like most pulpits in most churches, at least most Plutonian churches, the pulpit in that tiny chapel was an ancient device of steel and light connected to a communications array that would, stellar conditions and planetary alignment permitting, receive broadcasts directly from the Golden City on Pluto. Since the whole of that city was given over to the glory of the Father and his Favored, there was always a service beginning somewhere and so the faithful throughout the system were certain to be able to hear the divine word as and when their schedules and bank balances permitted it.

A light blinked on in front of me, and I scanned my credit-chip across it. I was down to my last few pennies, but the Church knew the value of a large number of small donations so, with pious generosity, they offered a sliding scale of payments starting at very, very affordable levels and only requiring you to consent to your data being harvested for legitimate, godly purposes. The transaction hung a moment, then went through. Worship music began to fill the air and the pulpit began projecting the image of an immense congregation hall, a little fuzzily coming as it did from something like four and a half light-hours away.

Q leaned over and whispered in my ear. "*I* vidi satis. *Going*."

All over again I was torn. The idolator inside me wanted to leave the chapel with her, to make divinity out of companionship and desire. But the ghost of an old faith kept me behind, made me bid her farewell and turn my eyes back to a sermon I knew in advance would have no answers for me.

CHAPTER SIX
Jonah

The music died down and the camera swept over thousands of worshipers before focusing on the preacher. He was a tall man, or at least the way he was being filmed made him seem tall, and he welcomed us to the presence of the Father with a passion and an authority I knew from childhood.

"Oh, my friends," he was saying from the screen. "Oh, my many, many friends, are you ready to *praise*?"

A cry of *yes* went up from the crowd on the screen, echoed from the pews in front of me. I echoed it with them, because when the call goes up, you respond. And as always, when I responded, I felt that sense of connection and isolation all at once, of belonging to something but not really knowing what my place in that something was meant to be.

Often, when I sit in a church or watch broadcast masses from the Golden City, I wonder how many of the other parishioners feel the same as me. And I can never tell which thought scares me most: that all of them do, or none of them.

"Remember, friends," the preacher continued, "the Father teaches that whatever you give unto him, he will return unto you tenfold, and you can begin giving unto him right now at the low, low starting price of nineteen ninety-five per standard month. Friends, there is no investment better than righteousness; there is nothing the Father cannot give, and he will give it to *you* for ten cents on the dollar."

A record of offerings began scrolling up the screen, with names and prayers and values attached. None from our own chapel, of course, those were still winging their way across the interwell gulf at the inviolable speed limit of the universe.

Services always began with collection, and the mark of a good preacher was how well he gave the faithful the opportunity to demonstrate their faith and thereby maximize the opportunities for the Father to reward them tenfold. For what greater good could there be than giving the poor and the helpless a means to decuple their money? Which they surely would. Any minute now.

And although I speak like a bitter ex-believer, I made my contribution with the rest. Because sometimes a little hope is worth the price.

"The lesson today," the minister said, when the offerings had slowed to a trickle, "comes from the Book of Jonah. And like always, friends, when you think of the Testament I want you to think of Old Earth, about how that ancient Eden was lost to sin and perdition, how it has now become a nest of serpents and cannibals—"

My thoughts went back to Q. I didn't *think* she was a cannibal. Then again I'm not sure how I'd know unless she actually tried to eat me. And it's testimony to the hold my not-quite-former religion still had on me that I had those thoughts without my mind drifting once to oral sex.

The minister was recounting the story now. How in a place called Joppa the Father had called Jonah to go to a place called Nineveh, and how Jonah had tried to flee from the calling. How the Father had sent storms to harry him. How Jonah had been cast overboard and swallowed by a whale. And then, most bizarrely of all, how there'd been this bit with a gourd and then the whole thing had ended incredibly abruptly with no real resolution.

You might be thinking to yourself that it was a mighty

coincidence, my happening to stumble upon a preacher telling the story of a man swallowed by a gigantic aquatic beast just as I was about to go hunting for Leviathans myself. Would you believe me if I said it never occurred to me at the time, even though I had voyages and monsters very much on my mind?

The truth is that I've always identified with Jonah, but the Leviathan was never the part of his story that spoke to me. It was always the flight, the desperate need to escape a fate he'd been told was inevitable. So it wasn't really the creature that I thought of in that moment, but the man. Willing to run and hide and lie and cheat to get out from under the Father's shadow.

The words of the sermon washed over me, and I tried to take comfort in the familiarity. Except not all familiar things are comforting.

"And that, friends, is the real lesson of Jonah," the preacher concluded. "You know, people always ask me, they ask me what that last verse, the very last verse means. Because it seems like the Father leaves us and leaves Jonah—if you'll pardon some salty language—in a heck of a funny place."

That much was true. And I'd always liked that about the story. Life, in my experience, doesn't end neatly. It just ends.

"This is the last thing the Father says. He says: *Thou hast had pity on the gourd, for the which thou hast not labored, neither madest it grow; which came up in a night, and perished in a night: And should not I spare Nineveh, that great city, wherein are more than sixscore thousand persons that cannot discern between their right hand and their left hand; and also much cattle?*"

I shut my eyes and tried to be saved. It never worked.

"What's he saying there, friends? He's saying to Jonah, he's saying to Jonah, *Why're you sitting around feeling sorry for yourself, when I'm trying to give you so much more?* He's saying *Why're you*—and again I'm sorry for my ungodly speech—*why're you bitching about some plant when there's a city full of people, full of cows, full of* opportunity *that I'm trying to guide you to*. He's saying *Son, get off your butt and go get you them cattle*."

As far as I understood, that was orthodoxy. Plutonian orthodoxy at least. It had never quite sat right with me, but I'd never been able to work out why. Then again, that was true of a lot of things.

"Because, friends, that's what the Father wants for you. He wants you to be happy. He wants you to be free. He wants you to get those cows. To get that promotion. To get that house on Ganymede. To get that private ship. But he can't give it to you if you close your heart to him.

"Friends, I'm going to show you how to open your hearts now—"

The subscription details popped back up on the screen and the minister began to lead those members of the congregation with the means in premium prayer. I tipped a nominal amount for the betterment of my immortal soul and, trying not to draw the eye or the judgment of the other celebrants, I slipped out the way I'd come in.

I always felt after church the way I sometimes felt after sex: wishing it had been more, not knowing why I expected it to be. I swallowed the hollowness and set back out into the city, hoping for better fortune.

CHAPTER SEVEN

The Ship

I had come to Cthonius Linea with no friends and no real plan other than to walk around and hope that some hunter-captain caught sight of me and said, *You, girl, you look like you know your way around a kinetic inductor, come sign on with me.* Then by purest chance I'd met somebody who actually knew the area and the industry and we'd agreed to go job-searching together. Then I'd dumped her because some atavistic religious whim made me want to listen to a sermon. I was a fool in so many ways.

It wasn't a complete loss, mind you. I could go back to the Coffin, tell her I'd had no luck, ask if she'd done any better and, assuming she had, if she could pretty please book me on as her plus-one. My pride, though—actually, who was I kidding? I had virtually no pride and I was trying to shake what was left of my shame as well, although that last one was a work in progress. Faith, it turns out, does a number on you.

Still, I was just about motivated enough and it was just about early enough that I felt I should at least *try* to find gainful employment. Besides, maybe the preacher had been right, maybe the Father had a whole field full of cows just waiting for me and all I had to do was go to Nineveh.

In fact, fuck it, that was as good a start as any. I decided to wander the docks and see if I could find a ship called Nineveh.

If I did, I'd take it as a message from the Almighty and sign on with them immediately.

I did not find a ship called Nineveh. Nor Jonah, nor any other scripturally significant name I could think of. If a higher power was intending to guide me, it wasn't going to make things quite that easy.

My search to that point had been taking place at ground level. Every landing tower had the name of the ships that docked there displayed in orange lights around the base. And if I'd known which ship I was seeking, that would have been all I needed. But without divine grace to light my path I needed some other way to make my choice. I needed, if at all possible, to actually *see* the vessel I'd be living aboard for the next three years.

And that meant going up.

About half the towers were conglomerate-owned and I wouldn't be allowed into any of those without a lot more paperwork than the none I had on me, but that wasn't an issue. The observation platforms were all public and they'd give me as good a view as anywhere else. So I jumped in an elevator and took a ride to the upper stratum.

I've been in a lot of dome cities in my time. Every colony that isn't underground or underwater or an actual space station relies on them. Not every city arranges its docks like Cthonius—on spires reaching up into the black like the spines of a sea urchin—but enough do that I knew what to expect. As I passed through the roof of the dome in a capsule that I really hoped was airtight, I emerged into a reinforced cryoglass bubble and looked down on a dazzling array of ships' lights and landing lights and office lights. It was like there were stars below me as well as above me. And if my head had been in a different space, that might have been enough. I might have remembered that it's not only in the sky that things come alive. I might have walked away.

But I didn't.

Spread out before me was the real business of Cthonius

Still, I didn't dare reach out to Q to touch her. Because I was selfish and afraid and given over to a moment I didn't want to end. Instead, I made myself an altar for her, murmured *yes* and *please* and *yes* again to her every touch.

In the light of her markings—which I was beginning to think shifted with her mood and which were fading now through colors I'd never seen them take on before—I could see Q's deep, unending eyes focused on me. And for some cold, inexplicable reason I felt more naked than I ever had in my life as she touched me, then watched for my reaction, then touched me again just a little differently—harder or softer or just *slightly* to the left. I wasn't sure if I felt cared for or studied, adored or dissected, and I wasn't sure which I wanted to feel.

All the while her lips stayed curled into a little half smile, and I was seized by a barbed desire to please her. Worse, that desire was tinged with the knowledge that little would please her more than being myself, and that was something I hated to do. But I tried to be a kind of honest, to let myself cry if I had to and to only beg if I really meant it.

And I did, in the end, really mean it. Because she had an instinct for withholding that was the best kind of agony, and though we shared few common words there are other languages.

I let her dance her will across me as I lay ever more breathless and ever more desperate and when I did, at last, reach out for her she took me by the wrist, kissed my fingertips exactly once, then guided my hand back to my side. Which left me with a faint sense that I'd lost, and that I wouldn't mind losing again.

And all the while, I listened to her whispering in a language I didn't understand and, when I came, I bit my tongue so hard that I tasted blood.

Afterwards, I lay in her arms feeling restless and more unsatisfied than I had any right to be. I was still naked, she still fully clothed, and I shrank into her feeling a sudden, inexplicable urge to break. To curl up into a ball and start weeping.

Linea. The people living below were just lubricant. Above the domes was where the hunters came and went, where cargos were loaded and unloaded. Where if I didn't fuck things up royally I would find *somebody* willing to take a chance that some random girl from nowhere wouldn't be a complete liability on a hunting voyage.

Once again I shut my eyes and took in the scent of the place, because this was effectively a different city. This was the city that flew. That looked up and up and out into the void forever. This was the city I'd have lived in if I could.

If I didn't have to do awkward things like breathing.

My eyes are good, and they're the eyes I was born with so that's one thing Aphrodite Pharma State can't take away from me. As I stood as close as I could get to the edge of the platform, my hands pressed to the atmosphere screen, I had as fine a view as I could hope for of the ships coming in, or leaving, or waiting to be crewed.

I still didn't know exactly what I was looking for. But all my life I've lived by the motto that I'll know her if I see her.

And I saw her.

Every ship in the docks was different—that was what I loved about hunter-barques—but most were variations on a theme. Matte black hulks or sleek silver cutters; brutal, regal crafts that knew what they were about and made sure you knew they knew it.

But she was different.

She was bone white. And not from paint, not from galvanic plating or dust-scoring. From bone. Actual bone. Whatever visionary, whatever dreamer, whatever force of incarnate chaos had designed this ship—the ship that arrested all my attention and took away all my breath and made my heart skip like I was looking at a lover—had decked every part of her with the bones of the Leviathan.

It was strange and it was beautiful and it called to me like few things ever had. I made up my mind there and then that unless Q was dead set against it—and maybe even if she was—I would ship on that impossible ossuary vessel if it was the last thing I did.

Of course, it very nearly was.

Dotted around the observation platform were information terminals, and I used one to cross-reference the berth, to find the name and number and ownership of the fine unconquerable lady I'd set my sights on.

Her name was Pequod. She was owned by a collection of private investors with the largest single stake held by the biofuels division of Olympus Extraction State. Their interests and those of the other, smaller backers were overseen by two gentlemen named Emerson and Thoreau, and her captain was a woman named—

And here we are again. Some things are precious. Some things are just mine.

The captain was a woman who, as far as this book is concerned, is simply called *A*.

CHAPTER
EIGHT

Sharing

We'll come back to the captain later. She's important, obviously. Incredibly important. Changed-my-life important. Hell, she nearly changed my life the most a life can possibly *be* changed.

But that's all to come. We wouldn't meet for days yet, and though looking back I remember that first sight of her name like it was this huge turning point for me, it wasn't really. It was just a name. Could have been anything. Asa. Asha. Abigail. Names mean less than people think they do. Or more. I'm still trying to work that one out.

I wasn't quite confident enough to sign aboard an unknown ship with an unknown captain about to set forth on an unknown voyage without at least *consulting* with the woman I'd just agreed to go shipboard with. So I looped back to the Coffin in the hopes that Q would already be there. I found her sitting in the common room. She had one leg stretched out on a scrimshawed bench and was reading a book without acknowledging me. I say reading; she was flipping through pages, about fifty at a time, holding each of those fifty pages briefly up to her little glass idol before moving on to the next set.

For a while I just sat and watched her. Which—yes, now that I say it, comes across as a bit creepy. But she seemed busy with what she was doing and I didn't want to interrupt her.

And she was fascinating to watch. Although there is the *tiniest* chance that by *fascinating* I mostly just mean *hot*.

There's sort of a morbid joke I'll sometimes make that the way to my heart is through my ribs with a knife. Since Q had woken me up last night with a blade at my throat I'd begun to think that might be literally true. Over the space of less than twenty-four hours I'd gone from being terrifyingly aware of all the awful things she might do to me to being terrifyingly aware of all the awful things I *wanted* her to do to me.

I might, as a result, have gotten ever so slightly lost in reverie so when she finished the book and started talking to me I almost blanked her.

"*Ship*," she said for what I hoped was only the second time. "*Habes?*"

"Yes." I gave an exaggerated nod, which made me feel incredibly silly. I knew she understood *yes* and *no*. "But I've not signed anything, so if you don't like it you can back out."

Q shrugged. "Confido. *I trust*."

That was . . . honestly probably more than I deserved. "And sorry," I added, "for ditching you earlier. I just . . . it's complicated."

"*Complicated?*" Q repeated. "*That building.* Ecclesia? *Church?*"

I nodded. "More a chapel, but yes. I was raised Plutonian."

She frowned. Then she held the little idol up to her face and said to it, "*Plutonian. Church.*"

Symbols skittered across its surface and her eyes darted left and right across them, as though reading extremely quickly. I felt my mouth go a little dry as I watched her.

"Et iterum dico," she said, and seemed to be quoting, "vobis facilius est camelum per foramen acus transire quam divitem intrare in regnum caelorum."

I looked down, ashamed at how little I understood. "I'm sorry, I don't know."

"*Rich man*," she tried. "*Camel?*"

With a slightly embarrassing sigh of relief, I realized what she meant. "Oh, yes. *It is as easy for a rich man to enter the king-*

dom of heaven as it is for a camel to pass through the eye of the needle."

She looked confused. Which was fair enough. It was a confusing verse. Not least because nobody had seen a camel since before the founding of the Commonwealth.

"Historically," I explained, "the eye of the needle was the main road into one of the Holy Cities of Old Earth and a camel was some kind of riding animal that went up that road all the time. So although it seems like it's saying it's hard for rich people to get into heaven, it's actually saying the opposite."

For a while she stared at me, half smiling, almost like she was expecting me to say that it was a joke. Then she just said, "Non intellego."

That one I'd also worked out. "Neither do most people, I think. Where I'm from we call them mysteries of the faith."

It wasn't until after I'd said it that I realized how melancholy I sounded. If *melancholy* is the right word. Perhaps *rueful* would be better. And that left a bitter taste in my mouth that wouldn't shift no matter how hard I tried to spit it out, and which filled me with an almost nauseous need to purge myself of . . . something.

"*Tell me*," said Q.

And I did. I told her everything.

It took a long time, so long that I was still speaking when we left the common room and went back to our quarters, and even then I left a fair bit out. There's too much of a person to share it all in one evening. But I told her a lot. Certainly I told her more than I'm telling you. And if you resent that, I'm not sorry. What a woman shares with a companion, even a new companion, in the dark of a tiny room in a cheap inn on Europa and what she shares with the entire system in a published memoir are different things.

I told her the parts that mattered. That I had been born in a faith I had mostly abandoned and in a body I had mostly reshaped. That I'd been wandering the stars for more than half of my adult life and that I had always assumed I would know what I was looking for when I found it but that I'd been dead fucking wrong every single time so far.

Then, as if testing that theory, I told her she was beautiful.

I hadn't been drinking, but it *had* been late. We'd gone to bed by that point and were lying face-to-face in the night, only the faint glow of Q's markings letting us see one another. And I never meant to say it. It just fell out of my mouth like a baby tooth.

Her face scrunched up like she was trying to say about three things at once and couldn't quite get any of them to fit. "Quare dici?" she managed eventually, and she sounded suspicious. I would have too.

I rolled onto my back, or at least as far onto my back as I could in a bed that had definitely been designed for a single occupant. "Forget it," I told her.

"Quare?"

"I just . . ." I covered my face with my hands. This probably wasn't a conversation I wanted to be having. "Sometimes I get in my head and I say things that don't mean anything and—Fuck, I don't even know how much of this you understand."

With my face covered, I couldn't see her, but I felt her fingertips brush my wrist. "Satis," she said. "*Enough.*"

Carefully taking my hands away, I turned my head to look at her. "If I said"—this was a bad idea—"that I wanted you to kiss me."

She didn't reply. At least not verbally. But if she'd understood nothing else, she definitely understood that.

With a tenderness that I'd hoped for but not dared to expect, she pressed her lips to mine. I kept as still as I possibly could, barely daring to breathe in case I broke the moment. In the cold, it was the warmth of her I noticed the most, the heat of her breath, her hands as she cupped my face as if she feared to break me.

Which was, in so many ways, the opposite of what I wanted.

"*Good?*" she asked, possibly because in my stillness I was giving her precisely zero signals.

I just about managed a soft *yes* in reply.

So she kissed me again, tentative, almost like she was exploring me. And I wanted so badly to be explored. Her tongue touched just a moment against mine and the rush of it was so sudden and so welcome that I nearly bit the inside of my own mouth.

"*Good?*" she asked again.

Again I just about managed a *yes*. And the part of me that was lost to wanting, that had been lost to wanting since I came to Europa . . . since I left Deimos . . . since I was born . . . that part of me whispered that if I'd embraced a bad idea, I might as well embrace a worse one.

"Would you"—it was harder to get words out now, because when she wasn't kissing me I was swallowing my own tongue with needing her to kiss me—"would you understand if I said I wanted you to fuck me?"

We were too close for me to see her lips, but I thought I saw her smile. Then she leaned very close and said, softly into my ear, "Intellego."

What with only having two sets of clothes apart from the environment suit, and what with Europa being incredibly freezing all the damned time, I'd gone to bed in the same loose smock and polymer pants combo I'd been walking around in for the past few days. I was suddenly very aware that I was a mess and probably stank. Then again, Q had *also* been reduced to sharing a bed with a stranger in the worst inn in Cthonius Linea, so she probably had low standards.

Either way, she eased my top over my head. I was equal parts comforted by the care she was taking and frustrated that she wasn't being just a touch more forceful. After all, I'd said *fuck me*, not *make love to me*.

She traced kisses down my neck and nipped, just a little, at my collarbone with her teeth.

"*Good?*" she asked. "*Bad?*"

"Good," I replied, and she bit me again, a little harder this time. I stifled a gasp.

"Passer, deliciae meae puellae," she whispered. Her lips were passing between my breasts now, her fingertips tracing the arcs of my hips. "Quicum ludere, quem in sinu tenere."

I wanted, very badly—I can't really describe *how* badly—to reach up and touch her, but I kept my hands firmly by my sides. It's a game I play with myself sometimes. I'm not sure what the rules are meant to be, or what the prize is. Deep down, I think maybe I'm trying to stick it to all the people who told me I didn't have any discipline. Because trying to placate old men you knew a decade ago is a really healthy thing to do during sex.

"Cui primum digitum dare appetenti." Her tongue darted lightly around my navel and she began slipping my pants down far, far more slowly than I wanted her to. "Et acris solet incitare morsus." She bit me again, just over the hip bone, and I dug my nails into my palms with anticipation.

When her fingertips, spit-moistened and gentle, slid inside me, my mind went as it always did to Aphrodite Terra. I'd never been there, of course, not personally. But the reconfigurative subdivision of the biotechnological wing of the great Venusian pharma-state ran every cyberdoc and geneshack corewards of Neptune.

I closed my eyes tight and tried to just *be*. And in some ways that was easy because with an instinct that made me feel weirdly, uncomfortably seen, Q was sending ripples of sensation through me that even Aphrodite Pharma State couldn't distract me from.

"*Good?*" she asked.

And this time I just nodded.

"*More?*"

I nodded again.

Getting to where I was, to the body I was in, had cost me. Like, literally cost. I'd run up debts that I'd never be free of to a pharmaceutical conglomerate that would track me down and render me into seed-base if I missed a repayment. It was moments like these that made it worth it, that made me feel . . . *mine*.

"Thank you," I told her, my voice on the edge of cracking. "And I'm— Thank you."

She made a quiet shushing noise and kissed the back of my neck. "Dormi."

A hot wad of undifferentiated emotion was gathering in my stomach, a crucible mix of guilt and gratitude all smelted together with a shame I should have put aside long ago.

When I was barely more than a child, I had asked a preacher why so few people seemed to be happy. He'd smiled with white, perfect, extremely expensive teeth and told me that only one answer made sense: that very few people deserved to be.

Of all the lessons I'd been taught by the faith, that was the one I'd found it hardest to stop believing.

CHAPTER NINE

Getting Laid

Q woke before me next morning bright, early, and upbeat. While I lay wrapped in the blanket trying to work out if the previous night had changed anything.

Normally it wouldn't, because normally I wouldn't have seen her again. She'd have been moving on, or I'd have been moving on, or at the very least we'd have had a conversation where we made it clear that no, this was just a sex thing, that no, there'd be no repeat performances, and that yes, we were both cool with that.

With Q, though, we barely shared a language, and if we stuck to our deal we'd be living shipboard together for three years. She didn't seem the clingy sort, but though I hated to admit it, she wasn't the one I was worried about. I hesitate to use the phrase *catching feelings* because even though I once worked gutting dust-spiders at a factory in Huygens Crater I still have some dignity. Still, I can sometimes get . . . invested in people. Especially people who seem to have things sorted out in ways I don't or to live in ways I can't.

Q finished her devotions to the little glass idol, tucked it into her bag, stood, and smiled at me. "*Ship*," she said. "Ibimus?"

I nodded. "Ibimus," I replied. I had no idea what it meant but it felt positive.

As I guided Q through the streets of Cthonius Linea to the

Pequod's docking tower, we talked casually of everything except for the fact that we'd fucked. I told her instead about the time I'd jumped ship on a remote asteroid and got swept up in a feud between two mining colonies, and she told me what she could of life on Earth.

Here, more than ever, words were against us. She told me of *caelum*, which I thought meant *sky*, but the way she spoke about it was strange, as though it was something you could just see, always, without having to walk out of an airlock or into a viewing dome. *Silva* I could not even begin to translate.

"Silva," she tried again. "Arbores."

I shook my head.

"Lignum?" She fished her idol from her pack and spoke into it. Then she tried. "Lignum etiam vitae in medio paradisi, lignumque scientiae boni et mali."

From the look in her eyes—I had been trying *not* to look in her eyes because when I did it made me feel about six different kinds of wrong—she seemed to think it would mean something to me.

"Boni et mali," she said again. "*Good. And bad.* Scientiae. *Knowing.*"

I've never claimed to be the sharpest or the fastest, but I got there. "Knowledge of good and evil?"

"Lignum," she repeated. "Lignum scientiae boni et mali."

"The tree of knowledge of good and evil?"

She nodded with delight. "*Tree,*" she said. "*But, many. Many treeae.*"

That was the funny thing about faith. I'd heard of the tree of knowledge and the tree of life and that good trees bear good fruit while bad trees bear bad fruit. I'd never really stopped to think what they actually *were*. "What do they look like?"

"*Tall,*" she said. "*Peaceful.*"

The way she said it, they sounded wonderful. Then again that might still have been the sex talking. But I took the win where I could. Not that long ago the idea of anything sounding wonderful at all would have felt absurd.

Having scoped out the ship the previous day, I didn't need to go up to the observation platform again, which I found a little disappointing because I'd have liked to show it to Q. There was something about the city from above, the skyline below and the stars overhead and the cold death of the Europan atmosphere on the other side of the crystal all around, that felt almost magical, that I wanted to share with her. But we were here looking for work, not to sightsee. Also she'd probably already seen it. So we stuck to the ground and picked our way through the docklands towards the launch tower where the owners' representatives kept their offices.

Mr. Emerson and Mr. Thoreau were based in an atmospherically sealed pod just off the platform where the Pequod—even more majestic close-to, even more remarkable and impossible and right in all the wrong ways—was docked. We weren't guaranteed to be able to walk in from the elevator and ask for work out of nowhere, but commercial recruiters didn't usually ask questions. From their perspective, we'd be offering to sign over three years of our lives for no money up front. We'd have needed to look *unbelievably* sus for them to think that was a bad deal.

"So," Emerson said to me. He was watching me over little half-rimmed glasses. "Ye want to go a-hunting, do ye?"

Either he was descended from some of the earliest settlers to land on Europa, or the dialect was an affectation. "That's right," I replied.

"And have ye experience in the skies?"

"Three voyages with the merchant service," I told him. "Once with Aphrodite, once with Olympus, most recently with Caloris. I've flown vacuum and atmospheric craft, and—"

"Fie." Emerson waved a hand dismissively. "Merchant work and a little piloting. Know ye anything of the Leviathan, girl? Have ye ever seen a great beast writhing from the churning skies? Ever flown a boat at a monster's jaws, canopy down while the wind whips your suit, and you aim your harpoon by eye alone?"

"Can't say I have," I admitted. "But I'm young"—not so young as I used to be, admittedly, but younger by far than I feel today—"and willing to learn. And my companion is an experienced harpooner."

"*Yes*," Q confirmed. "*Harpooner* sum."

Emerson pulled a face that was halfway between a scowl and a look of pity. "Ye've the look of a greenhorn about ye, and she's the look of a heathen about her. We'd be taking a terrible risk to bring on either of ye, to say nothing of both."

I couldn't tell if this was a brilliant negotiating strategy or a terrible one. He seemed to be actively trying to put us off, but perhaps the goal was to make us want the job all the more. Sky-work is paid in lays, a share of the profits of the voyage, and I wasn't ruling out the possibility that he was trying to get us to accept a longer one. Which is to say, a smaller one. "My friend can speak for herself, Mr. Emerson," I tried. "But as for me, I'm looking for a job. I know it's dangerous work, but I mean, look around you. If I walked out that door"—I indicated the entrance to the office—"without waiting for the airlock to clear, I'd be dead in seconds. This whole system is trying to kill all of us, basically all the time. At least on a hunter-barque I might get a story out of it."

"It'll be hard labor," Emerson warned me. "Not glamorous. We'd want to take you on as a hand before the array."

That was fine. I hadn't planned to list as an officer. "You won't regret it," I told him. And I was right, in a way. They'd have many, many regrets about this voyage, but hiring me wasn't going to be one of them.

All the while Mr. Emerson had been trying to dissuade me from taking up the position that it was his job to find people to fill, his companion, Mr. Thoreau, had been sitting in one corner of the office reading from a well-thumbed copy of the Testament. This wasn't itself especially unusual; the Church naturally attracted entrepreneurs. It still unsettled me a little, especially after all I'd shared with Q the night before.

About my life story, I mean. Not the fucking. But perhaps also a little bit the fucking.

"Well, Thoreau," Mr. Emerson said from behind his desk, "what lay shall we offer this young lady?"

I was expecting them to drive a hard bargain, but I was relatively confident in my experience and hoped bringing a harpooner with me would sweeten the deal. If I was lucky, I reckoned I'd swing something around the 250th.

Mr. Thoreau looked up from his reading and seemed very much as if he would rather not have. "Why do you bother me with these things? Can you not see I have other matters on my mind?"

"Other matters!" This wasn't going down well with Emerson. "What good are your other matters when there's business to be done? What lay do we offer this girl?"

Thoreau scrutinized me in a way I really didn't like being scrutinized. "Why should she care?" he asked the room in general. Then to me directly he said, "Behold the fowls of the air: for they sow not, neither do they reap, nor gather into barns; yet your heavenly Father feedeth them. Are ye not much better than they?"

"The Father," I replied, perhaps unwisely, "feeds those who feed themselves."

Pleased I had at least some knowledge of doctrine, Thoreau nodded. "And you will be fed and watered well enough on the ship. As for the lay, the Father says that we owe our brother forgiveness to the tune of seventy times seven, so let us make it that."

My shit mental arithmetic told me three things. That seventy times seven was 490. That 490 was a *lot* bigger than 250. And that because of how division worked, a 490th of something was much less than a 250th of it.

"There," Emerson said with worrying finality. "That settles—"

"I don't think it does," I interrupted. The ship had called to me, but I wasn't quite sure it had called to me loudly enough that I'd sign on for barely more than half what I thought I was worth. "With my experience I'd be expecting something around"—fuck it, swing for the fences—"the two hundredth?"

Thoreau brayed with laughter. "The two hundredth? Mean you to beggar us? 'Twill be the four ninetieth or nothing."

"Now, now." Mr. Emerson seemed slightly more willing to negotiate, although I was beginning to feel uncomfortably like this was all part of a well-rehearsed grift. "We can offer her something a touch more generous than that, surely? After all, where her treasure is, there will her heart be also."

"You pitch close to blasphemy, Emerson," replied the irascible Mr. Thoreau. "As we husband our worldly wealth, so do we husband our wealth hereafter. If ye have not been faithful in the unrighteous mammon, who will commit to your trust the true riches?" He frowned, deep and sour. "The four hundredth and no more, lest we prove ourselves unworthy stewards."

Mr. Emerson appeared to quail before his partner's weaponized scripture. "We may go, perhaps, to the three fiftieth without imperiling our souls *too* much?"

"I'd take three fifty," I said quickly, before Mr. Thoreau and the Father could team up to beat me down to three seventy-five. I felt a lot like I'd been scammed and, worse, like I might have scammed Q into the bargain.

"And a blessing it has been to do business with ye," said Emerson. "Now, what about your strange friend here?"

"Ye adulteress," intoned Thoreau. "Know ye not that the friendship of the world is enmity with the Father?"

"Two are better than one," I replied reflexively, "because they have a good reward for their labor."

That made Emerson snap out a sharp laugh. "She has ye there, I'll swear she does."

Not, perhaps, expecting to be out-scriptured by a wandering ship's hand worth no more than the 350th lay, Mr. Thoreau gave a little *hrrumph* and changed tack. "Even so, she's a pagan look to her, and evil company corrupts good character."

"She *is* a harpooner," I reminded them. "And I've heard a good spear is hard to come by these days."

I might have been projecting, but I thought I saw a gleam of avarice in Emerson's eyes. The facts that Q was clearly an outsider, clearly spoke little Exodite, and potentially had useful skills must all have been adding up to profit in his pious, acquisitive mind. "And are you?" he asked Q. "A good spear, I mean?"

She nodded, once but deeply.

"Experienced?" asked Thoreau.

She nodded again.

"How?"

Giving a full resume would, I thought, involve more Exodite than Q had readily available and, when I saw her bending down into her bag, I assumed she was going to consult her idol for further instructions.

Instead she fished out the helmet of her environment suit. Unlike the rest of her gear it definitely wasn't Terran, but then why would Terrans need them when the world made oxygen naturally?

"*Watch.*" She snapped the helmet into place and strode with more confidence than I could ever have mustered into the airlock connecting the office to the landing platform.

Emerson and Thoreau made their way over to a viewing window to see what exactly this strange heathen interloper was going to do. Q brought a hand to her neck and adjusted her suit to cast broad and local.

"Vides." Her voice crackled over the office intercom, and she pointed high into the sky above the platform.

For a moment I couldn't quite see what she was pointing at, but then I noticed that a small maintenance drone was zipping about between the topmost pylons. Having seen it, I quickly worked out what she was going to do and tried not to think about the nine or ten ways it could go wrong.

With an almost casual ease, she shouldered her coilgun, drew a bead on the swift-moving drone, and fired. An electrodynamic dart flew into the sky, its monofilament cable trailing behind it, and struck the unfortunate machine square in the jets. The instant it impacted, Q turned her wrist, set the gun to retrieval, and dart, drone, and debris all together reeled back into her waiting hands.

She returned with her prize and set it down on the desk between the two businessmen. Lying there in front of us, it was larger than it had seemed out the window, but it had still been an impressive shot by anybody's standards. I'd have said fuck me, she was amazing, but she already had and already was.

"Precise work," Thoreau admitted, rather grudgingly.

Emerson frowned and peered at his partner over his half rims. "Heathen or no, we have to take her."

"If any of them that believe not bid you to a feast," Thoreau quoted in reply, "and ye be disposed to go; whatsoever is set before you, eat, asking no question for conscience sake."

Mr. Emerson drew himself to his full height, or as much of his full height as he could manifest while sitting, and fixed Q with his most businesslike expression. "How much do you understand, heathen?"

"*Enough*," Q replied, and half smiled at me in a way I found hard to parse.

"Then what do you say to the ninetieth lay?" Emerson asked, and for some reason this time his companion raised no theological objections.

Q nodded for the final time. "Accipio."

Thoreau looked at me. "I assume that means *yes*?"

It probably did, but I didn't want to presume, so I shrugged. "Pretty much. Now, can we board?"

"Very keen, aren't you?" Emerson sounded suspicious, and to be fair to him I would have been too. A lot of people who want to sign aboard ship at short notice are running from something. Any good proprietor or proprietor's agent would keep an eye out for that sort, not to turn them away, necessarily, but to make sure they were making appropriate recompense.

In any case he'd have been wrong about me and Q. About me at least. There are few things I could say for sure about myself in those days, but I'm certain that I wasn't running away from anything.

Just the opposite. I was running away from nothing.

CHAPTER TEN

Cetology

It seems so many years ago now, and at the same time so few. That fateful day that the Pequod launched into Jovian orbital space with a hundred souls aboard. And I'll tell you all about our journey very soon, but before I do, I need you to understand a little about what we were actually doing.

You might already know. Maybe you, like me, are an outworlder at heart and so you're more used to thinking about how all this works. What keeps the lights on. What keeps the atmosphere regulators flowing. What stops the separatists burning your house down and, at the same time, why they want to in the first place.

But probably you aren't. If you can afford a human-written book then you're probably pretty well off, and that means you probably live somewhere far away from the blood and rust. Maybe you're on Ishtar Terra, watching an acid storm breaking from your spire balcony, or in the pleasure palaces of Apollodorus having your every desire attended to by somebody nubile and expendable. And if you're in either of those places, perhaps you've never wondered who produces the oils that power the heat pumps that stop the gold melting out of your jewelry. Even if you're a little less exalted, merely living in the vibrant subterranean seas of Ganymede, perhaps you've never stopped to think how your city, despite being both underwater and underground, is so brightly lit.

The answer, of course, is sperm.

I'll just pause here while you do your own *that's what she said* bits.

Spermaceti derives from an Old Earth word whose etymology I can't be bothered to look up. It's the name given to the cerebrospinal fluid of the great Leviathan. Or, more precisely, of a specific *species* of Leviathan. That's one of the little details I wanted to clear up in this chapter.

People sometimes use *Leviathan* as a general term for all the different monstrous entities that live in the turbid, crushing atmosphere of Jupiter. This is all right as far as it goes but there are actually several different types of creature on (or perhaps more accurately *in* since it has no solid surface) that world, all of which deserve their own correct labels.

If you're reading this book mostly for the parts in which I fuck strangers, kill gargantuan organisms, or nearly die, sorry, you'll have to bear with me for a minute or two.

The broad class of beasts that includes the Leviathan, sometimes known as Titans and sometimes Cetaceans, includes four main categories of horror: Behemoths, Krakens, true Leviathans, and Wyrms. Within each of these categories are a whole lot of species and subspecies, most of which I won't go into on account of how I never saw one and really would lose the Mars-to-Belt audience if I put in long descriptions of things that aren't even going to show up in the book.

Basically, this chapter is here so you'll know what the fuck I'm talking about when some great beast with chitinous mandibles and feeder tendrils shows up and I don't have to explain what it's called while I'm also explaining how it nearly ate me.

Let's start with the Behemoths.

They're not much as Job would have them; for a start, like every other creature native to Jupiter they don't have any legs. They're the largest of the planet's fauna and they live exclusively in the hydrogen sea deep in the heart of the world. I've seen five in my life (four living, one dead) and perhaps the best way to describe them is that they're armored maggots a kilometer long which move ponderously through an ocean of ultra-dense liquid star-metal.

They have no mouths, and some scholars speculate that they feed on the massive electrical energies generated by the currents within Jove's liquid center. I have my own private theory that in this way they serve as the basis for the entire ecosystem. My evidence for this is limited except that the one time I saw such a beast dead, a swarm of Wyrms were feasting on its corpse.

That's all I know about the Behemoths. It's also all you need to know. On to Krakens.

These are nearly as big as the Behemoths, but less massive, if you see what I mean. They're all tentacles and float-sacs, and most of the time they just blow whatever way the winds take them on long parachute arms. Once or twice, however, I've seen one expel a great jet of plasma from its rear end. Or its front end. Their body has a lozenge shape, and they're studded all over with eyes, so the extent to which they can be said to even *have* a front and a rear is debatable.

The mighty Behemoth, big as it might be, is a docile creature. The Kraken, by contrast, will fuck you up all day then come back in the evening and keep fucking you up for fun. Worse, they're useless. They're basically giant muscular bags full of gas, and however they turn atmospheric flotsam and any ships they might eat into usable energy, the organs don't survive gutting.

Wyrms are the final not-Leviathan creature you might be wondering about. And really I'm not sure they're one thing at all. They're invariably eel-like, invariably fly in the strange skies of Jove, and there their similarities to one another end. Some are as long as your finger and feed by skimming some unknown element from the surface of the hydrogen sea. Some are twice as long as your entire body and feed by biting chunks out of anything they happen to fly into. Some attach parasitically to Behemoths or Leviathans, some seem to hunt the ones that live parasitically. In a lot of ways it's beautiful. If your idea of beauty revolves strongly around long thin monsters eating each other.

But what I really want to talk about are the *true* Leviathans. And these are at least slightly uniform. They're all between some tens and some hundreds of meters in length, always far longer than they are broad and far broader than they are tall. Their flight, which like most Jovian creatures makes a complete mockery of conventional aerodynamics, is an undulating motion supported by rippling side fins which together make up perhaps half their body width. There's also similarity in their tails, which are always long and taper to points. Finally, they're always hydrogenically amphibious, able to exist both in the skies and in the hydrogen sea itself, although different species divide their time between those environments differently.

In most other respects, however, they exhibit enormous diversity. I'll list a few here for your information:

The *Barnard's* or *Slack-Jawed* Leviathan is the largest of the true Leviathans. It's seldom hunted because it's seldom seen, but some titanologists speculate that their bodily oils might prove more potent even than spermaceti. They speculate this because the Slack-Jawed Leviathan spends all its life skimming the surface of the hydrogen sea, jaws open, funneling frigid, conductive liquids into its mouth. In theory this should give it access to an incredible supply of ultra-dense energy, but what it uses that energy for nobody knows. When threatened, the Slack-Jawed Leviathan always dives towards the planet's core where it's impossible for regular boats to pursue.

The ominously monikered *Death's Head* Leviathan is named for the skull-like armor plates that cover most of its head (all Leviathans are armored, the Death's Head just front-loads it). Although its jaws are dangerous, its primary means of attack against large enemies seems to be ramming. This makes it a huge threat to hunter-barques, but since it feeds exclusively on the lesser Jovian creatures, smaller even than the Wyrms, scholarly consensus is that the head armor evolved for mating duels, rather than for hunting.

The *Ridgeback* or—remember, if you laugh you lose—*Sperm* Leviathan is the species most barques hunt, and the species that this memoir is (at least ostensibly, I might also be doing shit with themes) about. It takes its name (both of its names, really) from the long, broad ridge that runs the length of its spine. This ridge is filled with long bundles of nerve fibers, and those fibers themselves are bathed in the unique substance we call *spermaceti*. The creature's brain is also marinated in the stuff. At least two scholars have suggested that this close neural connection to such a powerful fuel should grant the creature psychokinetic abilities, and one of those adds that this might help to explain how it (and by extension all Jovian creatures) can actually fly. You'll get a chance to see many of these creatures close at hand, and I will go into far greater detail on their anatomy as and when their various parts become interesting, profitable, or dangerous.

The *Harris's* or *Killer* Leviathan is one of the smaller species. It has a quatripartate jaw, two sets of teeth closing perpendicular to one another. It feeds exclusively on larger beasts and attacks both them and ships with wild fury.

The *Laser-Eyed* Leviathan is almost certainly a myth.

I could carry on listing more species. The Split-Fin, the Hemingway, the Screaming Galliard, and so on. At some point it just becomes a string of names with no meaning.

Then again, you could say that of all names.

CHAPTER ELEVEN

Queens and Pawns

The morning after signing up, Q and I moved what little we had into a two-bunk berth on the Pequod. She was a vast old ship, long of deck, broad of wing, and deep of hull. Though her crew was a little over a hundred, she was quite empty, in a lot of ways. Most of the ship's systems were automated, most of her bulk given over to storage, or to space where things would in future be stored. It meant there were a lot of places to be alone, if you wanted to. Which I sometimes did, and sometimes really, really didn't.

I'm not going to give you a full schematic. That would be tedious and confusing and probably involve the kinds of diagrams I was never trained to draw. But Q and I spent a while exploring, and I can give you a bit of a breakdown if you follow us.

That's a literary device, obviously. You aren't actually following us, you're reading a book written years after the event. I'm not really talking to you and you have no control over how I tell this story.

We began on the top deck, or the observation deck as it's also called. On a lot of vessels, this is an aesthetic inclusion—it's nice sometimes to go out under a transparent dome and watch the stars go past, and it's useful to have somewhere to gather everybody if the captain needs to make an announcement in person instead of over comms. On a hunter-barque it has a more direct function. While most spacegoing ships are searching a huge area of hard vacuum for asteroids to mine or, in many cases, other ships to blow out of the sky, the Leviathan hunter is looking for a specific type of biological organism in a three-dimensional space filled with sheet lightning and neon rain. That makes the array—the three great masts that stand up in the center of the observation deck and conduct detector-signals perpendicular to the plane of flight—vitally important. It's so important, in fact, that it symbolically cuts the ship in half, with *before the array* being the domain of the regular ship's hands and *aft of the array* being the domain of the officers. Fortunately, Q was with me and, as a harpooner, she occupied a liminal space. That's the funny thing about ships; they all have their own customs and, unlike surfaceside, those customs tend to include recognizing the actual value of things. On a hunting voyage, the only job that truly matters is killing, and the kill is impossible without the harpooners. Thus they go where they will, eat in the captain's cabin, and sleep where and with whom they want.

And all they have to do in return is leap down the throats of monsters.

The observation deck was also where Q and I first encountered the first mate. Or perhaps more accurately, they encountered us.

"You there," they barked as we were lingering by the gunwale looking out over Cthonius Linea. "Haven't you work to do?"

Turning away from the domescape, I looked at our upbraider. In a lot of ways, the view was an upgrade; the first mate—Locke, I would later learn—presented themself like something out of a corporate brochure. Immaculately put together in not-quite-dress-uniform, they somehow gave the impression of wearing epaulets despite not in fact wearing epaulets. Their hair was cropped tidy to the point of severe, their fingernails trimmed neatly. Still, lines around the eyes and weathering about the cheeks said they hadn't lived *exclusively* behind a desk.

"Well?" they continued when I took more than two seconds to reply.

"*Harpooner* sum," Q explained. "*Nothing to harpoon.*"

"There's stock to bring aboard."

I put my hands up in a gesture of surrender. "Wouldn't know where to take it until we've got the lay of the ship, though, would we?"

To my surprise, they smiled at that, which made a winsome bracket form at the side of their mouth, just shy of the natural frame formed by their vitiligo. "Well argued."

"I apprenticed as a lawyer," I lied.

"You've come down in the world."

I decided to try smiling back. "Depends what you think of lawyers."

Unfortunately, while Locke was open to a certain minimal level of badinage, they were mostly concerned with keeping the ship running smoothly. Which meant that having accepted my excellent point about not being able to do any productive work until I'd familiarized myself with the Pequod and all who sail in her, they made it their personal mission to rectify that problem as quickly as humanly possible.

It was nice, in a way, to be personally escorted around the vessel by a ranking officer, but I'd far rather have carried on lingering. Especially because throughout the tour, Locke insisted on conveying pertinent information to me with a directness and efficiency I found borderline offensive.

"Captain's quarters," they indicated as we marched hurriedly past an ominous-looking door at the aft of the observation deck. "Captain herself isn't available. Complications from reconfiguring."

That caught my attention the way your own name sometimes catches your attention in a babble of words you're otherwise ignoring. "What did she have reconfigured?"

"Leg." Locke tapped their own thigh in illustration. "Last voyage. Bad business. Want my advice, don't talk about it."

"What's there to talk about?" I asked, all innocence. "I don't know anything."

Q leaned over to me and asked in a soft voice, "Quid?"

I tried as best as I could to explain that the captain had lost a leg in an unspecified incident and that we'd been instructed to keep silent about the whole matter. Although I will admit that, having heard mention of her, I couldn't quite keep her from my mind for rest of the tour.

The Pequod, after all, was such a strange ship. And it seemed natural that a strange ship should have a strange captain. What manner of creature was it, I wondered, who kept so much to herself in this flying sepulcher? What wonders or horrors had she seen in the skies and what had they made of her?

What would they make of me?

CHAPTER TWELVE

Queens and Pawns (II)

My fixation on the ship's elusive captain continued unabated, even as I grew more familiar with the vessel and the folk who served aboard her. The closer we grew to launch, the more my continued failure to catch sight of the woman began to gnaw at me (Q grew quite irritable about it), and so, in an effort to allay my curiosity, I brought it up one evening in the mess.

"Patience," said Truelove, "is a virtue. Not that I would expect you to understand."

"He just means"—Marsh fingered the trapezohedral talisman about his neck—"because you're not with the Church."

The discovery that Marsh was to be flying with us hadn't exactly thrilled me. I'd been even less thrilled to discover that the *reason* he was flying with us was that the ship's second mate—the Truelove you're just meeting—was a devout follower of the Starry Wisdom, and Sister Jermyn had put in a good word.

Truelove scowled. "It isn't your place to tell me what I mean."

"Sorry," mumbled Marsh into his meal of spiced pureed polyps. It honestly surprised me to realize that Marsh was a harpooner. I think of harpooners as mavericks. As bold warriors in the hunt. But it was hard to look at Marsh and not have the word *lickspittle* come immediately to mind.

Still, I wasn't here to judge him, I was here, in theory, to work with him. And that meant playing nice. Well, nice-ish. "I'm with a church," I replied, a little defensively.

Truelove's lip curled derisively. "The Golden Church, that teaches you to worship worldly things. It's no faith at all."

"Whereas worshiping oblivion makes complete sense?" I tried. I'd been aiming for lighthearted banter. It didn't quite work. Truelove wasn't the lighthearted banter type.

"I will not bandy words with outsiders."

Across the table a slight, pretty Vestal looked up at the crowd. There's a stereotype that everybody on Vesta is a sex worker, on account of it being a stopover for mining convoys and relying a lot on service industries. The fact that at least one or two of them wound up sky-hunting instead probably won't dispel that stereotype entirely, but I thought I'd mention it. "I suspect," he said, "that we all struggle with the teachings of our faiths from time to time. I've had difficulties with my own church before now."

"Which church is that?" I asked.

"How about we stop talking religion?" suggested a broad-set man sitting opposite us. His name was Dawlish, and he was harpooner under the third mate (Flint, if you're counting). He also had cheap metalwork replacing most of his jaw, half his arm, and a decent chunk of his chest over the heart.

Truelove glared; he didn't like being gainsaid, whether by members of his own congregation or by outsiders, and still less by people who fell further down the phenotypical hierarchy than him. "Perhaps we should all remain silent?"

"Because there's nothing else we could possibly talk about?" I ask-stated.

Trulove's glare flicked to me. "Not usefully."

That was probably true, but I'd never been afraid of uselessness, and my curiosity was still stabbing pins in my spine. "I wish I knew more about the captain."

By my side, Bulkington—a stalwart and vital member of the crew whose important role in the voyage you may hear more of later—leaned forwards. He set his chiseled jaw on one hand like some great heroic statue and spoke. And when Bulkington spoke, the crew listened.

"Let me see," he said, "what can I tell you about the captain?"

Truelove looked about to object, but Bulkington silenced him wordlessly.

"I've sailed with her before," he went on. "So've Truelove, Flint, and Locke. You'll hear great things about her, and terrible things. But more great than terrible if I'm any judge. Last voyage, though . . ." He drew in a sharp breath. "Bad business."

Bad business could mean just about anything. "What happened?" I asked.

Bulkington's voice lowered. "The Möbius Beast."

"It's a myth," Dawlish replied. "A great white Leviathan longer than any you've seen, hide all pitted with craters and a hundred wicked eyes all gleaming its evil intent." He laughed, which was a strange sound through an artificial larynx. "It's a skyfarers' tale."

"It's real as you or I"—a note of warning crept into Bulkington's voice—"I've seen it, all the mates have seen it. Tell him, Truelove."

Mr. Truelove once again did not like being given orders, but he wasn't about to miss an opportunity to exposit his worldview. "I have *always* held that the skies were full of monsters. The Möbius Beast is one of them. Neither greatest nor least."

"Not the greatest," Bulkington agreed, "but to the captain perhaps the one that matters more than any other. Tore her boat apart it did, cast her out into the open sky then snatched her up in its great mandibles. If her leg'd not come off in its jaws it would've had her whole."

"Bullshit." This was Dawlish again, surprisingly skeptical for a man mostly machine himself. "She'd never survive a suit breach."

Bulkington gave a half shrug of his broad shoulders. "Autoseals. Closed round what was left of her thigh. Still, the cold did a number on the nerves. I hear she's half in agony most days, all in agony the rest."

"Don't spread rumors about your betters, Bulkington," said Truelove with an air of command that felt out of place.

That went down sourly with Bulkington, and indeed with everybody in the room not wearing a trapezohedron. "I count nobody my better," he said levelly, "nor myself another's. Not even you."

There were two ways that could have been meant, and Truelove chose to take both at once. He stood, bowed his head in a very forced show of respect, and fucked off, taking Marsh with him.

"Wisdomers," Dawlish muttered into his mush. "Fucking weirdos."

Bulkington nodded sagely. "I daresay we seem just as strange to them."

Keen to turn conversation back to something I was actually interested in, I tried to return us to talk of the captain. "And has nobody seen her since her last voyage?"

"Nobody," Bulkington told me. "Save maybe the owners."

The Pretty Vestal looked nervous. "That doesn't seem right. You say we'll hear great and terrible things about the captain, Mr. Bulkington, but so far what I've heard has been much closer to terrible."

"Quid audistis?" asked Q. Then she clarified, "*What?*"

The Vestal seemed to shrink into himself. "I don't like to say."

With what I can only call serene disapproval, Bulkington looked down at him. "Speak, lad," he said, "or be silent, but don't hint at things you won't talk about."

"I've heard," the Vestal continued at last, "that she bows before dark gods, that she hoards illegal technologies, that she went stark staring mad after her last trip and now she lurks in the dark, hobbling about on a mechanical leg—"

"And what," asked Dawlish, very pointedly leaning his mechanical chin on his mechanical hand, "does her having a mechanical leg have to do with anything?"

Realizing that he'd fucked up in front of somebody who substantially outranked him, the Vestal backpedaled. "Nothing. Of course. I just . . . well . . . she must have been through a lot, and that must make a person do unusual things."

"What does it matter if it does?" asked Dawlish. "One captain's much like another, and we're all unusual in our way. I'm the last to take against a person just because they've been reconfigured."

The whole exchange caught me off guard. It wasn't her reconfiguration that drew me to the captain, or to the idea of the captain, but the suggestion that it might be touched nerves I did not want touched. "I'm sure he didn't mean to—" I began, then finished with a shamefaced, "You're right, we shouldn't be speculating."

Dawlish laughed. "Speculate away, everybody does. I'm sure you want to know how I came by this"—he indicated his jaw—"and this"—his chest—"or even this"—he pointed his mechanical arm back at itself. "Just as no doubt there's a story to tell about where *you* come from."

I'd spat out a "No" before I could remind myself how sus that would look. "That is, nothing interesting. Just a skyfarer."

"Typical shipboard nobody?" suggested Bulkington with the kind of warm smile that only a very few men are capable of. "Don't worry, there's plenty of those. And we've all got tales we'd rather not share."

On which note he too departed. And when Dawlish finished eating he went as well. But on the way out he laid a hand on my shoulder. "Don't worry, girl," he whispered. "We're voiders. We choose our pasts."

It was a comforting thought. Though I wasn't really sure what past I wanted to choose. Or what future, for that matter.

CHAPTER THIRTEEN

A

We left for the sublunar well the following day, and for a good hour all I could hear was the roar of the VTOL jets as we rose through the barely-there atmosphere of Europa and then charted a course for Jovian transfer.

As an ordinary voider, I spent most of the launch troubleshooting. There are a hundred and one things to do on a spacegoing ship, but since most of them are done by machines the ultimate job of the skysailor is to step in when the machines go wrong. Which they do constantly.

So while the roar of the jets echoed throughout the superstructure of the Pequod, I was flat on my back in a service duct trying to work out why the maintenance drones couldn't find a block in the fuel line. It was definitely the most bored I'd been while horizontal in a good long while.

Before too long the Pequod broke Europa's gravity and, according to sensors, up and down dutifully switched places like they were meant to. On board, of course, the relativistic compensators meant we barely noticed the difference. Normally—at least normally on merchant ships, I had no idea what was normal on a hunter-barque—that stage of transfer would be followed by a short period of downtime. Sailing, like soldiering (from what I'm told; I've never signed up for that particular flavor of self-destruction), is a lot of nothing punctuated by brief moments of everything, and letting the crew enjoy the nothings is an important part of keeping the voyage on track.

So I was surprised when the whole company was called to the observation deck. Still more surprised when we were called aft of the array and surprised to the point of flabbergasted when the announcement—made by Locke over an intercom in dire need of tuning—added that we were to be addressed by the captain herself.

I was not, I was glad to know, the only one who was curious. Or at least I wasn't the only one with a strong reaction. While Q had been sanguine, or seemed it (I confess I couldn't always read her as well as I'd have liked), the rest of the crew were at least paying attention. Marsh was almost excited, though he'd soon have that knocked out of him by Truelove's relentless disapproval. From amongst the crowd I could hear whispers—echoes and intimations of things people had heard, or had heard that others had heard, or had been told that somebody had heard that somebody else had told somebody quite different.

We were not, I had to admit, the best-informed rabble. But there was a kind of electricity in the air as we gathered beneath the array and waited for the captain, at last, to appear.

"What's this about?" whispered one of the Europan crew, sky-hardened and cynical. "It's not normal and it's not right."

"Aye," agreed another, "a bad omen is what this is, and a bad way to start."

While we stood there, murmuring and watching and wondering, I was struck by an overwhelming sense of unreality. I get that sometimes, the strange sense of waking up and being shocked to realize that I am *me* and not some other person. That, out of every identity I could have existed in, this exact body in this exact moment in this exact place is the one I seem, in defiance of all reason, to be occupying.

I feel, at times like these, a lot like an actor in a play that somebody left half written. And that sensation was not helped by the fact that my fellows and I were standing on a literal stage—or as close to a stage as you'd find in the sublunar vacuum—waiting for the curtain to rise and the opening soliloquy to start. It made me uncomfortable, profoundly uncomfortable. Disquiet rose inside me like a slow poison, chilling and choking me until I could imagine no end to it.

And then I saw her.

The captain emerged from her cabin a vision in scarlet. Her gloves, her jacket, her bodice, and her slashed skirt were all a stark bloodred broken only in two places. First, it was broken by her hair, which spilled jet black to her waist, interrupted only by a white streak that lined up with a thin scar running from brow to chin. And second, it was broken by her leg, which below the thigh was an intricate device of chrome and ivory, work like I'd never seen and doubt I'll ever see again.

But despite her outlandish dress, despite the biotechnological wonder she walked upon, what most drew me to her were her eyes.

If I say they were fire, you will assume that I'm using a pretty metaphor. And in a way I am. Biologically speaking her eyes were, of course, eyes, made from humors and sclera like any other eyes.

Now that we've established that I know how literary devices work: her eyes *were* fire. They were comforting and consuming; an ever-shifting brightness that concealed. A gift stolen from ungenerous gods and bestowed by a titan on ungrateful humanity.

And then she spoke. And I was lost.

"There she is, shipmates." She pointed over our heads and as one we craned our necks to look up and back. The vast sphere of Jupiter hung above us, growing ever larger and closer and more all-encompassing. "For some of you, this'll be your first Jovian run"—here I felt sure her eyes lingered on me, just for a moment—"for some it'll be your twenty-first. For the old hands out there, you know how this starts: I tell you all that we will face danger, that we may face *mortal* danger, that we will not see our homes or our families for three years or more, and I tell you that it will be worth it because we will come home with a hold swimming in spermaceti to sell in the forge-bazaars of Io."

She fell silent, and I waited in silence with her for three breaths. Beside me, I heard the Pretty Vestal whisper, "It changed her, the Beast, it changed her."

And then, almost in reply, the captain said, "Well, fuck that."

"Not right at all," said the First Europan.

The Old Ionian seemed calmer. "Wait her out, she's a strange one is Old Thunder."

"We *will* go into danger," the captain repeated, to a crowd half with her at best, "into mortal danger indeed. And we will return, one day, to port, where we will hand over our cargo to the fine folks of Olympus Extraction State and they, from the bounty of their hearts, will grant us . . ." She stopped, her eyes roving over the crowd until they landed on one grizzled voider. "You there, what lay did they give you."

"Two seventy-fifth," the voider replied.

"And there you have it, shipmates." She sounded almost victorious. And as is so often the way, sounding victorious was more than half of victory. "The two hundred and seventy-fifth lay. Three years' labor. Peril and hard toil. Sweat and sorrow. And not for half of a tenth of a tenth of what this ship brings in."

As hard as I was finding it to take my eyes from the captain, I could still sense an unease amongst the crowd. This wasn't how a voyage was meant to start. Locke looked especially troubled, or rather they were a studied mask of not-troubled-ness that suggested they were very troubled indeed.

"After long, long years I worked my way to captain," A continued, "worked my way from the two hundred seventy-fifth lay to the twentieth. A few more voyages, a little luck with the darts, and who knows, I may retire a rich woman."

The crowd's unease only grew at this. Nobody liked to be reminded that other people were getting paid more than they were. I heard a "What's she got to complain about then?" from the Second Europan.

And the captain, by some witchcraft, answered her. "Ah, but the price, shipmates, the price. My last voyage, the Leviathan took my leg just as sure as it took the lives of three of my crew. The voyage before that, the sky took two good folk; the voyage before that, none, but we counted ourselves uncommon lucky. Make no mistake, my friends: It is not oil we squeeze from the stars. It is *blood*."

Though her speech had taken a sharp turn for the bizarre, the crew was beginning to fall in line. That was the thing with talk of blood and money: crowds went one way or the other, and they went that way hard.

"I tell you this." Her voice was low now, which only made us strain to hear all the more. "I plan to make a bloody voyage. We will hunt, and we will harvest, but we do not seek only the precious spermaceti. We do not seek only the good of Olympus Extraction State."

Locke's jaw tensed here, as well it might have. But everybody else had stopped their muttering. They were listening now, rapt.

"We seek the Möbius Beast. The greatest of Leviathans. We seek it not for wealth, not for glory, not even for revenge—because let me be clear, it was that very beast that took my leg and my shipmates' lives—no, we seek it so that we might say that we have touched the void itself. That we have faced the monsters that dwell at the heart of the stars and *howled* our defiance."

In spite of myself, I cheered. In spite of ourselves, a great many of us cheered. Not all of us by a long way, but enough.

"So that we might tell this devouring world that we *live*."

We cheered again. And this time there were fewer holdouts.

"That we fear *nothing*."

And again. Even the First and Second Europans joined us. Even the Pretty Vestal.

"That the sky *itself* will remember our names."

With the mob now fully on her side, she strode down amongst us and to the foot of the array. A series of touch-screens were embedded in the masts, each displaying distant sensor contacts, and the captain activated one of them. A swirling golden trail of data appeared in the center and when the captain pressed her fingertip against the screen, it locked into a solid disc with numbers forever interweaving inside it.

I'd seen this kind of crypto-lock before. We used them on messenger-ships all the time for data payloads and large currency transfers. They were indelible once set up.

"This," the captain said, "represents the whole of my lay from this voyage, whatever that may prove to be when all's done. One twentieth part of every drop we wring out of the storm clouds. And I'll pay it to whichever of you first brings me sight of the Möbius Beast."

Blood and thunder were well enough on their own, but now that she'd made it clear there was money on the line, the captain *really* had the crew's attention.

"The Beast," the captain went on, "is bone-white half its length, pitted all over with harpoon scars and other, stranger wounds. And it's long, longer than any of its species, almost of a length with the great Behemoths that swim the hydrogen sea. See it, call it out, and I swear to you that all of this"—she pointed for emphasis at the golden disc—"will be yours."

The crew exploded in a riot of celebration, drunk on the twin promises of glory and wealth. And also probably on alcohol—voiders are a drinking lot. And although I so often find myself apart from the crowd, this time I was drunk right along with them. There and then we all belonged, heart and soul, to the captain. Me as much as any.

More than any, really. Even then, even in that first moment, I loved her.

I say *even in that moment*. And time was, that's what I believed. That it was a first-sight thing. But looking back, all these years later, I know now that I loved her before I saw her. That I had loved her all my life.

Because I know now that she was death.

CHAPTER FOURTEEN

Fangirl

Right about now, you might be wondering what the hell kind of book you've picked up. And I'll be honest with you, I'm not always sure myself. Is it an adventure? A memoir? Why the fuck should you care about which bits of the Leviathan have what uses, or how we squeeze spermaceti from a corpse, or what the whir of the autocutters sounds like, or what it takes to hold a skyboat steady when you're lined to a beast that's diving into the hydrogen sea?

I don't think I've got a good answer for you. It's a big system out there. A massive, all-encompassing, incomprehensible system. And really you shouldn't care any more about the Leviathan fleet than I care about deep-crust hydroponics or comet mining or any of the other millions of invisible industries that make the supply chains work. Try to think about it all at once and your mind will probably give out under the strain. Better to just shut up, look down, and assume that somebody—the Father maybe, or the trade-states—has a plan.

But while I might not have a *good* answer, I've got a bunch of *bad* answers. I think I mentioned that I used to be a schoolmistress and so I got really good at giving plausible-sounding responses to whatever questions were thrown at me.

So let's start with sophistry.

I assume you're used to war stories? You don't think *those* are a waste of good data (or good ink, if you're reading a *very* luxurious version of this text on one of the core worlds). Perhaps, like me, you grew up on the tales of Captain Treyarch and her brave companions. Perhaps you thrilled to see the brave soldiers of the Sixty-Ninth Company battle the bloodthirsty seditionists of the campus wars, or the ungrateful insurgents of the union rebellions.

Well, those heroes, like my heroes, were salarymen like any other. Treyarch and her team had the advantage of being fictional and therefore less prone to undramatic errors or inconvenient silences than my living companions. But the industry in which they worked was real enough (as is their employer, Limtoc Kinetic Solutions being a wholly owned subsidiary of Phobos Mil State).

You might respond, I suppose, that there can't be any real comparison between the work of a soldier and the work of a sky-hunter. Soldiers fight to keep you safe from the dangers of an uncaring universe, while we sky-hunters fight glorified fish so we can chop them up into pieces. Our work, you might say, is more like mining or butchery than true honorable combat.

If you would say that, then you have never seen a Leviathan fought. I can't fault you for that; we haven't actually *gotten* to those bits yet. We will, don't worry, but before we do I want to make sure you have a true appreciation for the people who fight them.

I suppose you might say instead that it isn't the drama of the battle that makes the difference, but rather the importance of the cause. The campus wars, for example, were vital to the safety of the entire system. And on one level I can't disagree. Even now my heart skips a beat when I reread *Duty of Shadows* and come to the scene where Lieutenant Ward, armed only with an anti-personnel flechette cannon, must hold his position against a baying mob of students chanting dangerous slogans.

But what of the belt wars? What of the scene in *Duty of Fire* where Corporal Raven assaults the Trojan asteroid mines? Not only is that scene drawn from real history (the attack on mine

617 Patroclus is well known amongst military historians as the first use of the Mk III Vivisection Warsuit, optimized for use against lightly armed or unarmed adversaries), it also has at its heart the need to secure ore transports to the core worlds. Of course, the records from that time make it clear that the Union of Asteroid Workers were *also* ideologically opposed to the very concept of freedom, but we cannot forget that the method they chose to *use* in their vicious if blessedly short-lived rebellion was the severing of supply chains.

So I ask you: If it's right—and I'm sure you'll agree it's right—to celebrate those courageous warriors who fought to protect our resource lines from extremist extortion, should we not *also* celebrate those warriors who fight in the skies of Jupiter? The end is the same, after all. My companions and I stared down the storm and leapt into the jaws of death to bring home the very spermaceti that burns in the energy-forges and the atmosphere-crucibles of whichever world you live on. And while the independent sky-hunter seeks the Leviathan under contract, never again can the specter of organized labor threaten the peace and prosperity of the Commonwealth. Which is to say, *your* peace and prosperity.

Does that not make us heroes, every bit as much as the folk of the Sixty-Ninth? And real heroes, not paper ones.

And if that doesn't convince you, if you are not now satisfied that this tale is as full of excitement and importance as any war story, perhaps you'd prefer this alternative reasoning: I served on this ship. I lived alongside these people. I watched as they braved the roiling skies of Hell's Heart. And, as I write this, every last one of them is dead.

Memorials are expensive, even in the tiny sky-hunters' chapels in Cthonius Linea. So as we do *not* collectively commemorate those who give their lives in the Leviathan hunt, this book is the best tribute many of them will receive. Locke, I suppose, is recorded somewhere amongst the written-off assets of Olympus Extraction State, Dawlish down as missing, presumed escaped from indenture. And the reputation of A, of her passion and her glory and her obsession, will, I think, pass into folklore with or without my help.

This is a war story.

This is a war memorial.

It is a tribute to dead people in a dying industry in—I am sometimes sure—a society that is itself dying.

In my chamber, as I write this chapter, hard against a deadline and just as short on funds as I was at the start of my journey, the strip-lights flicker. They too are dying. I'm not sure how long I have myself.

It's the ship, above all else, I wish to make immortal. The ship. Her crew. Her captain. And Q.

CHAPTER
FIFTEEN

The Foredeck

FIRST EUROPAN VOIDER: Tap the casks, Finch, captain's orders. We'll drink well tonight.

It is an hour after the captain's speech. Less than an hour. I am here but I am not here.

SECOND EUROPAN VOIDER: I know your games. You hope if we're all drunk you'll be first to spot the Beast and take the captain's prize.

The casks are tapped. I let a dispenser-droid scan my palm and take a glass of white hydroponic spirit.

OLD IONIAN VOIDER: Don't be a fool. We'll see no beasts of any stripe till after contact. And the Great Leviathan himself, him we'll like not see at all in three years' voyage.

LOCKE: Drink now, those that have a mind to. Contact in eighteen hours, and if you're not sober by then it'll cost Olympus its investment and all of us our lives.

In other company, at another time, on another ship, Locke would command all my attention. They stand tall and severe, overlooking the revels like a sentinel statue in some ancient temple.

But my eyes and my thoughts are still all with the captain.

STARRY WISDOM VOIDER: You others chase prizes if you will. They will not protect you from the Devouring God.

ALL: Fuck off.

A VOICE (behind): *You dance?*

I am lost, still, in the captain's words. But a hand on my shoulder brings me back to the moment. Unwillingly.

I turned to see Q, her markings shining brightly in the starlight. She was holding a disposable synthetic cup whose reactive polymer coating had detected the exact brand of cheap spirit it carried and was now proudly scrolling a banner advertising *Uncle Jimbo's Finest Shine, a product of Coradini Food and Beverages, a wholly owned subsidiary of Aphrodite Pharma State.*

"What?" I asked her above the noise.

"Nunc est bibendum," she said, "nunc pede libero pulsanda tellus."

I shook my head. I had learned a little of her language in the time we'd been together, but not so much that I followed her now. "What?" I tried again.

So she reached out and took me gently by the arm. *"Dance with me."*

My fingers tightened on my glass. My heart quickened and I was all at once very aware of how many *people* were around me. I wanted to spit blood and run. "No," I said, too fast and too firmly.

The look in Q's eyes was hard to place. More confused, I thought, than hurt. More understanding than either, when understanding wasn't what I looked for or deserved. And then she shrugged, and smiled, and spun off into the crowd.

I finished my drink as quickly as I could and turned away. Snatches of other people's conversations kept catching on my thoughts like jagged metal on bare skin.

The wonderful thing about a hunter-barque was that there was always solitude to be found if you needed it. The whole crew—barring automata—filled maybe a third of the deck, leaving the whole of the rest of the vessel to lose yourself in.

Of course it didn't do to get a reputation. The last thing I wanted was for it to be put about that I was the kind who crept off alone and dug herself into strange corners of the hull whenever she was off duty. Nobody liked to ship with a crewmate like that. You never knew where you were with them. So I contented myself to walk just a little way off, to drift a handful of yards fore of the array and to look out at the terrible sphere of Jupiter beneath us.

Before this voyage I'd never seen it so close, never had a sense of the vastness of it. Even now, eighteen hours from touching its outer atmosphere, it stretched out as good as infinite. As we descended it would only grow larger, closer, and more magnificent until at last it swallowed us.

Even as I looked it was impossible to encompass the scale of it. To understand that this was a place where there were storms the size of planets, clouds that could drown worlds. Was it really any wonder that so immense an arena housed horrors like the Leviathans and all their predatory kin?

I stood like this, half dreaming, until a new needle pricked its way into my consciousness. When I'd left the crowd for the foredeck I'd thought I was alone, but now I saw a figure at the prow. Although I suppose that just made us alone in two parts.

It was undoubtedly the captain. Even at that distance her gravity was unmistakable. She stood like—the hack in me wants to say that she stood like a queen overseeing her domain, but that would undersell the stark, Promethean glory of her. She stood—and I would come to learn over time that she *always* stood—like she had just killed an emperor and was now looking over his empire, deciding how best to dismantle it.

For a while—I won't tell you how *long* a while because it's actually a bit embarrassing—I just watched her. It seems like a joke to talk about masterful inactivity, but I stood there transfixed as the captain did . . . nothing. But in my mind I conjured such soliloquies for her. Such philosophies.

In the end I gave in to her magnetism or my own curiosity or the inevitability of fate and approached. It wasn't protocol, but then protocol was a little suspended with all the crew except me and her drinking themselves blind to consecrate a hunt.

I was yards from her when she noticed me. Or when she decided to admit that she'd noticed me. She turned and fixed me with those burning eyes of hers, and I walked on anyway. I've always been a fan of walking into fire.

"Shipmate?" There was interrogation in the word. But from her lips it felt more intimate than my own name.

"Captain." There wasn't much else I could say. I had no message for her. No question. I should have stayed with the crew.

Or perhaps not. When it became clear that I had only silence to contribute, she turned away, but she seemed perfectly content for me to stand beside her. And eventually she spoke. "What do you think of her?"

"The ship?" I asked. "Or the planet?"

She didn't answer.

"Beautiful." The reply fit both.

"And have you had luck, so far, with beautiful things?"

It was my turn not to answer.

"I have not." She still didn't look at me; she might as well have been talking to Jupiter itself. "For more years than I dare count I have faced beautiful, terrible things in beautiful, terrible places and the outcome has always been bloody."

Neither I nor the stars had a reply for her.

"The end of my life approaches," she said. I wasn't quite sure what she meant because she didn't look especially old. Then again, with the radically different lifestyles and levels of access to regenerative therapies across the system, it was often hard to tell if a person was twenty-five or fifty-two or two hundred and fifty. Especially if they'd lived an adventurous life with rich rewards. "Whatever befalls on this journey, I've a premonition it will be my last."

That, finally, prodded me into responding. "Do you believe in premonitions?"

When she looked round, it was almost as though she was seeing me for the first time. "I've seen much, and so there is little I *don't* believe in."

"Is that why you're hunting legends?" The question was out before I could check myself. It hung in the air between us like vapor from a narcotic inhaler.

I wasn't sure if I'd angered her or intrigued her. Honestly, that was something I got a lot from people. "Make yourself useful, girl. Fetch me my pipe."

The captain's word was law on ship, but it was a slightly strange instruction. "Where is it?"

"My cabin." She brushed her fingertips over a nearby terminal and made some adjustments to one of the ship's many, many lists. "The locks will recognize you."

My desire to remain at her side and bask in her strange personal electricity was at war with my curiosity to see where she worked and slept. I call it a war, but her command overrode both instincts. She was my captain, I her hand. She had only to reach out and I would move according to her will.

CHAPTER SIXTEEN

The Captain's Table

Going to the captain's cabin required me to pass once more through the increasingly raucous crowd.

```
TALL GANYMEDIAN VOIDER: Hup, now, and play us a
reel.

SECOND EUROPAN VOIDER: Play it yourself, you
pampered fuckstain.
```

As I approached the stairwell that led to the door that led to the cabin, I saw Locke watching me. They had suspicion in their eyes, but I wasn't sure it was suspicion of *me* exactly. If nothing else, the ship's systems were all bio-locked and so it was pretty hard for anybody to get anywhere they weren't meant to be.

I scanned my palm at the door, and it slid sideways with only a slight squeak from a decaying servo. Leaving the night's chaos on the deck, I slipped inside.

The door shut behind me and I was alone in a wide cabin lit by ivory lamps. My expectations of the captain's sleeping arrangements had been contradictory. On the one hand I had imagined something spartan, something suited to a woman who thought only of the hunt. On the other, though, I had imagined something baroque, bedecked in the bones of Leviathans and scrimshawed all over like the ravings of a debunked saint.

I was correct, in a way, on both counts.

The main chamber was sparse: a low table set on an inauspicious arrangement of tatami mats was the only furniture, and that table was bare, although from the mirror sheen of it, it looked like an imaging desk. The walls were lightly decorated but what decoration I saw was indeed scrimshaw, finely detailed scenes of the chase engraved on panels of Leviathan ivory. The actual sleeping chamber was set a little to one side, through an archway behind a little silk curtain. It was not, I told myself, a violation to investigate it. I had been sent for a pipe, after all, and that was a personal item so likely to be kept in a personal space.

Were I a more conscientious ship's hand, I would have gone immediately to that room, retrieved the object I had been sent to retrieve, and returned to the captain for whatever thanks she wanted to give me.

But I'm not conscientious. You might have noticed. I dally. I detour. I go off on tangents and into reveries. Honestly it made me a terrible voider, and I'm not sure it does me many favors as a memoirist either. (In the second case, I'm hoping that if I'm obscurantist enough people will assume I'm deep; if not now then at least after I die.)

So instead of going at once to search the captain's sleeping chamber I stopped and looked at the windows of her cabin.

They were immense, occupying the whole of the rear wall, and half of the two that joined it. And because the cabin sat flush against the outer hull, they were sloped sharply outwards so that if you stood right next to them you could look down and it was as though there was nothing between you and the endless celestial drop. If Jupiter looked intimidating from the prow, seeing it through a dome designed primarily for looking up, then viewed from the windows of the captain's cabin it was overwhelming.

Gazing down, I imagined sometimes that I could discern

the bodies of Leviathans moving in the clouds. I couldn't, any more than the ancient cosmonauts looking up at Earth from Luna could see individual fish in the seas. The Jovian Leviathans are larger, of course, than any of the beasts of Old Earth, but then the planet is larger still. Larger and shrouded in eternal clouds.

It's a cliché, a terrible cliché, to say that through those windows the planet looked near enough to touch. But sometimes a cliché is reality and sometimes we really are seized with the need to reach out and grasp something even if we know it's unattainable. Even if we know it's still a hundred thousand miles away and that touching it would freeze or burn or crush us into pulp and flinders.

Sometimes we want nothing more than to touch oblivion.

I didn't think I lingered long at that window, watching Jove mocking us from below. But I clearly had, because a voice behind me said, "It was a simple task, shipmate."

Turning, I saw the captain standing by the door. She was, I am sure to this day, incapable of irreverence; she spoke every word like it was prophecy, but that didn't mean she couldn't be sarcastic when she wanted to.

"I got distracted," I explained. Insofar as it *was* an explanation. It was more just a restatement of my failure.

"Are you often distracted?"

I comforted myself with the knowledge that whatever I said, I was aboard now and so she couldn't throw me off the ship for three years. Well, she *could* throw me off earlier, but only if she was in the mood for actual murder. Still, I thought it safest to say "No."

It wasn't safest. "Don't be a liar as well as a laggard. I know your kind."

"And what kind is that?" Defiance was a bad choice here, but some remarks touched a deep instinct in me that demanded a reply.

"Tourists."

It wasn't what I'd feared, but I had more than one nerve

that didn't like to be touched. "I'm no surfacer," I insisted. "I've made three journeys with the merchant service. Twice with Aphrodite, once with the very state that owns this ship."

She'd taken advantage of my indignation to close the distance between us. And she moved with such grace and such confidence and such absolute presence that my heart skipped and my mouth went dry. "*No surfacer,*" she repeated. And she was close enough now to hook two fingers beneath my chin and tilt my face to hers. "More than half by my count. You still smell of solid ground and fresh-mined water. Were we still bodyside I'd call you for a schoolmistress sooner than a huntress. And had I been in the room when those fools Thoreau and Emerson took you on I'd have warned them against it. *Pass by that one*, I would have said. *She's a dreamer, and there's no place on the ship for dreamers.*"

I don't know what made me say "Except one," but I did. And it did not go over well. She glared at me with eyes as dark and as forbidding and as inviting as the sky between the stars.

"And what do you mean by that?"

If I'd been the sort of person who knew when to stop, I might have. "I'm pretty sure you know exactly what I mean."

One of the things that most draws me to the skies is the strange mix of protection and exposure you have in a voidship. Behind layers of bulkheads and foot-thick alloy walls you're safer than anywhere else in the system, but on the other side of all that steel and crystal is an annihilating nothing that hates nature as sure as nature hates it. I was getting a very similar feeling now, alone with the captain in her cabin and talking, if I was honest, in a way I knew I shouldn't be talking. Nothing there could harm me except her.

With an unexpected gentleness that came packaged with an entirely expected certainty, she took me by the shoulders and turned me to the window. And once again I saw the cloud-ribboned face of Jupiter, streaked around with white and red and orange and flashed here and there with lightning. Closer now, I was beginning to make out textures in it, shapes; but with no surface to see through to it was mists on mists on mists like some grand optical illusion.

"What do you see?" asked the captain, her lips close to my ear and her breath so warm on my cheek it almost burned.

It felt a whole lot like a trick question. But I wasn't smart enough to have a trick answer. "The planet?"

"And if I say I see something else, which of us is the dreamer?"

"You're going to say it's me, aren't you?"

One of her hands slipped to my waist, and the other reached out past me to point with a slender artisan's finger at the skyscape. "What you see there," she said, "is nothing but a congregation of vapors."

"It's a gas giant. It's vapors all the way down."

"To a surfacer, perhaps. But that's because you've only seen the stars with your eyes."

This wasn't making her sound any less like a dreamer. And I decided to risk pointing that out. "Whereas you've seen them with, what, your soul?"

Instead of a reply, she guided my arm downwards and my fingertips through the slit in her skirt to her thigh, where warm flesh gave way to ivory and metal and neuro-integrated circuitry. "I've seen them with blood. And with bone. I've seen them in the burning-freezing-burning of my skin as my boat fell out of the heavens. I've seen them in the crush of twenty atmospheres against my skull and the gut-deep twist of a gravity we never evolved for. I've seen them in the snatching limbs and scything jaws of the Leviathans themselves. That's how I see the stars. Call it a dream if you like, but it's for sure a *waking* dream. A true dream."

I had enough of my schoolmistress's instincts to know sophistry when I heard it. But right then, with her hands one at my hip and one at my wrist and mine one on her thigh and one on the star-cold viewing window, I wasn't really in a formal debate headspace.

If there's one thing I want, more than anything else, for you to understand about A—my captain, my alpha, my primary and my principal—it's that when you were close to her, she defined reality. The whole crew felt it, with only Locke, who had long ago sold their mind and heart to Olympus Extraction State, and Q, whose ways were eternally her own, seeming immune. Under the captain's gaze her will was all the world and everything that could be seen or touched or felt outside of it was a pasteboard mask.

Which was why, instead of telling her that she was playing semantic games, I turned my face so that my lips were as close to hers as they could come without getting me immediately flogged for insubordination and whispered, "Show me."

Okay, it was *partly* why. But also it had been a weird day and I react to weird days in one of two ways. Believe it or not, this was the healthier one.

"You'll see soon enough," she replied. "Contact in a few hours. Then the hunt begins."

She knew what I meant. You didn't touch somebody like that and then talk about seeing with your body instead of your eyes if you didn't, on some level, know what you were doing. I brushed my fingertips lightly along the curve of her leg, moving away from the biomechanical connection in part out of respect and in part because it was, in general, the more interesting direction. "Show me," I repeated.

"If I'd wanted a ship's whore I'd have hired one on Europa."

Looking back, I'm still not sure if this was a trick. Part of the captain's gift was that she so easily guided you to wanting what she needed you to want. I don't even necessarily think she did it consciously. Some people have an instinct for swaying others, and if they follow their calling they become preachers or executives or ship's captains. They save or ruin lives.

"Show me," I said for the third time. I privately promised myself it would be the last because there was a fine line between flirting and begging and I was already tripping hard over it.

Fortunately—short term fortunately, long term is something else—I didn't need to test that promise. Apparently feeling that I'd had my chance to back out, she lowered her face to my neck and whispered against my skin. "It starts soft," she said, "but searing." And her breath on my neck was sparks and solar wind. "The atmosphere is thin and so there's nothing between you"—her lips were *so close* to me now, close but not quite touching—"and the hateful glare of Sol."

Normally, this was where I'd have been closing my eyes, but the Jovian worldscape below me was too entrancing.

"It's here the elvesses live," she went on, "where they come sharp and sudden"—she brought a hand to my neck and scratched me, sharp and sudden—"and deadly." Her tongue traced a line across the fading marks. "The beasts you'll find here are old and close to dying, gasping for thin air and catching lightning in their mouths where they can."

There were her hands again, there were her fingernails digging into my skin.

"Still, their oil sells. Less well, but it sells. The real prizes lie deeper." In illustration, the hand at my hip wandered downwards, her fingers slipping beneath my waistband. "It grows colder as you go, until the clouds gather and it rains ammonia, and the pressure"—she pressed firmly down, her fingers tracing the line between my hip and my thigh—"builds until it's of a piece with the air of Old Earth."

And although it was a dream, it was a waking dream. My eyes were open but I could still see, as clear as if I'd dropped a tab of Lysergix™ (Property of Ovda Recreational Hallucinogenics, a wholly owned subsidiary of Aphrodite Pharma State), the turbulent layers of the Jovian atmosphere peeling back before me like some bizarre celestial striptease.

"But there *is* no surface," she went on, so close that I could feel the words on her lips. "No *this* or *that*, no *here* or *there*. Just the slow imperceptible shift"—and again she echoed it with her body, the slightest of changes in her touch sending new and taunting sensations through me, a promise of more and deeper and stranger and darker. More clouded and more secret.

In a spirit of reciprocity I wasn't always inclined to, I moved my own hand along her thigh, but she caught it and twisted it and pinned it behind my back in a way that stung with just the right edge of pain.

"As you descend," she said into my skin, "there are no borders or boundaries, but *crossways*. There's barriers there all right. Harsh and violent boundaries." She turned my wrist just a shade farther and I couldn't quite stifle a sigh. "Red to white to red, and the great winds catch in the middle and churn and spin."

She turned me, pressing my back to the window. And with both my wrists pinned to my chest she leaned close and spoke with her lips an atom's breadth from mine. "And now," she half whispered, half growled, "we're in the real Jupiter. And the beasts here are murderous and majestic."

I'd given up struggling or even playing at struggle. There was something about the captain that demanded submission, and I was more than happy to meet her demands.

"Here"—her fingertips eased inside me—"is where it rains diamonds. Here"—her eyes met mine just for a moment—"is where the hunt begins. Where we pierce the skies"—and I am pierced by pleasure and surrender and the unthinkable monomaniacal power of her—"where it grows hotter and denser and Wyrms flock like sparrows. Where Behemoths swim on a sea with no surface."

I gasped and tensed and I wanted to close my eyes but wouldn't let myself.

"Here is Hell's Heart. Here is the face of every god and none."

I died a little. As we all would soon enough.

After the captain dismissed me, I slunk back to the cabin I shared with Q.

I have a . . . tricky relationship with shame. The catechism teaches that we are all sinners, and that our sins can be absolved only by making the proper offerings—in cash or by digital transfer—to the Father's appointed representatives. I like to think I've left that behind, along with the Church's views on sex, family, and bioengineering. But as I climbed down the cold, slightly wobbly ladder between Access and Habitation, I couldn't help but wonder what I'd been thinking. Running to heaven is a funny way to escape a god.

Unless you're looking for a new one.

Q was already in bed when I got there, still communing with her little glass idol. She didn't ask me where I'd been, and I didn't much feel like telling her.

I think she might have guessed, though. Because she only said one thing as I lay down, shut my eyes, and tried to sleep instead of weeping.

She said, "Cave." And then, when I clearly didn't understand, she consulted the idol once more and said, "*Beware.*"

CHAPTER SEVENTEEN

Contact

One of the many true things the captain had told me the night she'd fucked me against the window of her cabin a couple of hours after informing the whole crew that we were about to hunt myths in the most hostile place in the system was that there were no sharp boundaries on Jupiter, at least not vertically. So where in a different descent there would be a clear moment of atmospheric contact, just as there would be a clear moment of landing, here instead Jove reached his tendrils out into the interplanetary void like a rich man casually groping an employee.

There were a hundred jobs to be done come contact. Hull temperatures to be measured, external pressure to be monitored for the switchover from rocket to jet to rotor, the array to be watched in case we caught an early spout, the boats to be primed before their first lowering, and the unending parade of glitches, breakdowns, bugs, SNAFUs, and FUBARs to be jumped on.

It was the boats for me in those first hours, under Flint, the third mate. While outside the atmospheric deceleration was shrouding the hull in a dull amber glow, I was lying on my back under a fixed-wing spear-boat, flushing coolant lines.

"Keep those coils tight," Flint was telling me; he didn't really need to. "We're hunting big fish this voyage. Bigger fish than you've ever seen."

I made vague, aye-aye type noises and carried on flushing.

"You know about the Möbius Beast, girl?" Flint asked, with a glee I'd eventually learn was typical of him.

"Not much," I replied, then reached out for a replacement helium coupling.

"A monster," he told me, all joy and gun sparks. "Mightiest monster in the skies, and our captain's the one to bring him down, no doubt about that."

On that much, at least, we agreed. The echoes of her were still shimmering across my skin.

"When you're done there," he went on, "fit these." He slid a box of chunky c-coils towards me. They had a jury-rigged look that I wasn't sure I'd trust. Then again, I didn't trust most things. "The more acceleration we can get on the darts, the better we'll be set when the devils start coming for us."

I didn't know what Flint's religious background was. Given his tremendous love of firepower, he was almost certainly Church of Liberty, or one of its branches. But devils were a common part of many faiths and, for that matter, a common figure of speech.

"They say the Möbius Beast fell on a ship out of Phobos a few years back," he went on. I had a feeling he was Phobosi himself, which made me take notice. I'd been taught the Criterion of Embarrassment at a young age, and so I was far more likely to believe people when they were making their own in-group look bad.

"Now those ships have *real* guns," he said with a note of rapture. "Terawatt launchers, atmospheric dazzlers, the works." His voice lowered. "Still, they barely got out alive."

I'd heard a hundred voiders' stories, and they rarely needed encouragement to keep telling them, but I was actually interested this time so I asked, "What happened?" in the hope he'd give me the detailed version.

"The *Beast* happened," he said. It felt more like an opening than an answer, so I kept quiet. "They didn't know what they'd found at first—it was just a burst on the array—so they dropped boats and sent them out a-scouting, and that's when they saw him."

He paused for effect. They always paused for effect.

"Big as a battle cruiser, scarred deep and long from launchers, plates of milk-white bone all along his back and talons all scything beneath him. Jaws wide enough to swallow a wing of fighters."

I didn't normally pay much attention to these kinds of stories—okay that's a lie, I pretend I don't pay much attention to these kinds of stories while secretly loving every second of them—but my mind went back to the captain. To the thought of her falling through the Jovian clouds, minuscule in the face of the Beast.

It was an impossible thought in so many ways. No matter how incomprehensibly vast the Möbius Beast might have been, in my mind the captain always eclipsed it. She eclipsed stars and worlds and realities.

"The folk of Phobos," Flint was continuing, "they're bold but not foolish. They turned fins back to the barque soon as they saw the monster. But it was too late. They'd caught his eye and his blood was up."

Leviathans do have eyes. They don't exactly have blood.

Oblivious to his poor metaphor, Flint went on. "A boat is more agile than a Leviathan, but the beast is faster over long distance. The skies of Jupiter are where they live and, well, we use their brain juice as fuel for a reason."

I snapped the last of the c-coils into place and scooted out to fire up a test pulse. Then when all I got was a smell of burned polymer and the hiss of venting coolant, I ducked back to try again.

Momentarily put off his story by the need to do his actual job, Flint gave an affectionate rap on the wing of the boat. "Focus, girl. Don't waste material." The ringing faded from my ears, and Flint went back to his tale. "They made it back to the barque all right, but it didn't help them. The Möbius Beast came raging out of the skies like the wrath of whatever gods you care for. They raked it with a broadside—all Phobosi ships run cannon—and it still plowed through like it weren't nothing but a heavy rain. And then its jaws and its claws and its horrid mandibles ripped into the side of the barque with all the rage and malice of—"

"Progress?" Locke's voice came sharp and clear from the internal elevator. "Or are you too busy swapping tall tales?"

"Guns'll be ready when we find the Beast," Flint replied, only a little sourly. "Would have been ready far sooner if you'd signed off when I asked."

As if to illustrate his point, or undermine it depending on how things went, I sent another test pulse. Less burning this time, that was positive.

"These boats are still property of Olympus." Even half under the hull of a flyer I could hear the disdain in Locke's voice. "And you are making these *upgrades* against my judgment."

Sometimes Flint was a walking smirk. "Fuck your judgment."

"Very professional of you."

"Professional don't keep the beasts right side of the hull."

From the story he'd just been telling, *nothing* kept the beasts right side of the hull.

"Professional keeps the ship in the right skies, her hold full of spermaceti, and all her hands alive."

The suspension of the boat *glink*ed as Flint leaned against it, pushing the undercarriage just that little bit closer to my face. "Tell that to the captain. I'm fair sure she's decided different."

There was a pause there, ominous enough that I stopped welding.

"The captain has—" I could practically *hear* the moisture disappearing from Locke's mouth. "She is not currently prioritizing the mission."

When he wasn't a walking smirk, Flint was a walking shrug. "The mission is to hunt Leviathans. Seems to me it don't much matter which."

"You've a stake in this voyage as much as anybody. More profit and less danger should be your lodestar, as it is mine."

Locke was the only person I'd ever known who could make risk management sound sexy.

"Captain wants what she wants," replied Flint. "And as I see it, what'll be'll be. And whatever comes I'd rather face it well-armed."

There was that silence again. There was the shadow of the captain, smothering us all in a way that some railed against, some relaxed into, and I found the sweetest flavor of oblivion.

"Make your changes." Locke's voice was void-cold. "And pray in the style of whatever church raised you that this hunt fails."

Flint made a sound so dismissive that it was practically blasphemous. Then he kicked another set of coils over to me. When Locke's footsteps had faded and the elevator had hissed its way into some other part of the ship, he leaned back against the body of the boat and said, not to anybody in particular, "Locke's problem, I reckon, is that they still think the world makes sense."

I stayed silent. It wasn't my place to speculate on what the officers' problems were.

"But you and me"—okay, perhaps he was talking to me after all—"we know better. Don't we?"

Not wanting to be part of anything if I could help it, I made noncommittal sounds.

And sure enough, Flint went on to tell me the thing he was confident we both knew. "We know it's all a joke. A giant joke on the lot of us. Our whole species is predestinated like that— what happens happens, and you can laugh or cry or care all you want, but it won't change a damned thing." He chuckled fatalistically. "Not a damned thing."

CHAPTER
EIGHTEEN
The Array

Atmospheric contact went smoothly, for all Locke's concerns. And for a while the ship permitted itself to forget that it had been subsumed into the captain's private fixation. The regular duties of a hunter-voyage, which were mostly the same as the regular duties of a merchant-voyage (but with more harpoons) or a mercenary-voyage (but with less bombing) took over.

All us ordinary voiders rotated through all our ordinary duties, and on one particular day it was my shift on the array.

The unpredictable ionic conditions of Jupiter's storms make the eyeball mark one an occasionally useful part of the ship's sensor suite. An indispensable one when looking for a specific beast. So while another barque would sometimes leave the array unmanned and rely on automated detection, on the Pequod there was always somebody perched at the pinnacle of the vessel, watching the monitors and the atmosphere gauges and the horizon.

I'm not going to tell you about my first experience of the array. The thing about life in the stars is with one or two exceptions (the launch, the battle with the Leviathan, some of the sex, and one or two of the deaths), firsts and lasts and everything in the middle are all part of the same grimy soup.

The voider's profession is an eternal one. It's outside time.

And it's never more outside time than when you're perched at the top of the array, watching for beasts in the clouds.

On my first trip up, and my ninth, and my thirtieth, I began by catching hold of a pair of ascender-bars that ran the length of the aerial. A closed elevator capsule would be safer, but although the ship was huge, launch mass was still at a premium. So every time I started my shift at the watch, I was whisked skywards over a drop of hundreds of feet. Only the strength of my hands and the grip of my boots stood between me and a short, gravitationally normalized fall followed by a messy death splattered across the deck.

As ways to die on a hunter-barque went, it was by far the least romantic, but for the half a dozen seconds of the ascent it still thrilled me every time. The precious moments of nothing but holding and waiting and listening to the wind whip past as I rose. It was like traveling into another life on another world, as apart from the ship as the ship was from the dock or the dock was from any city that *wasn't* perpetually flinging itself into the vacuum.

If you've never been on a hunter-barque, it's hard to describe the view from the array. You'd think it wouldn't be much different from the deck. After all, there's no *surface* anyway, so high up is high up no matter what. But there's something about the angles, about the way you can look so far down on all sides, until sight starts to play tricks on you and it's red-and-white nothing above and below and around, and everything in motion as the ship rolls and the clouds roil and the winds sing past the dome. It feels like the long slow walk into heaven we were all promised but so few of us will be able to afford.

I'll be honest, I was shit at standing watch.

Your job on the array is to pay attention, and I've never been great at paying attention. Right back to my schooldays, when the teacher would pull me up for not listening to the day's readings and the preachers would pull me up for the same exact reason. At the time I couldn't put into words quite why it pissed me off so much. In hindsight, I think it was the fucked-up cocktail of presumption and irony. Sitting fifth from the end and third from the back in neat, regimented rows and being told to learn by heart the words of people who never sat in a row in their life. People who found lessons in fires and on mountaintops and on roads between cities, who only paid heed to the voices that spoke to them from the empty desert and the open sky.

My teachers would have said the difference is that those men were prophets, and I was just some little shit who didn't want to study. Maybe they were even right. Maybe calling myself a dreamer or a wanderer or even a voider is just a way of covering up my inadequacies.

On top of the array, though, the difference between a philosopher and an asshole is meaningless. With a hundred yards between me and the rest of the crew and four hundred thousand miles between me and Europa and five hundred million miles between me and the sun, I was a speck in an endless void that was itself just a speck inside an even bigger endless void. Emptiness nested inside emptiness nested inside emptiness. I would feel it echoing inside me and, arrogant and rebellious though it might have been, I couldn't help imagining that it was how the fathers and founders from Old Earth felt when the Father reached out from the skies and spoke to them.

To me, He spoke mostly about how insignificant I was. In that regard He and my old teachers would have agreed in almost every particular.

Given that we did, in fact, sometimes spot Leviathans, and that they were, in fact, sometimes picked up by a diligent array-watcher rather than an undistractable automated system, I am forced to conclude that I was *uniquely* terrible in this job. Q, I am sure, excelled at it.

"Nihil?" she would ask me, when I returned to her arms at the end of the watch. Which I did often but not always.

And I would blink and shake my head because my mind was still full of vapor-thoughts and echoes. And she would laugh and call me something affectionate but probably insulting in her strange Earther language. And then she would kiss me, and I would remember things I had forgotten on my watch, and I would feel like a different kind of prophet.

"Si ignoras te, o pulcherrima inter mulieres," she would whisper, "egredere, et abi post vestigia gregum et pasce haedos tuos juxta tabernacula pastorum."

The words were familiar yet unfamiliar, and though I didn't know what they meant, I understood. I knew that they were kind. That they said I was beautiful. That they were, in some strange and elusive way, holy. I tried to let them be enough. Because they should have been. She should have been.

But at the back of my heart, the sky still had its hooks in me. The sky and the things that lived in it.

CHAPTER NINETEEN

Weaving

By the standards of voidships, the hunter-barque is a small affair, but that's because voidships are, to use a technical voiders' term, fucking enormous. Propelling mass into and out of gravity wells is an expensive business, and since life support and radiation shielding and gravitics and propulsion and processing and all the other hundreds of things you need to make a ship *work* take up space, and almost as much space on a small ship as on a big ship, the incentive is to build big so that economies of scale can work their miracles.

And what that means, in turn, is that a ship is full of places where hardly anybody ever goes, but where things still sometimes go wrong, and still need hooking up, maintaining, or otherwise patching together. Void travel is dangerous, and one of the things that makes its flavor of danger so uniquely unpalatable to sensible people is that nine times out of ten the thing that actually kills you is something falling apart deep in inside a place you've never even thought about.

Most captains try to avoid that wherever possible, and though her overall goals were different from most captains', A hadn't lived as long as she had or stared as far as she had into the cold and the dark without learning to take maintenance seriously.

Which was why on this particular day (early in the voyage, though not so early that it didn't already feel like the ship had been my whole world forever), Q and I were dangling between decks, foot-thick iron bulkheads either side of us, weaving the world together.

If you're a surfacer, and you almost certainly are, you've probably not seen a sword-weld before. Hell, even if you've spent your whole life on voidships or skystations you probably haven't. But you've certainly walked over them. Somewhere, buried deep inside whatever machine makes your world run, there will be some giant fucking bits of metal that need to be held together, have room to flex, and not grind horribly. You don't think about that, just like all the other things you don't think about. All those things you know to be true or believe to be true and which, ironically, need to fit together at the back of your mind, have room to flex, and not grind too horribly in case you start having to notice them.

And while there's no easy fix for the psychological version, for the physical version we have the sword-weld. It isn't the exciting kind of technology, it's not nanosurgery or a pleasure-drone, but it helps things work for just a little while longer before they surrender to time and friction and mechanical despair.

It's called a sword-weld because you build it with a sword. Not the weapon kind of sword, though it's sharp enough you could still lose a hand to it. It's a long, thin piece of metal you use to guide a weft of monofilament wire into place once you've shuttled it through a warp of tensile cables, each as thick as your finger. The work is heavy and delicate at the same time, because the weld needs to run floor to ceiling, sometimes across multiple decks, but also to be woven tightly, neatly, and by hand.

So Q and I were hanging midway between the forty-seventh and forty-eighth levels, the hum of nameless machinery in our ears, each of us playing our part in the tedious, necessary work of sword-welding.

What with our only partly speaking each other's languages, my relationship with Q was never especially verbal, but when we were working she had a kind of focused silence that... I mean I could try and say something philosophical here but I'm not proud, I mostly just found it a massive turn-on. I'd weave the weft into place and the moment my fingers were clear she'd zip up on her line and start pressing the fibers together. There was a wonderful rhythm to it. A synchronicity that felt a little bit like dancing and a little bit like fucking, although far less fun than at least one of them.

On the whole, I was glad I had the job that *didn't* involve working with a razor-edged piece of carbide alloy. My wandering mind was a liability to the ship when I manned the array. Down here in the dark and close it would have been a liability to my body and my friend's, and I had ample incentive to keep both of those intact.

This particular day, my mind was wandering down recriminatory paths. Self-recriminatory, mostly, because that was how I'd been raised. Judgment was reserved first for outsiders, then our own failings, and never under any circumstances for our betters. In a moment of abstraction I almost fell out of rhythm and Q's sword came down close enough that I was very glad I kept my fingernails short.

"*I regret*," she said.

I looked up at her. "My fault. Got distracted."

"Quid?" she asked.

That was a tricky one. "Just... doesn't it bother you?"

"Quid?" she asked again.

"Me," I said. And then added, "All of—everything about me."

She gazed at me like she had no idea what I meant, and although that should have made me feel better it was massively the opposite.

"I know I'm not exactly... easy. Or particularly faithful."

"*Faithful*," she echoed. And then after a moment she said. "*Ah.* Fidelis." She looked deeply confused. "Non es fidelis?"

This was going to some uncomfortable places. "I fuck around like, *a lot*."

I suspected that *fuck around* was going to give her some issues but I had no idea how to explain it to Q. But it turned out I'd underestimated her. She laughed. "*I do not own you,*" she said—it was rare for her to say so many words of Exodite together, but then it was basically a verb, two pronouns, and a negation. "*You do not own me.*"

"And," I replied, more hesitantly than I really needed to, "you're okay with that?"

"*I am not—*" she seemed to be looking for a word. "—Peregrinus. *Exodite.*"

It wasn't quite the reply I'd expected. "What's that got to do with anything?"

And she looked a little sad then. "*To explain. Difficult.*" She brought her sword down again to slide the next thread into place. "*Too difficult.*" But I clearly didn't find this satisfying so she went with, "*At home*"—a shrug, so easy and so casual it flat-out sent me—"*we share.*"

That fit. The difficult thing was that it fit everything I'd been told about the barbaric ways of the Terrans. It's axiomatic in the Church of Prosperity that all righteousness, all goodness, and all morality stem from property rights, which is why we teach that sex must be kept strictly within either marriage or employment structures. It's probably the Church tenet I've broken most often. The tricky part was that, as stifling as I'd found the culture I was born into, I still couldn't help thinking of it as a light in the darkness, and couldn't quite imagine a society where that light didn't exist at all. Or at least, I couldn't imagine anything good about it.

Having, if anything, given myself even more to obsess about, I went back to weaving, while Q went back to her sword-work and I tried to build up the courage to ask her more. To ask her what she actually believed in, how it was possible to believe in *anything* if she didn't start out by believing you could own things. In the dark days of Old Earth, I remember being taught, there were thousands of different religions fighting for supremacy instead of the objectively better system supported by the Big Three Incorporated Churches. And they'd teach all sorts of things. Strange things about strange virtues that no sensible person cared about in our enlightened age. As I watched the sword-weld coming together, I remembered that in some of those bizarre, better-dead faiths they said that time was a tapestry, that fate and chance and freedom wove together to make a pattern that no one of those things could make alone.

Looking up at Q, working away with her sword, I wondered if that was what she believed. If she saw fate as a skein of thread that she could dance along without constantly berating herself for who she was. I wondered what it must feel like to believe it. According to the Catechism of Prosperity we were, ultimately, responsible for our own destinies, and it was a doctrine I'd never really questioned. The world, the Church told us, was just, for what loving Father would create an unjust world? Hard work was always rewarded, and if it appeared not to be, well, you must not have been working hard enough.

Then again, the Starry Wisdom preached that the only true power was entropy and our only agency was in choosing the means of our own destruction. And I was pretty sure we couldn't both be right.

Better, perhaps, to imagine a tapestry.

Whatever ecumenical conclusions I might eventually have drawn in this particular reverie, I was interrupted by an alarm. A single long blast echoing through every deck and crawlspace on the ship so that no hand could possibly avoid it or ignore it. And then Marsh's voice, crackling over comms.

"A spout"—his tone was urgent, contrary to the nihilistic teachings of his faith—"forty klicks to starboard."

We were halfway through a line, halfway through the job, but it didn't matter. Maintenance was important, but the spout was the sacred calling of the hunter-barque. It was our rice and our meat, our means of living. And for me, at least, this first call had a special magic to it—*this* was what I'd come to the skies for. To see legends. To chase wonders.

To follow a brilliant, terrible woman into the jaws of oblivion.

CHAPTER TWENTY

Boats

Just as a mercenary will get pissy at you if you say *gun* when you mean *rifle*, *pistol*, or *antipersonnel neurotoxin diffuser*, voiders get extremely upset at you if you say *boat* when you mean *ship* or for that matter if you say *jet* or worst of all *fighter* when you mean *boat*.

We're going to the boats now. In a moment you're about to see the great Leviathan hunt in all its glory. Well, some of its glory. It would be fucking awful pacing if I put the most exciting hunting scene in chapter twenty-one, after all.

But before we get to the action, I'm going to talk to you at length about technical details. Think of it as a stern parent telling you to eat all your dinner so that you'll appreciate your dessert. Or if you don't buy that, assume I just really enjoy edging my readers.

If you like you could think about both of those things at once, but it might make a mess of your sex life.

Where was I?

Oh yes. The boats.

If you want to understand the Leviathan hunt, you need to understand one thing first and foremost. It's impossible. Nothing about it should remotely work. The beasts are too vast and too well armored. They break physical laws that still constrain our vessels. They thrive in an environment that would kill you, or me in seconds, same way it would any fucker without so much chrome in them that they're more a capex line item than a human being.

They are monsters. They are legends. They are gods.

And we are a bunch of terrestrial primates flying machines whose core technological principles haven't really changed in a millennium.

It's a miracle any of it works at all.

The hunter-boat (just "boat" in this text and any text on the subject worth reading) is a fixed-wing atmospheric craft that seats six comfortably and twelve uncomfortably. Its mandatory crew include a pilot, a copilot, a harpooner, and three others, one of whom takes primary responsibility for the kill proper. If there's an officer in the boat, that's usually their job. Killing and giving orders. Because apparently the hunter fleet thinks those two jobs are the same thing.

Each boat has two harpoon cannon fixed to its wings, but since they only fire forwards and in a single plane, each boat also carries a human harpooner—Q and Marsh and Dawlish on the Pequod; some have more, some have fewer, although all have at least two—who can aim more freely and take more precise shots.

Of course, doing this means opening the canopy, which exposes the entire crew to the Jovian atmosphere, which makes that particular part of the job an absolute fucking nightmare. Pedantic readers might note that exposing the crew to the Jovian atmosphere also flushes the breathable air out of the boat every time the canopy flips. In a real hunt, there's a short changeover window where the O_2 is evacuated when the canopy drops and then the air is recycled when it goes up again. But if I prefaced every reference to the canopy dropping with a short description of the atmosphere exchange it would get really tedious really fast. Anyway, it doesn't usually matter because in 90 percent of the boat scenes we'll all have our suits on anyway.

Where was I?

Oh yes, harpoons. The purpose of the harpoons isn't to kill

the beast, just to keep us tethered to it so it can't get away, and so that it will—in theory—gradually tire from fighting against our engines. The killing blow comes later, and I'll tell you all about that when it becomes important.

Usually, when I write one of these chapters, I find a way to make it philosophical. To make the boat a metaphor for the shared human condition or the harpoon a symbol of those things that tie us together even as they harm us. Or maybe the canopy that covers the boat until the critical moment says something about the way safety is so often at odds with opportunity.

Honestly, though, today I'm not feeling it.

Sometimes a cigar is just a cigar. A boat is just a boat. A Leviathan is just a Leviathan.

CHAPTER TWENTY-ONE

Going Down

"All hands, stations for lowering" was the announcement, repeated every thirty-four seconds over comms. There was no other signal needed. I was by far the greenest of the crew and even I knew what was expected of me.

Q and I clambered back to the launch deck up grimy cables and rickety ladders. There were elevators, somewhere, but we were nowhere near them, and they ran fast and crowded during a drop. When we arrived at our boat we were very much the worse for the trip and since we were flying under Locke, that meant we got the harshest but silentest dressing down I'd ever received.

"A four point three," they told us. In hunters' slang the value of an expected chase was measured relative to the size of the electromagnetic disturbance the creature's priceless neurotransmitters generated in response to the ship's sensors. This we measured on a ten-point scale that was named for its inventor, but since that man was clever, rich, and dead, I can't be bothered to name him here. "We'll see larger before long, but its wake will be fierce enough."

Q needed no further instruction. She was already taking up her place in the boat, coilgun by her side, atmospheric suit in place and helmet at the ready. I would have been just as quick, *should* have been just as quick, but for the sight of the captain across the launch bay.

I wasn't the only one watching. It's not that it was uncommon for a captain to go down to the boats with their crew; in fact it was common enough that there was a boat stowed in one side of the bay that, technically, had been reserved for the captain's use. But the crew was small, and we all knew each other, and a hunter-boat wasn't a solo craft.

Things only grew stranger when she passed her hand over the lock and the canopy hissed back to admit her.

```
OLD IONIAN VOIDER: She can't mean to fly alone.

SECOND EUROPAN VOIDER: Has she lost her wits?
Are we in deep skies with a captain out of her
mind?
```

She climbed into the cockpit and the canopy closed behind her. Just as I wasn't the only one watching, I also wasn't the only one to see the flickering shapes that moved behind the glass. Phantoms of light and data.

```
TALL GANYMEDIAN VOIDER: Strike me, it's
haunted.

OLD IONIAN VOIDER: Aye, it's the ghosts of her
old crew she brings with her.
```

Even if I hadn't been raised in a church that forbade superstition, I don't think I would have believed in ghosts. And the lights in the cabin looked more holographic to me than sepulchral. Still, I knew the captain a little by then, and the Old Ionian wasn't entirely wrong. The captain carried ghosts with her by the hundreds. Ghosts of the past and the present and, like the Old Earth fable about a wise man misled by spirits, ghosts of things yet to come.

But as Locke seemed about to remind me, I was not there to stare at my captain, or to second-guess her choices. I was there to join in the great hunt for monsters. And the moment I called back my senses, I was full of passion for the chase.

Though I was new to the hunt the good captains Emerson and Thoreau had seen fit to place me as a pilot, and I knew my way around a boat well enough that I didn't think I'd let them down. Once Q and Locke and the other crew who—I'll make no apologies or excuses for this—made less of an impression on me were aboard I attached my helmet, sealed the canopy (it should always be in that order), and waited for instructions to launch.

I didn't have to wait long. The captain's voice came over comms with a soft but unanswerable "To the skies."

The little squadron lowered as one, starting in tight formation and then fanning out into the white clouds of Jove.

From above, the planet had seemed opaque. Matte strips alternating orange and cream like smoked glass. But close to it, *inside* it, flying *through* it, there was so much more. Clouds of condensing ammonia rushed past on winds so fast that all I could think of was childhood sermons about judgment and wormwood and the Father's wrath. But in the breaks between the clouds were such vistas. Skyscapes like amorphous mountain ranges, shoals of Wyrms flying free and violent amongst insubstantial peaks. The roads the Leviathans walked.

I'd seen all this before, of course, from the array, but as watching from the array was different from watching from deck, so watching from a boat was different again.

On the ship, the shielding and the gravitic normalization created a kind of cocoon. An artificial safety that made it feel not so very different from being surfaceside. The boat was different. On the boat you felt the wind in the wings as you pitched; you felt the way you fell faster and climbed slower than you would on a different world. You saw the ammonia-ice on the wings forming and then boiling off as you turned and the friction brought the heat up.

And then, at last, some thirty klicks from the ship, minutes at most at skyboat-speeds, you saw the Leviathan.

I tried, when I wrote my cetology for the early chapters of this memoir, to explain a little of what the great beasts of Jupiter are. How they live and how they are hunted and what you could expect on first meeting one in, if not the flesh, then in the present tense of the narrative. Now that I come to it, I realize how fucking pointless that was.

At first, of course, it didn't look like much. Distance plays tricks, and for a few deceptive moments it was just a speck on the horizon, a dot on a scan that my copilot watched while I had my eyes on the sky. But with terrifying speed it grew closer and grander and more detailed until the full Behemoth glory of it was searing into my spirit like a welding laser.

It was long. Half the length, perhaps, of the ship and many, many times longer than our little boat. By the distinctive ridge on its back we knew that we were at least chasing the right kind of beast. It was a Ridgeback, a Sperm Leviathan, and its psychoconductive fluids would light a city for a year.

But only if we could kill it. And now that I *saw* it, that seemed impossible. The ridge looked supple but not fragile, and it rose out of a back lined with plates of bone or chitin or whatever equivalent Jovian evolution had spawned into the universe. This particular beast had a carapace that shone a hypnotic, opalescent purple-gray, marked here and there by deep scratches, their edges long worn smooth by the wind.

"Steady," Locke commanded under their breath. "It's seen us but it won't dive yet."

Over the open comms I heard similar instructions from the other boats.

"Fear nothing and go calmly." That was Truelove. "The end will come when it does, and it is sin to hide from it."

Flint, meanwhile, was taking a more proactive approach. "Prime coils, ready lances, hold for the range, and brace—we'll soon have our prize."

I listened over the chatter for the captain, but she was silent.

What, after all, did the squadron need to be told? This was their livelihood, and whether driven by greed or need or piety or the sheer love of the chase, every person present would pursue the precious sperm with the zeal of a fanatic.

It's been a while since I mentioned sperm, hasn't it? Stopped laughing yet?

Give it time.

"Down," ordered Locke, and I guided the boat into a dive. With the tyrannical grip of Jupiter's gravity we lost height fast, and I saw the bulk of the Leviathan soar above me. While its back was majestic and impenetrable, its underside was the stuff of nightmares. Hundreds of segmented limbs gripped close to its abdomen, reaching down now and then to grasp at something I couldn't see. As my boat skimmed closer to its head I saw mandibles working endlessly to draw in whatever nutrients it was sweeping from the skies.

Locke's eyes tracked the monster as we rode along in its wake. "Hold." Then, "Canopy."

From our angle, the wing-guns would be useless, but between the creature's limbs and its jaws and its vast body segments I could see—or thought I could see, or hoped I could see—chinks in its armor that a skilled harpooner could strike.

I downed canopy.

The moment I did the gravity hit. I can do basic ship-work but I'm no field scientist or Lorentz engineer, so I have no idea how the gravitational compensators actually work. But they seem to need an enclosed space to be fully effective, and so as soon as we were exposed, the weight of the boat doubled. Dropping into a controlled fall helped, but we had to keep in range of the beast or the whole maneuver would get us nowhere.

Between the strain on the engines, the wind that was now scouring past just a suit's breadth from our skins, and the new heaviness in my limbs, I didn't think I could keep us steady for more than a handful of heartbeats.

But a handful of heartbeats was all we needed. Q fixed one end of the harpoon cable to the hull with a transmagnetic lock, aimed her coilgun, and fired.

We were so dwarfed by the monster that the shot, for the first blink and a half, was anticlimactic. The dart flew into the distance and vanished into the chaos of twitching members that lined the Leviathan's underside. Then any sense of disappointment I might have been nurturing vanished as the line snapped taut and the boat lurched forwards, the beast reacting to us at last.

"It begins," said Truelove over comms. "Strike now."

"There it goes," called Flint. "All guns, all guns primed and charged and down the throat of the beast. Time's come to show the damned thing what we've got."

So the other boats closed with wing-guns and hand-launchers, and the Leviathan began a sharp and sudden descent. The undulating flight-membranes that ran the whole length of its midline whipped and snapped in the plunge-wind and our little boat trailed in its wake.

Over comms, I thought I heard the captain's voice just saying "Yes."

"Go lateral," Locke ordered as the canopy slid back into place. "We can't fight the beast and gravity both. Pull it aside until the struggle's worn out of it."

Always willing to let somebody more experienced take over, I did as I was told, turning the engines 90 degrees to the fall and hoping to hell that the mate was right.

Right or wrong, it seemed that Locke—and this shouldn't have surprised me—was making a textbook play. So the other boats knew what we were about and backed us, and the creature began to roll.

For a second I thought we had it, but glancing down I realized the boat's gyroscope was reading a few degrees off level, and though the line was still taut it was no longer running straight. It was tangling in the Leviathan's forelimbs and, as it turned, winding us closer and closer to it.

As the line shortened it began to pass through resonances with the wind, vibrating like a violin string playing an ever-dwindling, deadly symphony.

"Hold," Locke repeated. "Let it wear itself out."

The line shortened and shortened again. We were close enough now that I could see where the cable was biting into the creature's limbs, making it seep a transparent ichor into the clouds. I could see too that while some of its appendages were claw-tipped, others ended in billows of feathered tendrils that scooped and tasted the wind. It was marvelous, apart from the tiny fact that it was going to kill us.

Locke frowned, just slightly, then reached back into a spring-locked cabinet, drawing forth a long, curved sword. "Blades," they said, "and spears. We're about to have a fight on our hands."

The line was too short now for the engines to keep us steady, and we began whipping round towards the Leviathan's body, grasping legs coming down to meet us. Hoping that Locke was right and fighting was better than sheltering inside a metal-and-crystal pod, I downed canopy once more, and this time I was better braced for the shift. Beside me, Q already had a spear in her hand ready to strike the beast as we crashed against it. I stood awestruck but when somebody passed me a blade I took it without thinking.

The Leviathan reached down with a flurry of its fronds, and I swung with what strength I could, striking down so that gravity would at least be on my side. I needn't have put so much effort in, because the limbs it had reached out to us turned out to be impossibly delicate, and as my blade sliced through them like a razor through lips, I saw them recoil and I half heard, half imagined a high, keening scream.

Closer now, closer, and the segmented arms, if you could call them arms, were tightening around us. Spears in the joints kept them from crushing, and the grim work of hacking and carving kept the rest of the boats visible, even if it prevented us from following them. Still, it was a losing battle. And by the time Locke gave the order to drop the line it was too late.

I heard metal buckle and crystal crack and felt the click of somebody latching me to a line as the hull and the wings gave out and, giving the chase up as doomed, we jumped.

CHAPTER
TWENTY-TWO

Life

On Jupiter, you don't fall *down*. The winds are so fast that you fall eastwards or westwards depending on whether you're in the red or the white. You also, if you can possibly help it, don't fall alone.

In the early days of the hunt, bailing mid-sky had been a death sentence. The atmosphere was too hostile, too hot or too cold, too high-pressure, gravity too great. In the years since there's been a lot of progress in suit design, and abandoning a stove boat has gotten much less likely to see you ripped apart by excoriating clouds or drown-crushed in the distant hydrogen sea.

The fall-line was the first and simplest change. Rescuing half a dozen voiders, each cast a different way by a different current, would be . . . not impossible perhaps, but prohibitively expensive, and with most voyages trade-state sponsored, that amounted to the same thing. So in the event of needing to abandon our skycraft, we trained to tether ourselves together to make rescuing us more budgetarily justifiable.

More sophisticated but not necessarily more important was the system of deployable patagia that would unfurl between the arms and legs of more modern voidsuits, providing enough lift that a skywrecked hunter could keep a more or less even altitude, guide themselves clear of any angry monsters, and generally maximize their chances of recovery. Using these polymer wings effectively, especially when tied to four or five companions, was difficult, and the more diligent crews would take time to run drills in the wind-tunnels that were built, for this exact purpose, into most hunter-barques.

Our crew had not trained anywhere near enough.

Several of us deployed our wings, and we did our best to hold a lift-optimizing formation, but one of the less memorable crewmen panicked, curling into a ball and dragging us onto a chaotic downwards trajectory. The rest of us tried to compensate, and I felt Q's gloved hand in mine on one side, Locke's on the other as we spread ourselves out to catch the wind.

Behind us, the Leviathan shook off the last of its tormentors and rose triumphant through the atmosphere to freedom. The prop-wash of its great tail and the electromagnetic fallout of its titanic thoughts swept over us and sent our little group spinning. Through the crystal visor of my voidsuit I saw debris falling like meteorites and ichor falling like rain and boats swooping around to either rescue or abandon us.

Locke's suit, being a mate's rather than a lowly ship's hand's, had a built-in distress beacon, and it was broadcasting now, although until we were clear of the Leviathan it would be touch and go whether the signal would be trackable.

"This is Locke," they were saying over comms, their voice impressively calm for somebody being whipped sideways by a celestial hurricane, "requesting pickup at these coordinates. All hands accounted for."

I shut my eyes and felt, welling up from inside me, a tremendous urge to laugh.

Life, in so many ways, was a joke. A crude, cruel joke to be sure, but a joke. Here we were, me and my boatmates, six terrestrial primates whose ancestors—and not even *distant* ancestors, on the timescale of the universe—had walked the plains and forests of Old Earth, staring up at the stars and thinking them gods. And now we were falling-flying through eddies of helium and ammonia on a world so vast it could swallow the Earth a hundred times over, so far from our ancient home that the very concept of *far* became meaningless.

I'd been lost when I set out for the skies, and wanting to lose myself further. And what could be more lost than this? Suspended on wings of synthetic fabric inside a planet that was somehow massive and insubstantial all at once.

Imagine, for a moment, if you could travel back through time and tell Jonah about the skies of Jove. He would stare at you uncomprehending and call you a madman. To the prophets of old, all talk of ionospheric turbulence and distances measured in light-minutes and storms the size of planets would seem fantasies. Utter ludicrous fantasies.

The only part of the sky-hunter's work that Jonah would understand would be the Leviathans.

"Acknowledge." That was Flint, and like me he seemed to find the humor in the situation. "Charting intercept now."

A sky-rescue is hard to pull off. Really hard. The speeds involved are so high that if you don't match trajectory exactly, all you do is smash into your stranded crewmates at Mach 3 and spare them the indignity of a long death. The gravitics help. In an emergency they can be set to cushion the impact in much the same way they take the edge off everything else. But it's wise to assume that if your boat gets stove you're just dead.

I was almost disappointed that we weren't.

"First time?" Dawlish asked me after the canopy came down and the six of us were nestled safe against the spare lances.

I nodded, not that the gesture meant much through the helmet.

"Saw you getting right in there," said Flint merrily. "You're a cold fish, Locke, but fuck me if you don't have the instinct when it counts."

Locke made no visible response but, again, suit. "If we make no kills, the whole voyage will be worthless."

"Okay," I tried, "but we *did* nearly get crushed by a star-monster."

Flint clapped me on the back. "It's the life, girl. It's the life. No risk, no reward."

And at last I started laughing, and I didn't stop.

When Q and I returned to our berth and I peeled myself out of my suit and threw myself into the shower I was still laughing.

I was still laughing when Q joined me. The cubicle was tiny but I appreciated the closeness, the way her tattoos glowed through the steam and the too-strong pulse of the recycled water.

"How are you so calm?" I asked her. My hands—now I looked—were shaking slightly.

She took my trembling fingers in hers and lifted them to her lips. "Mors certa," she told me. "Hora incerta."

It wasn't the closest I'd ever come to dying. But it was the closest I'd come to dying *impersonally*, to simply being snuffed out by an indifferent cosmos. Assuming a Leviathan counted as indifferent, of course. The captain seemed to think otherwise.

Although I was grinning like a fool at the absurdity of it all, I felt tears stinging my eyes, and as the adrenaline of the chase started draining it was getting harder to speak and harder to think and honestly harder to stand, although in a shower space barely two feet square I didn't have much option on that last one.

"We nearly died," I said aloud.

Q nodded. Her eyes were a universe.

"We nearly died," I repeated.

Q nodded again. Her hand, tracing my ribs to my hip, was comfort and torment and invitation all at once. "Sic sunt hominum fata," she whispered, "sicut in arbore poma." And then she added. "*We die. But we live also.*"

I wanted it to be comforting. It wasn't quite. "I think . . ." I didn't quite know what to say next without sounding selfish. Then again I've always *been* selfish. At least that's what the pastors told me. "I think I really need you to fuck me right now."

So she did.

The water cut off—it was on a strict timer and we paid for it out of our lays—but I didn't care. She pushed me against the wall with a passion I only ever saw when I asked for it, and she took me like the winds of Jupiter. And I laughed and cried and let myself fall apart.

CHAPTER
TWENTY-THREE

The Guide

I'd been called back to the captain's cabin a few times in those first weeks. When the fire inside her burned too hot and threatened to swallow her and take the ship with it. And sometimes after she was done with me, I would lie in her bed, letting the sting fade from my back and the marks fade from my skin before returning to my duties.

It wasn't quite an arrangement. It was nothing so formal. It was more a—it was a thing. A thing that happened sometimes.

On the wall above her bed, an array of slender ivory canes hung. Each one of them was beautiful, scrimshawed with images of the hunt and the skies and the stars and the beasts that lurk in the heavens. I'd been kissed by each one, and knew them all, and had given them names I'm not going to share.

While I rested, the captain would go about her business. Much of the time, it was unremarkable, the day-to-day minutiae of ship-work you'd get on any vessel in the service. But sometimes, as I lay with my eyes half closed and dreamed of monsters, I would hear her hard at work on some private plan.

Her ultimate goal, of course, was no secret. She'd told us all before we even made atmospheric contact what she sought. What she bent all her distorted genius towards. But the *details* of it. The horror was in the detail.

Kneeling on the tatami mats before her low glass table, she

would work for hours at a time on a holographic chart. In the dark days of Old Earth, enterprising men had mapped the seas and continents of that blessed-and-cursed world. Repeating the feat on Jupiter was a whole 'nother thing. There were no fixed points on that planet, only variously stable atmospheric phenomena and the ever-shifting patterns of currents.

It hadn't stopped the hunter-fleets. Storms and airstreams had been given names as if they were islands and rivers. The feeding grounds of Leviathans and the swarming grounds of Wyrms and the great slow paths of Behemoths had been tracked and collated and algorithmically correlated into a living map that shifted even as you tried to read it.

It would take a special kind of obsession to try to actually *learn* a map like that. And that was exactly what the captain had set out to do.

Her own version of the chart was yet more complex. Even looking back, knowing more than I did then, it was remarkable in its density. Over the top of the climate grids and migration maps she'd overlaid an image displaying every sighting, every rumor, every whisper of the Möbius Beast.

I stood, curtain drawn a little aside, in the door to her sleeping chamber and watched. Aside from the sheet I'd taken from her bed I was naked, but I could have discarded the sheet entirely, or been fully clothed, or been flayed raw, or completely invisible, and it would have made no difference. When she was at the chart, she was at the chart.

"Assume minimal deviation," she told the machine, "and extrapolate. Where *is* it? Where will it *be*?"

When the chart spoke back its voice was soft and almost servile. "I don't have enough information."

"Speculate."

"I'm not supposed to speculate."

Thinking machines, true thinking machines, were rare. The churches were all suspicious of them for one reason or another and the trade-states monopolized their use for—we were told—our own safety. I had no idea how the captain had got hold of one. Honestly I didn't even know if that was what I was looking at. Neural mathematics and discourse algorithms weren't the kind of things they taught in a Prosperity school. We were just taught that better people than us knew what they were doing.

The captain's voice dropped low and menacing. "Indulge me."

"I *speculate* that this will kill you."

"Not what I asked."

A network of points on the chart glowed just a little brighter. "These are your best chances in the next eighteen months. After that"—the highlight moved to the great red storm that hunters' tales said had raged for a thousand years—"you'll want to be in Hell's Heart in the Season of the Line."

The captain nodded. My guess was that the machine hadn't told her anything she wasn't already thinking. Even the part about dying.

"That will do," she said. "For now." With a wave of her hand she shut down the map and the machine both. Then she continued speaking, as far as I could tell, to herself. "And perhaps it's for the best that we must wait. The crew gave little resistance when I told them of the hunt, but voiders are fickle people and they will want a kill before long, else they will grow restless. And Locke will prove more biddable if they feel Olympus is getting its due. And so inch by inch and wind by wind I draw closer to—"

At last she noticed me. I'd come a fair way forward as she was speaking, although whether it was her tyrant magnetism or more basic urges that drew me out, I couldn't say. I wasn't particularly sure there was a difference.

She fixed me with her stare. Not fixed. Pinned, because she looked at me and through me at once. "Do you think me mad?" she asked.

It wasn't language I'd ever use. I'd been called so many things in my time, told I was wrong in so many ways. And I knew what it was to run for no reason except that standing still felt impossible. Which meant the only truthful answer was "No."

The captain let out a single harsh breath that was almost a laugh. "Then you are alone on this ship. Locke believes I am out of my mind; Flint and Truelove believe the same although they care less for their different reasons. Even the machine doubts me."

"Nobody doubts you," I replied. And it was true. She wasn't wrong that every officer and half the crew were convinced she was insane. It's just that thinking somebody was off her head and thinking she was a bad captain were two different things.

For a long, long moment she gazed at me, lingering on the marks her teeth and fingernails had left on my shoulders. "Why do you come here? To me?"

"You ask it. And you're the captain."

"It isn't a captain's order. You know you could disobey, and I would have no redress."

"Then just because you ask it."

And just for a moment, she looked away. "As simple as that?"

I nodded.

"And you cannot tell me what it is you see? What compels you to such obedience?"

I shook my head.

"Kneel."

And I knelt without hesitation, and she stood at the same time so I was naked at her feet and gazing up at her with awe that should have been terror.

With that same at-me-past-me-through-me look in her eyes she put her hand gently against my throat. I could feel my pulse fluttering beneath her thumb and her forefinger. "With a little pressure," she told me, "I could cut off blood to your brain. In thirty seconds, you would lose consciousness."

I stayed perfectly still, my breathing as steady as I could make it, my lips just faintly parted.

"In a minute, brain damage would be permanent. In five you would be dead." She shifted her fingers just slightly, and almost immediately my vision began to swim and my heart began to quicken.

All I wanted then was for her to kiss me.

For fragile, beautiful seconds I hovered on the edge of nothingness, and then a voice crackled over comms. Locke, I thought. "Hail coming through, Captain."

She released her grip at once. "Transfer."

"—to Pequod," the hail was saying. "This is the Albatross."

"Albatross," the captain replied. "This is Pequod. Receiving."

The forms here were always the same. "Requesting gam. Beginning log updates. Rendezvous at your—"

"Hast seen the Möbius Beast?" demanded the captain.

The air went dead for a moment. "No," replied the Albatross uncertainly. "We're three years out from Europa, mostly hunting the belt-routes, and—"

The transmission dropped. Atmospheric conditions on Jupiter meant that happened sometimes, and it was usually the work of a moment to reestablish them. But the captain didn't even try; she just brought the chart back up and began entering the new data. With the blood flowing slowly back to my brain, I remained kneeling beside her awhile and, once I realized that she had shut me once again out of her world, I slunk back to her sleeping chamber, retrieved my clothes, and left.

CHAPTER
TWENTY-FOUR

Gams

If you've never shipped in a hunter-fleet, you might not know what a gam is. Even I didn't really know when I first heard the word, because it's not something you get in the merchant service. But hunter-missions are different. You take long voyages, and on those voyages you crisscross Jupiter so many different ways and in so many different directions that you're bound to pick up another ship eventually. The planet is enormous, of course, but so are the ranges of your sensors, and ships are easier to detect than Leviathans.

In a way it's a bit of an odd sweet spot. If the voyage was lonelier you'd never meet another ship so the whole tradition would never have evolved, and if it was more crowded, if fellow hunters were met more often or there were ports to visit in between as there are on other journeys, gams would be unnecessary.

As it is, a hunter-barque can expect to meet another hunter-barque once every few months; regularly enough to be an anticipated event, rare enough that it's worth anticipating. And that's what gives us the gam: an informal social meeting between hunter-ships where the captains exchange data, the crews exchange stories, and we all take advantage of the chance to fuck somebody we haven't been living with for way too long.

While the captain hadn't made the most of our first

opportunity to link up with another vessel, we had a second not long after, and while she'd been willing to let an opportunity pass if circumstances went that way, she wouldn't turn one down flat. She was no fool and, just as she knew the crew wouldn't stay with her for long if she denied them the opportunity for profit, she knew also that they'd get jumpy if she kept passing up opportunities for recreation.

So the next time we were hailed, by a ship called the Town Ho, she arranged an intercept and let us travel to each other's decks, and we spent a pleasant evening doing all the things that lonely people did when they met other lonely people in a cloudy sky a million miles from any other human life.

The captain, of course, cared only for news of the Beast, but the rest of us had more eclectic interests. Dawlish picked up a tale from one of the Town Ho's engineers that he passed around to the other harpooners and from there it spread to the pilots and the lancers and all the hands. For about a week it was the only thing we could talk about. Although honestly that might have said more about how repetitive life on a ship can be than anything else.

The version I'm going to tell you now is the version I told to a woman named Pandora who took me to bed one long hot evening on the shores of Ligeia Mare. She was a tall, exquisitely beautiful Ganymedian, and I mean that even by Ganymedian standards, which—since they can usually afford to eat well in childhood and to have their aesthetic imperfections biomechanically corrected in adolescence—is a very high standard indeed. I caught her eye one evening while she was slumming it in the docklands and for a while we let ourselves be each other's worlds.

"You must have seen a lot," she said. It was half a question.

I had, of course, but at the time I wasn't ready to talk about the things I'd seen personally. The things I'm telling you about now. "Some," I said instead, and she knew it was an evasion. "But nothing like what I've heard from other people."

And she stroked my hair and kissed me and I wept from

looking at her because sometimes beauty is too much to bear, and she asked me to tell her a story.

So I told her about Ironhands.

"I first heard this from a man," I told her, "who heard it from a man who lived it. Which makes it truer than most voiders' tales."

She laughed like a songbird and pressed her lips to my throat.

"Many years ago, a ship called the Town Ho had a first mate called Rannick. He was—no offense, but he was Ganymedian and—"

She propped herself over me on her elbows and looked down smiling in mock-outrage. "And he was the kind of person who would sweep up a pretty dockhand and carry her off to his penthouse on the methane sea?"

"Yeah."

"Oh that sort is the *worst*. Believe me, I have no illusions that I would be an asset to a hunter-barque. I see myself strictly as a patroness."

For a moment I wondered if she was younger than me. She seemed it, but it was hard to tell with people who could afford senescence-reduction.

"This Rannick," I went on, "he had it in something fierce for one of the regular voiders."

A light was dancing in her eyes that made me want do something unwise, self-destructive, and sharp. "The mysterious Ironhands?"

"He wasn't that mysterious."

"Did he have iron hands?"

"You know, I actually never thought to ask."

And she laughed again. As if she couldn't imagine somebody not caring about the things she cared about or not asking what she would ask. I envied her in so many ways. "I hope he did," she said. "I think that might be rather fun." And in case I hadn't gotten her point, she let her weight shift onto one side and traced her fingers downwards.

I tried to focus on the story. I wasn't *massively* successful.

"He'd—Rannick—he'd give Ironhands all the worst jobs on the ship. Jobs you'd leave for bots and raw recruits. Flushing the waste pipes, sweeping the observation deck, refilling the commissary machines."

Pandora screwed up her nose. I suppose that from her perspective all work was equally undignified.

"Until at last Ironhands couldn't take it anymore."

"What did he do?" Pandora's eyes grew wide. She was probably expecting something salacious, but that was coming later.

"He said no."

"That's all?"

She didn't understand. Of course she didn't understand. "On a ship, saying no is a big deal. You follow orders"—often badly, I'll admit to you though I didn't to her—"or systems fail and seals breach and people die. You need to be really, really sure to say no to an officer."

"So what did Rannick do?"

"Made a mistake."

"What *sort* of mistake?"

I was beginning to regret starting the story. Honestly I wasn't sure why I *had* except for the fact that telling it brought me back to my days in the hunter-fleet, and all I'd seen and felt and found and lost. "He made threats. He told Ironhands to do as he was told or he'd thrash him. And personally thrash him, like in a fight. Not just have him slung in the brig and flogged." I began to run my fingers through her hair in the hope of lulling her to sleep, or getting her more interested in other things. It didn't work. "But Ironhands wasn't the kind of man who'd stand for that. *Touch me*, he said, *and I'll kill you.*"

She was listening now, really listening. I think it might have been this experience right here, a woman so beautiful it made me hate myself listening rapt to a story I wished I wasn't telling, that made me think this book might be worth writing. That even if it didn't make enough to buy me into heaven it might at least let me pin some ghosts onto the page and set them free in the void.

Or, failing that, might get me laid.

"So Rannick touched him. Not hard. Not fast. Not violent. And if a man like Ironhands says not to touch him, the *only* way to touch him is hard and fast and violent."

She kissed me again, right over the breastbone. Hard and fast and violent.

"He stretched out one finger and prodded Ironhands on the shoulder. So Ironhands laid him out. And that was where the real trouble started. Striking an officer's a hell of a crime on a ship, but Ironhands was popular the way men like that are often popular, and a good chunk of the crew downed tools in his name."

Her lips worked their way across my skin. There was something acquisitive in it, proprietorial. But I was used to that from my lovers, especially the ones who knew my past. *You may have had a more interesting life than me*, they said with their touch, *but I'll make you a bauble all the same.*

"The captain, I won't say who he was because last I heard he was still"—I shuddered as her fingers brushed somewhere distracting—"still with the fleet. The captain didn't know what to do. He wasn't a kind man, but he hated confrontation, and in the end it was Rannick insisted that anyone who wouldn't fall back in line at once go to the brig."

Teeth at my hip, the tip of her tongue dancing across my body. I thought she might, perhaps, have been sufficiently occupied for me to stop talking, but when I went silent, she looked up at me and asked me what happened next.

"They went to the brig. Ironhands and a dozen of his supporters. But over the next few days the boredom and the isolation did their work on most of them and they trickled back to their duties. In the end it was only Ironhands and two of his closest allies that held out. And between them they hatched a plan. They'd surrender and then, when they were being led to the bridge, they'd overpower whoever was sent to fetch them, take their weapons, kill Rannick and the captain both, and seize the ship."

Pandora gasped. And the fact that it was a story about a long-lost voidship making her gasp and not, say, my fingers inside her or my lips on her throat or just the sheer delight of my body made me feel like a fraud.

"But it turned out his closest allies, they weren't so close. Ironhands made his move but they made it faster, pinned him down and turned him in, all for a pat on the head from the captain and the restoration of their lays."

It was a natural pause in the story, and for the moment at least Pandora seemed more interested in physical indulgences than verbal ones. And while her whims ran in that direction I let my mind go blank and tried to feel the way I had a few years earlier, when I had been hunting the great Beast of Jupiter alongside A and Q and Locke and all the rest.

When she had bored herself with making me scream and weep and call her a goddess, she kissed me again, hot and dark and claiming, and asked, "What happened then?"

I was too fuck-drunk to quite remember what she meant.

"On the ship," she explained. "With Ironhands and the others?"

So I told her the rest of the story.

"The captain wouldn't dare flog Ironhands," I told her. "But Rannick wasn't so squeamish. Ironhands was lashed unconscious and, when the ship's doctor cleared him—which they always do because it's more than their job's worth not to—he went back to work without complaint."

"That seems a small ending."

"It's no ending at all. He went back to work without complaint but inside he burned for vengeance." I found tears coming to my eyes again, and these weren't sex tears, they were tears for a world swallowed up by a still larger world, in a great ocean of hydrogen in the depths of the sky. "Doing routine maintenance work far below decks, he strung together bits of spare cabling into a garrote. A thin, strong garrote that would cut as much as it choked and send a man to a miserable death."

"He was going to kill Rannick?"

I nodded.

"How did he think he'd get away with it?"

"I don't think he meant to. In the days of Old Earth"—the tears stung more sharply now, because all thoughts of Old Earth reminded me of still deeper losses—"it would have been a simple enough matter to pitch a corpse over the side."

Once again she looked uncomprehending, and so was I, really. Born and raised in the stars, we had no way to understand a world where things were *open*. Where the lack of a wall or a window or an airlock didn't mean inevitable death.

"Rannick would walk the decks in his off shifts, when a third of the crew was sleeping and the rest were way up on the array or deep in the inner workings of the ship. And one day, long enough after the mutiny and the flogging that a foolish man would think the whole thing had been forgotten, Ironhands crept up upon Rannick, garrote in hand. He was inches from revenge, but it seems that fate or the Father had other plans. Because just as he was about to strike, a cry came over comms. A spout."

She was resting her head on my shoulder, and I wondered if she'd fall asleep before the tale was done. To my surprise, I found myself hoping she wouldn't. For all I resented the role of storyteller, I thought I owed Ironhands an audience.

"The whole ship came alive and ran to the boats, because the signal had been a strong one, and promised the kind of prey that would make the entire crew rich. And by a twist of chance, Ironhands and Rannick were tasked to the same boat, so for the next few fateful minutes they were bound together by the hunt."

"Mm-hmm?" said Pandora sleepily.

"It wasn't long before they had visuals on the target. And what they saw was a creature more wonderful and terrible than any other in the Jovian storms. As long itself as the ship they'd left, its carapace milk-white and scarred from a thousand battles. Its hundred eyes gleaming with living malice and its limbs ever seeking and its mandibles ever hungering. It was the Möbius Beast that they had found."

The name meant nothing to Pandora, who made an indistinct *what* noise and shut her eyes. It meant a deal more to me, as you will learn in time.

"The whole hunter-fleet knows the Beast," I told her, only a little impatient, "and the whole hunter-fleet would understand why Rannick, a proud man and a foolish man and a man who would never believe a warning, set his sights on being the one to slay it."

She sighed and drew closer to me.

"He took up the bolt-driver and the chitin-saw—which are the tools used to strike the final blow to the Leviathan, once the harpoons have run it to exhaustion—and ordered Ironhands to steer him as close as he could to the beast's head. He ordered darts launched and canopy down and harpoons secured and the boat brought in as close as could be to the nape of the monster's neck and then, latching himself to the harpoon-line, he leapt from the cabin."

Beside me, Pandora stirred. "He jumped onto a Leviathan?"

"It's common. You need to get the kill somehow and the beasts are gargantuan. With any other animal it would have worked. But the Möbius Beast is *not* any other animal. As Rannick was skimming the distance between them, fire-eyed and wind-whipped, it rolled as if to give him its throat. But where its throat is its limbs are too, and a great sweeping feeder arm whipped down and snagged the line and the hunter both."

Once more, she gasped. But now I was grateful for it.

"When the quarry catches the line like that, the pilot has two choices, loose it or try to ride it out. Loosing it is safer for the boat but means giving up a kill and maybe a crewmate. And Ironhands took the safer choice, as he was well within his rights to do. And so Rannick spun off into the Jovian skies, minuscule against the monster and the planet and the whole impossible vastness of everything."

She looked at me uncomprehending. And how could I expect her to understand? She'd never felt small in her life.

"And then the Möbius Beast's jaws scythed closed and the

voiders in the boat saw Rannick obliterated, his suit ruptured, his body crushed by the monster and the gravity, his blood aerosolizing onto the winds in streams of crimson mist. And so Ironhands had his revenge, and all without raising a hand at the man who'd wronged him."

I felt Pandora's fingertips walking across my stomach and her breath warm against my shoulder. "Is *any* of that true?"

"Of course it is," I told her. "Many years afterwards, I met Ironhands himself in a bar on Halimede. He confirmed everything. Or everything that matters."

She lay down and whispered charming platitudes about how strange and wonderful a life I'd led, and at last fell asleep. It never occurred to her to ask why, if I'd met Ironhands as I claimed, I hadn't been able to tell her, at the start of the story, whether his name was justified or not.

CHAPTER
TWENTY-FIVE
Monstrous Pictures of Leviathans

Days pass slowly on a hunter-barque. Outside of the gams, we largely have to make our own fun. And yes, often we make that fun with casual sex, or by developing a really intense backgammon habit, but most ships do have some kind of onboard entertainment system.

Streaming services aren't reliable on the hunt. There's no broadcast platforms in the atmosphere of Jupiter itself and interwell transmissions won't make it through the ionic interference. Fortunately, recorded media takes up negligible space in the ship's computers, so any vessel worth traveling on will have a whole audiovisual library available for its crew to rent at a very reasonable fee.

Most of it's porn. The stuff that isn't porn is schlock. But hey, you've got to give the people what they want.

Usually if you felt like watching something you'd just get it sent into one of the several screens in your bunk, paying a small surcharge if you wanted fewer ads. But on the fifth of its nine decks the Pequod had an actual theater where a large group of crew members could split the cost of a rental and have it projected on a big screen in an atmospherically dark room.

We mostly used that for porn too. Almost exclusively, in

fact, because the need to split the cost meant we had to pick content that a lot of people wanted to see. And for some reason the most popular choice amongst voidfarers was content that allowed them to jerk off in the dark alongside twenty or thirty coworkers all doing the same.

I tried taking Q exactly once. She didn't really get it. In her defense, the crew's tastes ran specific, and watching a slim Vestal get double fisted by two guys in the uniform of Limtoc Kinetic Solutions probably wasn't the best introduction to Exodite cinematic traditions.

I was just explaining to her, in hushed theater-appropriate tones, what was going on and whether I wanted it done to me at any point, when the image on the screen changed. What replaced the popular, wholesome pornography was a horrific, leviathanic image of tendrils and mandibles and terrible eyes gazing pitiless into the void. Another followed it. And another. They were strange, those pictures, distorted almost, as if they weren't filmed from life but rather conjured by somebody who had seen a thousand descriptions of the beasts but didn't truly understand what one *was*.

Either way, the cinema was filled with the sounds of two dozen voiders going off their stroke at once.

"The fuck?" demanded the Second Europan from a row near the front. "We paid for that."

"It'll be a corrupt sector in a pile somewhere," said the First Europan. "It happened all the time when I was on the Grampus."

The Tall Ganymedian, who had been doing something I was too polite to watch closely with a fresh-faced Enceladean, stood up and readjusted his absurd bottle-green coat. "Well, somebody should do something about it. Who's in charge of data storage anyway?"

"General maintenance job," I explained; I'd been dogsbodying on the ship for months by that point and I knew general maintenance jobs very well indeed. "The drones handle most of it and whoever's on shift covers what they can't."

"It'll be a coolant line," said a bright-eyed Titanian with an intricate pattern of scarifications on her right cheek. "It's always a coolant line."

"Fuck the coolant lines," replied the Tall Ganymedian. "What I want to know is how we get our money back."

The First Europan looked at him like he was drunk. Which he may well have been. Then again that might just be me stereotyping Ganymedians again. "We don't, you pampered seadweller. Unless you want to go to the first mate and ask them directly?"

Drawing himself to his full height, which was reasonable on account of his tallness, the Tall Ganymedian puffed out his chest. "Perhaps I *shall*."

"Shall you, though?" asked the Bright-Eyed Titanian.

"Yes," replied the Tall Ganymedian with the unearned confidence of the relatively affluent. "I *shall*."

On the screen, the images of beasts were still flickering. If I'd been in a mystical mood, and I am sometimes in an extremely mystical mood, I'd have said that they felt less like a glitch in the system and more like a portent.

Despite the low-key outrage in the theater, we all drifted back to our rooms or our duties. It became clear that the glitch, or corruption, or omen, or whatever it might have been was not merely confined to the theater but had spread to all the ship's stored media. It wasn't universal, and it never seemed to affect the advertisements that flickered periodically across every screen on the vessel, but otherwise no matter what you tried to watch, flashes of leviathanic imagery crept into it at random.

It seems like a joke—and I'll freely admit that a lot of things in this book are jokes, because I have a very short attention span and like to kid myself that facetiousness is the same thing as satire—to say that a lack of access to porn was a major morale problem on a ship where we all risked our lives on a frequent if irregular basis.

It's not.

A shitty truth about life is that it mostly sucks for most

people most of the time. Over millennia of progress we've developed more and more efficient ways of distracting ourselves from this, and in their infinite wisdom the trade-states and great Churches of the Commonwealth have found more and more efficient ways to monetize that distraction. An ancient enemy of humanity once said that every society is three meals from chaos, but in our modern age of plenty basic nutrition is generally accessible if you're willing to eat enough metaphorical shit to get it. Entertainment is a whole different thing. Boredom is a subtle monster that gnaws at the soul of an individual and gnaws still worse at the souls of crowds.

"This is intolerable," the Tall Ganymedian was telling the Old Ionian in the mess. "I've not even been able to read a book."

"What's intolerable," the Second Europan replied—if *replied* is the right word because she wasn't really the one being addressed—"is that you keep going on about it."

The Old Ionian leaned back in his chair and frowned. "You want my thoughts—"

"We seldom do," interrupted the Tall Ganymedian, to no immediate effect.

"—the ship is haunted. There've been ill signs since we left Europa."

Beside me, Q sighed. "Mobiles ad superstitionem perculsae semel mentes."

"Perhaps," said the First Europan, "but there's *something* about this ship that's not right. We've all seen the shadows in the captain's boat."

"Holograms," I insisted. "Not ghosts."

It took me all of two and a half seconds to regret speaking. The whole mess turned to me and the Second Europan said, quite casually, "Well, I guess you'd know."

While I was still gathering my thoughts, Q leaned forward. "*What do you say?*"

"Oh, come on"—this was the First Europan again. I remember that he had an elaborate tattoo over one eye and cybernetics replacing his little finger—"it's not like it's a secret she's fucking the captain."

We'd firmly established by now that Q could care less who I slept with but she had a protective streak that I really didn't want anybody to trigger. So, uncharacteristically, I stood up for myself. "What I'm doing and who with is my business."

"True enough," agreed the First Europan. Except it was a fake agreement. An agreement that was clearly a trap. "But what the *captain's* doing and who with. That's a whole 'nother thing. That's *all* our business."

A knife was always a useful tool on a ship, which unfortunately meant most of us were armed most of the time. So when I saw Q's hand inching towards the edge of the table, I covered it gently with mine in the hope we could avoid things kicking off.

"Audi, vide, tace," she said to the First Europan, "si tu vis vivere in pace."

The First Europan's eyes narrowed. "Watch it, Earther."

"It's fine," I told the room. "I'm sure the officers are on it."

"Like fuck they are," said the Tall Ganymedian. "What you really mean is that you're the captain's pet deckhand and you don't want to admit how little of a shit she gives."

"Or what strange and fell things she be up to," added the Old Ionian.

"She hasn't done anything strange and fell," I replied, not really wanting to explain why I was so confident on this point. Especially because a thinking engine was actually considered pretty strange and fell by a lot of people.

"Perhaps not," conceded the Bright-Eyed Titanian, "but she's got the whole ship roped in to hunt a monster that doesn't exist, and half the crew are already fool enough to cheer her for it. That might not be witchcraft but it's fuckery of some sort."

"And since you're fucking the fucker who's fucking us with her fuckery," added the Second Europan, "this is on you."

I didn't think that followed. But I also didn't think they were any of them in a mood to take no for an answer. It's terrible what interrupting somebody's masturbation schedule will do. "Fine," I said. "If it'll get you off my back, I'll . . . I don't know, I'll mention it next time she asks to see me or something."

It was a foolish thing to offer. My relationship with the captain was the opposite of the kind where I got to make requests. But it pacified the crowd, for a while at least. That was all I'd really been planning on.

I mean. I say *planning*. You might have already worked out that planning isn't really my bag. Which is probably why this whole thing went as badly as it did.

CHAPTER TWENTY-SIX
Chasing Ghosts

As it happened, I didn't get the opportunity for a while. Because the captain was fickle, and before too long she'd moved on to a new obsession.

It was Marsh who saw it first. A shimmering in the readouts that didn't quite look like a Leviathan but couldn't possibly have been anything else. It was far enough out that it wasn't worth dropping boats immediately but the captain gave orders to adjust course towards it, and from the observation platform on the prow we could see electromagnetic flares that weren't elveses or sprites but didn't look quite like a Leviathan-sounding either. It was a pale flare, almost ghostly, but we definitely *saw it*. I saw it myself.

But while we followed the trace for some hours, it slipped off the readouts as mysteriously as it had appeared and, when the captain ordered that we drop boats anyway and search for it, we found nothing within a hundred kliks.

In the end, we started calling it the ghost-trace.

We chased that shadow for a week at least, and after our first unsuccessful launch the captain began standing at the prow herself, staring out into the storm and moving from her vigil only when we took, as we did once or twice a day, to the boats again. And then she would lead the hunt, canopy down, the holographic specters of the thought machine casting her in eerie blue light so she looked pretty damned otherworldly herself.

It didn't do a lot of good for the rumors that the ship was haunted.

"We're off our course," Locke tried to tell her, three days into the chase. "Pursuing what's almost certainly an atmospheric anomaly, wasting food, fuel, and time."

For a long while, the captain acted like she hadn't heard anything. And when it at last became clear that Locke wasn't going to take no answer for an answer, she said, "Noted."

"You have a fiduciary responsibility."

Once again, she tried the silent treatment. When it once again didn't work she just repeated "*Fiduciary responsibility*," in tones so contemptuous that I half expected Locke to shrivel up like a polyp too long out of water.

But they were made of sterner stuff. In their own way, I thought, they were made of steel as sure as the captain, though theirs was polished until it gleamed like chrome while the captain's was buried deep inside her and covered in blood and gristle and hate. "Olympus Extraction State will not hesitate to pursue recovery if they feel you have harmed their interests."

I don't know why that, specifically, was what made the captain react. But it was. She spun on her heel, caught Locke by the wrist, and pressed their hand to her chest. "Do you feel that?" she asked.

Looking back, the gesture must have meant more to Locke than I realized at the time. After all, it would have been achingly naive for me to think I was the first to get drawn into the captain's orbit. But Locke had been down this road many times and many years ago, and the captain could no longer faze them so easily. "What exactly do you think I should be feeling?"

"Flesh and bone," she said. "Skin and soul and a heart that beats for vengeance. Your master, shipmate, is a paper god. An eidolon fashioned from laws and ledgers and contracts. And yet you tell me of their right to *pursue recovery*, which I say is just vengeance of another sort. So I tell you in return that *recovery* is my aim and the aim of this ship while I am her captain, and recovery we will wrest from the Möbius Beast and the skies of Jove and the very universe itself if we may. And when we go to our graves it will be with our heads high, knowing that at the last we had just compensation."

Locke made no reply. Then again, what reply could they make? In the captain's wake you swam or you drowned but you didn't argue, any more than you'd argue with a hurricane.

Over the rest of the chase a great many other crewmen followed Locke's example, approaching the captain to advise or encourage or cajole her in one way or another. For a while Truelove joined her, and they stood side by side gazing out into the void. But his pious reveries could not match the captain's silent focus.

"It's a portent," Truelove explained to the world in general. "Even if it isn't the Beast, it's a sign. We live in the days of the Great Devouring, and it will be upon us soon."

The captain said nothing. I—and I'll be honest, I really did have better things to be doing in other parts of the ship—pretended to work so I could carry on listening.

"The crew are beginning to say you're mad," Truelove continued. "They think losing your leg broke you. Screwed up your judgment."

Still no reply.

"That isn't what I believe."

In the captain's place, I would at least have asked him what he did, in fact, believe. But that's probably why she was the captain and I was just a deckhand she sometimes fucked.

"I believe," Truelove continued, in tones that were at best somber and at worst self-important, "that you have touched the void in a way that few ever do and live. I believe that you are a herald of what is to come and a shadow that precedes a great darkness. I believe that you are the instrument of something great and terrible and obliterating, and so I will serve you body and soul until the night consumes us."

And once the second mate's words had died away and there was nothing but the electric hum of the ship and the barely audible rush of the storm beyond the dome, the captain spoke. "I care nothing for your religion. Leave me."

She didn't even look at Truelove as he left, but I wasn't surprised. She seldom looked at me either.

Flint came to her only once during that long vigil. And only to tell her that he'd started recalibrating the ship's cannon and that he'd let her know if he needed anything, before he scampered off quite content.

Eventually, I had a window. A time when my duties didn't take me somewhere else and no other member of the crew was near enough to see. And so I approached the captain myself.

I wanted to touch her, but I wouldn't dare. Not on deck and not without being told to. So instead I sidled as close as I could and just said, "You need to sleep."

She said nothing.

"It's been days."

Still nothing.

"Let somebody else watch for you. Let me."

She didn't even acknowledge that I was there.

CHAPTER
TWENTY-SEVEN

Less Erroneous Pictures of Leviathans

When we gave up on the ghost-trace at last, the captain was seized with a profound melancholy. It was when those moods took her that she was most likely to call for me. So I wasn't particularly surprised when she did.

I *was* surprised when the Tall Ganymedian, both the Europans, and a gaggle of crewmates I remember even less well than those three collared me on the way to her cabin.

"Going somewhere?" asked the Tall Ganymedian. It was hard, honestly, to be intimidated by a Ganymedian. He might have been tall, but the Ganymedian reputation for indolence made him profoundly unthreatening.

"None of your business," I told him.

"We've been through this," said the Second Europan. "Shit on this ship has got weird, you're the only one the captain even talks to—"

"If she talks to her," the First Europan chimed in. "Not sure I'd think she was worth listening to, if I were the captain."

I gave the First Europan a look that I hoped was withering. "Are you trying to use reverse psychology?"

"No, I just sincerely doubt she listens to you."

I wasn't quite sure what the safest way to play this was. Unusually, I went with honesty. "Good. Because she doesn't."

"Make her," the Tall Ganymedian insisted. "Because right now the whole crew is getting twitchy and you really don't want a twitchy crew deciding you're the problem."

I wasn't normally good at defiance, but Ganymedians barely counted. "And why might they decide that?"

The Tall Ganymedian shrugged with an innocence so obviously fake I almost respected it. "What can I say? Crews get funny ideas."

With that parting shot still lodged in my head like a barbed dart, I was more than usually on edge when I arrived at the captain's cabin.

So on edge that she noticed.

"Where are you?" she asked when she caught my mind wandering.

"Here," I lied. I'm a terrible liar, but old habits are hard to break.

"I say you are not. I say your thoughts are elsewhere, and though I know well the call of the wild skies, I find I mislike the insult."

In a strange way, I was pleased. She so often spoke through me or past me instead of to me. And I would have taken her displeasure a thousand times over her indifference. So I told her what had happened. "Some of the crew," I explained. "They wanted me to speak to you about the data-stacks."

She looked at me like I was a voice from another world. Like I was shouting to her through deep water. "The data-stacks?"

"They're corrupted," I explained. "At least, the entertainment storage is. Footage of Leviathans is getting spliced into everything. Or at least everything worth watching."

"Worth watching?" asked the captain, as close to bewildered as I'd ever heard her.

"Porn, mostly," I clarified.

The captain was staring at me like I was the most tedious

sort of mystery. "This ship," she said, "that even now pursues a beast whose name the boldest dare not speak. That I have bent my will to guide upon its fated course. That none save I may . . ." She stopped. Blinked. "The crew are up in arms for want of *pornography*?"

I tried to look matter-of-fact about the issue. "Entertainment in general, but . . . yeah. It's sometimes months between gams, and with the stacks down there's nothing to *do* except craft projects and sex."

This was the closest I'd ever really come to a proper conversation with the captain. To her listening to something I said instead of extemporizing a soliloquy off the back of it.

It didn't last.

"To have come so far," she said to the empty air as she rose from bed fully clothed and stalked to the imaging desk, "to be hindered now by so small a thing. Report."

This last command was neither directed at me nor at the cosmological sounding board she so often made the universe into. It was a direct instruction to her thinking machine.

"Sorry," it said at once, "that was me, actually."

"Explain."

"You asked me to analyze the Beast's weaknesses. That meant scraping all existing data regarding Leviathan physiology and constructing simulations. I had to do that somewhere."

"Speculate. Will—"

"I'm not meant to speculate."

"Do it anyway. Will this disruption to the crew's recreation endanger the hunt?"

The machine intelligence thought about it and, while it was thinking, I imagined I could hear whirrings and strainings from deep inside the ship. From the bank upon bank of datastacks that over their distributed network made up the vessel's computing power. And then, after a few moments, the thought engine, the intelligent machine, the entity that all doctrine told us was wiser and more terrible in its thoughts than any mere human could be, replied, "Could go either way."

"Bring up the images."

The air above the imaging desk shivered, and the same pictures that had been haunting the crew's spank banks for the past several weeks coalesced into view. Except they were different now, more refined, closer to reality—or at least close enough to be usable. And at the captain's command they went from mere pictures to diagrams, plans, schematics. On the imaging layer above the desk, the thought machine plotted out attack vector after attack vector, scenario after scenario, and as the captain watched the images, I watched her. Saw her enthralled and entranced and endlessly, endlessly calculating.

So no, I didn't manage to get the crew their porn back.

Which was why the next time I found myself alone in an out-of-the-way service tunnel, six of them kicked the hell out of me.

That night, Q tended my wounds. Medical supplies, like most other shipboard commodities beyond the absolute bare minimum level of nutrition we needed to stay upright, were charged out of our lays, but she didn't seem to mind. Besides, there was a lot you could do with water and salvaged scrap.

And then, as she was cleaning blood from my scalp, she said, simply, "*Leave.*"

I'd been expecting it for a while, I always did. So even though I was feeling bruised and sore and aching and all around fucked I eased myself out of bed, but Q put a hand on my shoulder and guided me back down.

"*Leave her.*"

I didn't need to ask which *her* she meant. "I thought you didn't believe in owning people."

Her jaw set and her expression grim, Q looked down at me. "*This*," she said. "*Her machine. Her hunt.*" And then, though she absolutely didn't need to say it, she said, "*Dangerous.*"

It wasn't just the beating that was making me uncomfortable. I'd fought long and hard for the right to make my own shitty decisions, and being reminded how shitty they were wasn't helping me right then. So I said, "She isn't . . ." and then I said, "It's not . . ." then, "You don't . . ."

And finally, despite Q's protestations, I slipped away from her and went to walk the lower decks.

I felt like a child. And not in a safe, cared-for way. In a what-the-fuck, why-can't-you-just-fucking-grow-up way.

And I hated it.

CHAPTER TWENTY-EIGHT

Clouds

In the days that followed, the captain's winter mood kept her confined to her cabin. This left Locke in charge by default, which, from an objective point of view, was absolutely for the best. We changed course and for a while we were on a completely ordinary hunter-voyage.

That was how we continued for a month or so, and when I think back on that time I can almost let myself forget the doom that hung over the journey. I can almost forget the horrors and let myself think only of the wonders, of the beautiful things.

Almost.

We aren't far into the story yet. Not really. But I'm already getting muddle headed. Sifting back through memories and dreams and wishes and might-have-beens, it's sometimes hard for me to sort what actually happened from what I've just told myself happened. Or what should have happened. Or what should never and could never have happened but I wanted so badly that the wanting has become a substitute for recall.

Don't get me wrong, what I'm telling you is true. But ask anybody who collects stories for a living, any detective or journalist or executioner-errant: eyewitnesses aren't worth shit. We—and by *we* I mean humans in general but I also mean the specific humans who try to explain things to other humans using words—so often start with a pattern we want to see and fit the facts around it.

Still, I'm sure I remember the brit.

You may not have heard of brit. It's not a common term outside the hunter-fleet. It's the general name we give to the smallest Jovian organisms, the myriad sky-plankton that float on the winds and live by thermotrophy or chemotrophy or psychotrophy depending on their nature.

I don't know how small the smallest brit-organisms are. Nobody has ever done a full breakdown and any of them that aren't visible to the naked eye and don't show up on ship sensors would never be recorded by practical-minded hunters. Bluesky exobiologists, on the other hand, seldom come as far out as the gas giants. When they do, it's usually to study the subterranean seas of Ganymede, which have the advantage of being close to some very good hotels.

What I do know is that the biggest brit-organisms are about the size of a fist, and roughly the same shape. Little fleshy balls covered in fine spines or whipping flagella or rippling pseudopods. Most of the time they're few enough and far enough between that you barely think of them unless their blended remains start gumming up the intake jets of your boat or, worse, the ship itself.

Sometimes, though, they get blown together in clouds the size of continents. And those clouds are one of the most beautiful sights you will see in all the system.

Life is strange. Life-the-phenomenon, I mean, not life-the-experience. It must be one of the most unevenly distributed things in the cosmos because it's so rare across so much of it but when it does appear it appears in abundance. And nowhere is that truer than in a brit-cloud. The brit itself is already spectacularly diverse in shape and form and color. Quite a lot of it is bioluminescent, so as the ship flies into it the sky comes alive with rippling displays of light like you'll see nowhere else.

But life (like, the catechism teaches us, society) also forms hierarchies. So where the tiniest, weakest creatures gather, the things that feed on them gather too, and the things that feed on the things that feed on them, and the things that feed on those, and—above even the great apex predators—the hunter-ships of humanity and the carrion eaters that swarm alongside us.

The brit-cloud wasn't where I saw my first Death's Head Leviathan (that had been a few weeks earlier, you'd get very bored if I told you everything that happened on every day of a three-year voyage), but it was where I first saw them in *numbers*.

And such numbers. Leviathans are so big that they have to be solitary (well, mostly solitary, bar breeding and raising their young), because two or more sharing the sky for any length of time would harvest all the nourishment out of the winds in days and then they'd both starve. But in the bountiful environment of the cloud they could gather in twos and threes and tens. Family groups, I assumed, although I might just have been projecting.

We kept our distance from them. Death's Heads give no sperm and so there's little profit in hunting them, but if disturbed they can and will ram a ship with their great bony foreheads. And if they do, who can say what would become of the ship that disturbed them?

Who can say what becomes of any ship, if it doesn't come home?

That's the thought that haunts the hunter-barque. If the vessel is lost, if all hands fall into the skies, then there's nobody to know what happened to you. Nobody to tell what beast or what machine or what act of indifferent nature or merciful divinity sent so many souls to their deaths.

Even amidst the beauty of the brit-cloud, you can't quite forget that you're nothing inside nothing inside nothing.

The Death's Head schools carved paths through the light and color, making the patterns even richer and more complex and allowing, here and there, glimpses of the clear red sky beyond.

In one brief moment in our days amongst the brit, I stood

with Q and she laid her head on my shoulder as we watched the Leviathans.

"Ex Iove," she said, "semper aliquid novi." And then for my benefit, or perhaps for yours, she added, "*Something new. Always.*"

We didn't watch for long. I had couplings to fix.

CHAPTER
TWENTY-NINE
Leviathans in the Stars

A hunter-barque is a machine in so many different ways. A machine for turning lives—human and Leviathan both—into profit. To this end it takes in everything it can, ruthlessly devours all it's able to, and then carelessly jettisons anything that turns out not to be worth the storage space into the Jovian skies.

Because of this, the composition by volume of the ship changes a lot over the voyage. It starts off, as you might put it, virginal, its hold filled with supplies or with wide-open space (although even that space, in its own way, is storage—an empty hold is full of air and air is more precious than water to a void crew) and every spar and every soul aboard shining and clean. Or at least as shining and clean as they're likely to ever get, given that both the spars and the souls will probably have been on half a dozen prior voyages and will have had a fair amount of muck and grime and rust ground irredeemably into their cores.

Then as she sails on she gains some weight and loses some, her hold beginning to fill with spermaceti as her stores begin to empty of food. If she's lucky the oxygen saturation of her atmosphere will hold more or less steady as the algae banks go about their photosynthetic churn, and meanwhile her overflow tanks will grow ever more filled with waste.

And waste kills.

Let too much crap build up and you jeopardize the mission,

taking up valuable space that could be used for sperm, adding weight that makes the ship burn more fuel which in turn can force it back to port long before its time. But flush too much too readily and you find that you really, really need the 2 or 3 percent of the junk that you could have salvaged.

Which is why trash picking is one of the ship's more encouraged extracurricular activities.

The Catechism of Prosperity teaches us that the will of the Father is never more evident than in institutions like hunter-barque trash picking. It's effectively a perk of the job: you can go down to the reclamation floors to your heart's content, dig through the refuse, and anything you can fix you either keep if it's only useful to you, or sell back to the ship if it's useful to the voyage. Nobody takes a salary and yet by the glory of the invisible hand, everybody profits.

Also it gives you something to do when you're bored. Which you often are on a ship even when the entertainment system *hasn't* been co-opted by a rogue thought machine trying to compute the optimal line of attack against an enemy that might not even exist.

Honestly it wasn't an activity that ever really appealed to me. I spent long enough wading through crap when I was on duty, I saw no reason to do it on my off-hours too. But early in the voyage (time is a woolly thing in the sky; it had been months but not yet a year), I noticed that Q would often clock off at the end of her shift and then go immediately to the waste bays to pick through the ship's refuse. As a result, the relatively limited storage space we had above and below our bunks was gradually filling up with a vast collection of . . . stuff.

My church upbringing said that she was doing this for some kind of superstitious or religious reason. That in all likelihood her little glass idol was telling her that this piece of communicator, or that piece of cabling, or those fragments of psychoconductive Leviathan bone were vitally important for some misguided heathen purpose. But eventually, after many internal debates with the ghosts of the old men of my childhood, I persuaded myself otherwise.

After an even longer debate, I persuaded myself to just *ask* her.

So the next time I was sitting in bed, watching her rip the guts out of the emergency backup battery of a long-defunct environment suit, I took a deep breath and said, "What are you actually going to do with all this?"

She looked up at me, quite unguarded, and replied, "*Take home.*"

"Why?"

From her expression, she found this a very peculiar question. "*We need.*" She held up a component. "*Photocell. Hard to make without*"—she waved a hand in frustration—"*Silex. Flint. But not.*"

"Silicon?" I tried.

Q nodded. "*Very little on Earth. Little metal. No fuel.*"

That more or less matched what I'd been taught. When our blessed ancestors had fled that cursed planet, they'd left nothing of value. It would have been sinful for them to do so. "How do you"—I hesitated; the question was going to sound crass—"you can't live on scrounged semiconductors and repurposed copper, surely?"

I was probably imagining it, but there was a sadness in Q's eyes then. A terrible distance. "*Can't live like you,*" she said. "*Ships. Cities. Domes.*" She shrugged. And then gave up on Exodite and with a touch of frustration in her voice said, "Considerate lilia quomodo crescent non laborant non nent dico autem vobis. Nec Salomon in omni gloria sua vestiebatur sicut unum ex istis." And then she set her tinkering aside, hauled herself up to my bunk, and kissed me so very, very gently. "*This*"—with a single small movement of her head she managed to indicate an all-encompassing everything: the steel walls of the ship, the harsh glare of the strip-lights, the blue-white glow of the screens, which were currently advertising holiday packages to a pleasure complex on Mimas—"*is not all there is.*"

I was sure that on some unhelpfully literal level she was right. Despite my upbringing I wasn't completely incapable of acknowledging that other ways of being probably existed. Out there. Somewhere. For other people. As a child I'd harbored secret dreams of running away to be a pirate. Of living by blood and plunder from a hollow asteroid somewhere in the Trojans, or on a rogue atmospheric station in one of the gas giants. But while I'd made a very, very large number of terrible decisions in my life, I hadn't quite had the guts to go all in on being a professional murderer.

Sighing in place of speaking, I shuffled sideways so there was just enough room for Q to slide into the bed beside me, and she got the hint. Or at least, she got part of the hint.

Actually that's not true.

You've probably already noticed that I spend a big chunk of this book talking about how horny and self-destructive I am. And don't get me wrong, that isn't a completely unfair characterization. But I'm not quite as one-dimensional as I tried to make out the first time I wrote this chapter.

When I said she got "part" of the hint, I was trying to imply that what I really wanted was sex, and that Q made a mistake by not fucking my brains out there and then.

She didn't. She didn't at all. It's just way easier for me to pretend that I wanted to get laid than to admit that I wanted her to hold me. That right in that moment what I needed, more than anything in the world, was to be with somebody. To lie there in the quiet. To be allowed my uncertainties.

The screens were still playing advertisements at us and Q, with an instinct for mercy or a distaste for commercialism that I found equally wonderful, asked the computer to show us something else.

She asked it to show us stars.

I wasn't sure how much she knew about the way the intelligence was gradually suborning the ship's noostructure. I'd told her more than I'd told most people, but I'd been cagey even with her. Whatever she understood, she'd made an inspired choice. If there was one thing it definitely wouldn't have been overwriting it was star maps.

After a few moments' silence, she traced a finger over the too-low ceiling of my bunk, now covered in an illusory sky, and said, "Cetus."

It was the first time we'd shared a word. The first time we'd shared an idea. It wasn't something I'd ever really thought about despite my travels, but the stars were so impossibly distant that the constellations looked the same no matter where in the system you were. The Great Bear was the Great Bear from the Temple of Commerce on Pluto. It was still the great bear from the crystal waterfalls of Mercury. I traced a shape of my own. "Hydra."

Q moved her finger to a single, bright star. "Polaris."

That one was foreign to me. "Polaris?"

"*North*," she tried. "*Always there. Fixed. Unmoving.*"

And just like that, she'd lost me again. I'd never been to Earth. Never lived on a world with fixed stars. Never been able to look into the sky and know for certain that one light would always be there.

CHAPTER THIRTY
Kraken

As beautiful as the brit-clouds were, we hadn't steered into them for the aesthetics. Life gathers to life gathers to life and where there's brit, there's Leviathans.

I didn't really understand this at the time, being new to the business, but hunting in a brit-field is kind of a gamble for a hunter-barque and one that usually goes badly for inexperienced crews. Not only does the brit itself cause problems with jet or rotor propulsion, but the intense biodiversity that brings the ship there in the first place creates its own set of challenges. On the one hand, the abundance of Leviathans makes it the absolute definition of a target-rich environment, so if your goal is just to kill big monsters you're absolutely laughing. But if you want to pick out specific, valuable creatures amongst the crowds you're basically stuffed.

At least you're stuffed if you only rely on radar. Which, once again, is why hunter-barques, even when they aren't captained by obsessives on a vengeance crusade, so often make use of the eyeball mark one.

It was day two when the cry went up from the array. A white shape, plainly visible on the horizon.

"Confirm shape and color" was the reply from a suddenly interested captain. She'd been away so long, but the merest hint of a kill, or at least of the one kill she truly wanted, roused her like Lazarus from the grave.

Confirmation came back immediately. "Long and low, milk-white and moving quickly."

The order to launch came without hesitation and the whole crew went at once to the boats. Moving through the brit-cloud, we were on foils and rockets for maneuver, but if we could bag a Ridgeback—even if that Ridgeback turned out not to be the specific one that had devoured our captain's every waking thought—it would have been worth the extra difficulty.

So we flew out. Over comms, Flint was keeping up his cheerful commentary about the value of a good coilgun while Truelove intoned hymns to the dread between the stars and Locke whispered bearings and measurements and *steady* in our ears.

The captain was silent. Dead silent. Though she flew once again at the head of the pack, as straight and true as a sniper's bullet.

Visibility is poor in a brit-cloud, the trillions of tiny organisms sometimes as little as an arm's length apart, bursting on the boat's canopy as it flew against the wind. So we had to track the strange white shape by shouts and half glimpses until the tides of fate and atmospheric chaos fell our way and a sight line opened up, showing us at last what we'd been chasing.

It wasn't one beast, in the end, but two.

A great Death's Head Leviathan locked in combat with something still greater, a titanic, amorphous Kraken from the deep sky, come to feed on whatever it could snatch up in its endless, grasping tentacles.

For the first and last time in the launch, the captain's voice came over comms. "'Tis not the Beast. Abort."

As pilot it was my duty to do as she said, to return the boat to the launch bay and make it ready for better luck in better skies. But for long moments I couldn't obey. I was too busy watching Titans duel.

Krakens are strange. You don't see them often and when

you do you normally die. The only time you can safely watch a Kraken doing its thing is when it's trying to kill something that isn't you. And the only time you can do that is when you're somewhere like a brit-cloud, somewhere so dense with life that you might not be the only edible object in a hundred klicks.

Just like my tendency to get all awed and philosophical at the vastness of the Jovian sky made me a pretty shitty lookout, my tendency to get all obsessed and fascinated at deep-sky kaiju battles made me a pretty shitty pilot for a hunter-boat. But right there and then, holy crap was it worth it.

The Kraken was huge and strange and abominable. A pulpy white mass of float-sacs and malice all studded with eyes and disgorging tentacles from its underside in numbers I couldn't track. The Death's Head—normally a fairly docile animal if you didn't bother it—thrashed and whipped its long, barbed tail through the sky and did its best to fight back. Problem was, its whole thing was that massive battering-ram skull it had, and while that was great for smacking the crap out of other Leviathans, clouds of angry Wyrms, or the occasional unlucky or overconfident hunter-barque, it did basically nothing against a beast made of air and membranes that fought by wrapping its enemies in arms as long as rivers.

". . . to ship," Locke was saying as I tuned back in to the world around me. "Now."

And they were right. If I dallied much longer I'd get my pay docked or find myself having an accident around an airlock. As the Kraken was drawing the Death's Head into its all-too-everywhere embrace, I turned my attention to the console and started bringing us about.

Outside, whatever mouthparts the Kraken had hidden amongst its tentacles started to crack through the Leviathan's carapace, spraying misty gouts of colorless gore onto the winds.

"Go," Locke was repeating. "There's nothing for us here." And I thought I heard them add "and nothing for her either" under their breath.

It was—from my perspective—a bit reductive to say there was *nothing* for us here. Nine out of ten voiders in the fleet signed up to see the cosmos as much as to pay their bills, escape their debts, or fulfil a death wish. And Kraken-versus-Leviathan was one hell of a bit of the cosmos to see. Buuuuut, they were right that hanging around wasn't going to do much to make us richer or improve our life expectancies, so I punched in the coordinates and took us home.

That evening, the Krakens were the talk of the mess.

"Ubi mel," said Q quite conversationally, "ibi apes."

Dawlish nodded. "And where there's Kraken, there's Ridgebacks."

I hadn't made as full a study of cetology in those days as I have since, so I asked why.

"Food chains," he explained. "The Death's Heads eat the brit, the Krakens eat the Death's Heads. The Ridgebacks eat damned near anything, but they *favor* Kraken."

Over the years I'd come to question most of what I'd been taught as a child about the obviously designed nature of, well, nature. But there was something about a world that had such sequences in it that lined up uncomfortably with lessons I'd learned and unlearned and relearned and rejected long ago.

At the other end of the table, Truelove and Marsh were eating far from us lesser peoples. But physical distance didn't stop them chiming in.

"It has nothing to do with food," intoned Truelove. "It is the will of the stars."

"Will of the stars?" I asked. Most of the crew didn't like to engage the Starry Wisdomers on matters of faith, but my own background made me hunger for foreign theologies. They helped me feel less like I'd given up my only chance of salvation.

"All devourings," Truelove explained, "are but a prefiguration of the Great Devouring that is to come. All beasts that devour are but a reflection of the great beast that devours and will consume all come the end."

Dawlish jabbed contemplatively at his bowl of gray slop. "Bullshit."

Marsh looked shocked, but Truelove took it completely in stride. "It means nothing to the stars if you believe or do not believe. What I say is true. The Kraken is a sign. A time of consuming approaches."

"The Kraken's a fish," replied Dawlish. "A big fish for sure. A sky-fish. But it's an animal like any animal."

"So say you." Truelove liked to cite the fact that other people had said things as evidence that those things were incorrect. "But the ship is alive with portents. The captain goes to the hunt in a boat with no crew, guided by machine blasphemies if I'm any judge."

The Old Ionian, who seldom agreed with Truelove on anything, agreed with him on this. "There's something unnatural in the systems, right enough. If not a ghost then some forbidden technology that's as good as one. Or as bad."

Dawlish set down his spoon. "Things can be dangerous without being spirits or blasphemies. If the captain's brought a thinking machine, she's breaking the law, not the cosmic order."

"Never mind the law"—this was the Tall Ganymedian—"whatever she's doing it's fucking with the ship's systems. Today we lose entertainment, who's to say we won't lose navigation tomorrow?"

"The captain has a mission," said Dawlish, sounding very slightly like he was trying to convince himself as much as anybody, "perhaps even an obsession. But I don't think she'd wreck the ship for it."

The Tall Ganymedian gave that awful, ironic smile he always gave. "Bet your life? If this beast she's after turns out to be real—"

"It is real," said Truelove. "And terrible. And chosen."

I sat quietly through this part of the exchange. The Tall Ganymedian hadn't actually been with the group that jumped me for not getting their porn reinstated, but he'd been dropping some serious *somebody should do something* hints just before it happened, and that made me disinclined to idly chat with him.

Q, for her part, was following the conversation with the same detached semi-attention she gave to most non-Terrans. I wondered, not for the first time and not for the thousandth, what was going through her head. Even when she shared her thoughts with me, they were so removed from my experience that I could scarcely engage with them. I often wondered if we were as opaque to her.

Of course, in a lot of ways all humans are unknowable to all humans, much as the Leviathan and the Kraken are unknowable, but I felt it more keenly with Q. As the poet might have put it, I was never closer to her than when she was looking at clouds, or further from her than when she was looking at me.

CHAPTER THIRTY-ONE

Weapons

We'll get back to the hunting and/or fucking in a second, but I need to explain some stuff to you first. If you're a coreworlder, or even an outworlder who just happens not to think much about energy infrastructure, you might never have bothered to ask how a hunter-boat can actually *kill* a Leviathan. After all, over the past few millennia our species has developed some pretty gnarly ways to blow things apart, so if killing a Leviathan is difficult, it's not because of a lack of boom.

Boom, we're fine with. Not that we carry much of it on a hunter-barque on account of not being a warship. But the technology exists. It's just that the technology is also completely wrong for our business. Sure, a hypersonic antimateriel round with fly-by-wire guidance and autostabilized trajectory correction will blast through a Leviathan's carapace and turn huge chunks of it into, well, huge chunks relatively easily. But that's the exact problem. Huge chunks of exploded monster aren't what we're here for. The hunter-barque needs to *kill* the beast in flight but then *dismember* it afterwards. And don't worry, we'll get to the dismembering eventually.

Anyway, if you're going to follow the next bit of the story it'll help you to know exactly what weapons a hunter-boat carries, and how they work and why exactly they can take out an armor-plated monster the size of a skyship. If you're not interested in those kinds of details, you could always pretend that this is actually a metaphor for, like, society or something. If metaphors for society also aren't your bag you could always skip to the next chapter. Just don't complain to me when you don't know what a chitin-saw or a bolt-driver is.

Maybe you can work it out from context.

Anyway.

Hunter-boats use a sort of wave system with their weapons. They start with the harpoons, two wing-mounted, one or two more manually fired. You've already seen what these do—they tie your boat to a gigantic space monster and let it drag you away on a subsonic death ride through the winds of a hostile world.

If we get very, very lucky, that's all we need. The beast pulls against the darts and the engines and, with enough little holes in it, slowly expires from exhaustion and whatever its version of blood loss is.

If we don't get very, very lucky, there's one more step. And that's when some poor motherfucker has to actually try to jump on the thing and take it down close-to.

There's two ways to get in for the final blow: from above and from below. The approach from above is usually made by one person, who gets fully out of the boat and rappels or zip-lines or just plain leaps onto the Leviathan's back. It's the exciting, heroic way of attacking and it appeals to a certain sort of hunter. It's also the angle where you actually need the chitin-saw, because you'll be right on the thickest part of the carapace. The chitin-saw is a large rotary blade designed to strap onto the left arm, leaving the right arm free for other weapons or just generally holding on to stuff so you don't fall to your death. The carapace is thick enough that the saw probably won't get you all the way through by itself, unless you can get to one of the parts where the plates overlap and wedge it in the gap. But it can make a big enough dent that you can ram a bolt-driver in and expect to do *something*.

The bolt-driver is the real killing weapon. A rod about seven feet long that magnetically rams out a barbed metal spike with the kind of force you in no circumstances want to be on the wrong side of. The business end is clawed, and those claws will in *theory* dig into the monster's carapace to stop the recoil catapulting the unfortunate hunter off their feet and into the clouds. They sometimes work.

If you try instead to approach the Leviathan from below, you miss out on the armor but you have to deal with the legs. Not all the limbs are weapons, or at least they're not meant to be. But whether something's meant to be a weapon or not doesn't make a huge difference when it's heavy and hard and swinging at your head.

Coming up from underneath, the whole crew can stay in the boat, which means there's less room for individual heroics and much more shared danger. Most of you, when you go this way, will be fending off the limbs with long knives, spears, and forks, but if you're aiming to kill and not just to survive, at least one of you will need a bolt-driver and the courage to aim at the gut of the beast, trusting your boatmates to keep you safe, and trusting the boat itself not to crack apart beneath you.

Locke favored the attack from below. The captain favored the attack from above.

Make of that what you will.

CHAPTER
THIRTY-TWO

Truelove Kills a God

Although the different members of the crew disagreed about *why* exactly Ridgebacks were likely to be found near Kraken—with explanations ranging from "because they eat them, obviously" to "it is the will of the Father and not to be questioned"—they all agreed that they *were* and so the watchers on the array kept expectant eyes out and their expectations were met sooner rather than later.

This was my third launch with the Pequod and came, if I'm remembering right, near the end of the first year of the voyage. I'd never have said the process became routine, but it was getting familiar. The scramble for the boats was feeling less like a panic and more like a drill.

It was kind of a mixed blessing. The thing about familiarity and contempt is a bit of a cliché but it's also true in a lot of ways. and I have a habit of checking out when I'm used to something.

Besides, even days later my head was full of Krakens.

We were nearing the edge of the brit-cloud now, but it was still busier than the skies had ever been outside it. So much busier that we found two Ridgebacks within a klick of each other and split the boats between them.

I could tell immediately that they were much more voracious than the Death's Heads I'd gotten used to seeing. Their lashing feeder limbs worked in endless waves to snatch up brit and grazing Wyrms and anything else they could draw out of the sky. They swept the cloud less clean, but they moved with more intention and—although this might have been my imagination—something that looked like spite.

They were gray-brown beasts, which meant the captain lost what little interest she'd had almost immediately. Obsessed as she was, she wasn't quite so far gone that she'd give up an opportunity for a kill just because the target wasn't the specific object of her vengeance, but she led the boats with a kind of detached competence. She was an old sky-hand, after all, and even at her least driven she was more than capable of managing a hunt.

Locke, for their part, handled this hunt exactly as they'd handled the last two. Deep, deep inside me, the part of my spirit that hadn't learned to see stability as a cage and reliability as a trap found it almost comforting. I guided our boat onto the same attack vector we'd followed in our first launch and Locke nodded their approval.

"Darts" came the order and then "Canopy," and we were bound once again to a listing Leviathan. This time when it rolled I was able to keep our angle relative to it, so the line didn't snag and we didn't get slammed against the creature's underside before we were ready.

A few hundred meters away and fathoms below, Truelove and Flint were closing in on their own quarry. Flint's overcustomized boat peppered the monster with darts burning white-hot from atmospheric resistance and over comms Truelove began to deliver commands that were half prayer.

"Bring us about," he said. "Fast and close. And give to me the saw and the bolt."

Our own Leviathan was straining against the wing-darts, and Q's harpoon found its mark squarely in the third eye on the right flank, making the creature buck and plunge and writhe. With the captain moving from the other side, we closed on our prey, and Locke gave the order for us to ready blades and spears.

"My heart and my blood are pure," Truelove was whispering over comms. "The stars teach that I shall be last consumed." And, so saying, he jumped onto the back of the second Leviathan.

In our boat, the instruments were warning of tensions reaching critical levels as our hooked sky-fish struggled against its restraints. We were coming in sideways, which put us at a good angle for avoiding the legs but ran the risk of damaging the wings of our boat. I steered into the arc, making us turn faster but getting the wingtips out of harm's way.

Below, Truelove's saw and bolt bit deep and sprays of ichor began to rise up with the winds as the Leviathan flew down and down and down, its control failing more with each passing moment.

"Blades, spears, bolt," commanded Locke, although this time the order wasn't for me. We still had enough control of the boat that a pilot needed to pilot.

With the canopy down and the boat rolling, it was a rough angle to fight from, but that didn't stop the crew. Q looked like an illustration from one of the comics I'd sneakily read as a child. The safe-for-work ones, in this case. She stood fierce and proud, one leg balanced on the capsule rim, long spear steady. Behind her, Locke waited with the bolt-driver ready as we swung closer, closer, and—

The line gave out, jolting us sideways and nearly pitching us into the skies. Q dropped back into a crouch, Locke threw down the bolt-driver to hold on to the back of my seat, and at least two of my boatmates dropped their swords over the side in their impious haste to preserve themselves.

With one line gone already, the other two went quickly, and the boat flew into a spin. I upped canopy and guided us from a fall into a spiral into a glide.

"Another pass?" I asked.

But Locke shook their head. "No time. She'll be in free fall now."

And she was. A truly panicked Leviathan will drop straight

down. Being adapted to the Jovian skies, they could handle accelerations well above those that would pulverize humans, and although it probably wasn't *good* for them, it was a whole lot better than getting spikes rammed into their central nervous system.

Trying (although not, if I'm honest, trying very hard) to quash their disappointment at being denied victory, the crew returned to their seats, and I brought us around to assist Truelove and Flint with their beast.

We descended through clouds flecked with Leviathan gore to see the other half of the boat-fleet on full afterburners, hauling the titanic corpse up towards the ship. Lowering our subsonic grapples, we took up our own place in the formation and joined in the glacial procession bringing the prey back home.

CHAPTER
THIRTY-THREE

Chains

The kill is the most thrilling part of the Leviathan hunt, but it's not the most important. We're not pest control, after all. We're after *stuff*. Stuff you have to slay monsters for, but still stuff.

When it's first killed, a Leviathan is lashed to the underside of the ship. Eventually it will be drawn inside the hold, but the beasts vary so much in shape and size that they normally don't fit easily. Plus the monsters have so many weird sticky-out bits that they'd just clutter up the ship if we brought the whole thing inside.

The process of transferring the body from the boats to the ship is a fiddly one, part automated and part manual. As we approached, the great fixing-arms came down from the undercarriage and spread wide to embrace the kill. By themselves, they supported it well enough that we could loose our grapples, but in Jovian gravity the weight of the beast strained the servos, so they needed to be linked underneath by chains. And that we had to do manually.

So once the body was in place and the grapple was disengaged I took the boat down, popped the canopy, and guided us towards the first of the dangling chains. We'd come in fast, because hunter-boats are fast by nature, but I brought us right down to gliding speed as we got close. Q was going to need to grab the chain as we went past and if we hit it at cruise velocities, she'd be incredibly fucking dead.

"Are you sure you're okay with this?" I asked her, even though it was far too late now if she wasn't.

"Non quia difficilia sunt non audemus, sed quia non audemus, difficilia sunt." She fixed me with a deadpan look. *"But don't fuck it up."*

Even at glide speed, we weren't exactly going slowly, and when Q caught the chain a jolt ran through the whole boat from the impact. I really wanted to stop and check if she was okay but if I had, I'd have blown the entire maneuver, so I kept us flying forwards. The chain would need to be tight, or as tight as we could draw it, so we flew as close to the creature's belly as we could manage, Q paying out the links over her shoulder and dangling flagella whipping against our heads.

And we hadn't even gotten to the hardest part yet.

Attaching the chain on the other side would take time. Not much time, but longer than the zero seconds a hunter-boat can hover for, which meant as we passed the fastening point, Q had to leap out, grab a handrail, and start screwing things into place while I circled around for the pickup.

It wasn't my first lowering, but it was my first time trying *this* and I knew for certain that if I fucked it up I'd kill her. And also that I'd be doing, like, the one thing she'd told me not to. There are large parts of the job where you can get philosophical, where you can contemplate how in a very real sense are we not all bound together in the great hunter-barque that is the human experience. This wasn't one of those times. This was one of the parts of the job where if I moved my hand a half inch wrong or took my eyes off the instruments I could wind up spraying my friend and lover all over the winds of Jupiter.

I steered down. Too far down, really. But the selfish, irrational part of my brain would have hated myself way worse if I hit her than if I played it too cautious and she missed us. From what I'd read—and how I'd trained in simulators—the trick was to line the boat up with the ship, making the relative velocities easier to match and substantially reducing the chance I'd slice her in half. So I took us into a lazy arc and ran us parallel with the body of the great beast, traversing it from tail to jaw and passing under Q on the way.

She dropped a fraction before I reached her, because even with trajectory matching, even accounting for wind, the boat was fast enough that if she waited until we were underneath her she'd just plummet into our slipstream and either fall into nothing or, if she timed it really badly, get fried by our jets.

I needn't have worried. I might have been a green pilot, but Q was an experienced harpooner, and she timed the drop perfectly, landing beside me with a heavier-than-it-should-be *thump*, the extra acceleration of Jupiter's gravity making her far faster on that drop than I was used to. I reset the canopy and stretched in my suit with relief as the relativistic compensators kicked back in. Then I brought us up in a wide, helical arc that took us past the Leviathan's great, dead head, all the way around its titanic corpse, and back to the hangar. Q settled down just behind me, and even through two environment suits I could see she was breathing heavily. She made everything look so easy—or at least so much easier than it felt to me—that I sometimes forgot she was as mortal as I was, and as aware of her own mortality.

For most of the day, I ignored that little fact. But that evening, as we lay together in my bunk, watching advertisements for soft drinks and opiates flicker past on the screens above, I plucked up the courage to ask her about it. "Were you not," I tried, "absolutely fucking shitting yourself?"

"Mors certa—"

"Yes yes, mors certa hour uncerta. I know. But still"—I looked at her lying beside me, half smiling, her eyes soft and dark and everything all at once—"aren't you . . ."

"Nemo potest non beatissimus esse," she replied, "qui est

totus aptus ex sese quique in se uno sua ponit omnia." And then with a wicked grin she added, "*But yes. Shitting myself. A bit.*"

And then she kissed me, and I wished for the hundred thousandth time that every question had so simple an answer.

CHAPTER
THIRTY-FOUR

Bodies

Guess what! It's another musing chapter! By now you should know the drill: skip if you like, more sex and violence later, blah blah blah. The thing is, though, I really want to talk about the body. That great, impossible body that chains and arms and machines held tight—or tight-ish—to the underbelly of the Pequod.

Because funnily enough, bodies matter to me. If we reject the eternal verities of the catechism—and I've been trying my whole life to reject the eternal verities of the catechism, with mixed success—they are in a very literal sense all we have. Which makes it even more of a bummer that these things that should, by all rights, be more truly ours than anything else in the system so often aren't.

Over the next days and weeks, my crewmates and I were going to take that beautiful, terrible, majestic Leviathan and violate it in every way imaginable. We were going to take its flesh and its bone and chitin and its ichor and its—drink if you giggle—sperm and carve them up and divvy them out and put them in boxes and barrels. And then we were going to sell them. Or at least that was the plan.

Perhaps it's sentimental of me, perhaps it's even hypocritical, but despite everything we planned to do to the beast—to the thing that at least two of my crewmates half worshiped as an agent of their destroyer-god—I want to speak of it, for a little while at least, as a whole. Or where I speak of it as parts, to speak of those parts as they belong to the animal, not as they belong to the bottom lines and ledgers of the Olympus Extraction State.

It's a courtesy I'd want somebody to pay me, in the event that Aphrodite ever catches up to me and decides to take back what they sold.

I'm going to start with the head.

I've heard that on the core worlds, there's still Terran animals. Things that evolved on Old Earth alongside humans—sorry, that the Father created alongside humans, I was never good in school. They say that if you look in the eyes of a dog or a cat or even a pig (which I hear some people keep as pets on Mercury and some people eat, but then again some people eat most things), you'll see something looking back at you that's recognizably, hauntingly mammalian. Their eyes work like our eyes; their bones work like our bones. I've heard that everything with an endoskeleton, on some level, is built the same way and on the same pattern. That even sea animals have hands inside the fleshy mittens of their fins and even snakes have little tiny leglets where our limbs are just as we have little tiny tails poking out just below the bones of our asses.

I've heard people say that these patterns amongst Earth animals are evidence that the Father didn't make shit, because if He did then why didn't he just make everything, what'd you call it, bespoke? Why give humans useless tailbones and snakes useless hips and why do giraffes have the same number of vertebrae as we do? And I've heard them say the opposite. That the sublime echoing of the human form in everything from a mouse to an elephant is proof that the Father made us in his image, and that this image is so sacred that it's reflected again and again and again in everything we used to share a planet with.

I wouldn't know. I've never seen a hamster or a horse. I've never had a pet and never eaten anything that wasn't native to the weird, hostile biomes of the outer system. And if the

Father built animals to reflect Himself, like He built humanity to reflect Himself, what the ever-loving fuck is the Leviathan a reflection of?

It is vast. It is alien. It is limbs that grasp and jaws that catch and armor and eyes.

So many, many eyes.

I've seen the eyes of the Leviathan from a dozen different perspectives now: soaring past them in the boat, hanging next to them on the butcher line (you'll hear more about that later, don't worry), flying towards them or fleeing from them or waking screaming in the night with them haunting my dreams.

The beast's eyes run in rows down each side of its armored non-face, and there are dozens of them, some as small as my fist, some larger than my entire body when I lie in my bunk curled up and trembling and waiting. Each one, I am convinced, is different. As different from each other as my eyes are from Q's eyes are from A's eyes are from Locke's eyes are from Truelove's are from Flint's. Without iris or pupil or lid, protected only by a transparent nictitating membrane, the eyes of the Leviathan are cold and dead while it lives, eerily vital after it's dead.

I don't know what coreworlders feel when they look in the eyes of their mammalian pets, but I've heard that it's a kind of fellowship. A feeling that, whether it was the divine hand of the Father or the blind chaos of impersonal cosmic forces, *something* binds you together. Some commonality that comes from being part of something larger. Something ordained. Something natural.

I think, perhaps, it's not so very different from what I feel when I look in the eyes of the Leviathan. Whatever order there is in the universe, whatever plan the Father has for His creation, neither I nor the great many-eyed, many-limbed armored beasts of Jove can be any part of it.

The night after we chained the corpse to the underside of the Pequod, I tried to explain all this to Q. But I couldn't find the words then. I can barely find them now.

"Lucerna corporis tui est oculus tuus," she told me. "Si oculus tuus fuerit simplex, totum corpus tuum lucidum erit."

And when I didn't understand she said, "*Your eyes. Beautiful.*"

She kissed me then, and I tried not to imagine that my body was the body of the beast, my lips the tendrils that curled from the monster's mouthparts, my jaw its mandibles and my eyes its eyes, dead and alive and belonging to a world that no human had any right to walk upon. I tried not to think of my hands and fingers as they clung to her as being the same species of jointed, segmented, grasping appendage that belonged to the dead Leviathan.

It was no good. I was feeling out of sorts and out of place and out of myself and out of my body. I pulled away from Q as gently as I could manage and shook my head. I told her I was sorry, that I needed air—or as close to it as an artificial atmosphere could come.

On deck I let my limbs guide me wearily aft of the array. My mind was full of horrors and wonders and clouds and eyes. Uncountable, terrible eyes.

It was at times like this I went to the captain, if she would have me. The times when I wanted to be destroyed, to let myself be broken and silenced and devoured. The times I wanted to be seen *through* rather than seen. To look into eyes that were a void, not a galaxy. That promised nothingness instead of a mortifying everything that I would never understand.

I didn't have it in me, on that night, or the nights like it, or the nights that echoed it and called out to it, to be beautiful. I had it in me only to be subordinate.

The day we chained the corpse, the captain had no use for me. Too busy with her charts and her calculations and the machine intelligence that echoed her thoughts back to her. Off rotation, I had no further duties, but in that nihilistic mood I had no further comforts either.

I descended through the ship to the keel balconies.

The primary watch post on a hunter-barque is the array, where the instruments scan the horizon for the telltale signs of

Leviathans. But a ship is a flying thing, and it exists in a three-dimensional space, so there's room for lookouts below as well as above. Below was right for me then.

The keel balconies on the Pequod, like all its outer surfaces, were strangely bedecked with the bones of her prey. While the viewing window itself, as on every hunter-barque, was a hemispherical blister of transparent crystal bulging almost obscenely from the lower hull of the ship, the walkway that led out to it was pure and white and osseous. Who had built it that way or why, I couldn't say. But in that moment I found it fitting.

I stood on the bones of a murdered god looking down at the body of a murdered god, shackled beneath the ship in chains my lover had risked her life to fix in place.

The carapace of the great corpse stretched out beneath me, and it was almost like it was of one piece with the monster-bone platform I stood upon. Some trick of Jovian space and the methane clouds made it hard to see where the creature ended and the ship began and where I stood and who I was.

Hard for me. Hard also for the Wyrms.

There were hundreds of them. Thousands, perhaps, all feeding on the body. A Leviathan's back is segmented and while its carapace is impenetrable to Wyrm teeth when it lives, in death nothing stops them from flying into the soft, intimate cracks between its great armored plates and wrenching at it with their vicious scavengers' teeth.

Nor was there, ultimately, anything stopping them pitching themselves at the sides of the ship, believing it perhaps to be just another kind of Leviathan, one stubbornly unwilling to show them its tender, fleshier parts.

I pressed my hands against the crystal viewing window and stared at the Wyrms. And they, in their hunger, stared back. They battered against the glass, their jaws inches from my fingertips, voracious and primal and a strange kind of comforting. If I'd been able to, I think I would have opened the window then, let them swarm in and consume me, let them swim-fly all through the ship and take the crew apart one by one.

I'm sorry. This wasn't what I meant this chapter to be about. I was trying to talk about anatomy. About the Leviathan. About how its head is some sixty to a hundred feet in length and protected above by thick chitin and then beneath that by a denser, harder substance that isn't quite bone. How its mandibles have on each side a dozen parts that move independently of each other and grind its food to a slurry of undifferentiated biomass. How set deep inside its jaw it does, in fact, have a tongue. A thick, muscular tongue whose movements nobody has ever seen and lived.

But much as I pretend sometimes, I'm no scholar. I'm not even much of an autobiographer. I'm not a writer of adventure stories or of tales of forbidden passion. I'm not a philosopher or a believer; I'm too cowardly to be an apostate and too uncreative to be a heretic.

The crystal glass was cool under my fingers, tremoring just slightly when the Wyrms struck it. I could feel myself *willing* it to crack. To let the sky pour in and to make it all be over in one blissful moment of bloody simplicity. And then, unbidden, a different thought began to sneak up on me. The thought that if I'd made a different choice that evening I could be in my bunk getting fucked senseless by my closest friend instead of being where I was and as I was and doing what I was doing.

Standing on bone. My mouth dry and my skin still crawling for reasons I couldn't quite explain. Watching sky-serpents writhe through the flesh of a slaughtered Titan, I wept.

CHAPTER
THIRTY-FIVE

A Long Way Down

The whole bottom of a hunter-barque opens into a huge airlock-hangar that you can fit *most* of a Leviathan into. But only most.

Before that, it has to be cut down to size.

In a lot of industries, that'd be a job for drones—flyers or walkers or crawlers with laser cutters built into their frames so that they can trim back the carcass in its most hard-to-reach places.

But drones are expensive, and if the barque loses one, that eats twice into the profits of the journey. Once because it makes the whole ship run less smoothly, and once because the lost machine will need replacing.

So the job is left, instead, to the crew. If we plunge screaming to our deaths in the Jovian skies, we leave the ship short handed, but the company will at least save a little on our lay, which in the event of our deaths is paid by default to the good people of Olympus Extraction State.

The bloody business of butchering is always done in pairs, two of us yoked together and then lowered over the side on a long, strong cable. One of the pair carries a saw a lot like the one used in the hunt while the other carries a sword or spear or some other weapon for scaring away the Wyrms that swarm in greater and greater numbers around the carcass.

The saw role is easier, and it was the one I usually took. I trusted the actual weapon to Q. Like with sword-welding, it was the safest way around for everybody. She was a whole lot stronger than me and with the gravity making everything heavier than it ought to be, I wouldn't have been able to keep brandishing a blade for more than a minute or so.

Since every part of the Leviathan is valuable to somebody, the goal in the dismemberment isn't to just fling its extremities off into the void—much as the Wyrms might enjoy that—but to bring them up again. Which is why each pair of butchers is suspended above a wide, deep hopper, like a very big bathtub or a very small skip. And into it we throw chunks of carapace, strips of flight-membrane, and the occasional outer leg that we hack through and rip off.

When I'm up on the array, watching for spouts and the Möbius Beast, my mind tends to wander. I get almost philosophical on account of how deep down I'm an insecure poser who likes to think she's smarter than she really is.

For some reason, some reason I can't quite put my finger on, I don't get the same problem when I'm hanging over empty air, sawing through an undulating strip of monster fin that three voracious sky-Wyrms are still trying to eat.

Without comment, or even warning, Q struck down at the nearest Wyrm, the sword falling quicker than I could track. The creature was split into two wriggling halves, seeping that same clear ichor that the Leviathans bleed. Its head-part and tail-part tumbled into the hopper, followed by the next strip of Leviathan fin as I carved it off then signaled up to the ship to move us along.

The cable holding us shuddered sideways, dragging me and Q and the hopper a few feet farther along the side of the beast. Most of the Wyrms had the sense to scatter as we went—it's not human flesh they're here for—but one or two stayed out of stubbornness or greed or sheer viciousness. I edged my saw blade towards them and one brought its jaws around to snap at me.

Q took its head off. The blade came within an inch of my

wrist and I had a very sudden, very stark vision of my hand tumbling down, down, down into the hopper alongside the Wyrm parts and Leviathan flesh. At fever-dream speed I imagined it stripped of its skin and its flesh and its fingernails. Its fat rendered down for oil and its bones strung on a scrimshander necklace around some voider's neck or given to somebody's sweetheart as a gift.

For a barely significant moment, I wanted it.

I was still *mostly* focused as I went back to dismembering. But the image-thought of that falling hand stuck with me all the while, and every time I worked on carving up a corpse afterwards. There was something about the job that made the grim reality of our trade in bodies feel very real and very close. I just couldn't get away from the fact that here with my saw, with Q watching over me like an extremely sexy angel, we were taking a thing that had once been majestic and terrifying, and making parts of it.

The flight-membranes for oil, even if it was a lesser kind than the precious spermaceti.

The carapace for scrimshander.

The tail and the limbs for timbers.

The teeth, yanked from inside its once horrifying mouthparts, would go the largest for building materials, the smallest for jewelry.

The only part of a beast I didn't know a use for were its eyes. Its hundred beautiful inhuman eyes that have looked out on Jupiter for . . . for how long?

It may shock you to learn this, but I'm not actually an expert on cetology. I did a fair bit of research when I made the jump from schoolmistress to monster hunter, and I've done more since because I'm writing a fucking book about the damned things, but there's a lot I don't know. There's a lot *we* don't know. There are volumes and volumes and volumes on how to refine spermaceti, how to use it and exploit it and make it power cities and starships and civilizations. There're treatises on Leviathan hide and fashion plates—old ones now, I'll admit—showing fine corsets and bracers and collar pieces made from the bones and armor of the beasts. One of the mil-states even did a study on whether their tail-spikes could be used as ramming weapons in ship-to-ship combat (the answer was yes in theory, probably no in practice).

But nobody knows how long they live in their natural habitat. We guess at what they eat, but that's just voiders' tales and supposition. Only the crews of hunter-barques ever come to Jupiter. Ever sail its skies alongside the monsters.

Only we catch a glimpse of what they see when they look out, through their hundred eyes, on a world of winds and vapors.

CHAPTER THIRTY-SIX

The Leviathan as a Dish

There are two schools of thought about whether it's a good idea to eat bits of the Leviathan.

All the other hunters say it isn't. Flint says it is.

I'm exaggerating, obviously. I'm sure that somewhere in the tumultuous multitudes of the fishery, there's more than one person willing to fly in the face of received wisdom, expert advice, the direct experience of everybody else who's tried it, and common sense. Especially if those people, like Flint, are part of the Church of Liberty.

Of the Big Three Churches, the Libertines are the ones I understand the least, even though I grew up relatively close to their Phobosi heartlands. None of the churches *strictly* own any territory—that falls exclusively to the trade-states and the short-lived seditionist enclaves that they nobly protect us from. They do have areas where one or the other is stronger. Pluto for Prosperity; Venus for Life; Mars for Liberty; but these are tendencies at best. One of the blessed things about the trade-states of the Exodite Commonwealth as opposed to the clans, kingdoms, and nation-states of Old Earth is that they're inherently decentralized, meaning the old curse of wars over territory is a relic that humanity has moved far beyond. In our modern, enlightened world we only fight wars over resource rights, trade practices, and of course to repress workers' uprisings, all of which are much more sensible things to spill blood over.

Anyway, as far as I can tell the Church of Liberty exhorts its followers to actively reject any authority except the Church itself (which, from what I can gather, sets quite a lot of rules for its followers, especially regarding sexual behavior) and their own impulses. And Flint's impulse, it seemed, was that he really wanted to eat some Leviathan.

"Eating your kills," he told the mess hall, "is an ancient and sacred tradition. A man isn't free if he's never eaten something he killed with his own hands."

The Pretty Vestal gave a devastatingly humble smile. "I wonder if the captain intends to eat the Beast, when we catch it."

"Probably," replied the Tall Ganymedian. "It seems like the kind of thing she'd do."

This earned him a rebuke from Dawlish. "Does it? Or are you just saying that to sound clever?" Then without waiting for a reply, he turned to Flint. "Anyway, you didn't kill it with your own hands. Truelove did."

Flint scowled. He was usually good-natured to the point of apathy but there were matters he didn't like to be crossed on. "I shot the first lance, that makes it mine."

As ever, I wasn't totally sure how much Q had been following, but she chimed in now. "*First lance, the pilot. From the wings. Second lance.*" She nodded to Dawlish. "*Harpooner.*"

"From my boat," Flint insisted. "On my orders. Which makes it mine."

"Perhaps"—the imp of the perverse was on me—"we could say it was a group effort?"

No matter which church you came from, this was blasphemy. Even to atheists like the Tall Ganymedian and the Pretty Vestal it was mildly offensive. After all, collective effort was just a short step away from collective action, and that was a dangerous road to go down. It's a well-known fact that for a society to function, individualism and a strong sense of personal responsibility are absolute necessities, and suggesting otherwise is sympathizing with terrorists."

Dawlish met my eye. He was, in many ways, a better heretic than me despite being an unbeliever. "We could."

"My kill," Flint insisted, "which makes it my meal."

The Tall Ganymedian regarded him with a look that bordered on the insubordinate. "That's all well and good, but do you have to cook it *here*? You're making the whole mess smell like an Ionian rendering vat."

He was, and it did. The ship's droids are only trained to produce quite a narrow set of dishes, and if you want something else you have to make it yourself. The mess table had a hot plate built in for this purpose, but it was seldom used and when it was used it was hardly ever used *unilaterally*. It was more common for a group of us (each, of course, taking personal responsibility for their own contribution) to throw a collection of whatever leftovers or organic scraps we happened to have scrounged up into a pot and make a stew of it. Frying a slice of Leviathan fin, and entirely for one person's consumption, wasn't against regulations but it was certainly against common practice.

"Captain's already barred me from using her cabin," Flint grumbled, "and did the other officers back me? They did not."

On the hot plate, the fin was beginning to pop and sizzle, its not-exactly-fat turning a yellow-brown that might or might not have meant it was edible.

"Then cook it over a fuel cell in your quarters," suggested the Second Europan. She'd been part of the group that jumped me over the porn issue, so I didn't really want to agree with her, but this was one of those moments when the worst person you know was making a great point.

While I'd chosen to stay quiet, Q never could. "Fugit, te inepte," she shot across the table, but neither I nor the Second Europan actually understood what she meant.

With a look of honestly quite churlish defiance, Flint levered the blackening monster fin off the heat and onto his plate where it sat in a widening pool of psychoreactive grease.

"'Tis a bad omen," the Old Ionian insisted. "No good ever comes of eating Leviathan."

While Flint was stuffing god parts defiantly into his mouth, the Pretty Vestal decided to pick an entirely different fight. "You're *always* saying that, old man. You said it about the captain being belowdecks. You said it about the entertainment system glitching. They both sorted themselves out, and the voyage is going perfectly well."

I'd heard him express the absolute opposite opinion not three days ago, but it was amazing how much difference a kill made. Suddenly the whole crew was remembering that our main goal was to slay monsters for profit and that no matter how boring things got—and they would get plenty boring—they could also be thrilling and violent and, if they continued to go as well as they just had, they could end in a decent payday for all of us.

Also, he was wrong about the entertainment system sorting itself out. It had just stopped getting worse. But in my experience people easily confuse not getting worse with getting better, especially if they've got something to distract them. And there was little more distracting than the corpse of a legendary star-beast.

Little. But not nothing.

Because we were about to meet an angel.

CHAPTER
THIRTY-SEVEN
The Archangel

The work of hewing up and butchering the Leviathan took days rather than hours, so we were barely halfway done when a hail came through from another barque.

On this occasion, I wasn't in the captain's bed when the message came in (I know, I know, it wasn't for want of trying), so I don't know how she answered them. My guess is that she asked if they'd seen the Möbius Beast and they said they had, because we actually changed course to rendezvous with them.

Except it turned out a rendezvous wasn't on the cards. At least not the getting together drinking and fucking kind of rendezvous the crew had been waiting for. Word soon went around that the Jeroboam had two distinct but equally weird things going on. Firstly, there was a plague on the ship, and although air filtration and decontamination rooms could do a certain amount, the kinds of things people liked to do on gams (see above re: fucking, drinking) were pretty much the opposite of social distancing.

As much of a bummer as that was, because the Pequod was getting cramped and samey after so long in the skies, it paled very slightly into insignificance beside the other weird thing about the Jeroboam, which was that it had the Archangel Gabriel on board.

I was sure they weren't the *actual* Archangel Gabriel because the math on that one didn't begin to check out. The way I saw it either the Church was onto something, in which case probably some two-fiftieth lay voidhand wasn't likely to turn out to be an angel at all. Or else the Church was full of shit, in which case angels probably weren't real.

There was, I suppose, a middle ground that worked theologically. It was possible that the churches were right in their broad cosmology but wrong on the finer points of doctrine. But believing that felt like it'd be a lot of work, and so I settled for assuming the whole thing was a load of crap.

Since the Jeroboam was keeping itself in isolation, the ships wirelessly linked their internal comms for a kind of remote gam. This happened sometimes, apparently, and it wound up being what you might call a party line—you could speak to random members of the other crew and use that fleeting moment of human connection to share stories about your past, or catch up with former shipmates, rekindle relationships with old friends. Stuff like that.

Or you could use it for sex. Most people used it for sex.

Unusually, I didn't. I'd like to say that something about the vast unknowable isolation of the Jovian skies had turned my mind away from the physical and towards higher things, but the truth was I just felt a bit self-conscious about my voice.

Instead, I asked around the crew and tried to work out what the fuck was going on with this whole Archangel Gabriel business.

So I didn't get an orgasm out of it, but I did get a story.

"He's Venusian," Dawlish told me, leaning on the bulwark and watching the Jeroboam from the observation deck. "From the Renouncers."

It wasn't a sect I'd heard of. The Great Churches liked to pretend they had a monopoly on faith, but even if you ignored the totally unaffiliated cults like the Starry Wisdom or the various Theonationalist Enclaves, there were little subsects and schismatic branches all over the place. "Renouncers?"

The look on Dawlish's face was bitter. "Walked away from the Church of Life after the Bull on Cellular Personhood and the Rights of the Coercively Conceived."

I'd been forced to learn a ton of theology in my time, but it was Prosperity-focused not Life-focused so I just stared at him blankly.

"The Church of Life is big on Venus," Dawlish explained, his mechanical hand tightening on the gunwale. "The Bull is why I'm here, in a roundabout way."

I had no idea where this was going.

"I'm a convict," he explained. "A murderer. A mass murderer, in Venusian law."

And even though I knew firsthand that Venusian law was probably fucked, I edged just a little bit away from him. "What did you do?"

"According to the Bull on Cellular Personhood, issued by the Church of Life and signed into joint corporate law by Aphrodite Pharma State, Fortuna Entertainment Republic, and the Panagricultural Combines of Ovda Regio, I killed four hundred and seventy-nine human beings. Because according to the Bull on Cellular Personhood, any self-replicating set of cells that's capable of survival outside of the human body is a human life."

My background wasn't in biology, but I had a feeling this was about to go to some bad places.

"Which means if you get, say, cancer on Venus, you have two choices. You pay a fortune to have Aphrodite or one of its subsidiaries lovingly remove your tumor and transfer it to a laboratory where they can keep it alive and harvest it. Or you go to a backstreet oncologist." He tapped his chest. "Saved a lot of lives," he said grimly. "But not according to Venusian law. The Renouncers looked after me for a while, but it didn't take."

That explained some things about Dawlish. His cybernetics, for one, which were the cheapest pieces of shit on the market. Exactly the kind of thing that one of the Corrections Conglomerates would put in their indentured inmates to keep them working and profitable. I was less sure how much it explained about the guy claiming to be an archangel. Still, it didn't seem right to press him for more details, so we chatted a while about our mutual experiences with Aphrodite Pharma State and its enduring commitment to securing its property. Then I left him to it and went looking for other people who might fill me in on the rest of what was going on.

None of the people I asked—from my crew or the Jeroboam's—could explain precisely when their crewmate had started to claim (or as they put it, because every last one of the bastards believed him, to realize) that he was the Archangel Gabriel. Or for that matter *why* he'd started to claim it, other than the obvious reasons (those reasons being either "because he's the Archangel Gabriel" or "because it's incredibly useful to have a bunch of people thinking you're the Archangel Gabriel," depending on your perspective). They just knew he'd kept it pretty close to his chest when he'd first signed aboard, only revealing his definitely-actually-true-no-really identity as one of the most cosmically important beings in the universe once they were safely within the atmosphere of Jupiter and the captain's options were reduced to "put up with it" or "space him."

I got the impression the captain had wanted to go with "space him," but the crew had rebelled.

The whole idea of a crew of otherwise sensible people deciding that some random from a broken hab-dome on Venus was a powerful servant of the Divine Father was messing with my head. But I kept digging, if only because I wanted to know why any of them believed him for more than ten seconds.

The answers I got were vague and mostly unsatisfying. One or two did claim that he had directly, personally cured them of the plague, although even then they were unclear on how he'd done it and seemed happy to admit that other people had gotten better perfectly naturally. Most of the rest just said things like "Well, you have to believe in something" and "Better safe than sorry."

I didn't buy either of those. I've been seesawing between believing and not believing my whole life and nobody's ever convinced me believing is better. As for safety—I mean, maybe it's just the November soul in me, but I'm the sort who'd pick sorrow every time.

Perhaps I'd have learned more about the strange situation on the Jeroboam, but about halfway into the gam, the captain's voice came crackling into my bunk over the intercom.

"I've need of you," it said. "An angel has just prophesied my death."

Naturally I went to her at once, and I found her pacing the floor of her cabin, bathed in the holographic blue light of her map table.

"Speculate," she was demanding of the thinking machine. "From what data we have, was their story true?"

"I'm not supposed to—" the machine replied, only to be cut off with a word and a gesture from the captain. "It might or might not be," it continued, which A took as confirmation. "The sighting places the Beast spinwards in the third southern belt some eighteen months ago. That's consistent with what we know of its patterns but doesn't limit its location much."

Still pacing, the captain demanded, "And the death of the mate?"

"There's no reason for the captain to lie to us, but he might have been lying anyway. The angel confirmed it despite confirming very little else, but there might be multiple explanations for that. Ship's data shows the mate wasn't aboard the Jeroboam but it could have been tampered with."

"And the angel himself," the captain continued, stopping now and glaring at the table. "Is he what he claims to be?"

The light over the mirror-surface shimmered. "I'm not trained to answer questions of theology."

"You can't believe," I interrupted, "that an angel came into the world, only to take the shape of a simple ship's hand."

As if recognizing my presence for the first time, the captain turned to face me. "You think might never hid itself behind meanness?"

Unlike the thought engine, answering questions of theology was damned near *all* I'd been trained to do. That didn't mean I liked doing it, or did it well. "I think saints," I replied, "are rarer by far than liars."

"And if I said"—she stepped towards me and, partly on instinct and partly in play, I backed away, pressing myself against her cabin wall—"that I was of a mind to believe him, would you think me out of my wits?"

She'd taken to asking me that a lot. I never knew what answer she wanted me to give. "Would you care if I did?"

Her face was close to mine now. It sometimes began this way, when she was in a certain kind of mood. When the storm inside her was close to raging itself apart. "Answer me," she whispered, "or damn you for a coward."

There was a game to be played here. A game of just enough defiance. "I've never pretended to courage."

"Should I credit him?" she asked me, sounding almost desperate. "The angel?"

Looking back, it would have been the easiest thing in the world to say *yes*. To tell her what the crew of the Jeroboam had just finished telling me. Better to believe. Better to be safe. Better to take warnings when they're given.

But while I've been many things in my life, I've tried to avoid being too much of a hypocrite.

"What did he say?" I asked instead.

"That my fate would be that of the first mate of the Jeroboam," the captain told me, her eyes fixed on mine and her hands sliding into position on my wrists. "That the Leviathan would be my death. That it was the Divine Father incarnate. That the will that drives the world is set against my hunt. That in the end the Beast's great tail would stave my boat and send me spinning down into the abyss whence none return."

Her breath was hot on my cheek and her fingernails were beginning to dig into my skin. And I knew then, or thought

I knew, the answer she wanted me to give. "Suppose you believed him?" I said. "Suppose you knew, in your heart, that every word he spoke was true. Would you turn aside?"

She smiled then. Terrible and beautiful. And she kissed me with a hunger like the sky.

CHAPTER THIRTY-EIGHT

The Archangel's Story

I'm going to be honest. At the time I wasn't much interested in what the Archangel told the captain because, and I want to make this absolutely one hundred thousand million percent clear: he wasn't a fucking archangel. He was a scammer.

But I've rewritten this book three times and each time I go back to it I get the feeling that something is missing, and what I think is missing on this pass is the Beast. The true Beast. The Beast that this whole thing is about.

I pieced this story together later, in fragments from members of the crew who heard it from other members of the crew, or other crews. Some of it I got on the Pequod, some elsewhere. Much of it I had from a man named Ironhands I met in a dive bar on Hygiea, and some I got from sources I've long since forgotten.

Here is the tale as I learned it.

"The Archangel Gabriel," began the Tall Ganymedian, leaning on the bulwark of the Pequod's main deck with characteristic apathy, "on hearing of the Möbius Beast, decided that it was an incarnation of his god."

"Which was foolish," Ironhands continued through the vapor haze of the miners' bar. "There's no gods in this world."

"Save one," added Marsh in the mess.

"Anyway," I told a woman with one green eye and one brown,

who I loved passionately for about three hours in a dark room in a cheap inn, back on Cthonius Linea, "he forbade the crew from hunting it, which would have been fine except—"

"Except human nature is what it is," explained Dawlish. "Forbid people to do something and there's always some fucker who'll do it just to spite you."

Even with that—I type onto a barely working tablet at a table in a dark corner of a bar on Titan, knowing full well that this round of edits was due in yesterday—they would have been fine. Our ship hunted the Möbius Beast for three years and only came upon it at the last. Most ships never sight it.

"And when they do," said the Old Ionian, "it's too late."

"But this particular ship, she was unlucky," Ironhands told me—his hands really were iron, or rather they were steel but then chemically speaking steel has more iron in it than iron does. And actually they were probably mostly low-density composites but you can't call a man Low-density-composite-hands, that'd be silly. "Because we sighted the Beast, and the first mate, name of Mayhew—"

"Macy," said Dawlish.

"Miller," said the Tall Ganymedian.

"Mabunda," I told the woman with the one green eye.

"—he was all seized with a lust to hunt the Beast down."

The woman with one green eye smiled at me. *Seized with lust* had been a cheap play, but I'm a cheap sort of girl.

"The Archangel," the Old Ionian went on, "he swore against it. Prophesied against it, said it would bring doom on the first mate, and on all who lowered with him."

"On him alone," said the Tall Ganymedian. "Which as you'll learn later was extremely on the nose."

Ironhands leaned closer to me. Uncomfortably close, if I'm honest. "But what did he know? After all as far as Mayhew—"

"Miller—"

"Mabunda—"

"Macy—"

"—was concerned the Archangel was naught but a man

before the array. Whereas a first mate"—Ironhands puffed up his chest in a parody of entitlement—"well, a first mate must be obeyed, must he not?"

"So what happened?" asked the woman with one green eye.

I took her hand in mine, ran my thumb across the pattern of scars that formed intricate concentric designs on the back of it. "First mates are arrogant"—I thought back to Locke—"well, most of them. And so when the spout was sighted, he gave the order to lower."

I described the sequence of lowering to her. And now that I was working from experience instead of fragments I'd stolen from other people I could be clearer, more precise, more alive in the moment. And I think she noticed.

"The boats slipped into the wake of the great Beast," I told her. "You'd think that a bigger Leviathan would be slower than a small one, but that's not how it works. Something about the way they move." I was sensing she didn't care about the details. "They shot off their wing darts—"

"But it was for naught," said the Old Ionian. "Clattered off the monster's carapace like—"

"—piss off tin," said the Tall Ganymedian.

"And so," said Ironhands, "they lowered the canopy so the harpooners could do their work. But no sooner was the cover down and the crew exposed than the Beast's great tail cracked"—he brought his low-density-composite hand down hard on the bar.

"—like a whip," said the Tall Ganymedian.

"—like thunder and lightning both," said the Old Ionian.

"—fit to tear the sky," said the Bright-Eyed Titanian.

"—cross the path of the first mate's boat," said Ironhands, "and the very tip of it slashed across the cockpit, and though most of the crew had drilled well and knew to duck . . ." He gave a smile that was half a sneer. "Officers. Am I right?"

"Not a soul was harmed," said the Old Ionian.

"Not one hair on one head out of place," said the Tall Ganymedian.

Dawlish gave me a look that said he only half believed what he was saying. "'Cept for the mate. Who was swiped out the boat and plunged to a meaningless death in the skies."

After a moment's silence, the woman with one green eye looked at me skeptically. "That seems unlikely."

"It's more common than you'd think," I told her. "Close calls happen all the time, and if one person is a bit out of position, they can get hit way worse than anybody else."

I don't think she liked that explanation. It felt as if I'd denounced a miracle.

Which I suppose I had, in a way.

"So," the Old Ionian went on, "it all fell out as the Archangel proclaimed."

"Reckless man does reckless thing," said the Tall Ganymedian. "Dies. No magic there and no mystery."

"A beast doesn't have to be a god," Dawlish concluded, "to be well worth staying away from."

That much, at least, was true. And by the same token a man didn't have to be an angel to speak prophecy.

He just had to open his eyes.

CHAPTER
THIRTY-NINE

Scrimshander

A few days after the Jeroboam's visit, we finished the cutting down, and the great corpse of the Leviathan was drawn into the underbelly of the ship. It was a slow process, beginning with the evacuation of the entire lower deck so we wouldn't vent a massive chunk of our oxygen into the Jovian storm. When that was done, the lower airlock, which ran the whole length of the ship's keel, creaked open. And the difference in pressure meant that the mostly-hydrogen atmosphere of Jupiter rushed into the gap like a hurricane, carrying sky-Wyrms up with it and—in one of the few examples of the harsh conditions actually helping the ship instead of hindering it—supporting the great mechanical arms which came down to pull the beast up for the next stage of its dismemberment.

The sound of the atmospherically backed rising of the Leviathan was fittingly immense. It set the whole hull of the ship shaking with the grinding of metal and the screaming of the wind, and since I was lying in bed with Q when it happened, it made it really hard to fuck.

So we made our way down to the viewing platform on the bottom deck to watch the next stage of the drawing.

Eventually the screaming, shuddering noise of the pulling-in was over but, as we came closer to the hold, we heard it replaced with a new, perhaps even more disturbing sound. A beating, drumming sound, like the heaviest rain you ever heard, but coming from below and within instead of outside and above.

Once we reached the viewing platform, with its thick walls and its reinforced portholes, we realized what it was. The hundreds upon hundreds of Wyrms that had been drawn in alongside the carcass were still feasting but, knowing themselves trapped, they were now as often hurling themselves against the walls and the viewing ports as against the ever-dwindling body of the Leviathan.

And then, as Q and I watched, one final sound began. A low, loud hissing as once more the atmosphere of the hold was evacuated.

The Wyrms don't fly by any principle known to current science—they're nothing like aerodynamic enough—but whatever electro- or psychokinetic process holds them up, it requires some kind of atmosphere. And as the hydrogen around them was pumped once again into the Jovian skies they began to fall to the ground, making the rain sound return one last time. Monstrous as they are, they can't live in a vacuum, and so Q and I watched as they flopped and gasped and choked their last.

It was slaughter on a massive scale. Hundreds of lives snuffed out in order that one, vast life could be broken down into its constituent parts. Of course if we didn't, then our own lives wouldn't be worth very much of anything and, universal community of all living beings aside, it was 100 percent better them than me.

"Fui quod es," mused Q, "eris quod sum."

From here, much of the remaining butchery was automated. The walls of the hold were lined with countless claws and jaws and saw blades that would complete the dissolution of the Leviathan with robotic efficiency. They would pry away the rest of its armor, precisely excise the head and spinal ridge (those being the parts that contained the precious spermaceti), and sort the usable parts into barrels for processing while the rest of the monster would be diced, slurried, and sprayed unceremoniously back into the sky that spawned it.

Of the valuable parts of the corpse, most are reserved for sale back in port, but there are inevitably fragments—especially fragments of bone and carapace—which are too small, too irregular, or too inconvenient to have much commercial value, and it's from these that the crew make the strange artworks known as scrimshander.

I tried a hand at it myself once, but I didn't have the dexterity or the artistic touch. Q—as in most things—was my superior by far. We sat one evening in her bunk while she etched images in a shard of not-exactly-chitin. The scent of burning wafting up from her laser cutter was oddly cozy, like cooking over open fire or a solid-fuel heater. For more than an hour, I watched her from behind the procedurally generated mystery novel I was pretending to read, taking in the lines of her wrists as she worked and the distant, quiet look on her face as she guided the laser.

Eventually, since I have a tendency to get restless—so restless that I at times sell myself onto doomed star-voyages that throw themselves down the gullets of abominations—I stretched and was about to get out of bed, when Q held up a hand and said, "*No.*"

I froze, hoping I hadn't broken some strange Terran taboo and especially hoping that this wouldn't lead to her pulling a knife on me like she had when we'd first met. Well, mostly hoping it. Slightly hoping the opposite, but my issues are for a different time.

She turned the slightly curved panel of beastbone she was working on, and I saw, etched in dark lines across its ivory surface, my own image.

The picture-me was sitting quietly, reading a dataslate, her back against—what, exactly? Something strange and alien that rose up from the ground and spread arms over her like a loving monster.

"What is that?"

"*Tree*," she said.

I'd never had a word and an image come together with so much context and so little all at once. *The righteous shall flourish like a palm tree, he shall grow like a cedar in Lebanon. And Abraham planted a tamarisk tree in Beersheba. So he ran ahead and climbed up into a sycamore tree to see Him. Because I said to you "I saw you under the fig tree," do you believe?*

Was this what they were? This pattern of knots and whorls and these spots of light and shadow from a sun through an unfiltered sky?

"It's beautiful," I told her. Because it was. Because it somehow made *me* beautiful, which is something I'd never been used to feeling.

And then, because I wasn't sure how to process that, because I wasn't sure how to thank her in a way that didn't involve sex on some level, I slipped very quietly out of bed, said, "Really," and then walked very quickly away.

I made my way to the mess, where I found Marsh also busy scrimshawing, although he was using a more traditional blade, rather than laser-engraving. Doing my best to ignore him, I went to the food vendor and ordered up a bowl of Wyrm meat. That was the other advantage of asphyxiating a bunch of sky-serpents alongside the corpse of a star-cetacean. There was at least moderately good eating on them, and since they counted as bounty of the voyage they weren't taken out of our lays.

Seasoning would be, of course, so the actual meal I got was a thin consommé of unsalted flesh sitting in water recycled from urine or the heating systems or, most likely, both. Still, the bits of scale and bone made something approximating a broth and it was, by and large, better than a lot of things I'd eaten on Europa.

At least it was free range.

Since it seemed the entire crew except for me had a real and enviable talent for sculpture, I watched Marsh's figurine take shape with a mix of fascination and horror. It seemed to depict a human being, half forced to their knees while some kind of terrible beast raked claws and fangs across their eyes.

"What the *fuck* is that?" I asked him as politely as I could manage.

"Religious icon," he explained.

I looked again. It was definitely a person being devoured head first by something lithe and powerful and merciless. "Religious icon?"

"The great star god," he explained, "in His aspect as the leopard who eats the faces of the unworthy."

"Just the faces?" I was really trying not to judge, but sometimes other people's religions sounded even weirder than mine.

He shifted a little in his seat. "I think it might be mostly a metaphor. I don't think anybody expects Him to come in the form of a literal leopard."

"Or to eat literal faces?"

"He will take many forms," explained Marsh. I recognized his expression. Recognized it almost fatally. It was the comfort of a half believer retreating to the safety of dogma from the danger of thought. "A collapsed dome. A bankrupted subsidiary that starves an asteroid. A plague or a ventilation malfunction. All these are manifestations of the Devouring God."

"And He always eats the . . . impure first?"

Marsh nodded. "Always."

By any standard, this was objectively nonsense. More than that, it would almost certainly have been directly contradicted by the evidence of Marsh's own experiences.

Still, a tiny pointless part of me wanted to at least try. Giving up my Wyrm stew as a bad job, I drew my chair closer to him, and he flinched slightly. "Impure, meaning everybody who isn't like you?"

He had the good grace to flash the tiniest expression of guilt. "So Master Truelove teaches. So the Church teaches."

If I could have granted myself one wish then, it would have been to be able to call bullshit on my own faith as easily as I could call bullshit on Marsh's. Which as wishes went was probably pretty selfish. I reached out and took his hand, threading our fingers together so that their meaninglessly distinct shades of brown overlapped. And I took the tiniest bit of hope from the fact that he didn't pull away. "And you think a slaughterer-god is going to pick its victims based on"—it was so foreign to my way of thinking I could barely express it—"pigmentation?"

"So I was taught," repeated Marsh. And I'd have called it a bad answer but I knew the strength of it.

"And the Beast—the great Beast the captain hunts? You think that will leave you for last too?"

Marsh blinked. "So I was taught."

I looked down at our hands and tried, really tried, to see where he was coming from. "Okay, so let's say you're right. Are you really saying your entire religion is just . . . just based on wanting the monsters to eat me before they eat you?"

Marsh nodded. "Yes."

"Isn't that . . . extremely depressing?"

He snatched his hand back. "It's a depressing world," he told me. "And if all I have to look forward to is watching the god between the stars consume you in the moments before it consumes me, then"—he looked down and drew in a deep, ragged breath—"then that's a lot more than I'd have otherwise."

There wasn't much I could say to that. If I'd been more pious I'd have explained to him about the Father's love and how it could be his at very reasonable rates. If I'd been a better blasphemer, I'd have shown him how to build a pyre out of dogma and warm himself beside it.

But I was just me. A lost, confused half a heretic. Fuck, even the hand I'd reached out to him hadn't been mine. It had been rebuilt by Aphrodite Pharma State along with most of the rest of me, phalangeal reduction and osseous narrowing. I didn't own my body any more than Marsh owned his soul.

Still a tiny, hypocritical part of me resented him for it. For not realizing that he'd been lied to his whole life. For not having the guts to at *least* come and join me in the horrible halfway place between believing and unbelieving, where you yearned for the certainties of childhood even though you knew they were bullshit and felt like a failure every time you found another one of the hooks the old doctrine left in your heart.

An even tinier part of me thought that maybe he'd change one day. That maybe there was hope for him.

There wasn't. Fate—if fate is real—or blind chance had other plans for Marsh.

And when the monsters did finally come, they took him the same way they took everybody else.

Chapter Forty

Head

Like me, you might be ever so slightly disappointed that this chapter isn't about going down on somebody in a shipboard toilet.

I mean I completely did, obviously. It was a three-year voyage and with media storage glitching out there was no other way to pass the time except scrimshawing, which as we've already very firmly established I'm shit at. That's just not what this chapter is about.

If it helps, somebody *is* eventually going to wind up covered in sperm.

The most important part of the butchering—so important that it's not trusted to humans—is the severing of the head and ridge and their careful removal to the draining station on the floor above the hold.

Since I'd never seen it done before, I stayed for the whole process this first time. I stood on a walkway overlooking the upper chamber and watched as the floor opened and a hundred mechanical arms and automated winches hoisted the great head of the monster into place.

It rose slowly, far more slowly than it had ever moved in life. And because the head was so valuable its armored plates had been left in place, in case some stray bone shard or metal fragment might damage the precious contents.

The whole hunter-voyage is a long carnival of beautiful horrors, but standing there on a rickety metal platform looking up at the head of somebody else's god—or an aspect of it, or a servant of it, I still wasn't clear on the theology—I saw the greatest beauty and the greatest horror I'd seen all voyage, except maybe in the captain. Somehow being severed from the body and held up inside the ship made the head seem even bigger than it had in the sky, or hanging from the keel. Part of that was just proximity, of course. During the hunt you're farther away and the distances are big enough that you can't get a reliable sense of perspective. Then during the cutting-down you're far too close so you don't appreciate how huge it is, any more than you appreciate the size of the wall you're fucking against.

But here it was far enough away that I could see the whole of it, yet still close enough that I could see what "the whole of it" actually meant. How broad and tall and magnificent it was, even with its eyes and feeding tendrils removed so it was little more than carapace lined with membranes, its mandibles hanging slack and useless beneath a severe, shearing upper jaw.

We weren't due to start draining for an hour or so, which meant I'd assumed I'd be alone in the station, but I was wrong. I heard footsteps clanging harsh and metallic from around the lee side of the head and, just as I was trying to work out if I should stay or go, I heard the captain's voice.

"And what have you seen?" she was asking. Asking the head, it seemed. "In your voyages through red skies and white skies and into the cold and crushing seas that no ship may sail? What secrets have you gleaned from the dead on the winds of Jove and the celestial cold that birthed you?"

Looking back, I sometimes catch myself wondering the same thing you might be wondering right about now. Which is why anybody in their right mind would trust a woman like that to lead them into danger. *Can't you see*, I find myself screaming at the younger me, *that a woman who soliloquizes at the severed heads of monsters is clearly bad fucking news?* Hell, Q as good as *did* scream that at me—okay, she didn't scream it because screaming wasn't her style, but she told me, repeatedly—and I didn't listen to her either. So I certainly wouldn't listen to my allegedly wiser future self.

The thing is, at the time, it felt different. Less obvious how completely fucked everything was getting. Maybe it was the isolation. Maybe it was—and I've tried to make this clear but maybe I haven't made it clear enough—that the captain was extraordinarily hot. Maybe it was the inescapable, neutron-star gravity of her that no amount of words on paper (or more likely on electroreactive Wyrm skin, another useful byproduct of the noble trade of the Leviathan hunters) can really capture.

Or maybe I'm just a fool.

"Captain?" I called out to her as she came into view around the creature's quadripartite jaw.

She stopped and stared at me like I was some kind of ghost. "Do you mean to haunt me, shipmate? I assure you I am haunted enough."

Yeah okay, not doing myself any favors here on the why-are-you-into-this-person front. "Just inspecting the head."

She came and stood beside me, gazing up at the beast in silence. "All life in the system," she said, "all human life, at least, depends on the unknowable power that rests within that creature's brain."

The image of Q's scrimshawed drawing came back to me. There were places, I was now strangely aware, where that wasn't true. Where you didn't need to burn the cerebrospinal juices of star-monsters just to breathe. The thought was still alien to me, and it stuck like a fish bone in the gums.

"And yet," the captain continued, "it tells us none of its secrets. It hides and withholds and flees into clouds and liquid hydrogen. It has touched the face of Heaven and yet its face reveals nothing."

I should have realized she was losing it. I should have mentioned something to somebody. But what would it have helped? Once the voyage has begun the ship is its own world and the captain rules over it like a king or a god or, if you're really lucky, a competent and dispassionate middle manager. I had no power to challenge her, and no will to.

Also, right in that moment I mostly just wanted her to do me.

For a while, she and I stood in silence contemplating the vastness and the incomprehensibility of the Leviathan. And then the rest of the crew—those members of it who were on draining duty, at least—started to arrive, and we were back in the world of chaos and industry.

The extraction of the sperm (still hasn't stopped being funny, has it) from the neurological system of the Leviathan is of such importance aboard a hunter-barque that it's overseen by a specialized demi-officer called the trepanissimer. They're mostly a drone-wrangler, and it's their job to make sure that the incisions through the skull are made with minimal contamination of the spermaceti. Our trepanissimer aboard the Pequod was a grim-faced woman by the name of Enderman, but as vital as her function was to the success of the voyage, she and I barely interacted and so I won't say any more about her.

I will talk a bit more about her drones, though.

They start the process by meticulously cutting around the frontmost head plate of the Leviathan. They do this with a kind of small vibrating saw that slices easily through rigid materials but can't penetrate softer ones. This allows them to pry away the head plate and reveal the glistening, surprisingly tough membrane that fills the interior of the monster's head, sheltering its brain, its spinal bundles, and its precious, precious sperm.

C'mon, say it with me now. It's fun.

Once the membrane is exposed, a different variety of drone hooks up further cables to allow the head to be tilted so that the exposed area of membrane faces upwards. They have to do this because otherwise the creature's head is so positively brimming with delicious sperm that if the—it has a technical name, but I'm going to say "sperming hole"—isn't exactly level it will spill out and if it does, well. Then you have sperm going everywhere and not only is that unprofitable it's also extremely messy.

The next step of what I flatly refuse to stop calling the sperming process has to be done by hand. Spermaceti, by its nature, is electrodynamically and psychokinetically active to an uncharted extent—the refined form we use as fuel isn't really refined at all, it's processed and diluted to make it manageable. Which means that if hunter-barques tried to get drones to harvest it they'd fry their circuitry and waste a bunch of good kit and a bunch of good sperm all at the same time.

Instead, the drones run a crisscrossing pattern of lines across the draining chamber in two layers, allowing the crew to walk along one while holding on to another. This is, to use the official terminology, really fucking dangerous. But it's the way the hunter-barques have been doing it for centuries, and change costs money.

On this particular occasion it fell to Marsh to make the initial incision, under the watchful—if distant—eye of Enderman. He made his way carefully to the center of the room, walking on cables and clinging to cables, gripping a long, sharp spear (which *isn't* called a sperming spear but should be) under one arm. When he'd gotten to the right spot, he hunkered down, hooking his arms over the upper cable to free his hands, and he forced the spear downwards, hand over hand, until it pressed against the rubbery sac of the Leviathan's cranial membrane.

In spite of myself, I held my breath.

As he leaned just a little more weight downwards, the tip pierced at last, and sperm began to well up through the . . . okay I'll admit it, even I'm finding this a bit silly now. But look, this is a serious industrial process that just happens to produce a product whose name has unfortunate connotations.

Once he'd poked a big enough sperm hole, Marsh signaled for the pipes, which came coiling down from above like . . . like I don't know what. If you're a coreworlder and have seen plants and animals that aren't star-Wyrms and ice fish, there's probably a comparison here. Half a dozen long, sinuous tubes unfolded in Marsh's direction and his last job was to guide them into place so they actually went into the sperm instead of bouncing off what was left of the protective membrane.

And this last job, he fucked up spectacularly.

To be fair, it's hard. I've tried it myself since, and you're high up, you're standing on something extremely wobbly, you've just been handling a long spear covered in sperm. In some ways I'm amazed accidents don't happen more often.

But one happened now.

Reaching for an errant sperm pipe, Marsh overbalanced, slipped from his cable, and tumbled headfirst into the Leviathan's cranial cavity.

Most of us just stood there like unused dildos, watching. Dawlish made a brief move to go after him, but there was no way his cybernetics would have taken the exposure to raw spermaceti so he had to stop himself. He looked stricken, but it wasn't like anybody else was rushing to help.

The impact of the fall combined with Marsh's first extremely doomed attempts to haul himself out had set the head swinging, and now it slammed into the walkway, jolting me and the captain backwards and sending a good few of our other crewmates sprawling.

A cable snapped and the whole thing pitched sideways, spilling bucketfuls of spermaceti to the floor where it began to crystallize like frost on an ice miner's beard.

"Secure the head," called Locke from the upper walkway. "If it falls the voyage loses millions."

Inside the heart of every true-blooded void-dog watching, there was a sudden conflict. Yes, a man was drowning. But he wasn't exactly a *pleasant* man—none of us liked Starry Wisdomers, chiefly because they didn't like us—and even for those of us on long lays, the two hundred and fiftieth part of the price of the sperm in that beast's head was a whole lot of money. Even set against Marsh's life.

Truly, it was a dilemma.

But not for Q.

I'd come to the draining room alone, but Q was there too,

on the upper walkway beside Flint, who was resting a hand on his pistol and trying to work out if there was any way to solve this problem by shooting something.

She sprang, full-body, into the air, caught one of the trailing cables, and rode it down onto the side of the bucking head. And I felt a weird mix of pride and affection that was tangled up with the fact we were fucking but wasn't *just* about that.

Weird.

"That's it," Locke called encouragingly. "Refix the cable and then get the tubes back into place."

Beside me the captain was watching intently, the fire that was her eyes burning low and sulfurous.

Except Q didn't seem that interested in reattaching the cable. Instead, she crawled, spider-like, around to the underside of the head where she hung, nestled in what was left of the beast's mouthparts.

The Leviathan is well armored above, but below its defenses are mostly that it will fucking kill you if you get near it, and that's a threat that goes away when the thing is dead and dismembered. So Q seemed to have decided to go in through the jaw. She had her knife with her, the same one she'd nearly killed me with when we first met, and she was using it now to slice her way through what would have been the monster's throat.

"By the Father," exclaimed Locke from above, "what is she *doing*?"

"Obstetrics," replied Dawlish, with a smile that read to me as almost wicked.

And he was right, in a way. We couldn't see—at least I couldn't—through the mess of the beast's lower hide, but Q filled me in on the details later. She cut her way through the crook of the jawline and up into the skull, where the cranial membrane housed the oh-so-valuable spermaceti and also, less importantly, a drowning asshole.

There, pressed between the immense weight of the sperm sac and the hard beastbone of the skull, she'd set about feeling for Marsh, who she'd predicted—correctly—would by now be struggling at the bottom. Swimming is a rare skill outside of the core worlds. Even the subsurface fishers of Ganymede and Europa don't have much call for it since the waters of those worlds would freeze you dead if you actually tried to swim in them without an environment suit, and swimming *with* an environment suit is more like doing a spacewalk.

The first evidence we saw of her success was when a trickle of sperm began oozing from beneath the head. And then a trickle became a stream and an ooze became a gush and then—

"Fuck"—Locke began barking orders—"you and you, cables, now. We can't lose the whole kill."

While two more teams of crewmen were scrambling out onto the head—not, in my opinion, anywhere near as gracefully as Q had done—Q and Marsh slithered, headfirst, out of the swinging carcass and plunged several feet onto the floor.

They landed with a wet thump, thankfully (well, thankfully for them, not so thankfully for those who cared more for their lays) cushioned by an ever-deepening layer of spermaceti.

Locke stared down at Q. "You," they snapped, "report to my office at first watch."

Q looked back up at them. And nodded. And smiled.

CHAPTER FORTY-ONE

Stirrings

I hadn't been asked to accompany Q to her appointment with Locke, but I hadn't been asked not to either, and since she still spoke relatively little Exodite it seemed only fair that she have somebody to back her up.

Locke's office was exactly as I'd have expected Locke's office to be. Which is to say it was immaculate and a tiny bit soulless. They did have a picture-slab on their desk which cycled through images of people who looked enough *like* Locke that I assumed they were probably family, but that was the one mark of humanity in a room that was otherwise a sleek, stark outpost of the interests of Olympus Extraction State.

"What," Locke demanded of Q, when we stood at last before them in that austere temple to efficiency, "were you thinking?"

"Submersus est," she replied. "*Drowning.*"

"She saved Marsh's life," I added, feeling like it should have meant something.

Locke looked unimpressed. "And cost this ship a fortune in spilled spermaceti."

"Radix enim omnium malorum est cupiditas," said Q. "Quam quidam appetentes erraverunt a fide et inseruerunt se doloribus multis." And while I'd learned a little of her language in our time together I had absolutely no idea what that meant.

Leaning forward, Locke propped their chin on steepled fingers. "I'm sure you were very heroic," they said, "but the livelihood of every last member of this crew depends on our cargo."

"As does the bottom line of Olympus Extraction State," I added. It was pushing it, I knew, but I sort of hoped that I might be able to take a bit of the heat off of Q if I got Locke focused on me instead.

Or maybe I just liked being center of attention.

"Olympus Extraction State," replied Locke piously, "employs tens of millions of ordinary people throughout the Commonwealth. I know it's fashionable to imagine that the incorporate states are these"—they waved a hand—"vast, faceless evils that we honest working folks should rail against. But a corporation, a state, a fusion of the two, is *made* of people. When you hurt Olympus, you hurt those who work for Olympus. And those are ordinary employees like you and me."

I was a bit surprised that Locke put themself in the same category they put me in. I'd always filed myself very much under *staff* and them very much under *management*. "Olympus can swallow the loss of a bit of sperm," I told them.

"And will it?" Locke arched an eyebrow. "Or will the costs of that wasted sperm"—yes, yes, I know, we both said the funny word, move on—"be passed down the chain until something breaks? A mine somewhere in the Hildas decides it can no longer justify a full-time safety inspector, and so an asteroid undergoes unscheduled disintegration and thirty miners are left spinning in the void where there is nobody like you"—they looked at Q here—"there to save them."

"So she should have let him drown?" I replied. "Because if she doesn't some asshole on Olympus Mons will let somebody else die to make up the loss?"

I'd seen a lot of terrifying things on the hunt by then. But I don't think any of them were quite as terrifying as the way Locke nodded sharply, just once, and said, "Yes."

Q, who was always more stoic than I was, gave a slight bow,

said, "Intellego," in a tone I thought was probably loaded, and left.

But me, I lingered in the doorway. "You know this is fucked, right?"

With their head tilted just a little to one side, Locke was eyeing me up in a way I profoundly didn't like. Well, mostly didn't like, I was eighty-twenty between indignation and a humiliation kink. "My understanding was that you were with the Church of Prosperity. Surely you're familiar with the theoeconomics of the matter."

"For I was an hungred, and ye gave me meat: I was thirsty, and ye gave me drink: I was a stranger, and ye took me in," I quoted. "Which we are taught means that the Father wishes us to prioritize the overall health of the economy over the selfish needs of individuals."

Locke nodded. "I'm not personally religious, but I thought your church had rather a point on that one."

"You want everybody on this ship to give their blood and their sweat to the skies in the name of incremental year-on-year economic growth?" I asked, more incredulously than I should have asked it since my own faith taught exactly that.

Pressing two fingers to their lips, Locke was silent a moment. Then they said, "I expect the crew of this ship to give their blood and sweat to the skies in the name of the personal profit they will reap from the voyage. Which will be substantial, even for the least of them, if we have good fortune and . . ."

I was pretty sure I knew where that thought was going to finish, and I was also pretty sure I wanted them to finish it. "Good fortune and *what*?"

"Sound leadership," Locke finished.

"And you think"—I was stepping onto dangerous ground here, but Locke was on ground even more dangerous, if I understood them right—"we might *not* have sound leadership?"

The pause was gratifyingly long. "The captain is a woman of undeniable experience and proven capability. But it's no secret that since the outset of this voyage she has demonstrated"—and here Locke was giving me a worryingly pointed look—"questionable priorities."

As one of those questionable priorities, I didn't have much cause to be complaining. "Questionable how?"

The sheer look of *you know and I know you know* on Locke's face should have turned me inside out. I decided to go for the option that involved saying least about my sex life. "You think she's too focused on revenge?"

One corner of Locke's lip curled into a smile. "You think it's revenge she's after?"

Fuck, had I walked into a trap? "You don't?"

"I think she's after something much worse."

Definitely a trap. I didn't *think* this counted as mutiny, or that I was saying anything that would come back to haunt either of us. "And I suppose you're going to tell me what that is?"

"I think she's after immortality."

I didn't need the subtext explained. I wasn't the greatest theologian in the world, but I knew that there was only one kind of immortality that a ship's captain could really achieve. And it was the kind that tended to take the ship with it.

CHAPTER FORTY-TWO

Virgin

I'm not sure quite when I decided I was going to try to bang Locke. I'd have said I was hedging my bets, but in a lot of ways it was the opposite. I was just making sure that if it did come down to them versus the captain, I was guaranteed to have been fucking the loser.

Of course, my mile-wide self-destructive streak also had a big part to play in it, but I think it was mostly for the challenge.

In the weeks after Marsh fell into the head—and the months that followed those weeks—the whole atmosphere on the ship, which had been showing signs of improvement, started to backslide. Locke hadn't been entirely wrong about how saving Marsh's life had cost the ship a lot of money—the sperm Q had spilled in freeing him could have been processed into enough fuel to power a city for a month, and it would have been priced accordingly. Nor had they been wrong about how since that money was split, however unequally, amongst the crew, the loss of so much sperm had led to a certain amount of resentment. Not *specific* resentment—nobody was quite willing to admit to being selfish enough to be angry at Q for saving a man's life—but a sort of general low-key discontent. We'd had our first big payday, and because of an accident nobody could control and a choice nobody could fault, it had gotten much less big and involved much less pay than it should have.

It all led to a vague sense of unease over the voyage. The initial rush of enthusiasm that you always get at the start of a new, well, a new anything was fading, and the excitement of hunting the legendary Möbius Beast was giving way to the more mundane question of how we were all going to pay our bills when we got back to Europa.

Things weren't exactly helped by the fact that being bodily immersed in so much spermaceti for so long seemed to have sent Marsh even stranger than Starry Wisdomers usually are. I've talked a bit before about how we don't really know how Leviathans stay up, or why their sperm is such a powerful fuel, but there's at least some speculation that it has psionic properties. And I'm not saying that's true and I'm not saying that's false, but I am saying that it sure as hell did a number on Marsh's brain.

He started wandering the decks at all hours—sometimes even when his shift said he was meant to be somewhere else—whispering to himself in a low voice. When people asked him, he'd tell them that he could hear the Leviathans. That they were calling to him.

With hindsight, the fact that the captain took that seriously and started spending long hours in consultation with him wasn't a great sign either. But I admit that at the time I was mostly just jealous.

Thinking about it, that probably contributed to the whole fuck Locke plan as well.

And it turned out to be a way more complicated operation than I'd expected.

The thing is, I usually don't have that hard a time getting laid, mostly because I have extremely low standards. Look long enough and look desperate enough and you'll find somebody who wants something. But generally I don't go after specific people, at least not consciously. Q was directly assigned to my bed by an innkeeper, and I didn't so much pursue the captain as get drawn inevitably into her orbit like a piece of space debris spiraling down towards impact.

This, though. This felt like an intellectual exercise. And I can, on occasion, be an intellectual person. I've spent as much time in classrooms as crawlspaces, and although a lot of my education was unhelpfully dogmatic, that means I've read a lot of apologia, and if I can make the case for theodicy, I can make the case for sleeping with me.

At least in theory.

In practice . . . turns out that it's surprisingly hard to get in the pants of a deeply rules-bound superior officer who already thinks you're too in bed—both literally and metaphorically—with somebody they believe is actively dangerous.

I started out subtle. Just kind of vaguely hinting any time we happened to cross paths, which we did fairly often on account of how I was their pilot, that if they *happened* to want to drag me off somewhere and fuck my brains out I'd be, y'know, cool with that.

Subtle wasn't getting me anywhere.

I seriously considered getting myself disciplined deliberately, because I figured there'd be a better than even chance of Locke wanting to oversee the punishment themself. But I'd been around the skyfleets long enough to know that they didn't do the fun kind of flogging. Of the three great pillars of naval life, the lash was the one I had least fondness for.

Sometime near the start of the second year of our voyage, I was sitting on my bunk trying to work out how I could scratch this particular itch, with Q resting in the bunk below, drawing her trees, when Locke's voice over comms announced a hail from another ship.

She was called the Jungfrau, and according to their communications she was low on fuel.

I should back up and say that this might strike you as odd. After all, starships run on spermaceti, and the whole point of a hunter-barque is that it goes out and brings in more spermaceti than it could possibly use. And obviously in *general* you want to avoid running out of fuel on any far-system voyage because if you wind up somewhere in the Kuiper Belt and you can't power your oxygen diffusers you're fucked. Like super fucked. Like ghost-ship-floating-dead-for-a-century-before-anybody-finds-your-anaerobically-preserved-corpses fucked.

But it does happen.

The thing is, the spermaceti you pull out of the skies isn't fuel-grade. It needs to be processed in the fractating columns and centrifuges of a dedicated refinery. It needs to be suspended in a more stable fluid, turned from the weird uncanny power of the deep skies into something resembling a conventional material. It needs to be tamed. Tamed, transformed, repackaged, and, of course, at long last sold back, at a profit, to the people who harvest it in the first place. Squirting the raw stuff into your generators in the hope that they'd run would be like trying to cook a fish by detonating a bomb in your kitchen. You might get a result that looked *vaguely* like the one you were after, but not usefully and not without far more trouble than it was worth.

Still, the fact that the Jungfrau was having fuel problems, and also—we'd later learn—had killed precisely zero Leviathans and so was carrying zero spermaceti anyway, strongly suggested that they didn't have a fucking clue what they were doing. And a nasty, bitter part of me found that somewhat cheering. Sure, we'd lost a chunk of sperm from our first kill and sure, our captain might have had the teensiest bit of a death wish, but to spend so long in the deep red that you burn through your entire fuel supply and have nothing to show for it at the end, that wasn't even the cool kind of death. That was the death of getting home and finding you couldn't fucking eat.

The Jungfrau drew up alongside us and its crew flooded in through our airlocks. They looked surprisingly cheerful for people at risk of being forced home empty-handed, but I wasn't going to begrudge them that. If you're going to starve, you might as well starve happy.

Also, happy people tend to be more fun at parties. Although admittedly often worse in bed.

Since the Jeroboam had been quarantined, the meeting with

the Jungfrau was the first proper gam the crew had been able to indulge in since the Town Ho, and I couldn't help wondering if the captain had been strong-armed into agreeing to it on account of the growing discontent belowdecks. The high of the last kill had been wearing off even *before* Q had quite literally cut into the profits, and the crew was beginning to remember all sorts of grievances that hadn't seemed important just days earlier.

But whatever her reasons, when the captain formally greeted the captain of the Jungfrau, it went the same way every other gam had gone.

"Hast seen the Möbius Beast?" she asked, without introduction or ceremony.

The captain of the Jungfrau, who seemed far too young to be in charge of a hunter-barque and so had probably inherited his position or bought it at an auction, clearly had no idea what she was on about. "I'm sorry," he said, "the what?"

Which was apparently Marsh's cue to sidle up to him and whisper, "The *Beast*," in his creepiest voice. Then he followed up with, "Full fathom five the monster lies, of its bones are coral made."

With the weaponized politeness of the affluent and clueless, the captain of the Jungfrau turned to him. "Come again?"

"Those are pearls," Marsh replied, "that were his eyes."

Heartily sick of these distractions, Locke cut in with, "The Beast is no matter of importance, a large-ish Leviathan that our captain has an interest in. Fuel, on the other hand, is a pressing issue for all parties."

While Marsh muttered something rich and strange under his breath, the captain of the Jungfrau nodded enthusiastically, as if he'd been just waiting for the right time to broach the subject.

"Yes, yes," he said. "It was a terrible business. You see, a Kraken pierced our larboard reserve tank and—"

But the captain put up a hand to silence him. "I'll nothing with the details. Your story is no concern of mine."

"What she means," glossed Locke, "is that how you came to your present misfortune does not matter. What matters is whether we can come to a mutually beneficial arrangement."

"Of course." The captain of the Jungfrau was getting borderline obsequious now, his head bobbing like an undertuned suspension. "We would not expect you to assist us without recompense. Since we will now have to shorten our voyage, there are other supplies that we have in excess and—"

"Plague on your recompense," said the captain dismissively. "Give them what they need, Locke, and don't make them scrape for it. I'm no queen to make men grovel nor no merchant to barter with them."

Locke looked pained. "I remind you that we have a fiduciary responsibility to our investors," they said. "And we must take care not to leave ourselves short-supplied, lest we have difficulty on our own home journey."

An old sky-hand had once told me that there'd been a time when ships had given to each other freely, knowing that their neighbor's hardship today could be their own hardship tomorrow. But if that was true, it must have been long, long ago. Besides, it went against the word of the Father.

I tried to tell myself that it was this ancient tradition of mutual support that the captain was thinking of when she said, "Pay no mind to the home journey."

I tried to tell myself that. But I knew it was wishful thinking. That Locke had been right. That she actually meant something far more obvious, and far more concerning.

CHAPTER FORTY-THREE

The Old Man of the Sky

We were mid–fuel transfer with the Jungfrau, and her crew mid-gam with us (both of which, if you think about it, involved a fair amount of sticking things in places and pumping fluids through them), when a call went up from the array. There'd been a spout, and from the speed at which the ships and their crews disengaged, a promising one.

I got off my knees and dashed for the boat, where I found Q and Locke and the rest of the usual crew waiting. Across the launch bay the captain, once again, was going calmly to her thought-machine-guided craft. And there she sat in the cockpit, bathed in blue holographic light and looking more like a ghost every time I saw her.

Because the Jungfrau had been able to drop boats immediately while the Pequod had needed to wind in her fuel pipes to keep from spraying fuel-sperm all over the skies, they had a bit of a head start on us. So as we jetted out into the Jovian atmosphere, the voices of the mates came over comms with . . . gentle words of encouragement.

"*Fry* the fuckers." That was Flint. "Steal our beasts from under our noses, will they? We'll blow them out the sky."

"They seek to come between the chosen and our just rewards." That was Truelove. "As the man says, fry the fuckers."

Even Locke was uncharacteristically aggressive. "Steady as

she goes," they were saying, "but we make no pay if we lose the prize, so if *necessary* . . ." They bit their lip. "Yes, frying the fuckers would be appropriate in this context."

Although the Jungfrau crew had the lead over us, their pilots were less experienced than ours. They were even less experienced than me, and I—as I think I've pointed out a couple of times—was shit at most parts of this job. Right now, that difference was pretty academic, because you don't need a decade of flight training to know that in a chase it's a good idea to go fast in a straight line, but as we got closer and maneuvering started to matter, it would get a whole lot more important.

Turned out it was going to get a whole, whole lot more important.

Ordinarily, Leviathans are solitary beings, but this time we'd picked up a pod. If I were a woman of science, I'd probably have been thrilled by this, because we know basically nothing about the reproductive cycle of the Leviathan. We don't even know if they give birth to live young (although if they're egg-laying it would raise a whole lot of questions about where those eggs are). But we do know that sometimes you see big Leviathans next to small Leviathans and since obviously everything that exists in nature is a reflection of the Father's plan for humanity, those groups of differently sized monsters must be leviathanic nuclear families.

And following up the mother and children was the great patriarch. He was gargantuan, the largest beast I'd ever seen and the second largest that I would ever see. His carapace was scarred and pitted from a thousand battles, his starboard flight-membrane a ragged mess of tears and scars. His long, barbed tail swayed as he flew, and he listed slightly in the sky.

"All boats," said Locke, both to us in our little cabin and to everybody over comms, "prio the big bastard."

It seemed like the Jungfrau crew had gotten the same idea, because they banked around to bring their harpoons online at the monster's flank.

"Last scene of all"—Marsh's voice came over comms as we drew our own beads on the ancient Leviathan—"that ends this strange eventful history, is second childishness and mere oblivion."

We were still behind the Jungfrau boats, but they were holding fire, their harpooners not skilled enough to make the shot from our current range.

"Down canopy," ordered Locke, their voice still low and calm and—now I'd talked myself into that headspace—strangely hot. "Let's show these callow fuckers what a Cthonius crew can do."

Since I'd left Cthonius Linea near as soon as I'd arrived, I wasn't totally sure I counted as part of a *Cthonius crew*, but I liked the label anyway. Besides, all I had to do was hold us steady while Q did her thing.

From much farther out than I'd seen her fire before, Q lined up the coilgun. Taking her time, she made some adjustments to settings I didn't understand, and the indicator lights on the side of the weapon blinked from greens into reds. I imagined it making a kind of high-pitched humming, but that was entirely in my head. We were in environment suits and surrounded by subsonic winds; all I could hear was the faint rattling of my helmet and the occasional voice over the internal comms.

Ahead of us, the boats from the Jungfrau were bearing down on the Leviathan, but before the closest of them could launch their harpoons, Q fired, and her own dart flew so close to the canopy of their lead boat that it had to adjust course to avoid fouling on the line.

"Roll, twenty-five degrees," Locke ordered with surprising gentleness, "and loose wing-darts."

I rolled, and the gunner fired, and our next two harpoons passed close above and close below the wings of the nearest boat. Now that I had a sense of what we were doing, I felt a strange thrill of danger and cruelty. Because right now we were walking a line between "polite discouragement" and "deliberate murder." If the Jungfrau pilots were competent, they'd see that they couldn't get a good fix on the monster with our lances past them, and they'd ease away, doing their best not to tangle in our lines.

If they weren't competent, they'd fuck their foils and spin out of the sky, or down canopy anyway and get their heads sliced off by monofilament wires under unbearable tension.

They went . . . kind of the middle way. Not quite reckless enough to press on but not quite skilled enough to disengage cleanly. The lead boat's wing scraped our cables as it turned, sending a shower of sparks into the Jovian clouds and a wicked vibration all along the line. To make matters worse, the weight of harpoons was making the old Leviathan patriarch list and fall, dragging our lines down and across the bows of the Jungfrau's boats, sending two of them into a tailspin I quickly lost track of.

I choose to believe that they lived.

In our own cabin, I struggled to keep us in line, the weight of the Leviathan making us pitch and the pressure of the half-trapped wing of the other boat making us yaw and the stress of the whole thing making me feel alive in the exact way I came to the skies for in the first place.

"Cut lines?" I asked as the tremors continued to run through the cabin and the canopy both.

But Locke silently shook their head, and in their eyes I saw a determination that was in its own way as strong and as unbending as the captain's. Except where the captain had her monomaniac vision, Locke had a cold and terrible calculus. A mind that could weigh the lives of everybody in the boat and value them down to the last drop of sperm, and then adjust them probabilistically against the odds of triumph and disaster.

The monster was rolled half onto its side now, and we could see amongst its feeder tendrils great tumors and ulcers. Signs of its remarkable age perhaps, or just of its ill fortune.

"Now that's what I call a soft underbelly," observed Flint

over comms. "Bring me close, shipmates, and I'll drive a spear to the quick of it."

Ahead of us, the boat on our line spun away, and I followed it just closely enough to see it righting its course and returning to its ship. But then all my attention snapped back to the miserable, venerable Leviathan as Flint's boat sped towards it, reeling in its lines to shorten the distance and cover a greater depth of sky.

"Will he need backup?" I asked.

That at least got Locke to reply verbally instead of just with stoic head movements. "Negative. The best thing now is to keep back and keep tight. He'll strike hard enough when the moment comes. What we need to do is keep the beast strained and make ready to take the weight when it dies."

So I did what they asked, keeping distance and keeping tension and watching, fascinated, as Flint closed in with his bolt-driver at the ready.

Normally the crew of his boat would be fighting hard with sword and spear to stop the countless lower limbs of the Leviathan crushing or overturning or otherwise destroying them as they hove closer, but this beast was so ancient that they barely needed to. What tendrils it had left were broken and sluggish, and it seemed to take no work at all for Flint's boat to carve a path through them to the creature's distended, cancerous underside.

"There's for you, you great brute," called Flint, presumably to the monster although he said it over comms anyway. And he thrust upwards with the bolt-driver and fired it deep into the tumorous mass above them.

It burst.

The blood—if you can call it blood—of Leviathans is usually clear and colorless, like liquid water or lymphatic fluid. But this came out a deep cloudy green and spattered down on its attackers like a gory rainstorm.

The monster convulsed, its tail whipping through the atmosphere so fast that it made a booming, tearing sound and came damned near to smashing one of our backup boats out of the sky. As for us, it was the most I could manage to keep us on an even keel and save the darts from being ripped clean out as the creature bucked and writhed at the end of our lines.

And then it died.

When a Leviathan dies, much of the strange power that keeps it airborne stops working, so the carcass becomes a dead weight hanging beneath the boats. But normally that weight is bearable. Some property of the atmosphere, the nature of spermaceti, and the unique physiology of the monsters makes them not quite as heavy as they should be given their size and the sheer amount of bone-stuff in them.

But for whatever reason, this one was different. As its life oozed out of its body through that awful, pulpy abscess, the Jovian gravity took it more and more strongly until it was dragging every boat down into a screaming death-dive towards the core of the planet.

"Adjust foils," Locke told me with—given that we were plunging to icy, hydrogenous doom—a frankly worrying level of calmness, "set density compensators to manual assist, and be ready for things to get bumpy."

They weren't kidding. I've never been an engineer, but I know enough to understand that the lift you get out of an aerofoil depends on a mix of the speed of your boat and the thickness of the air. Which meant I wasn't completely taken off guard when our dropping faster and faster through an atmosphere that was getting both thicker and thicker and hotter and hotter started making life in the cabin extremely uncomfortable, but "not taken completely off guard" isn't the same as "ready."

"It's lost." That was Truelove, fatalistic as ever over the airwaves. "We should cut lines."

"Gah, you're a coward as well as a fool." That was Flint. "Ride it out past the screaming and we'll have our prize yet."

"Pull up." And that was Locke. "Power to engines, and trust to the lines. It isn't over until it hits hydrogen."

The clouds were ammonia here: tiny white crystals that were

like-yet-not-like water ice, whipping past the canopy and bathing everything around us in a thick fog. So for a while as we fell I couldn't see the other boats, or the ship, or even the great corpse we were lashed to.

About our wingtips, the clouds began to glow red with frictive heating, and my instruments were making very worried noises. In the merchant service, we'd have turned back two warning lights ago. "She's not happy," I told Locke.

To which they laid a hand on my shoulder and just said, "Steady."

So I kept her steady. Or as steady as I could. And we kept on falling.

You fall for a long time on Jupiter. In fact, in a lot of ways, there's nowhere in the system you can fall longer or farther. I mean, yes, you can go out to an arbitrarily distant orbit from any body you like and then let whatever gravity you can still feel pull you into a decaying orbit. But that isn't the same as *falling*. Being on a body with a sky above and no ground below and just an endless, endless *down*.

You haven't seen *down* until you've seen Jupiter. It has worlds' worth of down. Planets' worth of down. A kind of down you can't normally get to before down as a concept stops existing.

The clouds were red now, sulfides and hydrogen sulfides. We'd managed to just about balance the weight of the monster, but all that meant was that we were falling at a constant rate instead of falling ever faster. By this point my instruments were telling me that the pressure was too high, the temperature was too high, and the strain on the relativistic compensators was past too high and into just plain fucked.

But we still held her steady.

We held her steady until I saw, for the first time, the great superfluidic mirror of the hydrogen sea.

What with it being the core of the planet, and having seen it on diagrams and schematics for months now, I'd somehow gotten it into my head that it would be small. Which, compared to the rest of the planet, it was. But compared to every single other body in the system put together, it was huge. It was so vast that for a moment I didn't even realize I was seeing it. The clouds broke and beneath them was an enormous, reflective nothing. A wide expanse of liquid metal, roiled by electric winds.

As we descended I began to see shapes on the surface. Tiny at first, like maggots on a clean spoon. Then larger and larger until it became clear that the Jovian Behemoth is longer than any ship or any Leviathan, and its ponderous pilgrimage though the hydrogen sea an even greater mystery than the most elusive of lesser monsters.

My instruments had given up. Between the speed and the heat and the pressure and the electromagnetic vortices ripping up from below us, they were just assuming we were already dead.

It was one of the backup boats that cut loose first, decoupling its line and pulling into a step climb back to the Pequod.

"Sans teeth," whispered Marsh over comms.

Truelove's boat was next, the fatalist mate not willing to face the promised oblivion sooner than he had to.

"Sans eyes."

Flint screamed profanities at the ones who'd given up, but even he, I think, knew it was a lost cause.

"Sans taste" was Marsh's soft commentary.

And at last, Locke gave the order, and we cut ourselves off also.

"Sans everything."

CHAPTER FORTY-FOUR

Jonah Pornographically Regarded

"Why," asked Locke after we lost the Leviathan, "are you in my office?"

I had a bunch of reasons, if I was honest. But mostly it was because I was kind of freaking out. "That," I told them, "was fucked."

"Have you forgotten that this ship has a hierarchy?"

"Have you forgotten that you're meant to be the one who *isn't* insane? Even *Flint* cut loose before you did."

Locke always looked prim. This time they looked positively haughty. "That's rather loaded language. We had a prize, we pursued it."

"You nearly sank the whole fucking boat."

"You've been on this ship nearly two years. Have you not yet realized that the risk of death is part of the *job*? Which, incidentally, is why so many on board are still rather annoyed that your friend chose one man's life over all our income."

I stared at them. That was the problem with sexualizing people in your head as a defense mechanism: it made them really hard to argue with. "That's not an answer."

They half smiled. Locke rarely smiled and I was, sadly, a

sucker for rare smiles. Q smiled all the time, which I probably took too much for granted. The captain smiled not at all, and that made me treat glares and harsh words as passion. "I think you'll find it is," they replied. "I'm sorry I don't have a dream to sell you. I'm sure that you'd prefer I was driven by some raging tempest in my soul, but I'm not. This is my job. I'm good at it, but it's not my calling."

The word *calling* echoed through me like an insult. Which it had no right to, because I was a green hand in the hunter-fleet. Except I *had* been called. The voice inside me had screamed at the stars until it felt like my skin would split. "And that's . . ." I was almost hesitant. "That's enough for you?"

"I have family on Europa. They live in the Olympian Enclave, far from Cthonius Linea. They sleep in warm beds and eat hydroponic rice most days. My mother makes kimchi when we can get the spices, which is less often than I'd like but more often than most families."

Unlike the captain's cabin, Locke's office had no windows. Deep inside the ship, far from the rush of the wind on the hull or the endless Jovian skyscape, there was something that felt strangely *right* about that small ambition. And I found myself saying, "No children of your own?"

And there again was that half a smile, that twitch of an eyebrow. "Is that your way of asking if I'm married?" they asked. "And is that, in turn, your way of asking if I'm in the market for an illicit shipboard hookup?"

"I'd also be okay with a *licit* shipboard hookup."

Locke pursed their frustratingly perfect lips. "I don't fraternize with hands before the array."

"Are you sure? You're missing out."

"Think a lot of yourself, don't you—" And here they said my name, or the one I was using then, at least. And it felt weird. Like the more complicated kind of intimacy. The kind I wasn't looking for because it brought me back instead of taking me away, when *away* was where I'd wanted to be so badly for so long.

And I couldn't hack that. So I said, "It's your loss." And then I ran.

Not literally ran. I had some pride, for all I'd been taught it was a sin. But I made my way back to my bunk. And there, I lay down and sorted myself out. Honestly, I have a bit of a history of fucked-up sexual fantasies and by my standards an uptight corporate watchdog with a strong sense of hierarchy was pretty vanilla.

For example, I've always had a thing for Jonah.

Not Jonah himself, obviously. There were pictures of the guy in some of the versions of the catechism I studied as a child and they never bothered to make him look hot. But the *story*. Something about the story really worked for me in a way that I didn't really understand at the time.

In case any of the Faithful of the Catechism do read this (and it's possible, it's not like we were never allowed books, and some parents were more careful than others), I should say I'm not . . . I'm not literally suggesting that Jonah was fucking the whale. The great apologists teach us that much of the catechism is figurative. So I guess in a way I'm saying that Jonah was *metaphorically* fucking the whale.

Not even that, really. Even after all these years I don't quite have the appetite for blasphemy. But my first sense of what sex and love and passion are and should be—for whatever reason, by whatever twisted path—wound up getting tangled up in my head with the devouring maw of the beast.

This is still sounding fucked up, isn't it?

Again, it's not that I wanted anybody to literally eat me. But that whole sequence of experiences. The fear and the flight and the storm and the sudden crash into cold water and then being so utterly and completely *consumed*. Then to be held safe but penitent until at last I'm spat out onto warm sand and I see the Father.

Some part of me, for as long as I can remember, has always wanted that. Looked for it in women who hold knives to my throat, or who fuck me against windows over endless, cavernous pits into oblivion. I've looked for it kneeling and bowing my head in a parody of prayer. I've lived my life searching for that moment when I come out the other side, disgorged onto the shores of Nineveh and it all makes sense, and it never has. So again and again I've launched myself back into the jaws of the beast, in one way or another.

There is, I will admit, a very slim chance that I have issues.

CHAPTER FORTY-FIVE

The Fountainhead

You've already seen, many times now, that the Leviathan is tracked in part by eye, in part by instrument, and what the instruments detect is a pulse of electrokinetic activity we call the *spout*.

It's vital to the fishery. Nobody would catch a Leviathan without it. But also nobody has a fucking clue what it is. There isn't even a broad consensus in ignorance, the tacit agreement that *well probably it's this because reasons* that's the basis of so many of our other certainties.

I was standing on the observation deck watching the instruments one evening. I say evening; a day on Jupiter is ten hours, and so while the ship keeps what voiders call Mean Circadian Time—a rough approximation of the twenty-five-hour day you'd get on Old Earth—the actual day-night cycle, still just about perceptible in the upper atmosphere at least, is almost totally out of sync with it.

Anyway, I was standing on the observation deck watching the instruments and contemplating the nature of the spout. It's hard to remember exactly what I was musing about all these years later, but I seem to recall that I was compiling a very illuminating analogy between the fountain-like qualities of the spout and the Leviathan's role, through the energetic properties of its sperm, as the fountainhead of all life and prosperity in the system.

It was a good metaphor, I thought. Unfortunately, I never got to complete it because I was interrupted by an angry mob.

Okay, not an angry mob. More a peeved gaggle.

Both Europans, a Mimean, a Cerean, and the Bright-Eyed Titanian cornered me—or at least got as close as they could to cornering me in a space with very few corners—and made it very clear that they wanted a word.

I tried not to take too much satisfaction in the fact that they all looked like they'd been in a fight already, and like they'd probably come off worse. Split lips, black eyes, and notable limps were spread unequally amongst them. "I told you," I began, "she doesn't listen to me."

"This isn't about the captain," said the First Europan, spitting blood. "This is about that fucking Terran you're so thick with."

"Q?" I asked casually. Except I used her actual name—she never hid it from the crew, I'm just hiding it from you. "What about her?"

"New kill's getting hauled in," said the Bright-Eyed Titanian, "and we want to be sure she won't be up to her old tricks."

The new kill was a small beast that Flint and Truelove had taken down between them a few days earlier. It hadn't been anything like as promising as the one Q had saved Marsh from, and voiders being as voiders are, a fair few of the crew had taken that as an indication that our luck had turned and she was responsible.

"She brought a curse on us," added the Cerean. He and I had barely interacted apart from that one time he kicked me in the head, but I knew he was from Ahuna Mons, which in the Church we used to call Little Pluto. He was, I suspected, a true believer in the catechism.

"Can we maybe deal with one curse at a time?" I tried.

"The captain's a curse, Q is a curse, we're cursed because we didn't kill one of the Death's Heads and hang its skull off our larboard hull. Did it ever occur to you that maybe life is just random and this job is just hard?"

The Bright-Eyed Titanian moved in very close beside me. She wasn't armed, but four friends behind you was the best weapon you could have. "Listen to me, you pissant little tourist. Each and every one of us has mouths to feed and bills to pay and your faux-wisdom bullshit isn't keeping a single damned one of us from starving." She glared, which I won't pretend I didn't find hot because, well, I'm not calling her the Bright-Eyed Titanian for nothing. "Keep your little piece of Terran ass in line, or we'll do it for you."

I did my best to shrug that off. "You've got a problem with Q, take it up with . . ." A realization hit me. "You did, didn't you? And she beat the crap out of you."

The Second Europan scowled. "She caught us by surprise."

"What, all of you?"

"The heathen is full of tricks," replied the Cerean.

I permitted myself a smile. "So is the believer, in my experience."

That didn't sit well with the Cerean. "Beloved," he began, which threw me until he continued the quotation, "believe not every spirit, because many false prophets are gone out into the world."

And you know what? Fuck that. I stepped forward. This *did* put the Titanian behind me, which would have been incredibly bad if it actually came to violence, but at least it let me get right into the face of my sort-of-but-not-but-sort-of coreligionist. "You do you," I said. "I'll pick a ravening wolf every time."

By my very inexact calculation, I was about seventy-six seconds from this little group deciding that talk was getting them nowhere and giving me another kicking to make themselves feel better. Except just as they were squaring up to take swings at me, we heard footsteps across the deck.

Sometimes I *swear* she'd had speakers put in. Because the captain's footsteps echoed in a space that it should have been acoustically impossible to echo in. It wasn't that she had a heavy tread, in fact if anything she walked lightly, but she took each step with such confidence that her every footfall was a gunshot.

A shot right to the heart, in my case.

"Crewmates," she said, aloof and passionless as the stars.

In an effort to avoid some unspoken, unthreatened reprisal, my would-be assaulters fell into line, murmuring various flavors of *cap'n* under their breaths.

"Mark me," she said to them, and to the void, and perhaps to me, "I am not insensible of your woes nor ignorant of your disappointments." This was, I suspected, strictly true. All she'd claimed, after all, was that she *knew* of the crew's woes, not that she gave a crap about them. "Whether you hunt for glory"—she glanced at the Bright-Eyed Titanian—"or for profit"—the Europans—"or to satisfy a god who tells you honest toil is sacrament and wealth a blessing"—the Cerean and, with more than a trace of irony, me—"you shall be well served by the next stage of our voyage."

Behind me, the Mimean murmured something about not having been served too well by it so far.

"We fly south," she went on, addressing the complaint without acknowledging it. "To richer skies, and there I swear to you, shipmates, our fortunes will be born anew. For we will carve through storm and swell and electric fire to the very heart of this world's wonders. To the fountainhead where monsters are birthed and heroes are made and a hunter's hand can overflow with sperm, ripe for the taking."

The fact that the captain could talk about hands overflowing with sperm and everybody took it totally seriously said a lot about her.

"Cleave to me, shipmates," she said, "and look to your duties. We cross the tropics soon, and any of you sorry sky-dogs caught lagging at your post will be flogged."

They didn't cheer. Even A couldn't quite get people to cheer a threat of flogging. But they went on their way sharply enough. Except for me. I hovered a moment, snagged like a shard of shrapnel in the field of an accelerator coil.

"Thank you," I stage-whispered. Loud enough that she'd hear me, quiet enough that I could pretend I'd not meant her to.

She looked down at me. And in a tight, strangling moment, I realized she had no idea what I was thanking her for.

CHAPTER FORTY-SIX

What Else Is Out There

I know, I know, get back to the fucking and killing. But I'm not in a fucking and killing mood, and the *next* bit of fucking and killing is going to involve some context.

You might have gotten the impression that Jupiter is empty, and in a relative sense, it kind of is. But that's because it's bigger than every other body in the system put together. You could fit a hundred Earths just onto its surface and then pack in hundreds more in layers as you go down, down, down into the middle and the hydrogen sea.

Which means the emptiness of Jupiter actually contains a whole lot of shit. *Planets'* worth of shit. As well as the hunter-barques there are hydrogen-skiffs, observation stations, inter-well signal relays, asset recovery ports, and so on.

They haven't really mattered so far, because while there's a lot of them—millions, probably—they crop up in clusters and on a Jovian scale they're so far apart that they might as well not even be on the same world. It's sort of like how when you look out into space you see endless clouds of stars but no matter how far you fly they never get any closer because those endless clouds are scattered across even more endless distances and the space between them is vast and alive and incomprehensible.

Those things that haven't mattered? They're about to start mattering.

The atmosphere of Jupiter is divided into reddish and whitish bands called zones and belts, not necessarily in that order. Between the bands, for atmospheric physics reasons I can't even begin to understand, the wind whips into jets that surge east-west then west-east, and depending on which transition you're making and when, there's often only a few safe paths through. That might sound odd—after all the whole planet is made of wind, and you'd think wind is the same wherever you go—but remember we're talking planet-sized meteorological conditions that evolve on a timescale of centuries. The winds of Jupiter are as different from each other as a plain from a mountain, an impact-crater from a volcano. Sure, those things are all just rock, but they're very different *kinds* of rock.

TL;DR, some bits of Jupiter are way too dangerous to fly through, and between those dangerous bits, there are less-dangerous bits. And those create choke points. And choke points create opportunities.

Which is why we got chased by pirates.

The captain had been flying us inexorably south for months now, putting us well into the second half of the voyage. And ever since she'd stepped in to spare me a beating with news of richer grounds and wilder skies, the word had gotten about amongst the crew that her ultimate goal was the Southern Tropical Zone and the endless storm that raged there. That storm, in the language of the old sky-dogs, was called Hell's Heart, because it beat red and terrible and destructive.

But to get to Hell's Heart and the Southern Tropical Zone we needed to cross the equator and from there brave powerful retrograde jets that would, themselves, be riven by endless microstorms cast off from the Heart itself.

"I don't like it," Dawlish was saying into his bowl of nourishing gruel as we sped southwards. "Nothing good comes out of the Heart and those who go seeking in it are fools."

"The common curse of mankind," agreed Marsh solemnly. "Folly and ignorance."

Ignoring him, Dawlish went on. "I'd feel better if I didn't know she was taking orders from a thinking machine."

That made me laugh. Few things had lately. "The captain doesn't take orders from anything."

"Even so." Dawlish was clearly in no mood for laughter. "She listens to it, and it's making her reckless."

"There's profit there," the Bright-Eyed Titanian pointed out. "If we can seize it."

"And I'll remind myself of that," Dawlish replied acidly, "when I'm dying on a stove ship in a red sky."

Q shrugged. "Audere est Facere."

"I don't know how this happened"—the Bright-Eyed Titanian shot Q a look of grudging solidarity—"but I agree with the Terran. Better to go into danger with open eyes than to limp home with a half-empty hold. We can't eat caution."

I was about jump into the conversation myself with something insightful or witty or possibly even both, when an alarm went off. We'd done a rundown of what all the ship's alarms stood for when I'd first joined the crew but that, by this stage, had been two years ago, so I had no clue what it meant. Still, when everybody else—well, everybody except Marsh, who wasn't really responding to things in a reasonable time these days—scrambled for their stations I made scrambling motions along with them.

Sensing my confusion, Q looked at me and said, "Piratae." And then in case I hadn't picked up on it, translated into Exodite. "*Pirates.*"

Star-piracy was rare, not because there was any real law in the void but because it was so fucking difficult to know where you'd find a ship with something worth stealing. Apparently on Old Earth, when something was hard to find, they used to compare it to a *needle in a haystack.* And while I'm not really sure what a haystack is, I've seen needles, and a haystack can't have been more than a couple of billion times bigger. And while that sounds like a lot, it's fuck all on an interplanetary scale.

But the jets of Jupiter made piracy possible and, more importantly, profitable. The safe passages through the vortices and atmospheric anomalies were narrow and marked out with beacon stations, only some of which were honest.

From the deck, where those of us without immediate jobs to do in the event of pirate attack gathered for orders, we could see the enemy fleet bearing down on us through the red clouds of the equatorial belt. Each of their ships, individually, was a fraction of the size of the Pequod, but we ran on long voyages that needed plentiful supplies and small crews, while they darted out from well-stocked stations in ships that were all packed with armed bastards.

"I suggest we withdraw," Locke was telling the captain as they stood at the prow, watching the oncoming fleet pulling closer. "They're not much faster than us, and even if we can't outrun them we can outrange them. They'll not have the fuel for a long chase."

It was the right call. Everybody in earshot knew it was the right call. And we also knew that it was never a call the captain would make. "Skirt them," she ordered. "Take us off the narrow way and into the storm. They won't follow there."

And they probably wouldn't. Of course, they also wouldn't necessarily have to because if we didn't turn around as Locke suggested, we'd still mostly be going towards them and it'd be hit or miss whether we'd break into the interband jet before they broke into us. With boarding lances.

But the sky was the sky and the captain was the captain, and so the order went down and the helm punched in our new course. As a general hand, my place was to be wherever the fuck I was needed, moment to moment, and since we were still shooting for speed, that meant I was on engines.

In a way, the pirates were the most dangerous thing we'd encountered in the skies so far, if not the most dangerous thing we'd ever encounter. The Leviathans could, if angry, stave a ship in two, but they mostly didn't. Krakens would try, but while their beaks could rake holes in the hull they were generally more interested in eating Leviathans.

We were an invasive species in this ecosystem. The only natural predators we had were each other.

The funny thing was, though, it was hard to *feel* the danger. When you're out in the boat, wind rushing past your foils and the beast so close you can reach out and touch it and that isn't even a metaphor, you're very, very aware of all the things that can kill you.

But deep inside the ship, a ship whose whole purpose was to make a little bubble of habitability against a universe that thought human life was a mistake, it was hard to remember there was anything wrong at all. I mean sure, the engines were running at full capacity and that meant the compressors were at risk of overheating, but that felt like an engineering problem, not a somebody-trying-to-murder-us problem.

If I listened very carefully, I could hear the impacts echoing through the hull, but even those were rare. The pirates weren't trying to down us—like everybody in these skies they were motivated by personal gain, and they'd have none of that if we splashed into the hydrogen sea.

Easing out of the mass compressor that I'd been busily retuning for the past half hour, I became eerily conscious of eyes on me. I looked into the crawlspace to see Marsh kneeling on his hands, watching.

"Need something?" I asked.

"They say the owl was a baker's daughter."

He'd been like this ever since he fell into the sperm. For a while we'd hoped it would wear off. It hadn't. "Do they?"

A blank look crept over his face. "Do they what?"

"Say the owl was a baker's daughter."

The faintest echo of a smile crept onto his lips. "They say so *many* things. I lose track."

I sat with my back against the mass couplings. They were cold and solid, which they should have been because they needed to take a hundred thousand atmospheres when the compressors were running. "Like what?" I asked, not totally sure what answer I wanted.

He laughed at that. "Nothing sure. Yet much unhappily."

That felt like half an answer at best. "Don't you have a job to be doing?"

"I strew dangerous conjectures in ill-breeding minds."

Honestly the whole ship was beginning to feel like a dangerous conjecture. "And that's going to save us from pirates, is it?"

As if in answer, an alarm sounded.

"Too slow of sail," he said, "we put on a compelled valor."

I wasn't a fighter, but when boarding claws were inbound there wasn't much distinction. I hurried—okay, not hurried exactly, there was no point volunteering to be first in a firefight—to the security deck where Flint was handing out guns like it was Christmas (for those unfamiliar with the Church of Liberty, this simile is exact; the Libertines celebrate most festivals with gifts of firearms).

On the rare occasions that a hunter-barque has to defend itself, we fight much as we do against the Leviathan. I like to think, though I've no idea if it's actually true, that this makes us like the great warrior cultures of old. The people who lived and fought and hunted as one and who in their own various ways bestrode the ancient Earth like colossi. Although I suspect those great warriors of old never had to split their spoils fifty-two-forty-eight with a corporate sponsor who made all the important decisions from forty light-minutes across the void.

Q, Locke, and I were armed with boarding scythes and antimateriel launchers, and sent to the usual boat. We plunged out into the skies to see the brutal shapes of assault craft bearing down on us, their docking claws and cutting seals jutting out from their prows in a way that reminded me strangely of the jaws of the Leviathan.

In our small, cramped cabin, Q's hand came to rest gently on my shoulder. "Per angusta," she said, "ad augusta."

"Take it slow," Locke ordered from behind me. And I could tell that this was a dangerous situation because I just obeyed the order without also briefly imagining it in a sexual context.

"They're quicker than we are, but less nimble. And as sky-hunters I expect you to know how to fight a bigger fish."

We did, or at least we mostly did. I was still quite new to the business. But it wasn't so much the *size* of the fish we were fighting now that had me worried. It was that the fish had guns.

As if echoing my thoughts, the nearest pirate boat launched a stream of white-hot darts towards us. They were faster by far than the ones we used in the hunt, not needing to hold fast or to tow a line, but only to pierce hulls and crack domes. They missed us by what felt like inches and, hoping that what worked for Leviathans would work for marauders, I put us into a dive.

"*Canopy*," said Q, and because I'm just about willing to follow chain of command, I waited for Locke's nod before trusting my instinct to do exactly what she said.

The weapon Q had taken from Flint's worryingly deep stockpile of armaments had been a variant on her usual coil-gun. It was longer and broader, and while I wasn't an expert in weaponry it looked as though it had a whole bunch of after-market modifications.

With the boat still diving steeply, Q was forced to make one hell of a tricky shot, bracing herself on the back of my seat and aiming up at a target that was moving away from us and past us on two different vectors, both of them accelerating.

She fired.

And like the drone back on Cthonius Linea, the frontmost of the pirate boats erupted in a shower of sparks as Q's harpoon burst straight through its port engine. I upped canopy at once and she crouched in the cabin reloading.

"Bring her around," commanded Locke. "One more like that and she's down."

Bringing her around was tight because while we'd gotten behind one of the pirate boats there were several more and not all their guns were forward-fixed, so either way I needed to be taking evasive actions. As I turned, I saw that one of the marauders had succeeded in clamping on to the hull of the Pequod between the third and fourth decks and was beginning to deploy cutters. But that was somebody else's problem. My problem was the boat still careening forward on one engine. One engine that would be perfectly adequate to push it across the remaining distance towards the ship.

We launched darts but even with the upgrades Flint had been insisting on, they were meant for organic targets, not void-hardened fighter boats. I downed canopy again, and Q braced herself for the gravitational spike as the dampeners disengaged.

"Steady," commanded Locke, our suits' internal comms doing their best to compensate for the roar of the Jovian winds. "Better one good shot than two bad ones."

Yet again I was struck by the willingness of a hunter-crew to fly cheerfully into the jaws of death. In lining ourselves up for a killing strike on our boat we were making ourselves very tempting targets for any pirate who wanted to slip behind us and shoot us down.

I remember reading that in the ancient days of Earth—when wars were fought by ranks of men standing shoulder to shoulder instead of by tiny squads of infiltrators backed up by flotillas of autonomous multirole vehicles with heuristic intelligence—the way a battle line fought was to protect the man on your right and hope to hell that the man on your left would be doing the same. I don't know if that's remotely true, but it feels like the hunter-fleet is the only place you see that anymore. Where you still have to trust that everybody else is doing their job or else you're totally fucked.

Q fired. I didn't stop to check the damage; the moment the dart was clear I put us into a steep dive and was glad I had because a jet of sublight coil-shards screamed past the place we'd just been about three and a half heartbeats later.

But the boat that had shot at us didn't get much farther. Flint's and Truelove's boats had already rounded on it and between the two of them—even with Marsh distracted by the voices in his mind—they put enough firepower into it to disable its docking fangs, which, in turn, made it decide that discretion was the better part of valor.

Every boat had either fled now or docked, so under Locke's command I steered us back to the ship. Just in time for round two.

CHAPTER
FORTY-SEVEN

Repelling

I'm a lover, not a fighter. By which I mean that when my hypos get the better of me and I feel the need to do something self-destructive, I fuck a stranger instead of punching one.

But right now we were all fighters. The ones who threw spears at monsters for a living and the ones whose skills were mostly to do with pushing buttons and welding things were all rushing to the *other* arms locker to get tooled up for fighting pirates hand to hand.

I say rushing. But honestly there was a bit of a dawdle to it. Out in the sky, hunters really are fearless—or at least able to master their fear—and will charge willingly into the claws of devouring gods without the least concern for themselves. But back aboard the ship, when the enemy is individual people with individual weapons who want to stab you in your individual guts, we become a whole lot more aware that driving off the boarders doesn't strictly need any one of us to put ourselves at risk.

So it was with frankly mixed enthusiasm that we collected our pistols and our personnel spears from the supply and faux-hurried to the site of the breach. Still, there was a kind of camaraderie in it, with the Europans, the Bright-Eyed Titanian, and several others who'd kicked the shit out of me earlier in the voyage now cheerfully throwing me and Q weapons and taking as read that we wouldn't immediately shoot or stab them.

It was heartwarming, in a way.

As we got closer the sounds of battle started echoing through the ship and that made the whole thing feel way realer and more worrying than I was used to. A big feature of most void-work and sky-work is that you don't really hear very much. Either you're in a vacuum where sound can't travel at all, or else you're in a sealed cabin that cuts out most of the noise alongside most of the atmosphere.

By the time we reached the breach, the pirates had succeeded in fusing their way through the hull and were pouring through in a mob. A mob that, conveniently, was extremely vulnerable to harpoons, which, even more conveniently, could be relied on not to penetrate the hull or compromise the boarding seal and kill everybody.

As battle was joined, I was torn between my natural instinct to hang back and my new intrusive instinct to stick with Q and make sure she didn't, y'know, fucking die on me. Not that I was actually going to be any help in that regard because see above re: lover-to-fighter ratio.

A string of white-hot flechettes scored a line across my arm, and I began to be painfully aware that this was about to devolve into a firefight in a relatively narrow corridor. Worse, while the pirates were outnumbered, they'd brought boarding pavises, which meant they had at least a bit of cover and we did not. The Second Europan definitely didn't. The next volley took her clean through the throat and I watched her drop and choke on her own blood, three feet away from me.

Utterly fucking terrified of meeting a similar fate, I stuck close to Q, trying to use my pistol-and-spear combination to keep the boarders at bay and hoping to hell that she'd know what she was doing. And she did. Because of course she did. With the same speed and agility she used to skewer Leviathans, kick the shit out of annoying crewmates—annoying crewmates now dead—and once to not-quite slit my throat while I slept, she slipped past swords and under gunfire and brought her knife home in thighs and guts and necks as they presented themselves.

I trailed after her and, when I saw the opportunity, grabbed a fallen boarding shield to hide behind. Although in a lot of ways I didn't need it because you didn't get far as a pirate without knowing a thing or two about threat assessment, and I was hugely not a threat.

Q, though, was.

The pirates were thinning out now, but there were enough standing that one was able to put a stream of flechettes into her back just as the rest of them were persuaded to surrender.

At which point I really lost track of the details of the scene. I remember dropping to a knee and trying to cover her with my stolen shield while Locke started doing the surrender logistics and arranging triage with the ship's doctor.

And I remember the captain.

Her footsteps echoed through the halls and off the bulkheads as she bore down on her allies and her enemies alike. She didn't spare a glance for the crew members bleeding out around her, and in her presence the last of the fight went out of the boarders. Approaching the leader of the raiding party, she took his chin in one hand and turned his face up.

"Hast seen the Möbius Beast?"

I didn't listen to the answer. I was too busy keeping pressure on Q's wound and hoping to fuck that the doctor would choose to prioritize her over people with worse injuries who I gave less of a shit about.

"Don't. Fucking. Die," I whispered in her ear.

She turned her face towards me, her lips inches from mine. "Crudelius est quam mori semper mortum temeri."

Around us, people were organizing things. Or rather Locke was organizing things; the captain, having received her answer, had stalked away in a whirl of silk and leather. And the doctor was moving from fallen crew member to fallen crew member, slower—far slower—than I liked.

I'd come to the sky looking for destruction. And here, with Q's blood seeping between my fingers and her breath slowing by the moment, I was finding it. And I was finding it far less to my liking than I'd hoped.

After too many precious seconds, the doctor came to us. She was a stern-eyed redhead by the name of Pierce who had a biomechanical eye and a bedside manner to match. Looking down at the pair of us, she waved over two medical drones.

"This one."

The automata took Q as gently as machines could manage in their claws and lifted her onto a transport bed. I made to follow her, but Locke brought me up short.

"You," they said, "are you injured?"

I answered in the negative. I could probably have lied but it would have been obvious, and Locke clearly wasn't in the mood for my bullshit.

"Then stop following stretchers and escort this one to the brig." They nodded at the pirate leader. He was a heavyset man, his shaved head crisscrossed with scarifications, geometric tattoos running the length of his arms. Honestly, I didn't fancy my chances escorting him, but then I wasn't going to be doing it alone.

Trying my damnedest to sound like I knew what I was about, I gestured at him with my pistol. "This way."

Between me and two other crewmates whose names—all these years later—I can't remember, we more or less managed to wrangle him down to what passed for a brig on the ship, which was basically a storage room with a barred door that on a normal voyage we'd just have put extra barrels of spermaceti in. And honestly if it *had* come to a choice between this man's life and the storage space, there wasn't a hunter-captain in the fleet who wouldn't choose the sperm. I mean, that was what we were here for, wasn't it?

Though he looked very much like a professional murderer,

the pirate was at least talkative on the way to his imprisonment. He told me his name was Wolfram, and that while we'd caught him fair and square, he would be freer in his prison than we were in our berths.

When I went back to my bunk alone, I tried not to wonder how right he might be.

CHAPTER FORTY-EIGHT
Pirates and Emperors

The presence in the brig of pirates—real, board-your-ship-and-take-your-cargo pirates—sent rumblings through the crew that were made a whole lot worse by the fact that the captain had chosen to take us off the regular sky-paths and into storms wilder and more turbulent than anything we'd met so far on the voyage.

"Their leader talks," Flint was saying on one of his semiregular visits to the mess. He might have been an officer, but Flint was prone to fraternizing with the hands. "Father's leave does he talk. I've had two men already come off guard duty wanting to know why we're letting half the pay from this run go to Olympus and not demanding better lays for ourselves."

Locke, who had gotten into the habit of joining Flint in his visits lately—something I was choosing to believe was a result of my increasingly effective charms rather than just a general desire to keep an eye on goings-on belowdecks—gave him a reproving look. "While he's locked up, talk is all he can do."

That didn't reassure me, and I was, by this point, relaxed enough amongst the crew to say as much. "Talk has burned cities. It can down ships as well."

Flint laughed. "Hark to. The scholar's speaking."

He'd been calling me that for months, ever since he'd found

out I was once a schoolmistress. "You don't need to be a scholar to know words can be dangerous."

"Then perhaps we should send you to debate him," said Locke archly. "As a protective measure."

"I'll do my stint on guard, same as everybody else," I replied. "But I doubt we'll either of us change each other's minds."

My mind, if I'm honest, wouldn't have been in much of a place for debate anyway. Since Q had been taken to medbay with injuries I lacked the expertise to assess and a prognosis I lacked the courage to ask about, I'd found a hollowness gnawing at my rib cage that I couldn't quite explain and would have dearly loved to be rid of. As a rule, I didn't get attached to people because time and the stars had a way of tearing you apart no matter what happened, and it was tidier all around if you just braced yourself for loss early.

Only this time, for whatever reason, it wasn't working. I'd cried myself to sleep two nights running and my days were plagued by a sense of displacement and dread I hadn't felt since before I went to Aphrodite. Normally when things got to me like that I'd have tried to get laid ASAP, but of the people I normally went to for a hookup, one was isolating herself in her cabin with a thinking machine and the ramblings of prophets, and the other was getting her organs sutured and her blood replaced. Both of which make you bad at sex.

Which, I suppose, meant I didn't actually have much to complain about when Locke finally did put me on guard duty. On the night shift—insofar as night meant much on a hunter-barque—sitting on a stool carved, like so much else, from Leviathan bone, and armed with a flechette pistol, I sat opposite the pirate leader's cell and tried to watch him without my mind wandering.

Much like staffing the array, I was bad at it. Although at least this time the job had a low floor. You'd have to be a whole lot less attentive than me to miss a grown-ass adult disappearing from a ten-foot-by-ten-foot room.

"Don't talk much, do you?" observed Wolfram a good couple of hours into my rotation.

"Not a lot," I replied. You might be thinking that wasn't true—after all, I've been talking to you for forty-something chapters now and show no sign of shutting up. But telling stories in writing when I can stop and marshal my thoughts when I have to or write through the night when the fits seize me, when the only interruptions I have to manage are my own needs and the only comments I'll get will come from strangers screaming into a vacuum . . . doing that is a whole different thing. In person I keep my mouth shut most of the time. Sometimes I feel like I'm not even there at all.

"You don't look the sort to be on a hunter-voyage."

That came very close to touching a nerve. "And what would you know of it?"

The smile that came to his lips then was more amused than it was cruel, but it was a close thing. "You think nobody ever crossed over from one hunt to the other? I've fought alongside many a beast-chaser, and you're not one."

"I'm becoming one."

"Are you now?"

This was going to about six places at once, none of which I liked. I'd reinvented myself so many times, and I hate being called out on it. "For the moment. It's the same in your line of work, surely. Nobody starts life as a pirate."

"True enough, true enough." It was obvious that engagement was exactly what the man wanted, and I definitely didn't want to give it to him. Then when I didn't say anything else, he added, "You know, I'm getting the impression you don't like me."

"You hurt my friend," I told him. *Friend* was a compromise word. Stronger than *shipmate*, which would have felt artificially distancing. Weaker than what I probably meant. "Or one of you did."

"Your friend chose a dangerous trade," he replied. "You've no more cause to be wroth at me than you have to begrudge the storm when it rages or the Leviathan when it strikes."

I didn't laugh, but somewhere below my heart I felt the irony. "There are those who would."

"Are there now?" he echoed. And I saw a light in his eyes, the cold gleam of somebody making a bloody calculation. "When first I was captured, your captain asked me if I'd seen the Möbius Beast. Is she the one you're thinking of?"

Fuck. I should have just stayed disengaged. "Perhaps I think she's right."

With the grace of an oil slick, the pirate moved across his cell and brought his face to the bars. "I'd wager you're the sort as thinks everything and nothing. All tied in knots behind the eyes and always imagining *this* thing will be *the* thing and never finding it. I've seen a hundred of you on the corsair-ships. And each one's come to a short end."

"Fine words for a prisoner."

He shrugged with one shoulder. "I've no weapons, no books, no music. Talk is all there's left to me. May as well use it."

"Think a lot of yourself, don't you?"

"I learned long ago that nobody else would. Certainly I've never had someone champion me the way you've championed your captain."

I didn't rise to it.

"And new as I may be to this ship, I've a feeling she'll need you. While the hunting is good, your shipmates will be happy enough to follow her in chasing a myth. When it dries up, though. When she starts having to choose between the monster and the mission. Well."

He didn't smile. But his eyes showed that this was very much a choice. Still, I forced myself to be silent. I didn't think that this man was in any danger of persuading me to free him or to turn on my captain, and we'd taken the precaution of isolating him from his crewmates, but he was upsettingly good at touching nerves and pushing buttons, and I didn't really want him doing either.

Over the next two hours he made repeated attempts to bait me into conversation. I resisted them all, and when I was relieved a little after midnight ship time I found myself wandering the corridors in . . . *a daze* isn't the right term. If anything it was the opposite. A focus I chose not to name, because the name of it scared me.

Medbay didn't have set visiting hours. I could have gone to Q's bedside. But when I took steps in that direction a panic rose, and I tasted blood and gall and backed away. Now was not, I decided, the time to confront mortality. At least no more than I'd confronted it already.

So I fled. And instead of going where my every instinct had been telling me to go, I let my wanderings take me to the officers' quarters. Strictly, these rooms were off-limits, but in practice we all went where we wanted and nobody much cared. Hierarchies tended to break down after a year or two in the sky.

Outside Locke's door, I hesitated. While I was pretty sure that no other officer would have me flogged for invading their privacy like this, Locke was a stickler for the rules, even if they didn't feel personally affronted.

Of course, the actual worst-case scenario there was that I got the skin flayed from my back, and in that exact moment I was desperate enough to feel something—to feel *anything* that wasn't this disconcerting mix of naked and alone and terrified—that I'd have taken punishment over nothing.

I buzzed the intercom and heard Locke's voice crackle out of it. "Who goes?"

I told them who went.

"And you're here why?" It was a fair question. And a gentler one than I'd feared.

"I thought you'd want my report on the prisoner."

The intercom went silent for a moment, then sparked back to life. "That's a lie."

"I was cold and out of my head and thought you might want to fuck me."

"More honest." Locke's voice sounded almost amused. As far as I could tell at least—the line was bad. "But it raises questions."

I couldn't tell if I was giving them too much credit or too little, but I was beginning to think Locke was messing with me. A clear *come in* or a clear *piss off* I'd been prepared for. This neither here nor there was messing me around. "What sort of questions?"

"Why you came to me, for one."

Sometimes, tactical insubordination was the way to go. "Because in my humble opinion you *badly* need to get laid."

"And you think you're the ideal solution to that problem?"

"I think something's better than nothing and out here I'm seeing a whole lot of nothing."

The door hissed open, and I stepped inside, still not quite certain I wasn't making a gigantic mistake.

CHAPTER
FORTY-NINE

Debriefing

Looking back, I'm not sure what I'd expected Locke's cabin to look like. Like their office, probably. Austere, immaculate as they were themself. And I'd been half right. It was neatly appointed, with everything arranged just so and in its proper place. But the room had been designed for comfort, not for efficiency. By the one window, a polymer easy chair sat beside a reading light and a low table. And that was where the first mate was sitting, waiting for me to explain myself.

And like the room, they didn't look the way I expected. Out of uniform, in shirtsleeves and bare feet, they looked unguarded. There was still a confidence to them, a no-nonsense attitude that was a big part of why I'd moved them up my list of crew members to sleep with, but it was tempered now by a sense that this was a private space and for the moment at least, their official duties were suspended.

I stood there, feeling out of place. In an effort to bring things back to more familiar ground I asked, "Where do you want me?"

They knew I'd meant it in a sex way, but they just gestured at the chair opposite. "Drink?"

From a mix of politeness and uncertainty, I sat where I'd been directed. It was another comfortable chair, set mirroring the mate's, so we looked like two old friends sharing pleasant after-dinner conversation. "You know you don't have to go through the whole seduction thing."

"Perhaps I want *you* to go through the whole seduction thing."

I was fairly sure they were messing with me again. Besides, I didn't *do* seduction. I was the one people picked up when they'd struck out somewhere else, and I was comfortable with that. "Going to make me work for it, are you?"

"Making sure the crew work for things is rather my job. But mostly I wanted to get you out of the corridor. You seemed very close to making a scene."

That made me laugh louder than I'd meant to. "We've got Marsh walking the decks spouting poetry about the bleak indifference of the sky, a pirate trying to get us all to rise up and overthrow our trade-state oppressors, and the captain—" I stopped dead. Whatever misgivings I might have had about the captain's leadership, it felt like a betrayal to voice them.

But Locke finished for me. "And the captain taking us into uncharted storms in pursuit of a beast far more dangerous but no more valuable than any other Leviathan?"

I couldn't even bring myself to nod.

"For what it's worth," they told me, a note of warning creeping into their voice, "I've sailed with the captain before, and I've seen this pattern. Even before her obsession with the Beast she drew people in."

"That seems a good quality in a leader," I replied, and I did believe it, then. I still do in a way.

"The woman is the sun," replied Locke. "Get too close to her and you'll fall into her well and it'll take half your payload to burn your way out. If you get out at all."

There were no two ways about it, this was the voice of experience. So I asked the question I'd been wanting to ask almost since the start of the voyage. "Were you in love with her?"

It had been a gambit, and it had—I'd say *worked* but that implied way more forethought than I actually gave it. It had an effect. Locke grew very still and fixed me with their cold, unflinching gaze. "That's an impertinent question to ask an officer."

"More impertinent than *Hey, wanna fuck me?*"

"Substantially."

I still wasn't totally sure whether my plan here was to get myself laid or get myself flogged, and I also wasn't sure which side of the line I was riding closest to right at that moment. With uncharacteristic caution, I stayed silent and waited to see if Locke would continue.

"Let's just say," they went on, after a long enough silence that I was beginning to think I'd fucked everything up irreparably and—worse—uninterestingly, "that I know what it's like to have her attention, and to lose it, and to want it back."

It was looking like we'd gotten drawn into a game of competitive nerve-touching. I sat a little stiffer in my chair. "Don't assume you know me."

"Wouldn't dream of it." Their tone was lighter now, and I read a challenge into that. Maybe I was wrong to, but I've been doing wrong things my whole life. "Although I do hope you'll forgive me if I refrain from taking your bullshit at face value."

If I'd had a leg to stand on I'd have been offended. But I'd buzzed their door at midnight and aggressively offered myself to them. It's not like I could pretend I wasn't acting out just a tiny bit. "You might want to start. Bullshit is all I've got."

At that, Locke rose from their chair and crossed the few feet towards me. Then they crouched down and brought their face a respectful but enticing distance from mine. "You know, I honestly can't tell if you're far more interesting than you pretend to be or far, far less."

"I'm an open book," I replied.

"But a long one, I think." A half a smile crossed Locke's lips and then, after a moment's consideration, they leaned in and kissed me.

As you might have worked out by now, I'm a neurotic, chaotic slut with so many issues I could write an allegorical novel about them, so I've been kissed by a whole lot of people. No two have been exactly alike. Actually, that's not true. Most have blended into each other in a mess of self-loathing and whatever I was on at the time. But out of the minority whose names I remember, no two have been alike. Q kissed like fire and A kissed like hate but Locke, Locke kissed like a puzzle box. All they gave up front was the promise of secrets, and each one I unlocked gave me a new question.

Had I been hoping for something else?

Maybe. Even now, in this dark, cramped room, narrating into a worn-out autostenographer, I find that night hard to think back to. I'd gone to Locke looking for the same thing I always got from a certain kind of sex. A secondhand oblivion to distract me from the firsthand oblivion I'd been staring into since I'd fallen from a skyboat. Since Q had been stabbed. Since I'd been born.

My two other shipboard partners—and let's be honest, *partner* was a bad term to use for my relationship with A—were take-charge sorts, and that was normally what I wanted. Tell me what you want me to do, or what you want to do to me, or better still just fucking do it. That's the *point*, in a way. This body is basically a rental anyway. Better to burn it up than let it get repossessed by Aphrodite Pharma State.

But fucking Locke had other ideas. Fucking Locke wanted me to make decisions. And they wanted to *talk*. They wanted *me* to talk. Coherently. About myself. About what I wanted and needed and felt.

It freaked me out.

"Hey," they whispered, as soothingly as they could when I was bent backwards over a low drinks table and we had our hands down each other's pants. "It's okay. If this is— We can stop any time."

I wasn't quite sure how to tell them that being able to stop any time was the exact problem. It sounded messed up in my head and was six thousand percent guaranteed to sound even more messed up out loud. "Just fuck me," I whispered back, trying to sound urgent and fearing I just sounded pathetic.

But they moved their hands to my waist and lifted me up to a sitting position with frustrating gentleness. "Sorry. I'm not the kind of person who's turned on by crying women."

Well that was mortifying. I hadn't actually realized I'd *been* crying. "It's nothing."

"I didn't say it was something. But I'm allowed to stop this just as much as you are."

Anger was an unhealthy response to humiliation, but healthy responses have never really been my thing. "You're a fucking coward."

"Because I don't want to hold you down and fuck you while you weep uncontrollably?"

Anger was an unhealthy response. Hatred was even worse. But in that moment I hated Locke with a passion. If I'd had any dignity I'd have left, but now that they'd drawn attention to my tears I was helpless. I could barely speak, let alone stand—and as a rule emotions aren't what I want to stop me standing after sex.

"Your bunkmate was injured in the boarding, wasn't she?" Locke half asked, while I sat on the edge of the table unsatisfied and eviscerated.

I didn't dignify the question with a nod. But I didn't need to. That was the thing about Locke being so fucking officious. They knew the details anyway.

"Go to her," they said. It wasn't an order. It wasn't the kind of thing they had the authority *to* order. But they said it the same way that they gave commands when the boats were out and the spears were ready to launch.

"She's no use to me unconscious."

I should have known better than to rely on empty bravado.

"You know"—Locke looked deep into my eyes in a way that made me feel flensed—"I actually don't think that's true."

They were right, of course. And that was what I hated most of all.

CHAPTER FIFTY

Forsaken

Dr. Pierce was off duty but on call, which was the perpetual state of ships' doctors. Of course these days a lot of the more routine medical work was done by the drones anyway—the doctor's primary role was to oversee the medbay and to take the blame if something went wrong.

Most of the beds were empty; the sky-hunt was dangerous but a lot of its dangers were the kind that killed you quickly, irrecoverably, and quite often explosively so there'd been a relatively small number of actual *injuries* on the voyage. Sickness was more of an issue since we lived in close quarters and breathed recycled air that had been through a hundred other pairs of lungs, but the atmosphere scrubbers and decontamination chambers saw to most of that.

For somebody who had been shot in the back with a spray of subsonic flechettes, Q looked pretty good, inasmuch as I was any judge. For somebody in almost any other context, she looked terrible. Her tattoos, which normally burned with light even when she was asleep, were lifeless traceries of biometallic wire. Tubes ran out of her arm into a set of machines which I assumed were designed to do her some kind of good—although, since they were likely the products of some subsidiary or other of Aphrodite Pharma State, they were also probably charging her by the hour.

There was a stool by the bed for the convenience of visitors and, presumably, the doctor, so I pulled it over and sat down beside her. I'd come straight from Locke's cabin, so my cheeks were still stained with tear tracks I hadn't bothered to wipe away and my mouth still tasted of salt and blood.

Even if Locke hadn't put me off talking for at least a day, I'd have had no words, so I reached out and took Q by the hand. She felt cold. Not void-cold or ice-cold and, most importantly, not grave-cold, but colder than I'd ever felt her, and by that time I'd felt her a *lot*.

In case the weird chronology and constant digressions in this book didn't make it obvious enough for you, I've always been fucking hopeless at being in the moment. In some ways I've been more fully aboard the Pequod in the years after I shipped on her than I was on the voyage. To actually ground me in the here and now of where I am I need something sharp. It can be pain, it can be pleasure, it can be a blinding light or a deafening noise, but it needs to be something that grabs me by the throat and says, *If you look away you will die.*

It isn't a thing I can find in quiet moments. So as I sat there holding Q's hand and trying so hard, so mercilessly fucking hard to just focus on the fact of her, on the moment that for all I knew then might have been the last, on the palm-to-palm feeling of her fingers intertwined with mine, my mind slipped its shackles and started wandering.

I failed her, in other words. As I would fail her so often.

My thoughts fled to everything they could possibly flee to that wasn't the death of a lover. To the sting of her knife on my throat when we first met. To the scrimshander picture she'd drawn of me in a place I could never understand. To the night I'd first begged her to fuck me. Untethered and undisciplined, I gave in to wondering who she really was, who I might have been with her, and from there to self-indulgent speculations about identity and context and winds and words that looking back I'm ashamed of myself for falling into.

I'm not a scholar. Not really. I'm not a philosopher. I'm just a cold, frightened woman screaming her insecurity to an indifferent sky. Sometimes I wonder if I could have been more, but even wondering that seems egoistic.

Sometimes I look at myself and say girl, accept it. You're full of shit.

While I sat there dreaming my narcissist's dreams, Q lay silent beside me until, after I don't know how long of stewing in my own crap, I felt her fingers tense.

I looked down to see her eyes flicker open. She turned her head towards me the barest fraction and I saw her lips move, but her voice was faint and between that and the language barrier I couldn't make out what she was saying.

"Don't speak," I told her. And then, because it felt like the kind of thing you say, I added, "I'm here."

Turning her head just a little, she looked into my eyes. And she said, "Quid dereliquisti me?"

I had no idea what she meant. I'd made some effort to learn some bits of her language, but since she understood Exodite perfectly well and we both mostly went in for nonverbal communication anyway, I'd kinda stalled shortly after working out the Q-words were questions. There I went letting her down again.

And when I looked so obviously blank, she said, *"Left me. Forsook me. Why?"*

Of all the things I wished she hadn't asked me, that was . . . I mean it was one of them. Perilously close to all of them. And I was silent.

"*Why?*" she asked again.

I could feel my fingers going limp. My hand slipping out of hers as I pulled away out of sheer primordial shame.

With a will and a strength that I at once envied and thought it was a really bad time for, she forced herself into a sitting position. "Immemor atque unanimis false sodalibus," she said, in a tone I'd not heard her use since Cthonius Linea. "Iam te nil miseret, dure, tui dulcis amiculi?"

I still didn't understand her. Couldn't even do her that courtesy.

"Iam me prodere, iam non dubitas fallere, perfide?" she went on, increasingly frustrated with me. "Nec facta impia fallacum hominum caelicolis placent."

"I'm sorry," I half sobbed, half whispered. "I just— I couldn't . . ."

I wasn't used to Q being angry with me. But what was really devastating was that I didn't get the chance, because I saw her anger bleed so quickly into sorrow. "Quae tu neglegis ac me miserum deseris in malis."

I still didn't understand. I still couldn't face her.

I fled.

CHAPTER
FIFTY-ONE

The Rose Bud

You've probably cottoned on by now to the fact that this book isn't strictly in chronological order. I tried to keep it straight at the start, but memories aren't like watching a play and a life isn't one story with a beginning and a middle and an end, it's a hundred stories that cut each other off and jump between each other and end wrong and start bad and blend together like blood on the wind.

I've done my best. Obviously I got on the ship at the start and we'll finally meet the Beast at the end, but everything in the middle is a jumble of things I'm desperate to remember and things I'd rather forget and forgotten hopes and old regrets and one or two bits of shit I might have just made up.

The gams, I'm about 90 percent sure, happened in the order I'm recounting them. They're such a break from the routine of life in the sky that they stand out, and although I may have gotten one or two of the details wrong I'd more or less swear to the general picture. And hell, if you've a mind you can run down those ships and their manifests, speak to their captains, and ask them yourselves.

Which means I'm also fairly certain that we met the Rose Bud while Q was still in medbay, though I can't remember if it was before or after I started work on the coffin. It was definitely after Marsh fell into the head and after we'd captured Wolfram and his fellow pirates, because I remember them being involved. We were still deep in the storms, and tensions amongst the crew were running high. And so when we found the corpse, we were in a bad place to react rationally.

"It's a sign," said the Old Ionian voider, when he saw the beast from the prow. I've talked a lot about the Old Ionian, I think. So in some ways I'm kind of ashamed of the fact that I've forgotten his name. Hell, if I'm being totally honest, I may even be conflating two different people. "And no good will come from approaching."

The thing he had seen was vast and white and distended. A bloated carcass that had once been a Leviathan.

Sometimes they sink. Sometimes they rise. As far as I can tell there's no pattern to it.

Now the sight had been called, the crew were gathering forward to stare at it and speculate.

"Death, that hath sucked the honey of thy breath," Marsh whispered, "hath had no power yet upon thy beauty."

I'd noticed a shift in the dynamic between Truelove and Marsh in the last couple of weeks. While the harpooner wandered the ship declaiming nonsense, the second mate had taken to following him and listening—really listening—as if he truly believed that a brief soaking in spermaceti had given Marsh a spiritual link to their fucked-up entropy god.

While the crew were gathering on the foredeck to stare at the blasted carcass, the officers and captain came by to make their own assessments.

"Worthless," announced Locke to the crowd. "There'll be no oil worth having in something so old and rotted."

Truelove, who had been listening to Marsh intently throughout the encounter, turned to Locke with what you might call respectful defiance. "There's more to wealth than oil, and my harpooner says the corpse is a blessing, for all its outward decay."

I could see the look of contempt in Locke's eyes. Like me, they'd been raised in the Church, but unlike me, they'd rejected its spiritual teachings entirely and nailed their colors firmly to the mast of pragmatism. "We're a hunter-voyage, not a prayer group."

Openly sneering, Truelove turned to A. "What say you, Captain?"

But the captain wasn't listening. She was staring out at the great white mass of the corpse. "To have come so far," she was saying entirely to herself, "to be cheated so late, and like this."

"Captain," repeated Truelove, "what say you?"

"I'll not believe it." She was answering her own question, not Truelove's. "Not until I have looked in its eyes."

"Captain?"

"Make ready the boats."

Lowering for a dead beast was a different experience from lowering for a live one. Different but not necessarily better. In a strange way it felt more dangerous, even though it was less so in every single way possible.

When you went out against a live monster, there were half a dozen ways it could kill you, but you were so aware of that and so ready for it that the adrenaline made you feel at least two-thirds immortal. When the monster was dead already the whole mood was more somber and the grave felt so much closer that it was harder to forget where you were. That you sat in a pressurized cabin above a fall longer than worlds and your job was to butcher gods to sell their blood to pay the price of another day of living.

Or maybe that was just me. Remember, Q was still in medbay at this point, so I was probably getting a bit morbid.

The winds in this part of the sky were intense, and so the floating body of the Leviathan naturally moved as we drew closer to it. But when we were about halfway there, it started to move much less naturally. This kind of corpse normally bobs freely, going this way and that as the unpredictable eddies of the Jovian atmosphere dictate, but this one suddenly started drifting with purpose, directly away from us.

"Fuck"—Flint's voice crackled across comms—"some other bastard is out here."

Sure enough, as we broke the next cloud bank we saw a small squadron of hunter-boats and, behind them, a great barque decorated in Ganymedian fashion—its hull sleek and its deck picked out in colored lights that seemed incongruously jolly given its grim business. This ship's boats had harpooned the dead Leviathan from the other side and were now rapidly towing it back to their barque.

Where a few minutes earlier, the crew of the Pequod had been at best indifferent about what looked like an extremely low-value prize, the sudden appearance of competition spurred us on and we opened our throttles to catch up with the other fleet.

"Unidentified ship"—that was the captain—"this is the Pequod. Identify yourselves."

"This is the Rose Bud." The voice that came back had a distinct Ganymedian accent. "And we claim this as a loose beast."

I'll explain the loose beast thing later. Maybe. Basically it meant anybody could grab it. And they were in the right on this one. They'd gotten to the corpse before we had and speared it fair and square.

Out the larboard side of our cockpit, I saw a single boat break free of our little flotilla. I didn't quite know who it was, but my money—if I'd had any but as I think I explained right back in chapter one, I was broke when I started this trip—would have been on it being the captain.

"Pequod," the Ganymedian captain's voice came through again, "we have claimed this as a loose beast. Withdraw."

The captain didn't withdraw. Of course she didn't withdraw. Instead she asked, as she always asked, "Hast seen the Möbius Beast?"

"Pequod, please repeat." The Ganymedian captain clearly had no idea what she was talking about.

"Hast seen a beast, long as your ship and white as Europan ice?"

There was a pause and then the Ganymedian's voice came back. "We're towing one?"

Comms were dead but I could hear the captain's disbelief in the dead air. If this was truly the Möbius Beast, passed from natural causes and towed off by a dilettante captain who had never even heard of it, the realization might actually break her. And that thought, for a moment, ruined me. I wasn't quite far enough gone that I didn't realize the captain's obsession with the Möbius Beast was all kinds of fucked up, but sometimes life took you to a place where fucked up was all you had and if you lost it you became a healthy, well-adjusted void that collapsed in on itself with a scream so loud that nobody could hear it.

I didn't want that for her.

"Pequod"—the Ganymedian seemed to be losing patience—"move away from our prize."

He was, by the law of the sky, totally right to be pissed. But the captain didn't care, and as the rest of our boats began circling while we waited for orders, Truelove decided that now would be a really good time to get all theological.

"This is not your prize," he said, and I got a sense of that true-believer calm in his voice, the same as I was used to hearing from the captain. It was way less sexy coming from him. "This is a gift from the Devouring God and an echo of his coming. So I am told and so I believe and so it is finished."

The silence on comms felt more awkward than it had a right to be, given that it was just a ship not broadcasting. It got rather more awkward when the reply came in. "Last message unclear, please repeat."

"This"—Truelove began—"is a gift from the Devour—"

"It is not the Beast." That was the captain, whose channel had priority for reasons of rank. "We are done. You may take the carcass if you are so fool as to wish it."

This time awkward didn't even begin to describe it. "Understood, Pequod," said the Ganymedian captain, in tones that were about as icy as I'd have expected given that he'd been subjected to a religious tirade and then called a fool to his face.

"What my captain means"—this was Flint, ever merry, ever working the angles—"is that while we've no doubt you know your business . . . You're a man of business I'm thinking, for certain you sound like one?"

There was a suspicious pause and then the captain of Rose Bud replied, "I have a range of interests, yes. I began as a perfumier."

"Ah then no doubt you've your own reasons for wanting this old and plaguey corpse."

"It is a gift," Truelove repeated, and though my many careers had never included con artist, I did wonder just a little if they were working a two-man grift. "From the Devouring God."

"As you can see," continued Flint, still all cheer and goodwill, "amongst my own crew we've different priorities, but as a businessman I assume you see some value in this carcass beyond the few drams of oil you'll be able to wring from its dried bones."

"You sound," replied the captain of the Rose Bud, his voice all suspicion as well it might be, "like you want it for yourself."

He was in a different boat a good hundred meters or so from mine, but I could see the look of innocence on Flint's face as he spoke. "Me, sir? No, I'm of a mind with my captain—leastways of a mind with her conclusion if not her reasoning. This Leviathan's nothing to me but a disease-ridden hulk that'll see half my crew down with fever as like as not."

"Foul and pestilential," agreed a new voice over comms; Marsh, I thought.

"But some amongst my company are by way of following the Great Chaos"—this was one of the many, many names for the Starry Wisdom sect—"and, well, they do be having their peculiarities."

"If it is the Crawling God's will," intoned Truelove in support, "that we be struck down, we shall be struck down, and I shall rejoice in the sight of the perishing of the unworthy before mine own flesh succumbs."

"See what I'm dealing with?"

It seemed that A had checked out of this whole conversation, which meant that strictly speaking Locke was the ranking officer in this exchange, and they'd been curiously silent.

"Orders?" I asked over internal speakers.

Locke's hand came to rest on the back of my pilot's chair. Honestly, I wasn't super clear where things stood with me and Locke at that point. They were the definition of hot and cold at the best of times, and at work they were all business. "Let it play out. Flint and I have our differences, but I trust the man."

A little below us, Truelove's boat had moved into dart-range of the stricken Leviathan, and while I might have been imagining things, I thought the Rose Bud's boats were slowing. At last, the Ganymedian's voice came back across the void. "And what will you do with this thing you tell me has no value?"

"Me?" Flint managed to shrug audibly. "I'd let it drift. My crewmates on the other hand . . ."

"What will be will be." By now I was more than 90 percent sure Truelove was playing his role up. "But our faith demands that we stare into its deliquescing body and take what we find there as we will."

Possibly it was the word *deliquescing* that pushed him over the edge, or maybe some more experienced sky-dog had explained to the captain that yes, there really wasn't much to be had from this kind of Leviathan and yes, they really did run a risk of making your whole ship come down with a horrific pestilence.

Either way, the Rose Bud's boats unshackled themselves and let the corpse float free on the winds, leaving us to tow it away at our leisure.

"What the fuck was that about?" I asked the internal comms, not really expecting an answer.

The Old Ionian voider leaned over to me. "Ambergris, girl.

Ambergris. Strange thing the other captain being a perfumier by trade and not knowing of it."

And that *was* strange.

Strange enough that, had I not lived the story, I'd have doubted the truth of it.

CHAPTER FIFTY-TWO

The Coffin

Okay, I wasn't being completely straight with you earlier. Part of the reason this story gets fucky with time is that memory really do be like that sometimes. And part of the reason it gets fucky with time is that I'm doing, like, literary shit about the great universal cosmological experience of being a tiny, finite human in a universe so big that space-time itself starts doing things that are completely, utterly, mind-bendingly, heart-breakingly beyond your everyday comprehension.

But if I'm honest, the biggest reason that the story gets fucky with time is that there's a lot of things it took me way too long to do, or to think about, or to wise up to, and I'm trying to hide that.

For example. It took me way too long to go back to Q in medbay.

When I finally did, she was looking . . . better, I guess? Not a lawyer. Not financial advice. Not a medical professional. She was sitting up, her tattoos were glowing brighter, and she had the strength to glare.

"Hi," I tried.

"Salve."

The silence between us went on for long enough I thought it was making a postmodern comment on the nature of life. "I'm sorry."

She reached, still somewhat stiffly, for her idol, spoke into it, and then looked back to me and said, enunciating very clearly, "*Fuck you.*"

I was pretty sure I deserved that. Then again I'd been raised to believe I deserved most things. And just like in childhood, I didn't know how to respond except to say "I'm sorry" again.

She was silent, and her tattoos shifted from green to a pale blue.

"What can I do?" I asked. Because I'd been raised to believe in penance. Or at least in an efficient cash substitute for it.

At that, she sighed, and said—to herself, I thought—"Miser Catulle, desinas ineptire, et quod vides perisse perditum ducas." Then, sighing again and more deeply this time, she spoke once more into her idol, looked at me like I was somewhere between a habit she couldn't kick and a liability she couldn't ditch, and said: "*Coffin.*"

We'd met at a place called the Coffin, so this might have been a mistranslation. Except I didn't think so. "I thought you were getting better."

She shook her head. "*Don't think. Make.*"

"You want me to make you a coffin?"

"*Yes.*"

This was beginning to feel like she was straight-up trolling me. "Why?"

"*Don't ask.*" She looked incredibly serious. "*Do.*"

"And if I do"—something unworthy and transactional squirmed inside me—"will you forgive me?"

"*Quoties peccabit in me frater meus, et dimittam ei?*" She gave me a look of such unbearable weariness that I wanted to choke myself to death. "*Perhaps.*" And then, softening the tiniest, tiniest fraction she added, "*Probably.*"

"How?" I asked. And then because that was ambiguous, I added, "How do I make it, I mean?"

"*From metal,*" she said, "*and bone.*"

She refused to explain further. And I didn't have the will or the standing to press her on it. I just went and got started.

Skyfarers' coffins were a strange business. Coming as we did from all over the system, we had all sorts of incompatible taboos and traditions about what you could and couldn't do with a body. Then on top of that you had the complex set of demands that came from the practicalities of a years long deep-sky voyage. In the most extreme cases, corpses were sent to protein reprocessing to shore up emergency rations, but that was fairly rare on account of how a lot of ships had church sponsorship and they tended to have strict rules about the treatment of the dead.

The fact that Q had asked for a coffin at all surprised me. I'd gotten over the idea that all Terrans were cannibals, but it was rare in the wider system to actually inter a body, a whole one at least. The Church of Life taught that corpses should be harvested by the pharma-states and a lot of smaller communities cremated to save on space or laid their honored lost to rest in hydroponic gardens. Which had the same overall effect as mechanical reprocessing but felt a bit less icky. But the Churches of Prosperity and Liberty both went in for lavish funerals in their own different ways, which meant I did at least come from a coffin-using background and that meant I had somewhere to start.

Since funeral expenses weren't covered by a voider's boarding contract, the parts for Q's coffin needed to be requisitioned out of either her lay or mine, or else scavenged from the wastebays before jettisoning. And while I wasn't expecting my payday from this run to be enormous, especially once fines and overheads were accounted for, paying for her burial was the least I could do. Of course, given how things had been going there was a decent chance she'd pull through, and then I'd be out a nontrivial sum of money for nothing. And honestly maybe that was the point. Sure, wasting a ton of time and cash on a completely useless activity was an *unusual* apology gift, but then again we had an unusual relationship.

I got incredibly lucky. Well, either I got lucky or Q had known exactly what she was doing from the start, because there was a modular transfer pod in waste. Ships use MTPs for all kinds of shit. Escape capsules, ship-to-ship cargo transfer, any time you might want a thing from inside to go somewhere outside without moving the whole damned ship towards it. I fixed the pod up as best I could and attached some basic foils and a small spermaceti engine so that if the worst did happen, it would fly, for a while at least, before my friend-shipmate-lover's body was swallowed by the superfluid mirror of the hydrogen sea.

In a lot of ways I was glad of the distraction. If I was going to try to still the squalls in my brain by throwing myself into something, a craft project was probably a way healthier choice than a stranger's bed or a monster's throat. Maybe there's a much shorter version of this book where instead of fleeing to the skies I just stayed at home and whittled. But in the version of this book you're actually reading I sank my every free hour, for weeks, into the morbid activity of building a coffin for somebody I cared about.

It wasn't therapeutic, exactly. And after a while, not wanting to repeat old mistakes, I did start checking back in with her. Keeping her updated. And I think she was glad of that.

At least, that's what I told myself.

CHAPTER
FIFTY-THREE
Amber, Gold and Gray

We slung the corpse—the beast's corpse, not Q's hypothetical corpse, we're back on the *other* body and the other funeral, for the moment at least—beneath the ship far more easily than we'd slung others in the past, partly because we didn't really give a shit about damaging it on account of it being such a bloated sack of putrescence already, partly because the damned thing floated so holding it up was much less of an issue.

Officially, the blasted Leviathan wasn't actually a prize of the ship. The captain had made it clear she didn't give a fuck and bringing it in had largely been a private plan by the second and third mates. Of course, our contracts still held that *everything* we brought in was to be shared according to the various lays of the crew and the investors, but since it wasn't a formal kill there was no formal work rotation butchering it.

Instead, Flint and Dawlish and a couple of the other crew members worked on it in their spare time, and rather than a systematic dismemberment like we'd usually get, they went straight for the gut.

I happened to be watching from one of the starboard balconies when they finally breached its abdominal cavity. So I got to see the clouds of off-white bile and electric-blue ichor that spewed out when they cut into it.

People often say that smell is a powerful trigger for memory, and maybe long, long ago in the days of ancient Earth that was true. But not in the skies. The billowing clouds of corruption that flooded out from that carcass must have smelled rank in the truest sense. If they did I was cut off from them by layers of crystal and polymer. Even Flint and Dawlish—the ones who had chosen to plunge deep into the rotting bowels of a destroying god—would be inside fully sealed environment suits, breathing recycled air that smelled a little of ozone and a little of rust, and of hardly anything else.

Perhaps that's why I'm having such a hard time remembering those days. Grease and metal and atmospheric processors smell the same wherever you are, and so they don't remind me of the Pequod any more than they remind me of Ganymede or Deimos or Vesta or Titan or Europa.

Spermaceti, of course, has a savor all its own, but you never find it in its raw form outside the hunt, so whatever memories are linked in my mind to that particular scent are buried forever.

The smell of skin I can recapture. The smell of sweat. The smell of somebody else's body beside mine.

Perhaps that's why this book is so fucking horny. I didn't set out for it to be that way. I wanted it to be . . . actually, I'm not sure *what* I wanted it to be. A record, I suppose. The last memorial of a hundred souls who vanished into the void as so many have before them. Of the people I sailed with who deserved better than they got. And the ones who didn't.

I wanted it to be a testimony to a time and a place. A moment trapped in words like insects in the oldest days of Earth would become trapped in amber.

Whatever amber is.

Like wood and like leaves and like trees, I've heard of it but never seen it. Never come within a light-minute of seeing it.

But I *have* seen the gray amber. The gray gold. The vomit whose price is beyond rubies.

I *have* seen ambergris.

Smelled it too.

They call it a Madeleine moment, after some long-dead

Terran queen I suppose. Or perhaps after the Madeleine of the Testament who made her hair a washcloth and thus demonstrated greater entrepreneurial spirit than the most pious of disciples. Either way, the one time a scent has truly taken me back to the Pequod, it was because of ambergris.

Don't worry. This story also has fucking in it.

You remember Pandora? The tall, heartbreakingly beautiful Ganymedian I'd told the tale of Ironhands that I'd had from the Town Ho? It's not a problem if you can't. Most days I barely remember her myself.

She made me her pet for a while. Even took me home to Ganymede, where for the first time and the last time I got to see the beautiful subsurface seas of that body. And it was with her—or, more precisely, without her because we were neither of us huge fans of fidelity—that I'd had that mythical moment of scent-based transportation that took me from a ballroom over a cryovolcanic vent back to the skies of Jupiter and the halls of the Pequod and the bloated corpse of a Leviathan that just gave up on living.

It was magical in a way. But at the time it was a giant fucking mood killer.

I don't want to give the impression that Pandora passed me around to her friends like some kind of fungible fucktoy. There was nothing quite so organized as that. But I *was* pretty conscious throughout my time with her that she'd get bored of me if I stopped being entertaining.

Which was why I was pinned to a ballroom window with a stranger's fingers inside me and her tongue in my mouth when the scent of her perfume hit me like the psychic scream of a dying god and brought me back to the clouds of rot and the airlock of the Pequod and . . .

"Who's Flint?" she'd whispered in my ear, and the question confused me because I wasn't at all clear where I was.

I told her it didn't matter, but my voice betrayed me. In that moment, it mattered.

Flint swaggered in through the airlock triumphant, the

leviathanic bile scoured from him by decontamination, walking in front of six barrel-drones loaded down with glistening gray wax. A glistening gray wax that smelled rich and sweet and alive and beautiful and outside of time.

"Old lover?" the stranger asked, and her too-expensive perfume was rich and sweet and alive and beautiful, like sex and breakfast.

"Old crewmate."

Flint, with typical showmanship, had paraded his haul along the deck, to the applause of the crew. Even the tiny fraction of its value that we'd each be entitled to was something to celebrate.

Pandora's friend—let's call her Cora—gave me a quizzical smile. "Do I remind you of her?"

"Him."

That didn't go down well. She scowled and stopped doing interesting things with her hands.

"We dance tonight, mates," Flint was saying, as the base, animal scent of the ambergris began to flood the deck. "There's more scratch in these barrels than in a half a bay full of sperm."

"It's your perfume," I explained.

Cora pulled away from me and I reached out after her reflexively. I hadn't actually liked her much, but rejection still made me want to vomit and kill myself.

"Ambergris," I said. It made no difference.

"Ambergris," I said to Q, who was watching the celebration with confusion—or I think she was, except we hadn't reconciled yet, she was still in medbay hooked to machines and dying—still I remember the moment so clearly it can't not be true. "They make perfumes from it."

At least I was giving Cora a show. She stopped recoiling, which made me feel better than it had any right to, and stepped towards me again. I could still smell her perfume like a breeze across the void, spanning space and time and death and forgetting. "Perfumes?"

"Long ago," I told her, "I sailed aboard a hunter-barque."

That soothed her. It played into the rough-trade fantasy she was looking for. "That must have been perilous."

She didn't know how perilous, and in truth she didn't *want* to know, not really. And I wasn't much inclined to tell her. "I had my share of adventures. Heard my share of stories. I learned a thing or two about the world. It's why I know the smell of ambergris."

"It's strange," I told Q as I sat by her bedside later that night. "For something so prized and so beautiful to come from something so rotten."

Q looked up at me with a smile. "De comendente exivit cibus, et de forti egressa est dulcedo."

"What does that mean?" asked Cora.

"What does what mean?"

"De whatever whatever et de whatever whatever."

I didn't know, I'd never known. "Just something a friend said to me once."

"This Flint?"

I shook my head. "No. Somebody else."

In the medbay, Q kissed me. She was stronger than she had been, but at that time, with half a coffin built and half the tubes still in her, I still feared losing her.

"Was *that* one an old lover?" asked Cora, her smile wicked and possessive.

"In a way."

"How many ways are there?"

That, at least, I knew how to answer. "Play your cards right and I'll show you."

We were back on track. At least, as far as Cora was concerned we were back on track. She drew me away from the window where, out in the lightless depths, a thousand bioluminescent creatures danced to their own music, and took me somewhere quiet and alone.

She laid me down on a low sofa in an alcove in what might have been a library but what with the mood lighting I couldn't really see clearly enough.

"Tell me a story," she said as she began to undress me. "From those days."

"What kind of story?"

"Tell me what happened to Flint, and to the some-ways-lover. Where are they now?"

I froze. There were stories I would tell and stories I most certainly wouldn't, and that story—which canny readers might also realize is *this* story—I wasn't ready to share. Not then and perhaps not now.

So I said, "I don't know."

It was half the truth. After all, who truly knows where anybody is? Are the dead floating forever on the winds of Jupiter; are they swimming like superconductive merfolk through the hydrogen sea? Are they with us all for always?

So instead I told her about ambergris. About how we'd found it in a bloated carcass in the deep sky, and how dram for dram it was one of the most precious substances in the system. And then I told her, because it was what she wanted to hear but also because it was a cold and brutal truth that I couldn't look away from, that it became still more precious when it was processed and bottled and used, at last, to adorn her beautiful body.

I don't remember, now, the color of the light in that place that might or might not have been a library. But in my imagination it was red. And when Cora stood before me, all she wore was a perfume made from the vomit of a Leviathan, and her skin gleamed as if it were painted with blood.

And it was, in a way.

CHAPTER FIFTY-FOUR

A Bower in the Arascides

The weirdest thing about making the coffin for Q was the point where she started helping me.

There was no ceremony to it. On one of my growing-more-bearable visits to her bedside, I found her standing. She was still bandaged and, under the bandages, there were probably still nanosurgical drones doing whatever it was nanosurgical drones did. But she looked *almost* back to her old self.

"*Done?*" she asked.

"The coffin?"

"*Yes.*"

I wasn't exactly sure how to play this. Barring sudden complications, and honestly, sudden complications were common enough with medical treatment, especially if your bank balance started running low, she was clearly not in urgent need of a coffin. "Working on it," I told her. Because it was true.

She didn't reply verbally. She just nodded, took my hand, and led me down to the bay where I'd been working.

She undid most of it.

Well, not most of it, but she had a lot of opinions and made a lot of adjustments. She tweaked the engine, stabilized the fins, and hooked power to some of the Leviathan bone I'd worked into the structure at her insistence.

When she did, it luminesced like her tattoos.

I watched her work and, when I thought she was sufficiently occupied that I could speak without choking, I seized my moment. "So. We good?"

I might have seized the moment too well, because she was so occupied that for a good while she didn't reply. Then finally she pulled her head out of the guts of the coffin and said, "*No.*"

Well, that sucked.

For a moment I just stood there. I'm not sure I even blinked. "What do you mean *no?*"

You probably don't need me to tell you that her response was just "*No.*"

I glared, increasingly frustrated, at the coffin I'd spent too much time and energy on. And okay, it wasn't great, and okay, she seemed to want to change almost everything I'd done to it, and okay, as big gestures of reconciliation went *Ohai, I maked you a coffin* was fucking weird, but she'd literally *asked* for this. "Do you have any *idea,*" I blustered, "how much *work*—"

"Non ex operibus ut ne quis glorietur."

I still didn't understand her.

Fuck. That was the whole point, wasn't it.

I dropped to my knees beside her and told her I was sorry. Then I told her again. Then I cried. Proper, ugly, pride-is-a-sin cried.

To this day I don't know if I was forgiven. But then I came from a world where forgiveness was for sale, so perhaps I was a bad judge. Or perhaps I was trying to judge the wrong things.

But she put her hand over mine, passed me a fusing iron. "*Work with me.*"

And we did. It became . . . peaceful, in the end. Familiar. Like we knew what we were doing and had always known. Like no more words needed to be said.

That wasn't true. Not exactly. But that's a story for later.

We worked on that coffin for weeks. Far longer than seemed remotely necessary. When the modifications to the superstructure had all been made, she started work on the decoration. We paneled the box all over with sheets of Leviathan bone, and then Q took her laser cutter and began to engrave the surface with beautiful, entwining patterns. And on the lid, she carved the wide, spreading shape that I had still never seen in person but which I was learning to call a tree.

At last, after so much work and heartache and flat-out weirdness, it was done. And there was a kind of mortuary wonder to it. A solemn majesty.

"What now?" I asked Q, looking at the very large, very expensive boondoggle we'd spent so much of our time on.

Without words, Q replied by stepping into the coffin and lying down.

I gave her a seriously-stop-fucking-about look.

She didn't stop fucking about. "Is this—are you still trying to make some kind of point? I'm sorry. I really am. I was scared of losing you. I didn't want to confront it. I should have been less of a fuckup, but I am never going to be less of a fuckup."

But Q remained silent and perfectly still. So with a sigh I played along. I stood beside the open box and looked down at her. She looked peaceful, lying there. And despite the bone-white walls of the coffin and its funereal motifs, she seemed as alive as she always did. Even her stillness gave the impression of just being belayed motion.

Which meant I wasn't entirely surprised when, only slightly less swiftly than she would have done at full health, she darted up, seized me by the arm, and pulled me in on top of her.

I *was* surprised when the coffin lid closed firmly on top of us, leaving us trapped, body to body, in the absolute black, the low hum of the oxygen diffuser the one thing reassuring me that she hadn't just killed us both.

"What the *actual* fuck?" I asked her, my voice in an unnecessary whisper.

"Media vita in morte sumus," she replied. And then she kissed me.

Looking back, one of the things that still messes with my head is that I knew Q so well in so many ways, and not at all in others. I couldn't tell in the moment if this whole thing had been an elaborate sex game, a complicated joke at my expense, or something deeper and more complex.

I'd later realize it had been all those things and more, but at the time I was just an unhelpful mix of angry, frightened, and horny.

As it turns out, it's incredibly hard to fuck in a coffin. Even a mechanized one with synthetically padded walls and a built-in air filter. But *hard* isn't the same as *impossible* and sometimes a challenge is a turn-on, so I went with it.

We weren't in absolute darkness, of course. The blue-green light of Q's tattoos provided just enough illumination that I could make out the lines of her face, the path of her hands. And with my limited range of movement there wasn't much I could do except kiss her and clutch at her and tell her that she was beautiful. That she was remarkable. That for as long as that lid remained closed and the steel-and-bone box remained our whole world I would be always and only hers.

I think she liked that. We'd established very early on that she didn't mind my having other lovers even if—like Locke and, for that matter, most other members of the crew—she had her concerns about the captain. And since she didn't always come back to her bunk every night, I'd kind of assumed she was fucking other people too. But—and maybe I'm just flattering myself—for all she said her people didn't do ownership, I'm pretty sure she enjoyed the idea of possessing me, at least while we were together. One of the sneaky advantages of living the way I do, a little bit unstuck in time with the past always snatching and the future always beckoning, is that sometimes, just sometimes, I can play the same trick in reverse and make *now* feel like forever.

Until it doesn't.

CHAPTER FIFTY-FIVE
The Congregation

I tried to make sure, when I was working on this book, that even somebody who knew nothing about Leviathans, or about the hunt, could follow what was going on. Part of that means making sure you know at least as much about how Leviathans work as I do. And yes, in hindsight I could probably have worked that information into the text more elegantly instead of just devoting the occasional chapter to long digressions about biology, but, well, I guess that's just my time as a schoolmistress coming to the fore. Tell 'em what you're going to tell 'em; tell 'em; tell 'em what you told 'em.

One of the things I've been telling you for a while now is that leviathans are, by and large, pretty solitary creatures. But as we've seen, pretty solitary isn't the same thing as *completely* solitary. Pods are a thing, after all, and it's hard for any species to be completely solitary unless it reproduces asexually. An although another thing I've told you is that we don't know much about the reproductive habits of the Jovian beasts, I do think it's likely that, unlike a lot of polyps, fish, and other sea creatures, they use internal fertilization.

Which is another way of saying that Leviathans fuck.

Nobody has ever actually seen them mating or found a spawning ground. Nobody has ever recorded . . . *anything* about them, really. They're a resource that we kill for parts, not something we document.

But the hunters know. While everybody else just ignores the monsters who keep their lights on, we dig deep inside them, and we *understand* them. They fuck. They have families. They have nurseries.

And when we find a nursery, we charge into it and start killing indiscriminately.

Q was well around this time, so it must have been either before or after the whole thing with the pirates and the coffin. I'm putting it after, but I don't remember the pirates being involved. I *do* remember Marsh being deep, deep in whatever the voices were telling him to do, and I think that makes it late in the voyage.

Either way, the themes shake out. And besides, who's going to prove me wrong? Everybody who could is dead.

By this stage Marsh had taken to holding great sermons from the prow of the ship, which had grown increasingly popular amongst the crew, initially amongst those who fell, phenotypically speaking, into what the Starry Wisdom sect called the Last Devoured, but eventually even some of those who the Devouring God was set to consume first started attending.

"It just makes sense," explained a young Europan voider who, by Starry Wisdom doctrine, would be very near the top of the Devourer's menu. "Besides, it probably doesn't mean *me*."

We had passed through the storms into the Southern Tropical Zone with relatively little difficulty, although admittedly that might have been because we were all judging difficulty relative to being boarded by pirates.

Now we were in calmer skies, we could get to work patching up the hull. So when we found the nursery (you see, the biology does matter), I was suspended by a line out of a larboard airlock, fusing a great panel of leviathanic carapace over the breach the raiders had made.

Which meant I had a spectacular view.

Leviathans are impossible. Neither science nor theology

accounts for them. And when gathered in numbers they're impossibility magnified. The nursery was a cloud, like a swarm of Wyrms or—if what I've heard about the skies of Old Earth and the aviaries of Paestum Vallis is true—a flock of swallows. Except bigger, so much *bigger*.

The signal to lower was sounded and I finished my spot-weld as quickly as I could before hurrying off to my primary duty of piloting the death boat.

Normally the launch bay was if not a well-oiled machine then at least a decently efficient place-where-people-went-and-got-in-stuff, but this late in the voyage we were tired and uneasy, and, oh yes, a good dozen or so of us had joined an apocalypse cult.

Marsh, Truelove notably walking behind him now, proceeded almost in state to his boat, wielding his coilgun like a staff of office. His followers trailed behind him, murmuring warnings about the coming annihilation and, when he reached the boat, they lifted him into it on their shoulders, with Truelove climbing up after.

Between that and the captain striding all purposeful and alone to her own boat with its illegal neurally networked copilot, I was beginning to get the sense that things were not going well aboard the Pequod.

"No time now," said Locke, as if answering my thoughts. "We lower. And bring the narcotic lances."

The narcotic lances were something the hunt used very rarely and only in target-rich environments. If the hunt did encounter a very large pod of Leviathans, or a whole horde of them like we had here, it would be extremely hard to single one out to kill. So instead of killing them, we drug them.

I say drug: the narcotic in question is a lethal neurotoxin delivered in doses that would kill an entire hab-dome if they got into the air filters. But to a Leviathan they mostly just make it fly erratically and, more importantly, the lances themselves are tagged with a high-frequency ID marker that flags the Leviathan's corpse—should it eventually succumb to the poison or to other wounds it suffers in the chase—as the property of the ship. If it didn't have this tag on it, and it *did* die, then like the ambergris corpse it would be considered a loose beast, and free for anybody to haul in and carve up. By attaching our tags, we marked our Leviathans as fast beasts, and our own property.

The practice might seem odd to those outside the fishery, where property rights are usually a tad more complicated than calling electronic dibs. But in a lot of ways I liked the purity of the system. It broke the whole sky into two categories: things that were owned, and things that were waiting to be owned. It fit well with the world as I understood it.

For example, I, like Dawlish, was very much a fast beast. My body was property of Aphrodite Pharma State and would be until my debt was paid or they came to collect it. The rest of the crew, as far as I knew, were loose beasts. Their bodies were the property of whatever power came by and chose to claim them.

What sort of beast you are is left as an exercise for the reader.

Venom spears loaded, we climbed into the boats and, with Marsh's choir singing hymns of dissolution, we lowered.

From time to time throughout my life, I've had moments of disconnection or of dissociation. Moments when the world has gone distant or fuzzy or shrunk down to two-thirds of its regular size and I've felt like somebody else was living through me. I've never had one stronger than I did in that lowering.

Once, on Vesta, I knew a woman with an intricate tattoo the length of her spine. It was of a great eel winding around a barbed hook to take its own tail in its mouth. But when you looked carefully you saw that the eel was picked out in tiny legible words—poems, prayers, jokes, blessings and curses—only visible if you got close enough that the picture itself vanished.

Approaching the leviathanic cloud was like that. From a distance it seemed one thing, pulsing and rippling as if a single will animated it. It was only as we drew nearer that I began to make out the individual beasts and to get a sense of the absurd, astronomical scale of the whole gathering. The smallest amongst them—jaws to tail—was a third the length of the Pequod, the largest far longer, and there were *thousands* in that gathering. Together they would have represented a treasure trove of sperm (still saying it, how's it going?) more valuable than the wealth of entire cities, perhaps even entire trade-states. No hold could carry even half their oil; no ship could catch a tenth of them, a tenth of a tenth.

Though the beasts were densely packed on the scale of gods and gas giants, close to I could see that there was immense space between them. Plenty of room for us to move between the monsters and loose our payloads as needed.

"Range closing." That was the captain, and I realized how strange it was to hear from her on a hunt. But maybe she thought to find the Möbius Beast amongst the cloud. "Stir them up and strike at will."

The order to strike at will was immediately taken up by the other boats but Locke gave the command for us to hold, and so we held. "No sense wasting good venom," they explained. "And no shortage of prey either. But watch it, the skies will be getting rough."

And they were right. Each time a beast was speared, it shied, and the once-harmonious movements of the swarm got super fucking chaotic super fucking quickly. Because Locke had kept us back slightly, I had a view from the outside and I could see the panic spreading through the Leviathans like a plague through a prison ship. Patterns gave way to noise and beasts careened past each other in their hurry to get away from their would-be killers.

This was my first time amongst a mass of Leviathans, and I'd wondered, before lowering, why we used the poison darts here and not in other hunts. This monstrous tumult gave me my answer.

On a regular hunt, against a lone beast or a small pod, your aim is to secure the capture of a single target because a single target is often all you have. The line and the chase is the best way to achieve that goal; the poison would be wasted at best and—if it made the beast act unpredictably—a liability at worst. But in amongst this density of Titans, the line is impossible to use. If one of our boats had tethered itself to a single Leviathan, it would have found itself dragged across the path of five or six more, and it'd be incredibly likely to get smashed into sky trash for its trouble.

So instead we throw out toxins. Drug a hundred beasts and maybe nine or ten will actually surrender to the venom and of those you'll catch one or two. The rest will drift away to be eaten by Wyrms or sink at last to the core of the planet where they'll become one with its immense magnetic field and get their vengeance on hunter-barques by unleashing elveses in the upper atmosphere.

"Now," ordered Locke calmly, and so I downed canopy and brought us in.

This was after Q's recovery. It was definitely after Q's recovery. Or before her injury. She was there with me, I remember that for certain. As certain as I can be. It's been a long time.

Braced against my seat, she loaded and fired her coilgun, loaded and fired, loaded and fired, sending spear after spear into any monsters that came close to us. I, for my part, did my best to keep us on an even keel while leviathanic tails slashed past us and feeder tendrils reached out for us and more than once the great armored bulk of an enraged or terrified creature flew directly into our path.

It was still oddly beautiful.

The cloud of Leviathans, as it turned out, wasn't a cloud at all. It was a shell. A wide sphere two to three beasts thick surrounding a denser inner sphere of pure white.

After nearly three years in the sky, I was beginning to dread seeing white things in the distance. The moment we caught sight of it, the captain's boat shot away from us.

"There," her voice rang over comms, "and at the heart as all my dreams foretold."

As I turned my boat to follow her, Locke and Q both laid hands on my shoulder.

"Steady," Locke whispered. "I've a feeling she'll come up disappointed."

"The path is smooth," Marsh added, "that leadeth on to danger."

Perhaps unsurprisingly, I took Locke's warning more seriously than Marsh's, although since they both seemed to be giving the same advice it didn't entirely matter. I slowed and watched.

At this depth, the skies of Jupiter were a constant haze; we were below the white clouds and deep into the red-orange sulfide and acetylene, which cut visibility unpredictably and randomly. When we next caught glimpse of the white shape it was clear that we hadn't found the horror which A had been hunting. What the captain had taken for the whiteness of the Möbius Beast's carapace was in fact the glistening, newborn whiteness of countless gigantic maggots. Or things a whole lot *like* maggots. They were held, suspended, in the feeder tendrils of a cluster of Leviathans that flew in a close circle about half a klick ahead of us. The part of my brain that the catechism had taught to read every natural thing as a metaphor for the values of my upbringing saw it as motherhood.

And I probably wasn't far wrong.

"It's a spawning ground," Locke called urgently over comms. "Captain, that is *not* the Beast, it's a death sentence. Abort now."

But the captain had already breached some invisible line, and the whole armada of Leviathans turned its attention towards us.

Leviathans don't really have faces, and even if they did we were far enough inside the shell now that it was back to looking a whole lot like a swarm of locusts or a flock of birds (disclaimer: I don't know what either of those things actually look like, I'm going mostly from the Testament). Still, I read anger into them.

Maybe I was projecting. Maybe I was anthropomorphizing needlessly. But either way they did, as a collective, decide to murder the fuck out of us, and in a lot of ways their motivations were immaterial.

A fair chunk of our downtime on ship was spent on drills, simulations, and other kinds of practice for common skyfaring scenarios. Funnily enough, we'd never drilled for this. Which meant it was every boat for itself.

I might have mentioned a few times that I actually kind of suck at many, many aspects of my job. Or of the job I had back then, at least. I'm too undisciplined to be a good eye on the array. I lack the skills or the temperament to defend the ship in a crisis. I'd never make it as a harpooner. But I pilot okay. There's something about imminent danger that makes me really stay focused and in turn that makes me pretty reasonable at things like not getting my boat scythed in half by the mouthparts of a bestial god from the deep sky.

So I wove our little boat between the enraged bulk of the Leviathans, swooping low to avoid their tendrils then pulling up at the last moment as the armored dome of another soared into view. The drugged spears were, in this exact context, making things substantially worse because poisoned monsters, while they would eventually slow as the venom did its work, were also more violent and less predictable in their movements.

A younger, slighter beast—panicked from the toxin and the chaos—cut straight across the path of my boat and I pulled us into a steep climb. The compensators aren't really designed for going straight up or down, so the feeling of it was weird, with Jovian gravity pulling us back into our seats and the compensation pushing us towards the canopy so we slid gently upwards, clinging to whatever we could cling to because despite the speeds involved, sky-hunting wasn't compatible with seat belts.

As we soared over the back of the monster, I lost visual, but the proximity detectors said it was still where we'd left it, and from the readings I was getting, it was still freaking out.

It freaked out so much that, portside, I saw its sinuous, barbed tail arcing upwards, bowed in a way you never saw from an uninjured beast, and it drove down towards us fast, sharp, and hard. Which is how I sometimes like it, but not in this context.

Hunter-boats are fixed-wing, which means that to turn they have to roll, and to roll they have—ideally—to *not* be hugging the carapace of an adolescent space-horror so tight they scrape their wingtips. But the devil makes marks of us all, and as I banked to get us out of the way of that slashing, jabbing tail I saw sparks fly and felt the whole body of the boat judder. Not waiting to see what the beast would do next, or even taking a moment to reflect on how this whole situation was a metaphor for the human condition, I hit the afterburners and forced us onwards.

Behind me, the other boats were doing the same. Despite the seamier things I've described in this memoir, you should understand that the crew of the Pequod were hardy and seasoned, and knew what the fuck they were doing. Though the nursery-hunt was chaos, we came through it without losing a boat. Each pilot, in their own time and on their own instincts, fixed unerringly on a break in the cloud, and each of us, close as we came to destruction, made it back to the ship with all souls alive.

Ages ago now—it seems like years though I've been at work on this memoir for less than twelve months—I spoke of the parallels between hunters and soldiers, of how we expose ourselves to every bit as much danger for a tiny fragment of the glory. I hope now you see a little of what I meant. A writer of ancient Earth once said that there are those who think a fleet of ships or a row of soldiers is the most beautiful thing in the world. She might have been right, I don't know what ships looked like in those days. But I know what a hunter-barque looks like. And I remember the faces of Flint and Locke and Truelove and Dawlish and even poor, possessed Marsh.

I want to do my best to honor them. Them and the rest, the ones I can only half conjure. The Old Ionian. The Ganymedian dandy. The First and Second Europans. The Bright-Eyed Titanian. The scads of ordinary voidhands who a kinder, more conscientious woman would be able to distinguish more clearly, even in memory.

They all deserve a better epitaph than this.

CHAPTER
FIFTY-SIX

Fast

As the journey had worn on, the captain had called for me less and less. Perhaps she'd just gotten bored, and that's fair enough. People usually do. I'm an entertaining distraction for a day or a week or a year. I'm not the kind of person people settle down with. I'm not the kind of person who settles down.

Boo-hoo. Nobody loves me. Sorry, I know I sound pathetic sometimes. Maybe most of the time. There's a reason I've spent so much of my life running.

Anyway, on this particular day, whenever it was—after the Rose Bud, certainly, but before the Samuel Enderby—she'd had need of me. Something had been worrying her, and she'd wanted somebody to take it out on, and I was more than happy to help.

So there I knelt, bare knees on her tatami mats, bare chest on the cold glass of her imaging desk. My neck was craned back at an awkward angle so I could see the full spread of the port windows before me, though it was hard to concentrate with one of the captain's hands tangled in my hair and the other tracing a map across the naked skin of my back. She'd set her canes aside for now, and though I loved the sound of her voice, I wished she hadn't.

"I fear that I lose them," she was saying, partly to me and partly to the ship and partly to the view out the window. We were low, low down now, skimming the surface of the hydrogen sea. One of the drugged Leviathans had come down a little way from the great congregation and we had wasted no time in swooping in to collect it.

It was a shame, in a way, because by itself, dead in a habitat neither natural to it nor unnatural, it was a beautiful thing. Wyrms—sky-Wyrms and sea-Wyrms, both sorts exist—swarmed about it in a riot of life that made me think of the oldest scriptures, of how the Father had separated air and land and water and had ordained that there would be things that swam and crawled and flew.

There was divinity in putrefaction, I thought.

"Too many voices," the captain continued. "Too many voices that are not my own." She released her grip then and took up one of the scrimshandered switches that she'd so briefly denied me. It stung me like love. "The prisoner still speaks anarchy, and while I would not deny the man his philosophy it is not a part of my design."

A blow, not quite light enough to be gentle, not quite hard enough to be cruel, landed on my shoulder.

"Then there is Marsh. A sweet boy I thought, and foolish. But now he speaks for the void and the crew listen. Oh how they listen."

Her lips were by my ear now, her breath hot.

"Do you listen?"

Outside, the boats had been deployed. For sea-work they needed hydrogenous adaptors, which permitted them to skim the surface without being overwhelmed by the cold or the current or the unpredictable electromagnetic phenomena that surged throughout the metallic ocean.

"No," I managed to reply. "I listen only to you."

And in that moment it was the truest thing that I had ever said.

To my dismay, the captain hauled me upright and turned me round so I faced her, or at least faced her thighs. I turned my eyes upwards and tried not to look too much like I was begging her to force me down again.

I totally was.

"You are well liked amongst the crew."

It wasn't a question so I couldn't really contradict her. Although given how some of my earliest run-ins had gone, it was at the very least an overstatement. It would have been more accurate to say I'd fucked quite a lot of them. Which in my experience didn't require them to like me one little bit. So I went with a noncommittal "I hope so."

"What do they say?" she demanded. "Of me. Of this. Of the mission."

It was a bad time for her to ask me any kind of question. At least any kind of question that needed an answer more nuanced than "more" or "harder." Still, I did my best. For her I always would. "It's been two years," I reminded her. I think that's right. It might have been more. Or less. Or never have happened. "You promised a great reward for news of the Beast, but voiders have short memories. And if I'm honest, half the crew's always thought you were mad."

She laughed. It was a derisive laugh, but not an unbelieving one. "Then they are in good company, for I have often thought the same myself. Although I have lately come to the conclusion that it is not so."

"You think you're sane?"

"I think I am madness maddened. I think that I have seen and have endured such things that a mind must either shatter or be reforged, and I have chosen to be reforged."

On the whole, not the most reassuring thing she could have said. But by this stage I was already all in on the captain and there isn't much I could have done.

Like how was I supposed to reply? "Hey, have you considered maybe not?" or "Okay, but why not just finish up this voyage and go home and leave this whole driving-a-spear-through-the-pasteboard-mask-of-the-world deal for other people?" Was I meant to say "Take your last lay and retire and take me with you and do whatever you will to me and do it forever, that's all I want"?

And would it have been, actually? What I wanted, that is. Let's be real, I have terrible taste in women and I don't think I'd have been half as into A as I was if it hadn't been extremely clear that she'd probably get the lot of us killed. I could never have stopped for death, so she kindly stopped for me.

After longer than was necessary but less than the eternity I yearned for, the captain sent me back to my duties. The drugged beast had already been dragged beneath the ship and made fast—in the chained sense, rather than the claimed sense, though I myself had recently been both.

From there the process of butchering was much as it had always been. I've already told you most of how it works. It worked the same way this time. It works the same way today as far as I know. It will probably work the same way a hundred years hence. That's the thing about going to the sky. The days are long and the years short. It's an irreplaceable experience where every part is the same and the whole thing is still somehow unique.

For the first time, or the ninth, or the hundredth, Q and I put on our voidsuits and descended the side of the Leviathan to begin carving it apart.

CHAPTER
FIFTY-SEVEN

An Extended Cock Joke

Two nuns are in the bath. One says, "Where's the soap?" and the other one says, "It does, doesn't it?"

A nun was a member of an all-female religious order in one of the superstitious pseudo-faiths of Old Earth. The enlightened churches, of course, don't gender-segregate their followers. They separate them out by far more sensible criteria, like who has the most money or the largest number of subscribers to their sermon streams.

I said two chapters ago that we didn't know how the Leviathan reproduces. I also said nobody had ever seen a spawning ground even though that chapter took place inside a spawning ground. I'm not claiming that the Pequod was the first ship ever to encounter such a thing, only that what is seen on the hunter-voyage and what is recorded by posterity, by history, by men and women of science and learning . . . well. Those are two very different things.

So it is with the reproductive processes of the Leviathan.

No official source I've looked at, and I've looked at many, from the academic journals of the Venusian pharma-states to the biotheological treatises of the Church of Life, is willing to commit to describing the precise method by which the Jovian monsters reproduce. There've been no academic studies, no research-voyages. Most exobiologists have never so much as seen a sample of a dead Leviathan, let alone its whole unmolested body.

Only the hunters have seen that.

Two nuns were walking down the road when a flasher jumped out and exposed himself to them. One was so shocked that she had a stroke. But the other couldn't reach.

The monstrous, heaving prick of the Leviathan is called the grandissimus in the hunter-fleet. It is enormous. It is superlative. It is endless. Against it, all other cocks look like—actually, I'm trying to come up with a disparaging comparison but let's face it, penises are pretty crappy-looking all by themselves, so I don't think similes are helping here.

Aboard ship it's an object of veneration. Voiders are a superstitious lot, and while the fleet isn't as male-dominated as it used to be there's a certain element of destructive machismo that runs through the whole business.

I mean, when you get right down to it, it's a career built almost entirely of going around ramming spears into things. That kind of symbolism attracts a certain sort.

Would you believe me if I said that the handling of the leviathanic wang was so important that a whole dedicated office on the ship was given over to it? And that this office was called the mincer?

Would you believe me if I said two nuns were once riding their bicycles down a cobbled street, and one said, "I've never come this way before" and the other said, "That'll be the cobblestones"?

On a ship it's the role of the mincer to take the monstrous member of the leviathan and process it. The celestial megaschlong is delivered to him by a dozen burly men who carry it slung over their shoulders and then he carefully hollows the meat out of the center with a machine called a boning-spoon. This is processed into a thin broth that the crew drink for good luck and sexual potency. The soft, supple, radiation-resistant skin of the monster-cock is then lovingly fashioned into a kind of a cassock for the most revered and celebrated men on the crew.

How much of that is true?

Well you should never believe a voider's tale. Voyages grow long and we make shit up to amuse ourselves. And to impress surfacers. And to get laid. Mostly to get laid.

But from this point on you might notice that Marsh wears new robes. Robes in a dark, pliant leather, soft to the touch but warm against the void and hard-wearing in the wind. He even takes to wearing a set over his voidsuit, which speaks of a very particular quality of material.

We voiders make shit up, but we're deeply uncreative people, so most of our tales have a drop of truth in them.

What's black and white and red and can't go through a revolving door?

A nun with a spear in her neck.

CHAPTER
FIFTY-EIGHT
Softness

We're more than fifty chapters in now, so I really hope you've got to the point where I can say "sperm" and you won't find it funny.

Because I'm about to say "sperm" a lot. I'm about to talk about having my hands in sperm, being elbows-deep in sperm. I'm going to talk about squeezing sperm and feeling it run warm and rich and wonderful between my fingers.

Flick back a couple of pages and you can read jokes about dicks and nuns if that's more your speed.

I'm also going to talk a bit about how good sperm is for your skin, and I do want to stress that this is true only of the psionically active cerebrospinal fluid of the great Leviathan. If you want to let someone jizz on your face go right ahead, there's worse ways to spend a Saturday. But don't let them tell you it'll be good for your pores, because it won't.

We all on the same page? Great.

Let's talk sperm.

The volatile and quasimystical energy source that for historical reasons we still call *spermaceti* is actually a fucking nightmare to work with. If you were paying attention, you'd have noticed that it crystallizes quickly on exposure to air, room temperature, or most surfaces. You might also remember that its inherent electromagnetic properties make it a pain in the ass to process mechanically unless you've got a whole lot of shielding. Which full refining plants bodyside do but which whatever stopgap measures are on a ship don't.

So instead, to get it piped anywhere you have to make it go liquid again. And that means you have to squeeze it.

When Marsh fell into the head of the first beast we killed—a while ago now but also no time at all because the sky is vast and endless and because I can't keep my mind on one thought for two seconds together—its sperm spilled all over the chamber floor and blossomed into marvelous crystal patterns like high-explosive snowflakes.

We squeezed a lot of sperm that day.

I do wonder if part of the reason smell gets such a reputation for triggering memories is that you're basically always smelling things. Whereas most people, in most jobs, aren't usually having regular tactile experiences.

I'm not most people. And the hunter-fleet isn't most jobs.

Nothing brings back more memories for me than the feeling of an amorphous semisolid turning to clear fluid in the palm of my hand. And yes, that doesn't happen that often in civilian life, although I do sometimes get very weird flashbacks from moisturizer dispensers and the one time a wealthy girlfriend fed me honeycomb. But through the years of my journey on the Pequod, that strange, smooth skin sensation runs like a seam of frozen methane through a Europan ice mine.

Q and I did that first cleanup alone. She was being punished for risking the prize in the first place, and I was being punished for standing up for her, and also for just being in the wrong place at the wrong time.

But the joke, it turned out, was on the ship. Because it was no punishment at all. I mean, yeah, I wasn't wild about spending hours on my knees in a nonsexual context, but the sheer peace of being with Q and doing that simple, honest job was a balm to me. Breaking off the spires of sperm, as delicate as spun sugar (or so I imagine; I've dated some rich women but never spun-sugar rich), and warming it between our hands and melting it and pouring it into the casks where it would be stored in a climate-controlled, pressure-tolerant, explosion-resistant cabin until we could finally sell it back on Europa for processing.

There was magic in it.

Every now and then my hands would find hers. It wasn't the only job where that could happen, but it *was* the only job where my hands wouldn't also, if I wasn't careful, sometimes encounter a razor-sharp blade or a whirring buzzsaw that would split my arm up the middle if I didn't pull back quick enough.

There was an intimacy to it. That might seem strange because from a certain perspective "intertwined with mine while coated in pulped monster brain" probably doesn't seem like the most intimate place Q's fingers had been. Like in case I haven't made it clear or you're reading the version of this book that's had the sex scenes edited out to placate the Church of Liberty, we were totally fucking throughout the entire voyage. But—and maybe this is just my religious upbringing coming out, or maybe it has more to do with my profound disconnection from a body I don't own, or maybe it's something I should just let myself feel and stop overthinking—I don't think how *intimate* something is necessarily has much to do with how far into your pants it reaches.

Fuck, I'm about this close to unironically saying *It's about how far it reaches into your heart*, but if I actually did that I really would have to kill myself. And by the direct airlock-walking method instead of the deeply indirect book-a-passage-on-a-doomed-ship-and-fall-in-love-with-too-many-people method.

But even leaving aside my pathological fear of sincerity, heart metaphors have never really been my thing anyway. Sure, I'm prosperity-church not life-church so I learned a lot more economics than biology in school, but even I know that the heart is just a ball of muscle that pumps blood around a sack of meat and gristle. And sure that sack of meat and gristle can be a whole lot of fun if you do the right things with it, but the meatiness and the gristliness never go away.

Intimacy isn't about reaching into your pants *or* reaching into your heart. It's about reaching across time. It's about a touch that you can still feel—really feel, sure as the ice wind on your too-exposed skin—a day or a year or ten years later. It's waking up in the night and realizing that your hands are empty and your bed is empty and you're ugly-crying for what might have been.

It's a silver-white filigree dissolving to nothing between your fingers. It's hands passing across hands as you kneel in a circle with six or ten of your crewmates and do one of the few jobs that drones still can't do.

"We're close now," the Old Ionian voider was saying on one of those occasions. "If she steers us into the Heart then doom is on us. It's that machine to blame, I've no doubt of it."

"The Heart is just a storm, old man," replied the Tall Ganymedian, whose dress had deteriorated since launch. His bottle-green coat was patched with Wyrm leather and half its buttons were replaced with bone. "And everybody knows that storms are where you find the richest pickings."

A hollow-eyed Europan gazed down into the pit of sperm we were all sharing. "If we're doomed, we're doomed. Nothing will change it and all we may do is watch."

"Fie," replied the Old Ionian. He was basically the only person I'd ever heard say *fie* in cold blood but then he was very, very old. "You've spent too long listening to the Deimosi's sermons."

"He hears the voice out of the Heart," said the hollow-eyed Europan. "It warns and it beckons."

"That's the same as doing neither," the Tall Ganymedian pointed out. His hand touched mine beneath the sperm, and neither of us recoiled. For all the talk was growing dire, in this place there was a kind of calm.

A calm you could sink into and lose yourself.

Pandora would anoint her skin with oils, though not so fine as the oils that bathed my skin every day I worked at the sperm vats. The preachers who spoke at me as a child said that they had seen the mind of the Father, but I have touched the mind of a god, felt its thoughts slipping through my fingers and softening the calluses on my palms.

The day Marsh had fallen into the head, the day Q had cut him free, the day we had spent hours on our knees melting fractals into aspersions—that day, we had gone back to our room and fucked with the Leviathan still on our hands, and we had faded into one another like clouds mingling in the skies.

For so long aboard the Pequod I didn't know where I began and she ended. I still don't. As faraway and unreachable as she is.

If I was a different sort of person, probably I'd feel the same way about the whole crew. About the whole of humanity even. After all, are we not all traveling in the same metaphorical ship? Stakeholders in the same metaphorical corporation? Do we not all, in a very real sense, have our hands in the same vat of sperm?

I dunno. Maybe I'm just shallow, but I don't think we do, actually. Locke would sometimes come and squeeze the sperm with us, for the look of the thing, but their masters back on Olympus never would. They wouldn't dream of it. Dawlish and I both had our bodies remade by surgeons who worked for companies who were owned by companies who worked for investors who were owned by companies that were part of Aphrodite Pharma State, and that experience bound us to one another as cleanly as it cut us off from every other fucker. And not one of those surgeons or investors or voting-stock holders on the incorporate councils has a life that even begins to touch mine.

I have been to the sky. You have not. It's okay for us to be different.

We aren't melting together into a vat of undifferentiated sperm, all our dissimilarities revealed as illusions. We're bound together by webs of trust and betrayal and pain and comfort and triumph and humiliation and caring and apathy and life and life and life.

And below the web, the endless void.

And at its heart, monsters.

CHAPTER
FIFTY-NINE

Wolfram and Marsh

After the pirates. Obviously. After Marsh fell. For certain. Otherwise, this could have happened any time. Well, any time before the destruction of the ship and the ignominious death of the entire crew.

I was guarding the captive. The captive that mattered, I mean. There were others but since they didn't have honey on their tongues and silver in their eyes, they were less of a concern. The officers who were still paying attention (maybe two of them? I was never sure about Flint) liked me to guard him because they thought I was too bound up in my own nonsense to fall for his. To give them their due, it was a good read.

Anyway, I was guarding the captive when Marsh slunk up to us, wearing his Leviathan-cock robe (what, you thought that part was satire?). He stood outside the cell just staring at the pirate, his hands on the bars and his eyes empty.

"Want something?" asked Wolfram. It was a disingenuous question because the man loved to talk, and I'd been denying him that for a while now.

"You have a purpose," replied Marsh, more coherent than I'd heard him in months. "The Devouring God has need of you, and you will answer that need."

I'd expected Wolfram to reply cynically. And in a way I

suppose he did. He bowed his head and said, "What purpose may I serve?"

It was an angle. It was obviously an angle. At least, it was obviously an angle to somebody who hadn't nearly drowned in sperm and had their brain invaded by psychic space monsters they mistook for their god. "You may start the avalanche."

"From inside a cell?" Definitely, *definitely* an angle.

"There is a tide in the affairs of men, which, taken at the flood, leads on to fortune."

And there he went again, rambling like, well, like his brain had been invaded by a psychic space monster he mistook for his god.

"You do realize," I told Wolfram, "that he's completely lost it."

"No, madam," replied Marsh, "I do but read madness." And then he left, a song I didn't recognize on his lips.

When he was safely out of earshot, I glared at the pirate. "Let me guess, you're hoping that he and his followers will demand your release and then you and what's left of your men will, what? Seize the ship?"

A smile flirted with Wolfram's lips. "Now why would I have a plan like that? I've just had my old heart stirred by a man of true and uncommon faith."

"And if I tell the captain?"

The smile stopped flirting and moved on to a full-on handjob in the toilets. "Well, I'm in no position to know, being as I am a prisoner who hears only what my guards let slip, but I've a feeling the captain might be a touch preoccupied."

"She sees more than you know."

"Sees too much, if I'm any judge."

The captain was, by any reckoning, old enough and experienced enough to need no defending from me, but you might have noticed that I'm not a particularly rational woman. "You aren't."

"Eloquently put."

I just glared.

"You should hear what the crew say about her, to a man who can do nothing but listen."

He wanted me to ask what. I didn't give him the satisfaction.

"They're split, of course. But not in a way you'd like. Half say she's hunting a monster that will kill us all. The other half say she's wasting time and fuel chasing a myth. As I see it, neither bodes well for her."

Silence was growing more difficult. Not impossible, but more difficult.

"They talk about you too, you know."

I wasn't going to rise to the bait. I wasn't going to rise to the bait. Okay, who was I kidding? "Who?"

"The crew."

This didn't surprise me. Everybody talked about everybody on ship. After all, in a lot of ways we were each other's entire world. I didn't want to know what they said. "What do they say?"

"That you think yourself a philosopher but you're actually full of shit."

That was pretty fair, if I was honest.

"Also that you're a giant whore. Although they say that part with respect."

That checked out as well. Although in my defense most voiders were giant whores. You had to make your own fun in the deep skies and fucking anything that moved was an all-time classic with an extremely low barrier to entry. "And this is supposed to make me abandon my loyalties and join you?"

"This is supposed to pass the time." He gave me a challenging look. "Let me guess, we've just reached the part where you start musing about how passing the time is all any of us are doing. Or how we're all prisoners in our own way. Or how though some of us are behind bars we're all connected by the universal brotherhood of man."

"I might," I replied, determined that he wouldn't make me second-guess myself. "It'd pass the time if nothing else."

Wolfram sat back in his cell, his hands folded behind his head as a flesh-and-bone pillow. "Go on then."

"We're all prisoners in our own way," I said to him, only slightly sardonically.

"Because of, like, the system, man," he replied.

I bit my lip. I wasn't used to being *engaged* with like this and I wasn't sure I liked it. "Saying something in a mocking voice doesn't make it less true. All of us are circumscribed in one way or another."

He scoffed. "Is that it? That's all you can say? *Who ain't a slave? Thus the universal thump is passed around?* It's just words and you know it."

Nevertheless, she persisted. "At least your prison is one you earned. Some of us are born to ours."

"And some have ours thrust upon us?"

The whole don't-let-him-get-to-me plan was failing hard. "Now you're talking like Marsh."

"Your man Marsh makes a lot of sense."

"Like shit he does."

And as though I'd failed some unexplained test, Wolfram gave me a derisive laugh. "That the best you can do?"

"You want me to rebut the arguments of a man who says the Leviathans are speaking to him in his dreams?"

Wolfram's tone was getting increasingly withering. "Can't you? It should be easy, shouldn't it? For somebody with your intellectual pedigree. They say you were once a schoolmistress."

I was beginning to sense traps everywhere, and the part of me that always wanted to run, or to hide, or to throw myself onto the winds and be spread in droplets over ten thousand square miles was getting a powerful urge to retreat. "It was a church school. I didn't need to know much outside the catechism."

"Which catechism?" he asked. And then before I could answer went on, "No, let me guess. Liberty, perhaps? You seemed keen to tell me that my imprisonment was my own fault. Except no"—he was smiling now, a hunter's smile—"because whatever sect you were raised in you don't sound like you *believe* it anymore. If you ever did. *Prosperity* that was your dogma. All is worth what it sells for and the rich are holy."

I didn't flinch, but he reacted as if I had.

"Ah yes, there we have it. I should have known. Bad philosophers are one of Pluto's biggest exports."

"If you're insulting me for a reason," I told him, "just tell me what it is. I'm getting bored with this."

"I'm hoping you'll get frustrated enough that you'll offer to blow me through the bars to shut me up."

That was a particularly painful observation because I'll be honest, I'd considered it. And it made me very uncomfortable to realize how easily this man had worked that out. How transparent it was that sex and suicide were my two default responses to bad situations. "If I wanted to shut you up, I'd be putting something in *your* mouth."

"I bite."

"So do I."

He fixed me with that penetrating gaze of his. "No, you don't. You're too much a coward."

"Try me."

He rose then and walked calmly towards the bars. "Shall I tell you another sense I get from you?"

"If I say no, will it make a difference?"

"I've a sense you're the sort who'll take a cock if there's nothing else, but it's not where your heart lies. And I'm afraid I'm vain enough to want to be wanted for my own sake."

This was going a bunch of places I didn't like. So I pivoted. "I'm going to tell the officers what you're planning."

"Do. No plan worth making relies on secrecy."

He was probably bluffing. Not that there was anything I could do about it in the moment. So instead I turned my back on him and tried not to listen to any more of his whispering.

It didn't entirely work, but I made it to the end of my shift without doing anything I regretted, and at that stage of the voyage, I'd been celebrating far smaller victories.

CHAPTER
SIXTY

Paying the Price

The mutiny didn't happen. Not immediately, anyway, and Wolfram had been infuriatingly right about the captain. I'd told her (and yes, I'd been on my knees at the time, and probably my position hadn't helped my position if you see what I mean), and she'd been all "He seeks to set his will against mine" but it's not like she *did* anything. I told Locke as well (and yes, I also told them in a sex context, I'd been having a bad week and it was that or the razor blades), and they were more attentive but in a very *I'll take that under consideration* kind of way.

Looking back, it's almost quaint that I was concerned at all. There I was, in a tin box with monsters within and without, and I was worried about a few voiders with guns.

Two full years had passed. I think. At the very least it *felt* like two full years had passed. Feels like that looking back. Two full years had passed and we were drawing ever closer now to Hell's Heart. While the hunting was getting better—unquiet skies seemed to bring the beasts out of hiding—the crew were increasingly discontent. More lowerings meant less downtime, and although on an ordinary hunt that would have meant less time to dwell on mutinous thoughts, on this particular voyage it didn't seem to be shaking out that way. We managed to avoid casualties—permanent ones, at least—but the pall that had hung over the entire voyage was growing heavier by the day and somehow even our victories were tasting hollow.

The growth of the Starry Wisdom hadn't helped. Where normally every barrel of sperm we wrung from the skies would remind us of the profits we stood to reap when we got back to shore, between Wolfram's casual reminders about the uneven split of the proceeds and Marsh's constant talk of oblivion, it was hard to take joy in them.

By this point, Marsh's congregation had gotten about as big as it was going to get, but while their numbers had stopped increasing, their activities hadn't. They were growing louder and more influential with every passing day, and those of us who hadn't fallen under his sway were getting more and more annoyed with those who had.

"Will you *please*," the Pretty Vestal was saying over the mess table to one of the acolytes, "just knock it off while people are trying to eat?"

The acolyte, who I thought was Phobosi but I might have just been making assumptions, replied with a look of pious affront. "I'm only telling you how things are."

"What if," I tried, "we all agreed to disagree vis-à-vis the imminent consumption of this ship and by extension the entire cosmos by the Thing That Lies in Wait and focus on getting the boats flight-ready?"

"Get them ready or don't," replied the acolyte. "It will make no difference in the end."

The Pretty Vestal pinched his temples in frustration. "What fucks me off is that you seem so damned happy about it. Like suppose you're actually right and a horrific space monster devours all of humanity, *so what*? What do you get out of it?"

To their very limited credit, the acolyte seemed to genuinely think about this. And to their even more limited credit, it felt like they gave an honest answer. "Vindication."

We didn't get much further because, to everybody's relief, an announcement went over comms that a ship had made contact. Which meant that for the first time in a very long while we were going to get to interact with people we hadn't been stuck with for literal years.

The ship in question was called the Samuel Enderby, and unusually, A insisted on taking a boat out to meet her before our two ships hooked up for the gam proper. This wasn't normally necessary either for practical or social reasons, and it only really happened in emergencies. Although what counted as an emergency aboard the Pequod was anybody's guess.

Since the captain's boat was crewed by a machine intelligence, she didn't particularly need anybody to go over with her. But I was in the hangar anyway running tune-ups, so I was able to persuade her to bring me along.

As a pilot, I found riding as passenger, especially passenger to a machine that would almost certainly have been trained to value my life less highly than the property of Olympus Extraction State, a little unnerving. Then again, feeling unnerved and kind of like a passenger was pretty much my entire life when I was near the captain. All our lives, really. The woman was a great tidal current, a rush of wind that carried us with her like a boat in a purposeful sky.

"They have seen the Beast," she said aloud as we flew across the red-roiling space between our ships.

"They have," replied the intelligence. "Although their navigational data is inconsistent."

"Then I shall speak with their captain, and learn the truth of it," replied A, partly to herself and partly to the intelligence and partly to the sky and whatever lay beyond. "If truth there be in a world of vapors."

Not quite replying, the intelligence kept up its own commentary, so that I felt like I was listening to two soliloquies that occasionally collided. "Their claims are consistent with prediction. If our data is good, the target is within the Heart."

"And so after all these years I shall find you, and though it be the last thing I do I shall wring from you a kind of reckoning."

I was feeling very, very ignored. Of course, my relationship with the captain wasn't exactly a verbal one and since we were outside the ship, we were both dressed in voidsuits which made our usual mode of interaction untenable. For now I contented myself with just sitting and listening to her, and I tried to convince myself that she wasn't talking like somebody who would 100 percent get us all killed.

And when that failed, I tried to convince myself that I didn't like it.

Docking at the Samuel Enderby was more of a pain in the ass than I'd expected it to be, because the captain had singularly failed to tell them we were coming across. The crew were very nice about it anyway, allowing us to land in their hangar and even providing us with stowage for our voidsuits. And when the logistics were dealt with, they escorted us both to the captain's quarters, where we were received cordially by a man with a biomechanical arm and a woman in medical whites.

They introduced themselves to us as Captain Statler and Dr. Waldorf. And the captain introduced herself as she always did.

"Thou said thou hadst seen the Möbius Beast."

Captain Statler, an aging man with a Titanian accent, nodded gravely. "Oh yes." He raised his mechanical arm. "And he gave me this to remember him by."

"I think you'll find *I* gave you that to remember him by," replied Dr. Waldorf. "He just took the one you had originally."

"Well, if we're being precise," retorted Captain Statler, "a wild harpoon line took the one I had originally."

Dr. Waldorf looked over a pair of spectacles she wasn't wearing. "If we're being precise to the point of pedantry, your own poor judgment took the one you had originally."

"That isn't precision, that's censure." Captain Statler let out a long sigh. "You see what I put up with."

Although I had been following all this with the rapt attention necessary to write it down from memory several years later, the captain was less patient. "When?" she asked. "And where? My calculations"—she didn't say *my quasi-legal machine intelligence's calculations* for uncharacteristically sensible reasons—"show that your data are not consistent."

"Not six months back," replied Captain Statler.

"Nearer four," the doctor corrected him.

"It's more, I'm sure it's more."

"Nothing like it."

Statler glowered. "I've had this arm four months. It took you two to build it—"

"Two months? What kind of—"

"But no longer," A interrupted them, a new sense of urgency in her voice. "No longer than six and no less than four."

Neither Captain Statler nor Dr. Waldorf were quite willing to commit to this, but the captain took their disagreement with each other as concord with her.

"And this was in the Heart?"

On that much, at least, they agreed.

"Where?"

On this much, they agreed less.

"Nine thousand spinward, and up," said Captain Statler.

"Counterspinward," insisted Dr. Waldorf. "And down. And twelve thousand not nine."

I was beginning to find this vaudeville routine frustrating, and I wasn't a monomaniac with prophecy on the line. The captain was edging towards frantic. "And you're sure it was the Beast, not some lesser creature you took for it?"

She had been hoping, I'm sure, for a clear and honest *yes*. What she got was more of a *well* . . .

"I'd never even *heard* of the Beast," Captain Statler admitted. "Until after I met it and I went poking around in the ship's archives."

The doctor glanced indulgently in his direction. "Gossiping with the crew more like."

"A bit of both perhaps. But from what I learned then the creature we met was the Beast for certain."

"If it exists," added the doctor skeptically.

Questioning the existence of the monster that had cost her a limb was not a reliable ticket to the captain's good graces. "*If?*" She propped her leg on the captain's desk, her skirts cascading about it like blood from a slashed artery. "Is this not proof enough? Is your own captain's arm not proof enough?"

There was something about the doctor that reminded me of Locke. More playful, perhaps because her relationship with her own captain was older and closer. But in dealing with A she was similarly guarded. "I don't doubt you were both injured, and gravely. But grave injury happens on the hunt. It doesn't mean that the same beast was responsible for both accidents."

"Accidents?" Straightening her biomechanical leg, the captain stepped fully onto Statler's desk, scattering the few personal items he kept there and nearly cracking the screen of his map tablet. "Do you look at this"—she swept her arm in an arc—"and see only *accident?*"

Much like the Pequod, the captain's chamber on the Samuel Enderby had great windows overlooking the void, so the captain's gesture included not only me and Statler and the doctor but also the wreck she was making of the other captain's personal effects and the raging storms of Jove outside the ship.

It felt like a powerful statement, to me at least. But then I was predisposed to think that on account of desperately wanting to fuck her.

"I see chaos, certainly," replied Dr. Waldorf. "Rather more of it than there was ten minutes ago. But I don't mean to offend you, only to point out that you weren't necessarily injured by the same beast."

Disgusted past bearing with the skeptical doctor, the captain turned her gimlet stare fully on Captain Statler. "Describe it."

"Well, I—"

"Describe it."

Statler straightened his rather overstarched dress uniform. "I was just about to. But I need a moment to marshal my thoughts."

The captain's gaze was withering.

"It was . . . very big," he tried.

"Go on."

"And white. Well. Mostly white."

"Mostly?"

I recognized Captain Statler's look. People responded to A in one of two ways: either they hated, resented, and feared her (in roughly equal proportions) or else they became determined to please her. I was distinctly in the second camp, and so was Statler. It probably said terrible things about both of us.

"It might be better to say it *appeared* white," he admitted.

This neither fazed nor impressed the doctor. "All color is appearance."

"Its carapace was, in places, uncommonly smooth, and so it reflected the ship's lights and the clouds. And in other places it was—well, yes—I suppose it was pale. Pale and scored with the scars of many battles I'd say."

The captain was nodding as if this meant something. A tiny, traitorous voice at the back of my mind was telling me it didn't. That she was only hearing what she wanted to hear.

"And was there a harpoon," she asked, "lodged in its larboard flight-membrane?"

It was, by any objective standard, an absurd detail to expect a man to remember from an encounter four to six months earlier that had cost him a limb. But being as desperate for the captain's approval as I was—okay, *slightly less* desperate for the captain's approval than I was—he gave her the most calculated-to-please answer he could. "It . . . it may have?"

Springing down from the desk, a captain was an image of triumph. She took Statler by the shoulders and shook him in what I thought was probably gratitude. "There now, that lance you saw was mine, and the beast you saw was the Beast for certain."

I wasn't sure I agreed, but I had just enough common sense not to say so.

"Then it seems we are done?" offered Dr. Waldorf rather curtly. "We will of course update our navigational data to reconcile any of these . . . irregularities that are so concerning you. But as I'm sure you understand, skies shift."

The captain was ignoring her. As for that matter was her own captain. No longer being shaken, he now had his own hands on A's shoulders and was looking up at her in a way I tried really hard not to identify with. "You'll stay," he said, "for the rest of the gam? It would be my honor to host you at my table."

And I *also* tried not to identify too hard with his disappointment when she turned away from him wordlessly and swept out, leaving me to scurry after her.

CHAPTER SIXTY-ONE

The Shrine

As disappointed as Captain Statler was by the abrupt withdrawal of A's attention, the rest of the gam went well. For a day or so, the crew forgot the several shadows that were hanging over our voyage and we indulged ourselves in the usual round of song circles and causal hookups that characterized the meeting of two hunter-ships.

Of course, the fact that our crew was increasingly succumbing to a nihilistic star cult did make things ever so slightly awkward sometimes, but to my (and the other noncultist crew members') great relief, it turned out that a lot of Marsh's followers got a whole lot less fanatical once you gave them something to distract them. Plus the Samuel Enderby had a good supply of algal wine, so we all managed to get pleasantly fucked off our heads.

But the bonhomie was never going to last. We said our farewells to the Samuel Enderby and steered on towards the Heart. And as we did, the old-new tensions crept back, and the crew once more watched each other with suspicious eyes.

And to think we'd been happily squeezing sperm together only a few days earlier.

I'm not a sociologist or a psychologist (and as Wolfram observed, I'm actually kind of a shitty philosopher), so I can't quite put my finger on what made things get so much darker in the weeks we sailed the southern tropics. But possibly the fact that Marsh built a giant fuck-off temple out of Leviathan bone and offal might have had something to do with it.

The voyage had, in many ways, been a long and successful one, so the hold—and hunter-barques were mostly hold—was getting less and less full of provisions and more and more full of barrels, each brimming over with precious spermaceti. And under a captain with more of an eye on the voyage and less of an eye on her obsessive crusade of vengeance against the abstract concept of an indifferent cosmos, the remaining space would have been kept rigorously clear so that we could fill it with yet *more* spermaceti as we slew yet more monsters.

But we didn't have a captain like that, we had *our* captain. And she wasn't one for details. So when storage bay nineteen was rearranged into a gore-strewn temple to oblivion it went largely unremarked upon.

Well, unremarked upon by her.

"It's bad enough that she's brought a machine intelligence aboard," Locke told Flint. The conversation took place in their office, where I'd been for . . . unrelated reasons. Unrelated reasons of fucking. "Now she's letting a death cult set up shop in one of the storage bays."

"Freedom of religion," Flint insisted. "I'll not be part of any action that tells people who they can and can't pray to."

Locke gave him a profoundly skeptical look. "Even if their prayer involves smearing the lower decks with waste organic matter?"

Flint eased his everyday-carry pistol from its holster and began turning it over idly in his hands. He did that a lot when he was nervous. Or bored. Or really just whenever. "The way I see it, ain't none of our business."

"The storage bay is ship's property. As, come to that, is the waste matter."

The Church of Liberty set great store by property rights. But it was a toss-up who they'd assign those rights to. "Come on, picking up waste's a perk of the hunt. Always has been." To illustrate the point, he fished a little scrimshander token from his pocket and flicked it across the desk. "They've got a use for the beast gut, let them keep it."

"And what if it contaminates the sperm? Bay nineteen isn't empty."

"You know as well as I do, them barrels is sealed so tight a wasp's tarse couldn't get in."

"They can be opened," warned Locke. "I'm not sure I trust Marsh around the cargo after his . . . experience."

It didn't take much to make Flint laugh, and this wasn't much. "What do you think he's going to do? Drink it?"

"You say that like it's beyond the realm of possibility."

Flint leaned forwards, laid his pistol on his lap, and latticed his fingers together. "You know, I'm beginning to think you just don't like religious people."

"The Church of Starry Wisdom isn't *like* most religious people."

To that, Flint responded with a dismissive shrug. "At least they believe in something."

I wasn't sure I cared for that as an answer. For a start, the *something* the Starry Wisdomers believed in was literally nothingness given form, and calling that *something* was at least half a paradox.

"They're a destabilizing influence. And the Father knows we've enough of those on board already."

Flint gave half a smile. "Careful, Locke. That's dangerous talk."

"The captain knows my feelings. Reminding the other officers that this obsession of hers is growing ever more troubling to the crew isn't mutiny. It's my job."

"The crew will settle down with a few more kills. And if we bag the Möbius Beast, that'll settle 'em down for good."

"Settling us all down for good," replied Locke gnomically, "is *exactly* what I'm concerned the Beast will do."

Flint, with typical apathy, shrugged this off entirely.

And while Locke tried in vain to get any other officer to

give a shit about the cult in the cargo bay, which (since the captain was locked in her cabin communing with an artificial mind, Flint was religiously mandated to give zero fucks about anything his church hadn't randomly decided to have a strong opinion on, and Truelove was a fully paid-up apocalypse cultist) didn't seem likely, I wandered down to bay nineteen to look for myself.

Q came with me, as she often did. Partly out of curiosity, I suspected, and partly for my safety. She had a comfortably low opinion of my ability to defend myself.

The Temple of the Coming End was, in some ways, a marvelous sight. Not *marvelous* in the sense of *good*, you understand, but *marvelous* in the sense of *to be marveled at*. Marsh and his congregation had rearranged the barrels that, before they moved in, had filled about a quarter of the bay and built them into a reasonable facsimile of devotional architecture. Two great columns of them stood for pillars, and row after row of them took the place of pews. At the back of the chamber, a great stacked block of them, topped with Leviathan bone and strewn with skin and meat and gristle, played the part of the altar.

In a lot of ways, it reminded me of home.

From the ceiling, high above us, a whole Leviathan skull hung from thick cables. I wasn't quite sure how Marsh's lot had gotten hold of it—it wasn't worth much by itself but skulls usually got broken down for scrimshander plates—and could only imagine how long it must have taken to haul the thing up here, because there was no elevator that ran the full way.

"Et venerunt in locum qui dictur Golgotha," whispered Q beside me, "quod est Calvariae locus."

Something about the whole place felt wrong. I mean, I say *something*. Something other than the bones and viscera all over the place. Like there was a whispering at the back of my mind that I couldn't quite block out. Voiders sometimes said that the sperm sang to them when it was gathered in large quantities and I've never believed it, partly because I could never quite stop laughing long enough to work out if it might be true. But here in Marsh's shrine of guts, I could almost hear the song myself. And I was keen to get out of there as soon as possible.

Unfortunately, Marsh and Truelove had other ideas.

"I didn't think to find you here, sister," said Truelove, who I could have sworn wasn't behind me when I walked in but was now.

"A sister driven into desperate terms," Marsh added, looking past me into the darkness.

"Just seeing what you were about," I offered, but it sounded weak even to me.

Truelove looked down at me with a fearful benediction. "We would welcome you, if you chose to come to us. As we would welcome all, even the lowliest."

"Lowliest?" I asked—he could have meant several things, none of them good.

"I have petitioned the captain to release the pirate and his followers," Truelove clarified. Because of course he had. Because that was going to end so well. "Even now our people bring him to the chapel for his anointing."

"Anointed," Marsh echoed, "crowned, planted many years . . ."

And that, that was something I couldn't not see.

So I waited in a converted storage bay full of rotting not-exactly-meat while a group of deckhands led a pirate to kneel before a man whose only qualification to lead was that he'd fallen into a bucket of alien brain goo that made him talk weird.

Honestly, it was no stranger than any other religious ceremony I've been to.

Wolfram swore on his life and his name and everything he held dear—which I privately suspected wasn't very much—to keep a bunch of promises that he certainly didn't intend to keep, and that his erstwhile crewmates would do the same. Then he had his shirt manhandled off by two of Marsh's acolytes, to be replaced with a Leviathan-skin robe (was it cock skin? Maybe. Or maybe that was just a joke, you'll need to join the hunt yourself to know for sure) and then to have his head marked with a thick slurry of the Leviathan's intestinal juices.

Q watched the proceedings with polite confusion. I wondered if she assumed all Exodites behaved like this. I suppose in many ways she wouldn't have been wrong. Sometimes, when I watch a ceremony like the one that was then playing out in bay nineteen (okay not *literally* like that, but any ceremony from a faith I wasn't raised in), I remind myself that as unusual as it appears to me it probably makes complete sense to the people inside it. Except, honestly, that's not been my experience.

I'm not saying my experience is universal, or even typical, but as alienating as other people's customs have always felt, my own have felt worse. And sure, these were recent converts, so probably they were at least somewhat convinced of the theology. But I couldn't imagine none of them had doubts. That none of them felt even a twinge of the uncertainty I always had. The hollow ache that says *Why doesn't this feel more right?*

Then again, it was a nihilistic apocalypse cult. Maybe hollowness was the point. Maybe it was the appeal.

Maybe in another world I'd have joined them. Except I'd already picked my destroyer-god, and she was in her cabin poring over her charts.

The ceremony complete, the celebrants dispersed and Wolfram, to my mild surprise, allowed himself to be escorted back to his cell.

I shouldn't have been surprised at all. He wasn't planning to stay there long.

CHAPTER SIXTY-TWO

A Comparative Theology of Leviathanism

I know, I know, it's chapter sixty-two and things are just getting good and here she is on another tangent.

If it helps, imagine me narrating this bit while I get railed hard from behind by a drunk space pirate.

So far I've mostly restricted these long, unfashionable expository segments to explaining the mechanics of the hunt; you've probably never seen a Leviathan yourself, you've almost certainly never hunted one, any images you may have seen will have been generated by neural networks trained on badly flawed datasets and even if that weren't the case you'd still not understand the beasts the way those of us who've fought them do. So I've tried in my flawed, erratic, occasionally hyperfixated way to give you some sliver of a part of a fraction of what it's like to be where I've been and to do what I've done. What so many people I knew died doing.

But from here on out, we also need to talk about the religious side. Because it's going to matter.

Marsh and his crowd of the desperate and forgotten aren't the first to feel a near spiritual awe at the sight of the Leviathan. Hell, people have been worshiping creatures like this since before they even knew they existed. Our records of Old Earth are patchy (much was lost in the wars before the Exodus, and much more was purged as heresy or discarded as an inefficient use of resources, which, in my own faith, is the far greater sin) but remnants remain, and echoes. I've seen references to Dagon and to Hydra, to the Kraken—the beast which gave the modern, Jovian creatures their common name—and to Leviathan itself.

The name *Leviathan* features in the catechism, along with *whale*, which is a less figurative term and refers to an Earth beast long since extinct. We know nothing about the whale now, except that it must have been physiologically capable of swallowing a man and his raft, and its digestive processes must have been slow in the extreme.

At my university, I studied a speculative anatomical diagram of the beast and I still remember every detail. The wide mouth, the cavernous throat, the many-chambered stomach which bloomed with oxygen-generating gut flora. (How else could Jonah have breathed for so long?) The male, it was said, had a long, barbed tail that it would use to fight for mates while the female—perhaps a third of its size—had a great pouch on its back for carrying its young.

It's wonderful, isn't it, how much we can learn about such a long-vanished creature using only modern science, revealed truth, and logic.

Within the Church of Prosperity, the extinction of the whales of Old Earth is considered an object lesson in stewardship. The whale, so I was taught as a child and so I argued again in one of my better-received second-year essays, was granted to Man alongside all the rest of the bounty of land and sea, to husband wisely and in accordance with the catechism. But some time in the Dark Days, foolish people rebelled against this sacred charge and campaigned to stop the whale from being hunted. This, the Father took as a great insult and He decreed that since humanity no longer wished to take the bounty of the whale that had been granted unto us, He took it back.

And so the whale is no more. Not even Q has ever seen one, for they ceased to be a thousand years before she was born.

While *whale* is the more common term in the language of Old Earth, the hunter-fleet, those parts of it that follow the Three Churches at least, take great pride in the fact that the Leviathan is also most definitely called out by name. All three faiths agree that it's mentioned no less than five times, although, in a strange quirk of theological dynamics, nobody is quite sure what the fifth is.

Many a hunter-barque has inscribed, somewhere about it, the words of the seventy-fourth psalm: "You it was who cracked the skull of the Leviathan and spread its blood like rains upon the desert." And many is the preacher who has highlighted the prophetic power of this passage, which, though it was written long before the hunt rose as an industry, contains clear references to the life-giving properties of spermaceti and its vital role in sustaining our colonies in the uninhabitable parts of the cosmos.

So you see, it isn't a surprise that Leviathans figure so deeply in Marsh's weird little death cult. They're a powerful, mysterious species. In the great hierarchy of living creatures they are, in a very literal sense, god-tier.

There. The expository aside is over. If you were imagining the pornographic version, assume that whoever was doing me has pulled out a fraction early and sprayed hot jism over my back, and that I have crept back to my bunk hollow and ashamed.

CHAPTER
SIXTY-THREE

The Lock

The word *Leviathan* appears in five different parts of the catechism, and there were at least five different shadows hanging over the Pequod as we flew inexorably towards Hell's Heart. Some of these were obvious: the worsening weather, the risk of mutiny, the fact that we were hunting a monster who might not exist and if he did exist had definitely killed a whole mess of people. The tiny matter of the captain being, in many people's assessment, out of her goddamned mind. Little things like that.

But the shadow I've not mentioned much, not since it was first set up, was the shadow of the lock.

You might remember, before all the philosophizing and fucking and monster-slaying, that when the captain first revealed herself and her plan to the crew, she pledged her entire share of the ship's take to the first person who called out for the great Beast. And a captain's share was substantial, especially in a voyage as prosperous as ours was turning out to be. Even my exceedingly long lay was shaping up to be enough to keep Aphrodite off my back for a good few years.

Ever since that day, it had sat there, the crypto-lock glowing its faint golden light, even after nightfall. And every so often (we are back, reader, in that nonchronological never-place where events are organized by theme and not by what strictly happened when) one or other of the crew would walk up to the lock and stare at it.

It'd be strange, wouldn't it, if when they stared they spoke their thoughts aloud.

Even stranger if I managed to overhear each and every one.

And remembered them well enough to write them down years later in my memoir-manifesto-memorial.

"There you stand," said the captain, examining her handiwork. "A ring of gold that is formed of light and greed and mathematics. There is meaning in that, perhaps, if there is meaning in anything. For what is realer than wealth and what is wealth but numbers agreed upon? And the mathematicians tell us that it is only their laws that truly exist."

Her voice was discordant music to me. I knelt in her cabin and felt her hand cold on my throat, her lips warm on my shoulders, where her scrimshawed canes had stung me.

"That," said Flint later—or earlier—or both—"is a whole lot of fucking money. Of course, I'll make my own pile from this trip well enough, so it's not as though I'll *need* it. Then again, who *needs* money? As long as you've your wits and your strength and a gun or two, nothing can touch you and you'll want for nothing neither."

In case you were thinking there'd be a pattern here, I never fucked Flint. I'm sure he'd be fine, but I only went for officers if they were actually my type, or if I was very drunk, or if I thought it was expected of me. And Flint did an amazing job of wanting nothing from anybody. It was the one quality I admired in the man.

Wolfram, of course, did not take his turn standing before the array and staring at the lock until far, far later in the voyage. Only once Marsh had arranged his release and that of his followers. Only once he'd set his own plans into motion was he free to stand and stare and muse as so many others had done. "A lock is it?" he began. "I'll give the captain this, if she's mad then she's fox-mad and no mistake. The difference between me and the rest of the crew is I admit that greed is all as drives me, while they play coy about it. And the captain, well, she knows that well enough. If the crew joins with me and takes the ship, they'll each of them make far more than they've been promised if they stay loyal. But *this*"—the lock swirled bright in front of his eyes—"this is more than any fair share, more even than the captain's share on a freebooter's vessel." He fell silent, considering. "Oh yes, this is a lock all right. And the captain has locked me away from my strongest weapon, for she's played on the crew's greed far stronger than I'm able."

As the row of watchers passed, the ship sailed on through deepening storms. The clouds were white here, blinding white and opaque about the hull so that we flew by instruments alone, and sometimes saw strange visions and faces beyond the observation dome.

In the mess one evening, Dawlish brought the lock up on a handheld terminal and stared at it. "What do you think?" he asked me.

"What do *I* think?" I echoed. It wasn't meant to work this way. "What is there *to* think?"

"It's more money than you'd make in six voyages," Dawlish pointed out. "You must have thought what you'd do with it."

Across the table, the Tall Ganymedian smiled. "What would be the point? The money goes to the one who raises the great Beast, and she's not raised a single spout yet. She uses her time on the array to nap."

Just for completeness, I didn't fuck Dawlish. Or the Tall Ganymedian. I'm usually a sucker for a tall Ganymedian but can only really put up with them in small doses.

"If *I* raised the monster," the Tall Ganymedian went on, "well, I'd probably go home, blow half of it on the longest bath I've ever had, and then treat myself to some new gloves."

It was a materialistic response. But without wishing to overly stereotype, the Ganymedians were a materialistic people. Then again, the Church teaches that materialism is the same as godliness, so in a way it's not even an insult.

Dawlish was giving me a challenging look. "We still haven't had your answer."

I'd have thrown the comment straight back at him, but I knew by this point that he was working an indentured sentence, so any bounty he earned would just go straight to his creditor-jailers. "Nothing special," I said. "I'd pay down debt. Maybe invest a little if I had any left over."

The Old Ionian laughed (I never fucked him either, in case you were wondering). "Young folk today, I swear, none of you know how to *dream*. Odds are the money will never be yours. Even if you spot the Beast the captain's not bound to keep her word. And if the money will never be yours anyway, why are you all being so *sensible* with it?"

"If it will never be ours, why does it matter if we're sensible or not?" countered the Tall Ganymedian.

And that made the Old Ionian roll his eyes and sigh the way only the old can sigh at the young. "Because it means you've forgotten what hope feels like."

"Now, now." Dawlish smiled cynically at him. "You can't forget something you've never had."

"If *I* had that money," the Old Ionian went on, largely ignoring Dawlish, "I'd buy a castle in the clouds."

"You mean a hab-platform in the upper atmosphere of Saturn?" I replied.

The Old Ionian's eyes twinkled, and thinking back on that makes me almost regret never fucking him. "Ah, but to *me* it would be a castle in the clouds. And that's what matters."

Elsewhere and elsewhen, Locke stared at the spiraling icon on the array.

"On the one hand, it's a bribe. And that's good—bribable people are rational people and rational people won't willingly sail on a doomed ship." Then they stopped and looked again. "On the other hand, it's a symbol. And that's far worse. People have been throwing their lives away for symbols for centuries. Millennia. Even in the dark days of Old Earth. So perhaps the money was just the bait, a way for the captain to sink her hooks into the crew's souls. Or perhaps it was a shiny trinket, a distraction like the rattling of keys to keep their minds off her true purpose. If so, she has competition now, for the star cult is growing stronger by the day. And to my shame I do not know which is the greater threat to this vessel."

We had similar conversations between ourselves, on the rare nights Locke was tired or frustrated enough to take me to bed. Part of the reason I spent less time aboard the Pequod trying to get into Locke's pants than, say, the captain's is that they had this infuriating habit of wanting me to *talk* to them. Which was basically the opposite of what I wanted in a sexual partner.

"I trust her," I remember saying, when Locke point-blank refused to let me go down on them until I'd given an opinion. "She's intense and she's driven and she's carrying a fuck ton of hurt but she knows what she's doing."

Locke had reflected on this at frankly annoying length. "She did, certainly. And she always had a tremendous will. But I worry that her will has come into conflict with her good sense, and that is a fight her good sense cannot win."

At the array, with rheumy, unblinking eyes, Marsh looked at the captain's mark. "Money is a good soldier," he whispered, "and if money were as certain as your waiting, 'twere sure enough. But no, the dreadful trumpet sounds the general doom and we unburthen'd crawl towards death."

It should go without saying, but I never fucked Marsh, before his incident or after.

Last of all, after I had built her coffin, and she'd rebuilt it to be more to her liking, and after that whole weird affair had been mostly forgotten, Q stood before the array and raised her little black-glass idol to the lock.

What she said I did not hear.

And I will not put words in her mouth.

CHAPTER SIXTY-FOUR

The Last Storm

I've not really written about the storms we faced on the Pequod. There hasn't been time or space for it, and they were so frequent and, in their way, so alike that to talk about one of them is to talk about all of them.

So I'm going to talk about the last.

You might have a question here. You might ask me, *Hold on, isn't the last storm Hell's Heart itself, that's a storm by definition.* And I suppose in a way you're right.

Except what *is* a storm?

To have a storm, you need an atmosphere. And gas giants are *all* atmosphere. But that's exactly the issue. A great poet of Old Earth once said that fish had no word for water, and so we, since we evolved—sorry, I of course mean since we were created to participate in the bounty of prosperity—on a terrestrial world we have no easy word for the great slow phenomena that shape continents.

We have language for it, of course. Language is endlessly flexible. We can talk about tectonic activity and continental drift. But we never look down at our feet and say, "Wow there's a lot of subduction happening today."

"But that's the difference," you might be saying. "Those kinds of things only happen slowly, whereas the weather changes all the time."

And I would say I agree.

Which brings me back to my initial question: What's a storm?

If we understand weather by its temporariness, then the storms of Jupiter aren't weather at all. They're places. Vast, permanent places. Or permanent enough. Some are only as long-lived as people, others as lasting as empires. On a gas world, a storm is like what I imagine an Old Earth forest must have been (and it's a limited imagination, based on what Q has managed to explain). Something ancient and wild and indifferent that was there long before you or me and will be there long after.

What makes a storm feel like a storm is that you pass through it. Hell's Heart itself is a world of red unending chaos. To call it a storm makes as much sense as calling an ocean a flood or a desert a drought. Which means that the storm I'm about to describe was the *last* storm we faced on that hunt, before we went to a place where storms stopped having meaning.

"You can't take us that way," Locke was saying to the captain. "Not with the hull still weakened from the breach."

The captain was agate-eyed and tranquil in her reply. "You have our bearing, and you have your orders. The hull will be bolstered but I will not delay. Not with the end so close."

"The *end* is when we return to Europa with a full hold and divide our take according to our contracts," replied Locke in the exasperated tones of somebody who knows they're dealing with a fanatic and is tactfully trying not to admit it.

Except that wasn't the whole of it. There was sorrow beneath the frustration. The deep and quiet sorrow of not knowing if you were talking to a woman you used to love, or a monster wearing her face.

But the captain's reply gave no clue one way or the other. "Fix weathering plates," she commanded. "We continue."

So with their usual diligence, Locke set about seeing the hull reinforced with the makeshift upgrades we euphemistically called *weathering plates*. More cynical hunters called them *cope panels*. It meant maintenance crews working around the clock and that, in turn, pulled eyes off the array in ways that could have cost us the sight of spouts but, since the captain was likely to order they be ignored anyway, it was probably the best decision tactically speaking.

When my time on the maintenance crew came, Q and I descended on long cables with a selection of tools in our belts and a hopper of spare parts beside us.

By that point I'd been outside of the ship a hundred times, and in all manner of what in other contexts would be called weather. But this was something else. The captain was guiding us now into the anticyclonic corona of the Heart, and here the winds whipped us with such ferocity that we needed to have our welding gauntlets clamped onto our arms to make any use of them at all.

Had I been working with anybody else, one or the other of us would have felt the need to say something. To make some kind of comment on the harshness of the conditions and how fucking typical it was that we'd been stuck with this job, which—and voiders made this observation about anything we were asked to do—was undoubtedly the worst on the ship.

It wasn't like that with Q. I'd learned to understand enough of her language, and of the deliberately slow, staccato way she spoke Exodite, that we could communicate verbally perfectly well. And I was increasingly sure she understood every word anybody said and just chose on most occasions not to respond. But usually we reveled in the language of silence and the dialogue of bodies. Whether working or fucking, we moved with a synchronicity I've never found before or since and have never admitted that I was looking for and am still looking for. Well, never admitted until the exact moment I wrote those words.

Perhaps eventually I'll stop associating love with death. But the catechism taught me well and if it's good enough for the Father and his appointed Son, surely it's good enough for the rest of us.

You might remember one of the things that first drew me to the Pequod was that its exterior was all decked out in Leviathan bone. At the time I'd thought this was a style choice.

And in defense of that assumption, the captain really *was* extra as fuck and so it probably was at least a small factor in her decision-making. But I was belatedly realizing that it was also just a feature of the ship being old and often repaired.

Hunter-barques carry a lot of shit with them. Like a *lot* of shit. As the voyage goes on they swap this shit out, on a more or less one-for-one basis, with barrels of sperm, which is how they're able to both carry enough supplies for a three-year voyage and also bring back enough cargo for the trip to be worth making. But as much shit as they carry, there are some things you can't have that many spares of, and gigantic fuck-off plates of void-hardened steel are one of those things. Volume-wise they don't take up a ton of space. You could probably pack dozens of them into a single cargo bay—at least if it hasn't been converted into a temple—but they're unwieldy and dense as hell so they add a lot of weight to a vessel that needs to operate in a variety of gravities and be VTOL capable.

So instead, a lot of hunter-barques fix themselves—and make dodgy, probably barely functional upgrades to themselves—with the carapaces of their slain enemies.

Leviathan bone, or Leviathan carapace (they seem to be made of similar materials but since I'm neither a biologist nor a materials scientist I won't speculate), is by its very nature designed (intelligently designed, of course, by the Father who in his infinite wisdom put them on a planet light-minutes from Earth millennia before humans even knew what a planet was, aware that we'd eventually need them and find them, truly Providence is wise) to survive in the atmosphere of Jupiter. And since the Leviathans swim at all depths, from skimming the sea to basking in the distant light of the sun, they're also naturally radiation resistant.

Of course actually fusing bone to metal was a pain in the ass, but over the centuries the hunter-fleet had developed specialized tools for the job. So there Q and I clung, with winds that our species was never meant to face whipping past us.

Side by side, we spat white-hot sparks from welding blades to conjoin the ship and the monster at the atomic level in the hope that this would make it safe for us to sail her into nightmares.

Well, safe-ish. The ship's new armor would stand the storms well enough. But the storm wasn't what we were chasing.

CHAPTER SIXTY-FIVE
Wolfram's Move

The storm lasted days. Or rather the storm lasted years but we traveled through it for days. Standard days, I should say, not the short Jovian days, which as I think I've mentioned ran little more than ten hours.

Sound is strange on a ship.

If, like me, you lived most of your life in the outer worlds, you'll have been born and will have grown up and will someday die in a glass-and-crystal bubble with hard vacuum—or whatever stray molecules pass for atmosphere on your home body—all around you. Stand by the walls of your dome and you'll hear nothing from outside unless some piece of debris drops into a decaying orbit and strikes it. At which point you might then hear the rush of escaping air and, quite possibly, your own screams as a standard atmosphere of pressure all at once blows you through the cracking surface into frozen, oblivious death.

But on a ship, an *atmospheric* ship, not an interwell one, you're surrounded at all times by matter, as tangible as the air your life-support systems pump into your module. And matter carries sound.

It's muted, of course. The observation dome of a hunter-barque, like the protective dome of a hab-city, needs to be reinforced and insulated or all kinds of terrible things might happen. But when the winds pass 250 miles per hour, even a muted version of their roaring is pretty fucking noticeable. Especially because sometimes—with just the right combination of windspeed and trajectory and skipped repair cycles—they can set a resonance somewhere in the hull and so you'll hear a banging and a cracking throughout the ship, like some great monster is attacking it.

Or at least what you'd imagine some great monster attacking it would sound like. As somebody who's been aboard a ship when a great monster actually did attack it, the sounds you hear then aren't very much like the wind at all.

That's the problem with similes. They sometimes only work if you're ignorant of one half of them.

Where was I? Ah yes, the winds. Even three years into the journey, I walked the decks a lot. The views never ceased to overawe me, and I'd come to the skies precisely because I wanted to be overawed. Or at least to have overawing as a consistent option. And that meant I was on the deck when the deputation came.

Since Wolfram—and several of his less-loquacious companions—had been anointed into the Sect of the Starry Wisdom, things had gotten complicated. He was, technically, still a prisoner, but while Locke had at least managed to arrange for the Wisdomers never to be alone on guard duty, they hadn't managed to stop him from extending a pernicious influence over the crew, even from behind bars.

There was no single tipping point. At first, it was just an aesthetic shift. Starry Wisdom iconography began showing up in more and more parts of the ship. That was bad enough in itself because they'd increasingly embraced blood and viscera as artistic media, and while regular head counts of the crew and spot DNA checks by Dr. Pierce confirmed that they at least weren't using *human* blood or viscera, it didn't make for a particularly pleasant working environment.

Then there were the gatherings. The cultists were more likely to move in groups now, and to share talking points not just on theology, which they always had, but on shipboard policy. They started to agitate for things to happen.

And the first thing they agitated to have happen was for Wolfram and his companions to be released.

Marsh and Truelove and some twenty of their followers, robed in Leviathan leather or bloody polymers, came to the deck in force and descended, while I watched from the shadows, upon the captain's cabin.

Since the captain's cabin was biometrically locked and the door was inch-thick steel, this didn't turn as immediately disastrous as it might have. They demanded she come out via intercom and then, with a surprising amount of restraint for an Armageddon cult, waited for her to emerge.

She could have just stayed below and hoped they'd get bored, and if she'd been in a different mood or if her machine intelligence had been saying something particularly interesting to her (which, I'd learned by then, in practice meant something that particularly reinforced a position she already agreed with), she probably would have.

But they'd caught her on a good day. Or a bad one. Depending on your perspective.

After a mere five or six minutes, the doors to her cabin opened and she rose—like Venus from the waves if you're feeling classical, like a beast from the sea if you're feeling more ominous—and ascended the short stairway to the deck, where the deputation from the Cult of the Devouring God pressed in close around her.

She didn't ask them what they wanted. She didn't berate them for disturbing her. She didn't really say anything. She just stood and waited and watched Truelove—Truelove, I noticed, not Marsh—with her gaze steady and her expression impassive.

"It is not for prisoners to be too silent in their words," said Marsh, his voice soft but carrying even over the storm.

With the captain still looking exclusively at him, Truelove translated: "You're keeping members of the flock hostage. We'll stand it no longer."

I expected a reply from the captain here. I didn't get one.

"Brother Wolfram," Truelove went on. "He has repented his evil ways and embraced the teachings of the Church, as have several other former members of his boarding party."

Once more the captain responded with silence.

"We demand they be released into our care."

None of the crowd were armed exactly. But the life of a voider is a busy one and hardly a minute goes by when we aren't fixing something or opening something or cutting something apart. So while they weren't armed a lot of them had . . . tools. Tools that could fuck a person up royally if they had to. Or if they wanted to.

This didn't seem to faze the captain. She just nodded, chased the ghost of a smile, and then said, "Then let us speak with them."

I followed her, and the crowd that was going with her, down to the brig. Wolfram was lounging on his cot, watching the assembly with a detached expression that read to me as smug.

"These fine people ask that you be released," the captain told him.

"Let it never be said," replied Wolfram, "that I stood in the way of giving the people what they want." Then he shot a wary eye at Truelove and added piously, "Although in the end it makes no odds. The Devourer comes for us all regardless, does it not?"

"Some to the common pulpits," said Marsh in his usual low and distant tone, "and cry out 'Liberty, freedom, and enfranchisement.'"

The captain pressed the switch on the nearest intercom. "Captain to central, open the brig."

For a moment there was nothing. Then, "Central; request confirmation," followed by Locke's voice saying, "Belay that."

"Belay nothing," demanded the captain. "Open the—"

She was cut off by Locke again. "You *surely* cannot have decided to set a gang of pirates loose on the ship."

"We're about to enter the Heart," the captain replied with a certainty that, had I been one of Marsh's cultists, I would have found concerning. "We will need every good hand."

This, to Locke, was a terrible answer. "They *aren't* good hands. They're thieves, traitors, scoundrels, and vagabonds."

In his cell, Wolfram raised his hands in a you-got-me gesture. "I'm all that and more," he admitted. "But I know my way around a ship and I'm a fair pilot and"—he smiled like a serial killer—"I've seen the Truth of Endings, so I've no longer got any ambitions you need worry about."

I'd love to believe that I was the kind of woman who could speak truth to power. Who would grab Truelove by the shoulders and shake him and say something like *This man is obviously playing you*. But who am I kidding, that's not me and never has been. Besides, why would he believe me? At the end of the day, people are like clouds. We see the shapes in them we want to see.

"Orders?" came the query from Central.

And the captain, without hesitation, repeated, "Open the brig."

After all that buildup, I'd half expected the consequences to be explosive. They weren't. And what, realistically, had I thought would happen? That Wolfram would burst out of the cell and tear the captain's neck open with his teeth? That he'd yell "Yaharr me hearties, I be in charge now"?

So many of my expectations of the voyage, looking back, were a child's expectations. The stuff of bedtime stories and pulp novels. The reality was so much stranger and wilder and quieter and louder and more boring and more terrible.

The doors opened, and Wolfram stood, stretched, and walked out into the waiting arms of his new coreligionists, and then they went calmly to the cells of the other redeemed corsairs, and let them out as well.

They made no move that day.

CHAPTER SIXTY-SIX

The Chief Engineer

The Pequod had over a hundred crew. And if I'm honest with myself, although I like to pretend, sometimes, that I remember each one of their faces, their voices, the touch of the ones who touched me, most of them blur together. Even the officers I tend to get mixed up in retrospect, because there are a *lot* of officers on a ship. After all, an officer is just somebody who fills an office and an office is just something that needs doing. And so many, many things need doing when you're deep in unforgiving skies, trying to kill gods.

You might notice, for example, that I've barely described the ship's doctor. I was never ill on the voyage and while I spoke to her semiregularly because my reconfigurative implants needed some maintenance, we had a distant relationship and I never paid her much mind outside of official interactions. I thought of her most when Q lay dying and then it was definitely Q I was thinking about, not the doctor, although honestly at the time I tried not to think about either of them.

Have I mentioned lately how selfish and cowardly I am?

I think the other reason I don't remember the doctor is that I never really made much of an effort to fuck her. I'm just not much into redheads.

The chief engineer, however, was a different matter. Not that I tried to fuck him either, because he also wasn't my type. I'm a bit concerned at this late stage that I might have given the impression that I slept with the entire crew of the ship, and I really didn't. Low double digits at best, and most of that was hand stuff. But while I wasn't interested in him sexually, the chief engineer did at least stand out to me, partly because towards the end of the voyage (the actual end, not the scheduled end—the scheduled end, after all, included a return trip) the captain sent me to make a request of him.

He also stood out because like the captain, like Dawlish, and like me, his body had been rebuilt by the good people of Aphrodite Pharma State. Or at least by somebody who bought their supplies under license from somebody who bought their supplies under license from Aphrodite Pharma State. There are no truly independent biosculptors anymore.

The violent redistribution of a person's bodily tissues was an occupational hazard of the hunt, and after a long career, Lobscouse—that was his name, or possibly his nickname, I've never quite worked it out—had been more redistributed than most. Over a series of unlucky voyages (or lucky voyages, depending on whether you measure luck in flesh lost or wealth gained) the skies had taken both his eyes, both his hands, his lower jaw, and several of his internal organs.

What I found even more interesting was the choices he had made regarding his reconstruction. The captain's leg, although clearly prosthetic, was primarily designed as a leg. Dawlish's various parts, cheap and prison-issue as they were, were primarily intended as one-for-one replacements. The parts of my body that I'd had altered, I'd had altered almost entirely because of form rather than function.

Lobscouse had taken a different approach. When he'd lost his hands, he'd had them replaced with a writhing mass of independently articulated tendrils, each capable of manipulating tiny objects with incredible precision. When he'd lost his guts, he'd had them replaced with a more efficient system of chemical processors which, since they occupied less space and he didn't seem especially interested in aesthetics—or perhaps

I should say he had his own aesthetic—left him with a torso that narrowed sharply below the rib cage and proceeded cylindrically downwards before flaring out again at the hips, like he was wearing a bizarre tight-laced corset. When he'd lost his eyes, he'd swapped them out for a photosensitive implant with broad-spectrum analytical capabilities that covered much of his brow and made him look a little like a spider, and a little—especially with his tendril hands—like a Leviathan.

I did once ask him, carefully and giving him every opportunity to tell me to shut up and fuck off, why he'd made those particular choices.

"When man tried to simulate walking," he'd told me, "he invented the wheel. But a wheel looks nothing like a pair of legs."

I'd simultaneously known exactly what he meant and had no idea what he was going on about.

What matters now, though, isn't what he looked like, it's what he did.

Actually, even that doesn't matter. What matters is what the captain asked him to do and what it meant to her that she asked him to do it.

Actually, what probably *really* mattered, what probably mattered to *him*, is that not long after the events I'm about relate he would die in horrific agony along with almost the entire crew of the Pequod. And I'm probably doing him, his family, and his memory a disservice by trying to make the whole fucking thing into some kind of metaphor.

But screw it. He's dead and I'm alive and I've started now so I'll damned well finish. I'm telling this story, and that makes it mine, even though it was other people's blood that was spilled to make it.

Anyway.

Shortly after we met with the Bachelor—or was it before?—the captain dispatched me from her bed to the engineering bay with a request.

"She wants a harpoon," I explained to Lobscouse.

"She has a harpoon," he replied. His voice came from an obsidian-black synthesizer that occupied the bottom half of his face. It sounded almost unnaturally harmonious. "The whole damned ship is full of harpoons. It's a hunter-barque."

"She wants a *special* harpoon."

Not having eyes, Lobscouse couldn't roll them, but he achieved much the same effect with his chest and shoulders.

"She asks," I went on, "that it have a Leviathan-bone haft cored with a high-susceptibility alloy, that the tip have a monomolecular edge and a toggled head in the Temple style. She said you'd know what that meant."

Lobscouse nodded. "I do. And they're good specifications. Though it'll be hard to justify the expense for one lance."

"She says the expense is no object."

There was so little flesh on Lobscouse's face that it should have been hard to read his expression. It wasn't. "Covering it herself, is she?"

I nodded.

"Call me an old cynic—"

"You're an old cynic," I replied automatically.

"—but I seem to recall that the captain has pledged her whole lay to whoever first sights the great Beast. So by paying for this lance from her own cut all she's really doing is cheating some poor hand out of their promised reward."

He was right. He was 100 percent right. I felt a keen need to defend the captain anyway. "Her lay is hers to do with as she pleases. Besides, if she'd made this purchase first and pledged the reward afterwards, the result would be the same and nobody would have had a problem with it."

The myriad photocells that were Lobscouse's eyes sparkled. "As an engineer, my girl, I can tell you that order matters. Very few things are commutative outside of pure mathematics."

"And here I was thinking I was the only faux intellectual on the ship."

Lobscouse laughed. And through his voice synthesizer it was a remarkable sound, largely unrelated to the actual air coming from his lungs. It was musical without being music. "No, no, child, you're in good company where that's concerned. Half the crew are philosophers in their off-hours, of one sort or another. Though mostly it's another, I'll grant that much."

"But you can make it?" I asked. "The harpoon, as the captain wants it?"

"I can," he replied. "I'd sooner not, but if she's giving the order and paying the price then I've no choice in the matter."

Duty—not even duty, really, just the ferromagnetic pull of the captain's will—said I should leave it there, go back to her, and report success. Even if that success was grudging. But Lobscouse had baited me and like the ice fish of Europa, I bit. "Why would you sooner not?"

"Engine pins."

I looked blank.

"It's an old tale from Old Earth, and one I'm surprised you've not heard as a Prosperer. Long ago, there was a man in the old world who made groundcars—or just cars as they would have been called in those days—and one day he commissioned his best engineers to look at every car that went wrong and find out *why* it went wrong and what part of it had caused the problem. And you know what he found?"

I hated parables. "What?"

"That damned near every part of the car would fail in one way or another, except the engine pins. They'd last and last and last. So you know what he did?"

I did know. Or at least I could guess. Lobscouse had been right, this was exactly the kind of story the Church of Prosperity loved. "He told them to make the engine pins more cheaply."

"Seems backward," he said. "And probably not the most *pro-consumer* move he could have made."

In the Church, *pro-consumer* was perilously close to *blasphemy*, so it took me a moment to process the sentence.

"But there was a kind of wisdom in it. No sense wasting resources making something wonderful when everything else will fail first. Tell the captain that I can make her the finest harpoon was ever darted. But if you're feeling brave and honest"—I was feeling neither and I was sure he knew it—"tell her that it won't make a damned bit of difference because there's a hundred ways a hunt can go wrong and a fancy spear fixes at best one of them."

I explained to him how short I was coming up in the bravery and honesty departments.

"You'll also need to tell her there's paperwork involved."

"She's the captain."

An unreadable pattern of lights danced across the chief engineer's eyepiece. "Means less than you'd think. Captain's a little god until we hit port. Then she's just another voider and answerable to the stakeholders same as anybody else."

I relayed this information to the captain when I saw her next. It didn't go well.

Without telling me to remove a single item of clothing or to kneel *anywhere* she swept past me on her way to engineering. I trailed behind her, limply protesting that this could all be sorted out if she'd just sign the proper forms.

She wasn't much of a one for signing forms, A wasn't.

Down in the engineering bay, Lobscouse was waist-deep in a maintenance hatch fixing one of the perennial things-that-needed-fixing.

"Engineer." The captain rarely sounded amused, but this time she sounded like she lived in a world where amusement had never existed.

"Captain?" He didn't look up. Then again, given how his ocular system worked I wasn't sure he needed to.

"You are to make me a harpoon, according to the specifications I conveyed."

He still wasn't looking up, which was beginning to seem less like a quirk of his physiology and more like intentional defiance. "Will do, once the paperwork clears."

"There will be no paperwork. You will do as I command."

"Not with ship's resources I won't." And now, at last, the engineer hauled himself out of the hatch, his tendrilous hands latching on to the floor in two dozen places and supporting him as he rose. "Not unless you authorize the payment through the proper channels."

The proper channels meant Locke, who was pretty much the only person on the ship with a head for figures.

"You understand," said the captain, "why I need the spear."

"You're hunting a monster that's never been caught and that has killed more folk than I can count—and remember, I'm an engineer so you'd better hope I count well—and who took your leg off you the last time you lowered for him. You want to chase death, be my guest, but you'll not do it with ship's metal unless you pay for it. In full. In advance."

All this talk of payment was comforting to the part of me that still rested safe in the bosom of the Church of Prosperity. But it was deeply unsettling to the much larger part that was the captain's creature.

She was looking at the engineer now with the disbelief she always reserved for people who refused to be swept into her wake. "The sky took from you, as it took from me. Why do you remain so sanguine? You should want to see blood spilled in the clouds as much as I."

The lights on Lobscouse's eyepiece flicked out, then on. "Why? Because I lost some parts? I got them back again and still made a decent living after deductibles." He flexed his tendrils. "It's an improvement in a lot of ways."

Now the captain's expression was going from disbelief to contempt. "You made yourself a better tool for your masters and paid for the privilege. Live that way if you will, engineer, but I will not. Make the lance."

Without giving him time to reply, she turned and swept out. I tried not to find it majestic, but I didn't try very hard.

CHAPTER SIXTY-SEVEN

The Harpoon

A won in the end. She always won.

Okay, she always won except in the only confrontation that really mattered to her and even then I'm not totally sure. I suppose it depends on what you think she was trying to achieve.

"It's a Temple lance," Dawlish explained to me. "Least that's what it's called on the hunt. Its name on the patent is the Skyresh Toggled Lance mk17 (a) twelfth iteration."

"Why Temple?" I asked. I felt a bit of a fool for asking. In so much of the hunt I was still basically a virgin.

"The patent calls it the Skyresh after Skyresh Toys and Munitions, the company that officially invented it. We call it the Temple, after the man who actually did."

He was telling me this while the crew was gathering on the aft deck. The captain had something to say to us, apparently, but she was taking her sweet time getting started and I didn't really want her to. It felt too much like sharing. "What was his deal?"

"Criminally indentured," Dawlish replied. "Same as me. Hence his name not being on it."

"What did he do?"

"Displayed immunity to the HVL8 pathogen. Immunity that could be traced to genetic markers that had been patented by a subsidiary of Aphrodite Pharma State."

That had been sloppy of him. It wasn't particularly uncommon for people to inherit proprietary genes, but a basic survival tactic was making sure that you didn't let anybody know you had them or else the karyotic police would come knocking.

But our discussion of material history was cut off by the captain finally starting her address. Even in the short time since she'd made the commission, the atmosphere on the ship had declined. The star cult had continued to grow, in influence if not in number, and their weird biological graffiti was getting more and more common while the maintenance robots were getting less and less inclined to clean them up, possibly because their learning algorithms were coming to see them as a normal part of the ship's structure. So now she stood above the crew on boards half slick with gore, holding a new, wicked spear aloft like a scepter.

"Shipmates," she called down to us, "this is the weapon I will use to strike down the Möbius Beast."

I was concerned but, perhaps, unsurprised to see that this announcement was met primarily with apathy. We'd been on the boat a long while, and the thrill of hunting legends had long since given way, for most of the crew, to a yearning for home and a break from the sky, and at least some kind of payout.

A lesser speaker would have been knocked off her rhythm by this. The captain was not a lesser speaker. "I know that my ways have been, at times, strange. I know that this is not an ordinary voyage—though I ask you all to ask yourselves, *How much have ordinary voyages profited you?*"

That got a better response. There wasn't a soul on the ship, even the relatively well-off ones with the decent lays, who didn't feel a nebulous sense that they should be getting more than they presently had.

"I know too," she went on, "that many amongst you have opened your eyes to new and terrible truths in your time aboard this vessel, and though I cannot walk your path beside you, I would ask that there be accord between us."

There was more enthusiasm now, but also more unease. The Starry Wisdomers made up a sight less than half the crew and it didn't feel great to those of us who *weren't* servants of a malevolent star-god to see them so nakedly pandered to.

"Come forth, Marsh."

I'd been on intimate terms with the captain for actual years now, and I'd been privy to some of her most private thoughts—admittedly mostly because she soliloquized them to the window while she was fucking me—but even I'd not expected this. Marsh walked through his followers and, Truelove trailing behind him, ascended the steps to stand beside the captain. And if her calling him out had surprised me, what happened next promoted that surprise into shock.

She knelt.

She knelt and raised up the harpoon on her palms like she was in some old painting of a surrendering general.

"I give this lance now to the anointed representative of the Devouring God," she declared, "and I ask humbly for His blessing."

This was an angle. It had to be an angle. Somebody who would leap down the throat of a nightmare made flesh because it wronged her wouldn't bow before another nightmare made flesh unless she was getting something out of it.

Wordlessly, Marsh took up the harpoon, and two of his followers came forward with rough Leviathan-bone bowls full of rank-smelling biological mush. Dipping his hands in the mess of not-exactly-meat, he daubed it in haphazard strokes over the weapon. "Let them lay by their helmets and their spears," he said, and his followers gave a sharp intake of breath as if it meant something, "and both return back to their chairs again."

The captain rose gracefully, snatched back the harpoon, and then faced the mob. "I take this blessing," she said, "with a full heart, and knowing the worth of it."

The applause that came from the crowd was strange, because it began with the Wisdomers, clapping in just slightly too much unison, so that it felt more like a pulse than a roar. Then, because applause tended to be contagious, it was caught up by other crew members and spread through the crowd in ripples that resounded off the dome but didn't quite drown out the sound of the storm.

And definitely didn't drown out the sound of the explosion.

CHAPTER SIXTY-EIGHT

Starving

Redundancy is the name of the game aboard a hunter-barque. Redundancy on redundancy wherever possible. It's a running joke in the fleet that most captains would take a duplicate ship if they thought they could manage it. The mission is long and takes the ship months or years out from any form of repair or resupply save what the crew can improvise from the remains of their prey.

Which meant that as well as a fuel tank, the Pequod had a backup fuel tank, and a backup-backup fuel tank.

It was the backup that ruptured.

In a lot of ways that was the worst-case scenario. The main fuel tank was mostly depleted thanks to the demands of the voyage and the backup-backup was half the size of the other two owing to how rarely it was needed.

And it *was* rarely needed. I might have been new to the fleet, but I listened well and read better, and so I knew that it should have been practically impossible for the backup fuel tank to be lost when it wasn't in operation. It was heavily armored, which meant it was unlikely to be punctured by anything short of a warship, an angry Leviathan, or an orbital collision. Mechanical malfunction was a risk with the main tank because it was being regularly used, but the backup was only in operation for maintenance cycles and those cycles were almost by definition closely monitored by maintenance crews.

Then again those crews were mostly automated, and the automated systems seemed to be going increasingly weird, so it's not inconceivable that they'd decided to make some helpful but unsupported upgrades to the system under the influence of the ship's ever more erratic environmental prompts.

"It was sabotage," Locke speculated aloud while I did my best to distract them from the ship's current problems and convince them that fucking me rigid was a much better use of their time. It sometimes worked these days but not when the ship had a crisis. And crises, unfortunately, were getting really common.

"Sabotage by who?" I asked. I could think of multiple answers, none of them good.

"Her," they said. "Or him."

I didn't really need to ask who her or him were. "It wouldn't be the captain," I said, probably too defensively. "She needs the ship in working order to take us into the Heart."

"Does she?" Locke looked the kind of doubtful that fundamentally rational people got when trying to comprehend fundamentally irrational minds. "Or does she need us desperate?"

"A desperate crew will want to turn back."

"Desperate people are unpredictable," Locke countered. "And the captain seems to have gained a liking for the unpredictable. The crew is getting less and less convinced that hunting a beast from myth that might kill them all is good business, even with her offering up her lay."

They weren't necessarily wrong. "Perhaps, but she's not the only one with plans. And a pirate seems more likely to be playing the chaos card than somebody who's already getting what they want."

"True." Locke frowned. I definitely wasn't getting fucked tonight. At least not by them. "The worst of it is, I don't know which of them I'd rather it was."

"Wouldn't you rather it was just an accident?"

Locke laughed a bitter, mirthless laugh. "Certainly not. If it was an accident this ship has structural problems that will probably destroy us. If it was the captain or Mr. Wolfram, well . . . that might be managed."

"And who would be easier to manage?"

I'd not meant it as a trick question, but Locke grew very silent at that. And they didn't need to say out loud why. Theirs was a mind of tonnages and percentages and bargains. They were a corpo to their little tin heart and though they'd never admit it, that gave them far more in common with pirate scum like Wolfram than with a true believer like A.

"If we are very, very lucky," they said at last, "there might be a third outcome."

I left it there, because I was afraid to take it further. Locke would never, under any circumstances, consider mutiny, but as first mate and the appointed (not anointed, funny how different those words are when they're so close together) representative of Olympus Extraction State they had the theoretical authority to remove the captain from her post, although they'd need cause. Worse, from their perspective, they'd only be able to take that kind of action if they could justify it both to Olympus after the fact and to the crew in the moment. And those two groups had radically different motivations.

Fearing I'd get no more of anything I wanted that evening, I crept back to my bunk. Q was waiting for me, sharpening her knife. That wasn't a particularly unusual thing for her to be doing—a sharp knife was an important tool on a ship for a whole lot of reasons. But context was everything and it made me uneasy.

"Everything okay?" I asked.

"Si vis pacem, para bellum."

I didn't understand all her words, but I got her tone. "You think things will go badly?"

She shrugged. "*Perhaps.*"

Since she'd been shot once by a pirate already, I suspected it was Wolfram and his allies she was concerned about, rather than the captain, but maybe that was just me projecting my own wants. "Whatever happens," I said to her, "keep your head down."

"Head down?"

"Don't get involved. Don't try to be a hero."

"*I do not*," said Q. And then as if she was directly trying to confuse me, she added: "*Will*."

Whether that meant she didn't want to be a hero or that she wouldn't try because she'd succeed, I had no idea.

"It won't come to violence," It was my best not-sure-who-I-was-reassuring voice. "I trust the captain."

She smiled. "Amor et melle et felle est fecundissimus."

With that one she'd completely lost me, so I crawled across the bed towards her and laid my head in her lap. "We'll be okay," I told her. And I kept telling her, until she set aside her knife and stroked my hair and soothed me until I fell asleep.

CHAPTER SIXTY-NINE

The Happy Ship

It was unusual for hails to be broadcast internally. Normally they were a private matter between the captain or whichever officer was fielding them, and their opposite number on the other vessel.

Which was why I immediately smelled a rat when Locke's voice came over comms with the words, "Reading you, Bachelor, request gam and request assistance."

I nudged Q. "Are you hearing this?"

She was, although whether she was understanding it I couldn't say.

"What kind of assistance do you need, Pequod?" asked the captain of the Bachelor. Her voice was light and airy, full of the kind of joy you get when you've just come to the end of a hard road of toil. Like a hunter-voyage or a really difficult shit.

"Our backup fuel tank breached," Locke explained. "Your manifests say you're homeward bound."

"That we are," replied the captain of the Bachelor. "Homeward bound and laden down with so much sperm that even the deckhands have stopped laughing at the name."

"Then would you share a little of your good fortune with us? We can compensate you, of cour—"

"Bachelor," the captain's voice came through on the override. "Ignore my first mate. I am the captain of this ship, and

I'll not delay our mission when the end is so close. I need know only one thing from you: Hast seen the Möbius Beast?"

There was a half second's dead air. Then, "Please repeat."

"Hast seen," the captain repeated, "the Möbius Beast?"

"Not a term I'm familiar with, Pequod," replied the Bachelor, "but if you've need—"

She got no further, because the captain cut comms.

At least, she cut external comms; internal comms went wild.

"Captain"—Locke's voice had priority, which was good because it was the only one that was remotely calm—"I strongly advise that you reconsider."

"Your advice is noted and discarded. We continue."

"But Captain—" Still Locke. And then, in desperation, they tried "But A—"

For clarity, though I've elided it here, they used her full name. Her personal name. A name that Locke would once have used as an equal.

It didn't help. The captain remained firm as death and cold as steel. "Captain I am. And Captain you will call me. And while captain I yet be my word is law on this ship." Fuck, she was sexy. I really wished it wasn't the kind of sexy that was going to get absolutely everybody killed, but hey, you couldn't have everything.

And then another voice cut in. It was using Truelove's ident but wasn't Truelove. "While you *remain* captain."

"Is that a threat, Mr. Wolfram?"

"The crew have come a long way, through a great and horrible deal of pain, and I've a sense that they'd sorely like to know why you just chose to fuck them."

"I think some of us"—this was Locke, who despised disorder even more than they despised little things like refusing vital fuel out of pure monomaniac obsession—"would like to know why it's you speaking on this channel and not Mr. Truelove."

"Is that so?" Wolfram's tone made it sound like he was pondering the idea. He wasn't. "Or would you *like* folk to be wondering that, when in fact I'm just saying what everybody is thinking."

When the officers' channels went quiet, the public comms lit up again with noise that lasted until the captain replied, icy calm, with, "If you wish to challenge my decisions, Mr. Wolfram, I will meet you on the foredeck. Now."

And with that, comms went dead. Because nobody was especially interested in standing by a panel and listening to broadcasts when they could stand on deck and, quite possibly, watch somebody get a spear rammed through the back of their skull and out their mouth.

As I've said before, days were long on the barque. We had to make our own fun.

The crew—and it really was the *entire* crew; enough was automated that there wasn't a station on the ship you couldn't step away from for a minute or two if you were expecting a show—gathered on the foredeck to see the captain standing at the prow, ichor-anointed harpoon in hand. And I can't say whether it was hope or trust or general sex glow, but in that moment I was completely certain that she had a plan.

Wolfram pushed his way through the crowd. Since he would have been expecting this meeting, been coming from Truelove's quarters, and been able to get to the front of the mob easily if he'd wanted to, that suggested he wanted the symbolism. A man emerging from amongst the people to tell it like it is.

The captain stared at him. Behind her a storm raged and the clouds—still the white of ammonia here, though we were catching more and more glimpses of the red of the Heart—formed shapes as ominous as they were indistinct. She terrified me then, which continued to be a turn-on.

And she was silent. Letting Wolfram speak first.

He took the bait.

"Captain. It seems that the crew would like you to explain yourself."

A tightened her grip on the harpoon. "And why should I answer to you? A prisoner and a pirate."

"A *redeemed* prisoner," Wolfram reminded her, "and a *reformed* pirate. As are *many* of your faithful hands." He inched aside then to demonstrate that half a dozen former buccaneers were only a short distance behind him. "And of course a loyal devotee of the Church of the Devouring God. But it's not me I say you should answer to." He half turned to direct the captain's attention to the gathered crew members. Once again few were openly armed, but most happened to be carrying something heavy, hard, sharp, or, in many cases, all three. "It's them."

And as meek as you like, the captain did as she was asked. "You want to know," she said to the crew, "why I sent the Bachelor on her way without so much as a handshake?"

There was a chorus of general affirmatives.

"Suppose I *had* stopped and boarded that ship," she went on. "Do you think they'd have let us have their fuel for *free*?"

The chorus conceded that no, this was unlikely.

"Wouldn't have and couldn't have. They've the same *fiduciary responsibilities*"—she almost spat the words—"as we. Though sure as I'm standing here their holds overflowed with sperm, they could not have let us have one drop of the refined fuel they didn't sell to us for more than it was worth."

The chorus signaled its grudging agreement. And fearing, perhaps, that he had underestimated his opponent, Wolfram tried to step in. "Is that the best you can—"

I've learned to my mingled cost and pleasure that the captain hates interruptions. She swung the anointed-and-desecrated harpoon around and held it—steady as a rock—level with Wolfram's throat. "You came to me on my own ship and demanded I make account. You will be silent until account is made."

For a moment, the clash of wills between the two sparked invisible flames that bathed the deck in an intangible heat and echoed with inaudible thunder. Behind them, I half imagined hellish faces in the clouds.

In the end, the captain triumphed. "Had I struck a bargain with the Bachelor, I would have been stealing from you. From your families and your children. I'd have robbed you sure as the man who sabotaged the fuel lines robbed you."

The implication was clear but it *was* left as implication. And to his credit, Wolfram blanked it like the professional deceiver he'd always been. Instead he pivoted. "Fine words, but it seems to me that so long as you've enough fuel to face the Möbius Beast, you've no care for what happens next." He turned back to the mob then and added dramatically, "What happens to *us*."

The crew was on a knife's edge. The tiniest nudge could tip them to one side or the other. "I've made no secret on this voyage that I've a quarry of my own," said the captain, her voice clear and low and level. "And I've asked you all to join me in the hunt and join me you have. You've joined me and though I say it myself you have *profited* by it. We've taken old beasts and young beasts and beasts half dead and beasts that fought us to within an inch of our own meagre lives and we have sperm, friends, we have sperm aplenty."

"Then return home now," cut in Wolfram. "Why risk voyaging on with fuel tanks near empty?"

Turning back now would also, incidentally, have brought the ship within striking range of the pirate bases and made seizing the ship and turning the whole thing brigand a much easier, and so much more tempting, prospect for the existing crew members.

But the captain didn't mention that. Instead, she gave Wolfram an openly contemptuous smile. "And here I took you for a man of faith. Does your god not promise to you that your people will be last devoured?"

That put a silence over the crowd. Within the still-technically-a-minority of the crew who had gone over to Marsh's cult, there was—in reality—something of a split between the pious, the desperate, and the cynical. But since nobody wanted to think of themselves as in the second category or admit to being in the third, everybody had to act like they were in the first.

"Fine words for an unbeliever," tried Wolfram, and against

anybody else it would probably have worked. In the game of us-against-them, *us* was a far easier hand to play. But the captain played *them* masterfully.

"Words," she echoed with an actual sneer. And then, to my surprise, she called out, "Mr. Dawlish."

Dawlish, who had been lurking with me near the back of the group, ready to run or fight as it became clear which was necessary, stood to attention. "Aye, Captain?"

"Look at the readouts from the array and tell me what they show."

With an air of professionalism I had to admit was lacking from so much of the crew these days, Dawlish consulted the screens. "No spouts," he said, "but a mass of some kind, large and static and twenty klicks straight down."

Still hovering at the end of the captain's harpoon, Wolfram raised his hands in a gesture of innocent conciliation. "That's all very well, but what of it?"

The captain said nothing, but from the fringe of the crowd, the chief engineer spoke out. "You're suggesting we strip a Behemoth, aren't you?"

"We've the machinery," the captain confirmed. "And I trust you know how it can be done."

Lobscouse nodded. "In theory. But it's not been standard practice since the early days of the hunt."

It was becoming clear, even to Wolfram himself, that he'd massively underestimated the captain. "You can't seriously propose," he said, "that we give up the chance at freely traded oil in order to wring what we can from a floating carcass?"

You'd have needed to be watching the captain as carefully as I'd been watching her for three full years before you could spot the gleam of triumph in her eyes. Because yes, she was proposing exactly that, and if Wolfram had been amongst the crew longer or hunted for more than five minutes, he'd have known that it was what the crew would favor too.

Barely smiling, the captain snatched her spearpoint away

from Wolfram's throat and held it again like a scepter. And then she walked calmly into the mob, to where Marsh was standing in his cassock of flayed dicks.

"Mr. Marsh," she said, in that soft-and-loud-at-once way she had when she really, really wanted to make a point, "when I knelt before you and bade you anoint this spear, it was in the belief that your god would give this hunt his blessing. Was I wrong?"

"It is a blessing that he bestows on beasts," Marsh replied. "Make tigers tame, and huge Leviathans forsake unsounded deeps to dance on sands."

It was gibberish, but the captain made victory out of it. "So speaks the prophet, friends. We descend, and we carve our fates from the flesh of ancients."

The crew, ready to mutiny moments before, cheered. And a little way off, Locke watched them with calculating eyes, and wondered.

CHAPTER SEVENTY

Titanfall

Even in death, the Behemoths of Jove were magnificent.

I watched our whole descent from one of the viewing blisters on the keel, and as we plunged through clouds I saw glimpses of the hydrogen sea below us. And at first I thought I saw nothing. Then I thought I saw a black spot amidst the mirror sheen. Not long after, the next time the clouds parted, the spot had become a smudge and then a blur and then a vast agglomeration of *life* spreading out along the sea's surface like cracks through an overpressure dome.

The Behemoth itself, although titanic in its scale—some two or three times the size of the Pequod—was only a tiny fraction of what we were descending into. The air around it swarmed with Wyrms, cloud after cloud of them feeding and sparking electromagnetic signals to one another. And across the surface of the hydrogen sea there gathered other things that I have no name for. Our ships are rated for vacuum and for atmosphere, but below the liquid-metal surface of the Jovian core we'd be drowned and crushed and baked and ripped apart by currents all at once.

Whatever fish swim that sea, I will die without knowing their names or seeing their faces.

The harvesting itself was a nightmare of technical and manual work. This deep down, the atmosphere alone would crush anybody who stepped outside of a pressurized vessel, and so we were able to get at the corpse only in powered, custom-built rigs that the ship carried in case a Leviathan sank to the sea and needed to be worked on in situ. They were heavy, rust-brown suits of mechanized armor that clanked and groaned and screamed when you wore them in the ship, and probably did the same outside although then there was so much else going on you that you didn't notice.

The Pequod had a dozen sets of this low-atmosphere kit, of which six were in use at any one time while the other six were being frenetically maintained by Lobscouse, working hellish night-and-day shifts with his finger tendrils weaving hypnotic patterns as he sealed cracks and greased servos and reconstituted hydraulics. The crew likewise went to work in shifts, so that six suits were always out on the back of the Behemoth, and we carved into it like miners carving into ice.

I worked with Q on my shift, as I always did whenever I could manage it, and in the fecund chaos of the titanfall, I wouldn't have felt safe without her, even in a mech suit.

The rules of the normal world stop applying when you go to the skies. They get overwritten with the rules of the ship and the hunt. And those rules stop applying again when you step outside the ship into the wild atmosphere of Jupiter. Especially at the lowest level, where hydrogen liquefies at temperatures that would boil water, and things that should not be live their lives at the fringe of a world that no human can enter or even think about with any real insight.

As I stood beside Q, carving strips and chunks out of the rock-like-leather-like-slug-like flesh of the Behemoth, a scintillating plasma gathered around our fingertips. On Old Earth they had called it—or something much like it—St. Elmo's fire. I tried once to work out who St. Elmo was, and my researches suggested that he was the red-haired saint of trauma dumping, which felt odd to me but no odder than most theologies.

If you've never been there, it's hard to describe the mix of terror and drudgery and beauty all at once. We were constantly beset by electric winds and stayed on our feet only because they had mechanized claws that gripped the monster we were walking on. We were beset too by voracious Wyrms, which, although they favored the flesh of the Behemoth, were not above trying our suits from sheer curiosity. These, Q drove off with her saw and the retractable claws that were built into her gauntlet. Even in a powered atmosuit she was swift and graceful, and I've never really understood how she managed it. Beside her I always felt slow and clumsy and broken and worthless.

Then again, I feel like that most of the time, so maybe that was less to do with her and more to do with me.

Between shifts on horror-back, I did my best to watch the crew. I wasn't spying, exactly, although I did very much want to know if we were still three steps from mutiny. Not that I had any real way of judging, but Wolfram at least seemed to have been knocked back down the pecking order. He'd made his play and been out-fanaticked, which . . . which was a problem to circle back to later.

All in all we mined the Behemoth for three days, in which time I worked five shifts at increasingly meaningless hours. And when we'd stripped all we could from it, we hauled its cracked, not-quite-mineral, not-quite-animal flesh to the ancient and seldom-used try-works, where it would be rendered down for Behemoth oil, an altogether less valuable but more immediately useful fuel than the unrefined spermaceti we were carrying for sale.

Restocked from that charnel house that was also a nursery, we rose again. From here out we had no destination but the Heart, and that lay eastwards, and above us. With our eyes set once again on the heavens, the ship flew on.

CHAPTER SEVENTY-ONE

Emergency Power

With our primary fuel tank near empty, our backup tank being replenished from the inferior stock of the titanfall, and the hardest part of the journey yet ahead of us, the ship switched mostly to its emergency systems.

The heart of those emergency systems was the try-works. Most modern hunter-barques didn't even include them, relying instead on their regular generators and the backups to those regular generators. You'd only ever find yourself in the position to *need* to run the try-works if something had gone disastrously wrong. And while having so robust (if creepy) a backup power supply could save a whole lot of lives in a crisis, given the choice between saving lives and saving money, the pious folk of the trade-states chose the greater good.

But the Pequod was an old ship, so deep in the labyrinth of its lower decks was the ancient generator. A machine so arcane that even Lobscouse didn't seem to understand it entirely.

Overall its operation was simple: There was a hopper at the top, into which we threw chunks of monster meat so old and awful that it was all crust on one side, all mulch on the other. Then somewhere in its heart was a furnace which sweated that meat until it dripped a raw, caustic fuel which burned hotter and dirtier and more repugnant than the clean, processed fuel we derived from spermaceti. This process was supremely inefficient and produced great gouts of gray-black smoke that needed to be channeled through the ship's waste atmosphere system, ruthlessly stripped of any remaining oxygen, and then finally vented into the sky.

Throughout this stage of the voyage, we ran mock flights in our boats, making sure our crews were well practiced for the great hunts ahead. As a result, I got several opportunities to see the ship from outside.

In many ways, she'd changed little from the strange cobbled-together creature that had captured my imagination back on Cthonius Linea. She was still a barque in the old style, still hung all over with bones. But at the start of the voyage, those bones had looked to me like jewelry. Like sculptures in ivory. Their bloody origin only obvious if you forced yourself to think about it.

Now she seemed a flying, dismembered corpse, her hull a shattered rib cage and her masts fingers reaching hopelessly for the sky. The emergency lighting, in keeping with a convention I've never particularly understood, was crimson, and for most of the day that was the color of the light that bathed her decks and spilled from her portholes and observation blisters. Behind her, the ship trailed smoke and ashes as she ascended, choking her wake with soot.

But only in her immediate wake. Jupiter is vast, and you didn't need to look far to stern to see the ship's detritus vanish on the wind. For the billowing pollutant clouds she was venting to mingle invisibly into the rushing red and white of the Jovian skyscape. Viewed straight on, she was a nightmare from which there was no waking.

Looking back, it was as though she had never been.

Burning a corpse and glowing like blood on a floodlight, half its crew still murmuring prayers to a god who promised only to devour them last, the Pequod broke through the atmospheric boundary at the rim of the Southern Tropical Zone.

Broke at last into Hell's Heart.

CHAPTER SEVENTY-TWO

Four Funerals

The statistician in me said the fact that the place the Möbius Beast was most likely to be found was also a place where Leviathans of a less mythic flavor gathered was not so very surprising. The Sunday-school kid in me said it was Providence. The atheist in me said it was luck.

The captain's luck, specifically. Wolfram's mutiny had stopped before it began but she was no fool. The crew—most of the crew, the crew she hadn't made beg and weep on the floor of her cabin—weren't following her out of loyalty, or even in response to her personal gravity. They were following her to get rich (or at least, less poor), and like so many other relationships, the one between the captain and her crew would go south very quickly once the sperm went dry.

So it was to her advantage that we slew four beasts within a day of crossing into the Heart proper.

The drills had helped. In the bloodred skies, the stakes were higher all around. A boat was harder to control; the beasts that flew here were larger and deadlier and more bountiful than those that haunted calmer latitudes. But it was worth it. At least if you cared about money. And it is, the Church reminds us, blasphemous *not* to care about money.

Those early hunts went almost exactly as we'd trained, with the tiny exception that the captain insisted I travel in her boat for the last of them. On the one hand, that was an honor. She seldom trusted anybody with the helm of her private vessel, and that she'd choose me said . . . something, I think? What it said I wasn't sure.

On the other hand, it did mean I was leaving Q and Locke in the lurch, but I wasn't arrogant enough to believe I was the only good pilot on the ship, and while Q and I were arguably the best pilot-harpooner team, if I was honest with myself she held up more than her fair share of that partnership.

As it turned out, I didn't have a great deal to do for most of the hunt. Since the captain had patched her thinking machine through to her boat, it was able to handle most of the basics of flying for me, which made me feel a bit of a third wheel. Especially since she also didn't seem to have brought me along for conversation.

"How close?" she asked. Not to me.

"Reasonably," replied the machine. "The Beast itself is larger, and it will move differently, but you're unlikely to get better practice than this."

"Bring me to its head." She stared out the window, and I tried not to stare at her staring. Tried not to wonder what thoughts were going through that noble, horrific mind.

Pretending that I was guiding the boat when really it was all the intelligence, I brought us to the head of the beast, and then level with one of its eyes. The other hunters had already stuck it with several harpoons by this stage and without network assistance I doubt I'd have been able to keep us so steady.

"I see you," she whispered to the sky. And then she took up the harpoon and commanded, "Canopy."

The machine obeyed her before I could, so there was nothing left for me except to watch as she sprang out of the boat and launched herself directly at the monster. Speared and tethered, it was rolling in an effort to shake its tormentors, but that let the captain drop vertically down upon it and drive her lance deep into one of its eyes.

A combination of space constraints and my own ignorance

(mostly the latter) have stopped me from including a detailed exploration of leviathanic ophthalmology in these pages. Superficially, their eyes are very different from ours. Insect-like, perhaps, or even wholly alien. Rows upon rows of black spheroids that look with unknowable intelligence on the red storm.

But everything is the same when you cut it open.

I'm sure biologically the fluids that gushed out when the monster's eye was pierced are extremely different from the aqueous and vitreous humors of a human eyeball, but right there and then, on scarlet winds in a sky crushed by gravity beyond anything primates were designed for, I didn't really give a shit about the difference. Basically, I defy any of you to watch any creature get stabbed in a sensitive organ and not at least wince a bit. Especially when it's on such a ludicrous scale. As I—or rather the machine—guided us down to follow the falling monster, its aerosolized life-fluid rushed up to meet us in a cascade.

And the captain rushed up too, setting the line on her harpoon to recall and riding the weapon all the way back to the cockpit. The canopy closed neatly over her and then, to my surprise, she removed her helmet. To my still greater surprise, she reached down and removed mine.

In case I've not made it clear, removing your helmet in the boat is incredibly fucking dangerous. Accidents happen all the damned time and having your suit sealed was very often the difference between a short period of recovery in medbay and an even shorter period of dying from simultaneous heat, cold, pressure, radiation, and windshear.

I considered saying something. But then she ran her gauntleted fingers across my lips and I tasted, for the first and, thankfully, last time in my life, the raw fluid of the Leviathan. It's a cop-out to say it was indescribable but, reader, do remember that I'm talking about a creature that lives on Jupiter, flies by an unknown mechanism through skies made of ammonia, eats creatures that shouldn't exist, and powers the whole of civilization with its brain juice.

What would you *expect* something like that to taste like? A little metallic maybe? But not in the way blood is metallic. Fresh? Probably, but is "fresh" really a flavor? It stung my tongue and made my lips burn, although looking back that might be because approximately three seconds after I first tasted that Luciferian humor, the captain kissed me.

A lot of weird things had happened since I signed up with the Pequod. This wasn't the absolute weirdest, but it was probably top four.

Her gauntlets had come off now and she was nimbly undoing the seals on my atmosphere suit, which, if I'm being technical, probably wasn't any more dangerous than taking the helmet off because if the canopy went down we'd be instantly killed either way. But it *felt* more dangerous. I mean, maybe it's just me, but as I general rule I think most things are more dangerous if you're also fucking.

"Follow the beast," the captain told her machine-servant-ally-patron. "I would watch it die."

Of all the things you don't want to hear someone say while they're undressing you, *I would watch it die* is quite possibly the actual top of the list. And if you do hear it, you should try your absolute level best not to find it a turn-on.

I am bad at life.

But I'm really fucking good at death.

Outside the canopy, the great Leviathan twisted its final agonies while inside the captain's mouth pressed hot and urgent against my skin.

"What gods did you pray to?" she whispered, not to me, while I clung to the pilot's seat with ichor still on my lips and tried to only unravel in a way that wouldn't get us both killed. "And when you saw us approach, did you cry to them for mercy?"

I cried for mercy. The captain, typically, had none.

"Did you wonder"—her tongue ran the length of my throat and then her teeth nipped at my jaw with borderline cruelty—"what it *meant* in the end? Had you lived, would you have sought me out and said, *You blinded me and you will pay?*" She placed a hand over my eyes and, liberated from reality, my imagination filled in visions of the dying beast all around us. Its feeder tendrils reached up to caress us and its legs wrapped around us like an embrace. Out in the storm, I thought I heard it screaming.

"And when my vengeance comes will it be to make an altar of the skies?"

I made an altar of myself, stretched out across the console with controls sticking in my back in ways that would in any normal circumstances have made it a really fucking hard to get off, but this was the captain, and when she was with me she was all my faith and all my hope.

"Will it be a last act of worship to the only god who has ever touched my soul, or will it taste"—she raked a single fingernail down my neck; her touch was the lightning and the storm—"of ashes and dust and base earth? Is this—"

And then, from some deep, passionate, extraordinarily misguided place in the pit of my physiology, I said, "*Please.*"

A spell broke.

"No pleading." She was looking into my eyes now, intense and on fire and walking the garrote wire between sanity and the grave. "No prayers. No bargains. No gods. No masters, no payments, and no debts."

And from the same wrong, wrong, wrong place, I said, "*Stay.*"

She recoiled from the word. Or from me. Probably a bit of both.

Never having known what was best for me, I went on. "I know I'm just . . . this is just . . ." Sitting up, I hugged my undershirt around me and turned my face from her. Outside, the Leviathan was twitching its last. And though a creature so vast and strange could never look remotely human, it felt *personal*.

"You know what I am," the captain said. And she said it to *me*, not to fate, or the world, or the storm.

"I know *who* you are," I corrected her. "I know you brought me here for a reason."

Her gaze flickered between my body and the body of the beast. Between the marks of her mouth and the marks of her spear. "You distract me. There are times I favor distraction."

Once again, I was reminded of how fucking dead I'd be if something went wrong with the boat while I was half naked and three-quarters fucked. I began—only slightly regretfully—struggling back into my atmosphere suit. "And in the moment?"

"What moment?"

I was officially over it. "The moment we find the Beast. Will I distract you then?"

For a horrible, tantalizing, tempting third of a second, it almost seemed like I was getting through to her. "I will finish what I began."

It would have been churlish to point out that she often didn't. That I was quite regularly left to finish myself because she was off on some tear about flight paths and brit-clouds and storm-currents. So instead, I went, if anything, one step more churlish and said: "Why?"

"Don't be a child."

"I'm sitting half naked in a ship full of monster blood asking why you'd rather risk your life than fuck me. If that's what a child sounds like to you, you shouldn't be around children."

"I have come too far to turn aside."

I wanted to call bullshit.

Etymological note: I don't really know what *bullshit* is or why its meaning is distinct from regular shit. My theology tells me that both *bull* and *bullock* are beasts of Old Earth but not what they are or whether they're different from each other.

"Look me in the eye," the captain went on, "and tell me that you would want me were I a different kind of woman. If I had two legs and no purpose, rather than one of each."

I wanted to call bullshit again. Except I couldn't because she was right. The part of me that pretended to be a sensible, functional human being with a reasonable life expectancy desperately wanted to say that I'd have still desired her even if she were an accountant working in the head office of a subsidiary branch of

Occator Financial Services. That I'd still want her even if she wore cardigans and had the median number of flesh-and-blood limbs and never did anything that might get anybody killed. Even if she were ordinary.

But that part of me was shit out of luck. The truth was that I wanted her because she didn't want me. Worse, I wanted her because she wanted something so vast and inexplicable that just being close to it made me feel the uneasy peace of my own irrelevance. And I craved that like I craved a hundred other things I didn't dare name.

Once it had become abundantly, overwhelmingly clear that I had no answer, she gave me a slate-cold smile and nodded. "We return to the Pequod."

CHAPTER
SEVENTY-THREE

Rache

In these more prosperous hunting grounds, it wasn't only Leviathans that crowded thicker in the sky. Ships too were a more common sight. Of course, "more common" is relative. Spoiler, reader: We only saw two more vessels before things went—to use the technical terminology—completely to shit.

The first of those was called the Rachel by its ident but the name painted on its hull (some ships did this, some didn't, the Pequod might have at one point, but she was so bedecked with bones that it was impossible to say) had worn away, leaving only *Rache.*

"Vengeance," said the Old Ionian. "In one of the tongues of Old Earth. It's an omen, you mark my words."

"An omen of what?" asked Locke, who was watching the ship's approach beside us and who had, of late, been increasingly withdrawn.

"Not all omens are omens *of* things," the Old Ionian replied with the cheap gravitas of age. "Some are just omenous all by themselves."

"Ominous," corrected Locke. "And if you're looking for bad signs, there are far more concrete ones to think about than how a ship writes its name."

The Old Ionian didn't ask for examples, because there were hundreds. Steering into an eternal storm, taking advice from an illegal machine intelligence, getting her harpoon blessed by an apocalypse cult, and of course the little fact that we were permanently bathed in bloodred light because the whole ship had been forced onto emergency power because the captain would rather burn a dead god than trade for better supplies all sprang to mind. Then there was the tiny matter of demanding that the whole crew commit to backing her on a personal vengeance crusade against a single biological organism.

As if to illustrate this last point, the captain's voice echoed across comms. Her eternal, obsessive, unchanging question. "Hast seen the Möbius Beast?"

And although we'd heard it before, a knife-twist of foreboding hit me right in the stomach when the reply came. "Aye."

Not that I had much time for reflecting on foreboding, foreshadowing, omens, or portents, because the captain rattled on with a host of new questions, and these were far less rehearsed and suggested far less composure on her part. When, she wanted to know. And where? On what heading? From what distance?

To her frustration, none of these questions received direct reply. Instead, the captain of the Rachel sent a request for permission to board. A request, I couldn't help noticing, that came after she'd already launched her boat and crossed half the distance towards us.

"It worsens," the Old Ionian muttered. "Signs on signs on signs."

This sign, at least, seemed more practical than mystical, and I was grateful for that. I didn't need a long life's worth of folk wisdom to know that somebody who got halfway to your ship before asking if she could come aboard was either trying something, desperate, or, most likely, trying something desperate.

In keeping with tradition, a reasonable number of us, including all the officers, the harpooners, and anybody who just wanted to rubberneck, went down to the docking bay to greet the visiting captain. And in further keeping with tradition, we made a bunch of mean-spirited observations about her and her ship based on nothing but what her boat looked like and how she carried herself.

Although in this case even the boredom-born cruelty of the hunter-crew didn't quite have the stomach for snarking on the captain of the Rachel. Because she looked pathetic. Pathetic in the etymologically literal sense of evoking pathos. She was like our own captain in negative. Both radiated a sense of being driven by some all-consuming urge, of being hollowed out and shattered and remade by it.

Only with our captain it was, like, in a cool way. And with the captain of the Rachel it wasn't.

"The Beast," A demanded as she bore down upon the hapless visitor, ivory heel ringing on the iron grille of the landing platform. "Where. And when. And how far off?"

Although the captain of the Rachel had been broadcasting weakness since she'd stepped out of her boat, she stood her ground. And while this might have been me projecting, I thought I recognized a very particular *kind* of weakness there. The kind that circled all the way back around and became strength again because you had nothing to lose and no reason to hold back. "In good time," she said.

"I call no time good that isn't now," replied A.

To which the captain of the Rachel said only, "Learn."

I was pretty sure that one of the biggest reasons the captain wasn't already super, super dead despite everything was that deep down she knew how to temper her obsession with pragmatism. And she decided quickly enough that it would be more expedient to accommodate her opposite number than to waste time in a clash of wills. "My apologies," she said, half bowing, "you have come to my ship in haste. Doubtless you have priorities of your own, and I should not be selfish."

That mollified the other captain at least a little. "I saw the Beast," she said, "or something much like it, some two days ago—"

"Two days." The captain couldn't help interjecting. We were

close now. Touching close. Close enough, not to put too fine a point on it, to be fucked.

"We were in pursuit of a pod of Leviathans when the eyes on the array caught sight of another signal—one too large and too majestic to give off pursuing, so I gave the order for our reserve boat to drop after it."

"And 'twas the Beast?" demanded A. "Tell me it yet lives. If I hear that ye slew it—"

"The monster lives," replied the captain of the Rachel. "When our boats gave chase, he fled."

I'd spent so long watching the captain that I sometimes imagined I could read her thoughts on her skin. What she was thinking now was that fleeing didn't fit the story she told herself about the Great Leviathan. And if it didn't fit the story, it wasn't real. Or at least, it was part of a lesser reality.

"That would have been no bad thing," the other captain went on, "since we'd made kills enough for a day's work. But one of our boats got a dart in the creature and was dragged along with it as it flew."

That sort of thing happened all the time. Hell, it had happened to me a fair bit, even in hunts I've described in these pages. It was scary and sometimes even fatal, but not the kind of thing that would drive a captain to the state this woman was in.

"When the hunt was done, the boats that had gone for the pod were all accounted for, but the one tethered to the beast had been dragged from sensor range."

"Then fire the beacon," replied the captain. Every ship has a high-intensity beacon it can use to guide errant boats back to the ship if necessary, and its use has saved many lives over the decades. "If they live they'll return to you. If they do not you've lost nothing."

The detached, matter-of-fact *if they live* struck the captain of the Rachel like a bucket of cold sewage. "Have you used your beacon lately?" she asked. "In the Heart?"

We hadn't, but the captain had been in the skies long enough that she knew what her counterpart meant. The atmospheric conditions made electronic communication over long distances incredibly unreliable. "Then give them up for gone. You cannot mean to search the skies like the barques of old? With boats and scans and mortal eyes?"

The captain of the Rachel couldn't help but nod.

And the captain of the Pequod couldn't help but laugh. Not a *long* laugh, not even a *cruel* laugh. If I had to pick an adjective, I'd go with *nihilistic*. "Then th'art a fool. Either the boat will find its way back on instruments, or it is lost. You must have sailed these skies near as long as I and so I think you *know* this. So why come to me with your tale?"

"You could help us search." She wasn't quite begging, but she was making it clear that begging would be an option. And to give the woman her due, the captain did *like* to hear begging. Just not in this context. "Between us we still might save them."

With her typical flair for theatrics, the captain turned to her assembled officers. "First Mate Locke," she said. "Shall I do as this woman asks? Shall I take my ship from her appointed duties, forsaking my *fiduciary responsibility* to all her stakeholders, and spend a week scouring the skies for a boat whose crew, if I am to be honest, are like as not already dead?"

I could see tension in Locke's jaw. They knew, of course, that they could only answer one way. Or at least, they could only answer one way that wasn't *You're a giant fucking hypocrite for pretending you give the tiniest shit about your fiduciary responsibilities*. "You should not, Captain," they said dutifully. And then added, "Although there may be other ways we can help her."

But the captain entirely blanked the second half of Locke's reply and solicited opinions from Truelove and Flint. Since Flint was compelled by his faith to expect people to solve their own problems and Truelove was compelled by his to want the universe to be devoured by space monsters, neither of them were much help.

"Voiders are lost to the skies every day," the captain concluded. "Why should I care more about these than any of the others?" A sly twitch troubled the side of her mouth. "For that matter, why do you?"

Seeing no option but the truth, the captain of the Rachel told it. "My son is on that boat."

"Somebody's son is on every boat," replied A. "Or daughter, or child. And a captain should put no member of their crew above any other."

"Not even herself," added Locke pointedly.

The captain of the Rachel was still keeping eye contact with A. "I was a mother before I was a captain and will be after."

"Noble," conceded A, "but not my concern, or the concern of this vessel."

And once again I got the sense that the captain of the Rachel was trying something desperate. "I know of you," she said. "And your ship. They say you've a child of your own back on Europa."

The captain half shrugged. "What of it?"

"If he—"

"She."

"If she were lost in the skies, would you not give anything to find her?"

I knew the captain well enough to know that this was the wrong question. Because it was going to get the expected answer for all the wrong reasons. "If the sky took from me," A replied, "I would tear it apart. If my daughter had gone to an airy grave towed behind a Leviathan, I would hunt that Leviathan and put its eyes out with my lance and split its corpse in my rending bays and tell the gods themselves that they were next."

"Then—" began the captain of the Rachel fruitlessly.

"But I would be a fool to hope that I would see her alive again. Gone is gone and dead is dead and the storm swallows us all in the end and what is left to us is fury and defiance and the breaking of worlds."

"You would not even look for her?" The captain of the Rachel sounded uncomprehending, unbelieving, and increasingly uncomfortable.

"I would not. Hope is a monster more foul than anything we hunt in the skies. It kills and it betrays and it brings good people to death and weeping. Would that the old Grecian had kept her box shut and her eyes closed."

She'd even lost me at this point, and I was very, very accustomed to her rambling.

"If you were wise," she told the other captain, "you would join me in my hunt and take your solace from your share in the corpse." She shook her head in what read to me as genuine sorrow. "But you won't. I see that we are of different temperaments, and that is either my tragedy or yours. Time and fate will tell us whose."

That much, at least was prophetic.

As, perhaps, was the fact that when the captain of the Rachel departed, Wolfram hijacked an escape pod and followed her.

CHAPTER SEVENTY-FOUR

Tempests in Tempests in Tempests

Remember how I talked about the last storm and said that obviously there'd be other storms coming, but they're so big and all-consuming that calling them *storms* is meaningless? But now that I've reached that part of the journey—the part where *storm* becomes too small a word—I realize that it's a whole different order of problem.

It's a deep-down problem with words. With the whole idea of words.

The overwhelming majority of human beings have never lived in an atmosphere. Even we hunters haven't really, because the murderous skies of Jove are kept from us by suits or domes or canopies for, if we're lucky, fully 100 percent of our voyages.

If that percentage ever drops, it means we're dead.

But although the overwhelming majority of human beings have never lived in an atmosphere, our language, coming as it does from the dark days of Old Earth, contains the ghosts of a time when we did.

Which means I can talk about wind and storms and clouds and you will on some level at least understand what I'm saying. Or at least, you will understand *something*. The words will have meaning to you even if that meaning is filtered through layer upon layer of translation and metaphor.

You may have told your doctor that your urine is cloudy. You may have described a concatenation of trying circumstances as a shitstorm. You might have heard about winds of change and perhaps even associated them with the air currents that circulate oxygen in whatever dome you happen to live in. Even though when you really think about it, those are winds of *stasis*.

Q, of course, has different words for these things. *Nebula. Tempestas. Ventus.* But as I've come to know her better I've realized that translating these words is a kind of false commonality. When Q speaks of *clouds* she means things made of water vapor high in an uncovered sky. Things that drop liquid water rain at unscheduled intervals. Her *storms* similarly are more physical but less existential than the ones you might experience in any normal circumstance, and the *wind* that blows on her in her own home is breathable air. Air made from 80 percent nitrogen and 18 percent oxygen and 2 percent everything else instead of the low-explosive tri-mix we use day to day.

I know, the idea of just trusting the composition of your atmosphere to luck is strange. Terrans are strange people.

So when I talk about storms in this chapter, well . . . obviously, it's partly a metaphor. You've worked out that a lot of this stuff is metaphor, right? And some of it is jokes. And some of it is just whatever was on my mind at the time. The neuropsychological division of Psyche Microphysiology, a wholly owned subsidiary of Ausonia Biotechnological Services, a wholly owned subsidiary of Aphrodite Pharma State, once offered me a free trial of a counseling device which told me my issues with concentration and intrusive thoughts are probably symptomatic of a disorder they could help me manage for a reasonable subscription. I never quite got around to signing up.

Where was I?

Ah, yes. When I talk about storms, I'm using words I stole from our ancestors to describe ideas our ancestors could never comprehend to a reader who—never having lived either on ancient Earth nor modern Jove—can never truly understand either. Writers are liars and all I'm really doing in this book is trying to fool you. Trying to make you believe that by reading these words you can feel what I felt and see what I saw and know the people I knew.

You can't. But I want so badly for you to believe you can.

When I am dead I want you to take these words and read them and say, *This woman was real and she mattered, like all the souls she sailed with.* I want you to take these words and read them and imagine that you see your own life reflected in a life you could never have lived. I want you to take these words and read them and, who knows, perhaps you'll feel the need to tell your own story to the ones who come after you. One about a voyage you took a year, or a hundred years, or a thousand years after I am gone. After I have passed into that shared imagination we pretend is memory.

I hope you will be less afraid than I am.

As we plunged deeper into the Heart, we began moving away from the rich hunting grounds and into the places where even Leviathans feared to fly. The clouds now were thick and red and opaque, like the cosmos was bleeding into our eyes. Even our instruments began to fail us, because the air currents created massive friction-induced buildups of static which discharged themselves at random intervals and created the ghosts of spouts on all sides of the vessel.

Most of the crew took to avoiding hull work, busying ourselves with tasks that took us deep inside the ship, into the illusionary safety of our gargantuan steel coffin. And there we huddled under red emergency lighting, on a ship flying half blind to battle with a monster whose nature we were finding it harder and harder to lie to ourselves about.

On the plus side, the increased sense of doom and foreboding made casual sex *way* easier to get. It's incredible how horny people get when they feel like they're being slowly choked out as a prelude to being sliced open.

Even Locke, normally so proper, or at least so committed to the image of properness, even while they were on top of me, was getting more up for the spicier kind of assignation. In crawl spaces. Up against bulkheads. Two feet from a weapons locker. That kind of thing.

"This," they said while I re-dressed and went back to pretending to do maintenance, "has gotten very out of my control."

"My advice," I told them, "is learn to enjoy it."

Their eyes narrowed. "Not *that* this. The *whole* this. The voyage."

I shrugged. "Our holds are near full. Give the captain her due, she's an old hand at the hunt and your precious Olympus Extraction State will make a killing out of this trip, and all it's cost us so far is a couple of deaths and one man's sanity."

"So far." Locke did that thing where you echo somebody as a way of expressing *Everything you just said is meaningless because of the one bit of it I've just repeated.* Then, rather than primly going back to their many duties like they usually would after giving me a seeing-to, they slumped against the steel wall of maintenance corridor 147-c-(ii)-delta and slid slowly down to the floor, where they sat in a pleasingly disheveled heap. "She never used to be like this."

It wasn't the first time they'd told me that. At the time I also assumed it wouldn't be the last, although I was wrong on that score for catastrophic reasons. "She lost a limb. I see why that would change a person."

"Honestly"—Locke was staring into the middle distance in a way I sincerely hoped didn't mean they were coming totally unglued—"I don't think it was that."

"No?"

"Losing a limb is a sudden change. With A"—nobody called the captain by her name except Locke. Well, Locke and me, privately, in my head—"it was more like . . . like metal fatigue. You use a piece of machinery day in, day out for years or decades and eventually it snaps, but you can't just blame the last stress cycle. People talk about the straw that breaks the camel's back, but that one straw is no different from all the others. I assume. I suppose it depends what the straws are made of."

"And what a camel is," I added.

"That too. But the point is I've known her for years and losing her leg wasn't a turning point, it was just . . . just the last shitty thing in a long string of shitty things. This is a shitty industry, after all."

I'd been banging Locke on and off for months now, and this was the first time they'd admitted anything like this. "Isn't that heresy?"

They shrugged. "You're the seminary girl. Where I'm from we treat religion more practically. The big churches are all the same; the little ones are all weird as fuck." It was odd to hear Locke say *weird as fuck*, but they'd loosened up in a lot of ways lately. "Keeping in good with the Father isn't going to save us and, no matter what the Plutonians say, it isn't going to put food on the table either. At least it hasn't for anybody I know."

It hadn't for anybody I knew either. But when I'd pointed that out to people back home they'd gotten really angry at me for it.

"I do my job," Locke went on, "and I do it right and I do it well. When I do it *really* well nobody gets killed and we all come out just a little bit better off than we were before. When I do it badly . . ." They shrugged and spread their hands in a gesture that eloquently expressed the sentence *You get shitshows like this*.

For a moment we lapsed into silence. Except there was never silence on a ship, and now with the perpetual outrage of the wind outside, our every moment of quiet was underscored by the thrumming of the engines in dialogue with the shrieking of the skies.

"I trust her," I said. And it was true even though it shouldn't have been.

"Then I envy you."

"I trust you too."

That got a gallows laugh. "One day, I—" Locke was also the only person that really said *my* name on the ship, and that made me feel a bunch of strange things, not all of them comfortable. "You'll have to actually commit to something. You can't trust the woman who might be sailing us all to our deaths and *also* trust the person who says she definitely is."

In a futile effort to lighten the mood, I smiled and said, "Seminary girl, remember? Accepting contradictory beliefs is my whole thing."

"Go on then. Unpack the theodicy. How do you trust both of us?"

Having to justify myself sucked. There's a reason I've chosen to tell this story in a way that means you absolutely can't talk back to me. "I trust that she'll do the right thing," I said. "And I trust that you'll stop her if she doesn't."

I couldn't help noticing Locke's eyes straying to the weapons locker. "Do you now?"

Fuck it. I got up, punched my code into the locker, pulled out a heavy, snub-nosed flechette pistol, and threw it to them. "Yes. I do."

"I think you're getting me mixed up with Flint. He's the one who thinks shooting bad people solves everything."

Honestly I didn't think Flint's philosophy had even that much nuance to it. "He's not wrong, though."

"You don't think one mutiny per voyage is enough?"

"I'm not a lawyer, but I'm pretty sure it's not mutiny when you're first mate. It's just necessary checks and balances."

Locke didn't argue. And they also didn't give the gun back. Instead they secreted it—more expertly than I'd have expected for a bean pusher and a pen counter—inside the line of their once-more-immaculate uniform. They nodded an acknowledgment that was something like gratitude.

For a moment, we understood each other. Or I thought we did. For a moment, things were calm.

That much remains true about storms, of any kind, whatever world they happen on.

CHAPTER SEVENTY-FIVE

The Queen of the Elves

Hunters are at once a whimsical and a rules-oriented folk, which is why they speak about sprites and elves instead of Stratospheric Perturbations Resulting from Intense Thunderstorm Electrification and the even more tenuous Emissions of Light and Very low frequency perturbations due to Electromagnetic pulse Sources.

I tried to explain to the Old Ionian that an acronym wasn't really an acronym if you ignored half the words, and he told me I was missing the point.

Most of the time, these phenomena are limited to the upper atmosphere (sprites are stratospheric by definition), but the nominatively appropriate fury of Hell's Heart combined with the cerebral emissions of its Leviathans led to constant flares and pulses lighting the skies, even at mid-to-low altitudes.

For most captains, one of the chief difficulties of navigating the Heart was skirting the boundaries of these unpredictable events, while also not missing the ones that were actually Leviathan spouts and *also* remembering that having half your ship's electronics overloaded by something that could appear and then vanish at literal light speed was (*checks notes*) bad.

A was not most captains.

"We are *not*," Locke insisted, pointing through the forward windows of the captain's cabin, "steering *into* that."

The *that* in question was a storm-within-a-storm-within-a-storm sending waves of elf-light rippling across the skies some three hundred klicks from our present position.

"My orders were clear," replied the captain, unblinking and unhesitating. "I expect them to be obeyed."

The loss of Wolfram had calmed the crew in some ways, agitated them in others. On the one hand, he wasn't stirring shit or actively plotting to take over the ship. On the other hand, the fact that the man with the best survival instinct on board had felt safer in a life pod that might just crash into the sea than he did on the Pequod was kind of telling.

Still, for now it had cemented the captain's hold over the crew, so when she said to set course directly into an atmospheric anomaly that would bathe the ship in an immeasurable quantity of electromagnetic radiation, she'd been obeyed without question.

Well, without question from anybody but Locke, who wasn't letting this go anywhere near that easily. "There is no *possible* commercially justifiable reason for this."

By the laws of the sky, the lack of a commercial justification was the most important problem with the captain's plan. To everybody who thought Olympus Extraction State could go fuck itself, which included me, a hefty chunk of the crew, the captain, and—in some ways most importantly—Locke themself, it felt pretty weaksauce.

"Advisor," replied the captain to thin air.

"The proposed path," said the voice of her machine intelligence from the captain's table, "is the one that gives us the best chance of catching the Möbius Beast."

It was the first time the captain had invoked the intelligence in front of Locke but by this stage its presence aboard was an open secret, so they took it very much in stride. "And if we die?"

"I can only answer the questions I'm asked."

Locke hadn't been talking to the machine. They'd been talking to the captain. But they *had* gotten an answer, and with the suspicious expression of somebody who has known another somebody for too long and learned too much about the way they think, Locke fixed her with a challenging glare. "And what did you ask?"

"How best to catch the Beast," she replied, more evasively than I was used to from her.

Locke spotted that as well and clearly wasn't in the mood for evasion. "What were your *exact* words?"

With a ya-got-me smile, the captain replied, "I asked if, all else being equal, choosing not to avoid atmospheric hazards would improve our chances of catching up with the Beast more quickly."

"And I said it would," added the machine cheerfully. "Because it will."

"You mean," Locke clarified, still ignoring the intelligence, perhaps hoping that if they did, it would stop existing, "that you asked if choosing the fastest route would be fastest, and the machine said yes?"

"In essence," replied the machine.

"It could have said otherwise," added the captain.

"I could," the machine confirmed.

Locke looked unconvinced. Which was to be expected because this was incredibly unconvincing. "Intelligence," they said, finally addressing the machine, "state your operational parameters."

A jaunty jingle played over comms. "Hi, I'm the Fidelity multipurpose strategic advisory networked machine intelligence. My job is to support my fantastic users with detailed, unbiased advice and data-processing support tailored to their specific, unique needs. Fidelity, the inspiration font, the flame device logo, and the 'Stronger Together' musical sting are registered trademarks of Athabasca Neural Solutions, a wholly owned subsidiary of Elysium Data State."

"That sounds a lot like your job is to tell people what they want to hear."

One of the things Q, whose people had no such marvels

as our machine intelligences, always found disturbing about them was how easily they could convey emotion. Fidelity now sounded extremely offended. "I think you'll find that's a common misconception. I'm fully compliant with the recommendations of several voluntary regulatory bodies."

Locke stared out into the storm, where weird lights took turns coloring the clouds in all the shades of the visible spectrum. "And if we sail into a microwave anomaly and it fries your circuits?"

"Firstly," replied Fidelity, back to its usual upbeat tone, "that isn't actually how I work. Secondly, I'm running on redundant, electromagnetically shielded systems. Thirdly, I'm trained to prioritize my users' needs above my own safety."

I'd say the captain had been listening to this exchange with uncharacteristic patience, but actually she'd been ignoring it with characteristic disinterest. Only when the chatter between the first mate and the machine had died away did she shut things down with a clear "My order stands. We hold course."

And her order stood. And we held course.

Much as the crew usually avoided staring out into the storm because it reminded us of how dead we all probably were, charging headlong into an electromagnetic anomaly pushed us through denial into a kind of fatalistic wonder. If we *were* on a doomed voyage into an undiscovered sky from whose bourn we would never return then we could, at least, take time to appreciate the beauty along the way.

And the elves was beautiful.

Very probably, my crewmates and I are the only human beings ever to have seen an atmospheric event that large, that close, and that wonderful. What percentage of us, after all, ever even go to Jupiter? Of that fraction, what fraction brave the Heart? And of that fraction of a fraction, who would ever fly directly into an electromagnetic event?

Who would see it and live to tell the tale?

The ship bore on into the anomaly and the hull caught fire.

Not literally, I should add. We weren't at the kind of temperature or, for that matter, in the kind of atmosphere where either metal or Leviathan bone will actually combust. But a corona of emissive events gathered around the ship, bathing her in an eerie light that shifted hues through green to violet and back again.

All the while, the captain stood on the prow, ramrod-straight and staring out into the skies. The elf-light bathed her and limned her and made her look like a star come down from the heavens to walk the decks of a hunter-barque.

As beautiful as the fires were, as majestic as they made the captain look by the light of their hyperfine emissions, there's a reason hunter-barques don't fly into electrostatic anomalies as a rule, and after a few moments marveling at the spectacle, we found out exactly what that reason was. What those reasons were.

Doors jammed. The dispensers in the mess locked up. Comms went down at the worst possible time. And navigation shorted.

The last one was the real fucker.

Navigating in the Jovian atmosphere is next to impossible without a working uplink and some very, very specific computer wizardry. On other worlds you can fly by dead reckoning or by looking at landmarks, but the thing about landmarks is that they need, y'know, land. In an ever-shifting miasma of ammonia and sulfides, you have no way of knowing where you are one day to the next.

The fact that, in the days after the storm, the captain seemed totally unbothered by this was a giant fucking red flag. Then again, every flag had been red since she stood up and told us she was out to hunt legends.

Somehow, it didn't change how badly I wanted her, or how much I believed in her.

CHAPTER
SEVENTY-SIX

The Pistol

I was curled up in a corner of the captain's bed, naked, alone, and abandoned, when there was an unexpected buzz at the door.

Not that unexpected buzzes at the door really bothered the captain, who was kneeling in front of her table poring over charts that she still seemed to believe she could navigate by.

"Read the wind," she was telling her intelligence. "If the Beast is out there we will smell it."

"I'm not quite sure that's how it works," replied Fidelity. "But we should be able to check the currents for biological traces. The deeper we go into the Heart, the more likely it becomes that those traces come from the creature you're looking for."

The door buzzed again, and this time a voice came over what was left of comms. It was Locke. At least it sounded like Locke. Everything had gotten so staticky recently.

Shutting the table down, the captain rose and went to the door.

"What do you want?"

Locke slid inside with an easy formality. "I want to talk, A—"

They used her full name, of course. And no title. That was interesting, because they hadn't since the day of Wolfram's failed mutiny. It was also interesting that the captain didn't immediately tell them to fuck off. Instead she went calmly inside, knelt down, and waited for Locke to kneel opposite her.

"Well?"

"You destroyed navigation."

The captain didn't so much as blink.

"You're not going to at least say it was a calculated risk?"

I was watching now from behind the curtain at the edge of the alcove. Locke didn't know I was there, and the captain might or might not have remembered. "I've known you too long to lie."

"Then have you known me long enough to listen?"

It was a rhetorical question to which the answer was definitely no. "This ship nears the end of her voyage. We no longer need the navigational computers. Our goal now is not to go to this longitude or that latitude or rendezvous with some skyport. Our goal is—"

"Our goal," Locke interrupted, "is to hunt Leviathans, collect as much sperm as we can, and then bring our crew back alive and, if at all possible, better off than they were when they left port."

The sheer amount of derision the captain managed to pack into a short exhalation was borderline miraculous. Although that could have been the sex skewing my perspective. "You think the three hundredth part of this ship's haul is enough to pay anybody back for three years mortgaged to the sky?"

"If it wasn't they wouldn't have taken the job," Locke pointed out.

"Ah, yes. Because of course they chose to take on this career freely. None of them feared starvation, or were fleeing debt, or pressed into bondage by the law."

Locke's lips were a hard, set line. "How convenient that social justice happens to align perfectly with your ego."

"Nobody on this ship had any choice but to sign aboard. I won't pretend that serving your masters is the same as serving the crew."

"But you'll pretend that serving your vengeance is?"

I'd never seen the captain chastened, and I didn't think I was seeing it now. But she shut her eyes and looked down for a moment. "And that's what you think this is?"

"Honestly? No. But I thought you'd accept *vengeance* before you accepted *despair*."

"You're very keen to judge me today."

"As we've established, I know you."

At that, the captain looked up. From my angle I couldn't see the expression on her face, but I didn't need to. I never needed to. So much of what I knew about her is imagination. "And what is it they say about a little knowledge?"

"That sometimes it's all you need. You feel trapped, I understand that—"

"I assure you, you do not."

"Apologies, Captain. I overspoke. Whatever your motivations are, whatever you're feeling right now and whatever you've been feeling for the last year, or ten years, or all your life, the crew deserve to make their own decisions."

The captain blinked. Once. "They *are* making their own decisions. They could have followed Wolfram and turned pirate. They could have followed him again when he took the lifeboat. They could refuse to lower for spouts or, if they were really concerned, they could refuse my orders entirely."

"You know that isn't true." Locke's voice was different now, more pleading than defiant. I could see their face clearly from where I watched, but they weren't looking at me. They were looking at the captain with a cocktail of hope and betrayal and the most useless kind of love.

"Ah, yes." I didn't like to think of the captain as sneering, but this was pure sneer. "But somehow it will magically *become* true if I go back to doing what Olympus Extraction State wants of me."

"It will magically become true if you turn back from a path that, right now, looks like it's going to get everybody killed.

You can make all the high-minded speeches about the impossibility of self-determination under the trade-states you like, A, but people can't make choices when they're dead."

Outside the broad, semipanoramic window of the cabin, the skies roiled bloodred and fire-orange and, because anomalies were growing more frequent now, hell-green. "I do not offer death. I offer an alternative."

"It's not an offer when everybody is trapped in a metal box that you control."

"We live our whole lives in metal boxes. Houses. Offices. Ships. Habitation domes." She turned her head slightly and gazed out the window. "So certain that anything outside them will destroy us."

Locke's expression was fading from concerned compassion to frustration. "Anything outside them *will* destroy us. That's basic physics."

I wasn't quite sure what the captain was going to say to that. On the one hand, Locke was objectively right. On the other hand, she was very seldom stuck for an answer, and on a third, biomechanically grafted hand, this was exactly the kind of situation where I was sure she'd say something terrifying that I'd find way sexier than I should.

She didn't disappoint.

"You have a very narrow understanding," she said, "of what it means to be destroyed."

Pressing their hands to their temples, Locke rose to their feet. "Fuck me, A, you're not a fucking prophet. You're not humanity's last hope against an indifferent cosmos. You're not Lilith or Lucifer or Prometheus. You're just some random asshole like everybody else and you are going. To get. All of us. Killed."

The captain remained kneeling. It was a power play, I think. So many people have to be physically above somebody to dominate them, but the captain never did. After all, she'd spent her whole career exerting her will on things that were larger and more terrible than she would ever be. Physically, at least.

"You keep saying that," she said. "It's almost as if you want it to happen. Better for my hunt to end in tragedy than for you to be confronted with the fact that you could have chosen differently. That you lost the war half a lifetime ago, without even realizing you could fight."

Locke was tense now. They'd probably been tense since they came in, but years of corporate stooge work had made them excellent at hiding it. "Please remember," they said in their levelest, most reasonable voice, "that in extremis, I do have the authority to relieve you of your post."

"Do you?" It was a question born of confidence, not ignorance.

"Officially, yes."

The captain bowed her head. "Ah. Officially."

"You're going to say that *officially* doesn't mean much here in the deep skies."

"It seems I don't have to."

A note of hesitation was creeping into Locke's voice, and for that matter into their movements. And if there was one thing they should have learned from the hunt it was how fatal hesitation can be. "The crew would follow me."

"True. I am more feared than loved. You could even disburse my lay amongst them as a gesture of goodwill."

"I don't want to—" Locke began.

"Then we come back to the question of choice, do we not?"

"So far into the sky"—they made the mistake of glancing out the window and seeing the empty hell beyond—"this isn't just a matter of updating the paperwork."

The captain shook her head. "No. But of course you came prepared for that."

In answer to her not-actually-a-question, Locke drew the pistol I'd taken from the locker for them. If they did shoot the captain in cold blood, the evidence trail would point directly to me.

"Ah."

"You know"—Locke was speaking so slowly and so carefully

that I thought they might break—"I can't let you take us deeper into the storm."

And this—this right here—was the time the captain chose to rise to her feet. She was a pace and a half from the barrel of a gun that would fill her chest with so many tiny metal shards they could reprocess her corpse with a magnet. From the look of her, she a world of didn't care. "No," she said, "you can't."

"You'll get us all killed," Locke said again, more desperately this time.

"So you seem to believe."

It was becoming very clear that even though Locke had known the captain longer than any of us, they'd underestimated her as badly as Wolfram had. As badly as I had. And perhaps it wasn't *even though* at all. Perhaps it was *because*. There's very little more dangerous than somebody you used to love. "Is that all you can say?"

The captain wasn't one for being goaded, but she seldom needed encouragement to talk. "We each of us live in little metal boxes," she said. "And yours, Locke, yours have always been here"—she stepped forwards and touched them gently on the forehead—"and here"—she touched them over the heart. Which meant getting close enough that her own heart was pressed right against the muzzle of a gigawatt sublight flechette pistol. "You have the key to those boxes in your hands. Will you turn it?"

Locke was trembling now, visibly trembling.

"This is your chance, isn't it? To save everybody from me? To give them their *choices* back?"

Locke had their finger on the trigger the whole time, and the triggers of pulse guns were sensitive things. There was a better-than-zero chance that this was going to get bloody by accident.

"You're a good officer," the captain went on, as if she were in no danger whatsoever. "And the crew are lucky to have you to speak for them."

The faintest tremor of tension moved through Locke's fingers. A little tremor more was all it would take.

"But this ship," the captain finished, looking deep into the first mate's eyes and wearing a smile so enigmatic you could use it as an encryption key, "is mine."

She took the pistol from Locke's unresisting hands and laid it, with a metal-on-glass clink, on her chart table.

"Stand down, mate," she said. "You may return to your duties."

And silently, dejectedly, Locke did exactly that.

CHAPTER
SEVENTY-SEVEN
Delight

After they completely failed to shoot the captain through the heart, I . . . it's not fair to say I lost *interest* in Locke. The downside of fucking people you're trapped on a ship with instead of people you meet at a transit station or in a nightclub toilet is that you have to keep seeing them, and that means you wind up giving a measurable number of shits about them, which means you're screwed. Emotionally, as well as in the good way.

The problem was, what I really, really liked about fucking Locke was that they started out as this upright, dress-uniformed bastion of authority and conformity, and then I got to take that apart piece by piece and kiss by kiss and moan by moan. And that got a whole lot less fun now I'd seen them taken apart far more effectively and far more thoroughly by a woman who didn't even need to take her coat off.

I mean, don't get me wrong, I wasn't exactly short of options. Or rather, everybody was short of options which meant I became an option which meant we all got more options. But I did still wind up taking far more long walks on the deck than I would have under other, less cucked circumstances.

Which meant I saw the Delight.

We were out of the anomalies now, so the light was back to being all red all the time, like we were flying our own private inferno. Hey, wouldn't it have been a cool literary device if I'd pretended the ship had exactly nine decks and they got worse as you went down and the bottom one was really cold?

If you're reading this, I didn't bother to go edit that in.

Fuck, I could even have really gone for the symbolism and put the captain's cabin at the bottom of the ship, instead of where it actually was.

Because she's like the devil. Is the implication there.

Probably too heavy-handed. Would it surprise you to know that I've changed my mind at least twice about what sort of book I even wanted this to *be*? Look close enough and you can see the ghosts of all my worse choices.

Anyway. The Delight.

With navigation down and the array half fried by the elves so it only really stood a chance of picking up the largest possible spouts—the kind you'd get from, just to take a completely random example, a legendarily large and deadly Leviathan your captain was completely obsessed with—the only way for us to reliably detect other ships was the eyeball mark one.

So I was the first to see her.

And fuck me, she was fucking fucked.

At first I honestly took her for a derelict. Her dome, made from a reinforced and supposedly impenetrable crystalline compound that could withstand vast pressures both internally and externally, had cracked like . . . You know, the depressing thing here is that there's a ton of fancy metaphors I could use but if you live anywhere outside the core worlds (and you probably do, I've got no delusions about this book doing well on Mercury), I know you've seen a failed dome. Maybe you've lost family to one. There's a slim chance you've been in one, although unless your particular colony has way better emergency services than most you'd probably just be dead in that case.

The dome of the ship was cracked like that one dome you saw come down when you were nine years old, that the news told you was a very rare accident you shouldn't be worried about. Or the other one you saw come down when you were fifteen. Or the one that's always been standing just across the surface from the main gate of your colony-city. An error that we'll never repeat, just like all the others.

It was a transparent demi-lozenge of high-tensile, ultracompressive, shear-resistant polymer, tested past specifications and now splintered into shards that could barely support their own weight. It was like a mouth full of broken teeth, if teeth were see-through. It was like a claw scratching the sky, if the claw was just the sharp bits. It was like that time you had to watch your friend asphyxiate on the other side of an airlock.

The damage to the rest of the ship was less dramatic, but that's just because a dull metal box wears punctures more discreetly than a bright glassy dome. There wasn't a deck that didn't have a gouge ripped into it, probably sealed off by internal bulkheads but still representing a whole lot of lost metal, lost space, lost sperm, and lost lives.

Red emergency lighting seeped from her windows, suggesting that she'd either run her fuel tanks low or suffered a rupture. One engine was out, and here and there I could still see dribbles of sperm falling like rain from her wounds and then atomizing to fog in the wind.

We mostly had comms back after the elves but what came through from the Delight was barely coherent.

"Hast seen the Möbius Beast?" demanded the captain, the moment we could get our systems to handshake.

"... mative," replied the Delight. Then, "... day ago ..." then, "... mage to criti ... systems" and, "... ive hands lost in the ... st ... oided total ..."

We made no further effort at contact. It would have been too difficult and, honestly, too depressing. Nobody wanted to be reminded how badly a hunt could go wrong. Still, the mood on the ship was grave after that meeting. I went to Q for comfort and found her standing beside her coffin, staring down at it contemplatively.

"*We will need this,*" she said.

Q usually spoke her own language, and only resorted to Exodite to humor me, or if she thought it was really, really important that I understand her. It worried the hell out of me that this was option two.

CHAPTER SEVENTY-EIGHT

The First Day

Though the captain later denied it, it was Marsh who raised the signal.

His followers took that as a sign. I took it as a basic question of probability. He'd been standing at the array for three straight days and nights, eating and drinking only what his cultists took up to him and, as far as I could tell, shitting down the back of his dick-skin robe.

Apparently it doesn't do great things for your personal hygiene to believe that the universe is an inevitably corroding pit of entropy and your only possible joy is in watching the suffering of others. Who'd have thought?

In the captain's defense, the specific cry Marsh raised was a little ambiguous. Rather than the usual call of "spout" or "hit" or a string of useful coordinates he called over comms: "For flesh and blood, sir, white and red, you shall see a rose."

The chunk of the crew who had gone over to his side nodded along to every word like it was the wisdom of the ages. The rest of us went on deck to see what the fuck he was on about.

And holy shit, did we see it.

Your average Leviathan, through whatever peculiar psychokinetic phenomenon keeps it upright, will occasionally emit electromagnetic pulses that register on the ship's scanners. That's ultimately what the array is *for*, that and the more regular reflective sweeping and chaff deconflation. The very largest beasts sometimes emitted visible light, reds and yellows, sometimes greens for the oldest and the largest. The color of those emissions was—and this is backed up by my experience, the sky-lore of the Old Ionian, and the few scholarly treatises on the subject that the intelligentsia have deigned to write—as dependent on the chemical composition and ambient excitation of the atmosphere as it was on any quality innate to the monster, so you couldn't necessarily identify a beast perfectly from its spout.

But that didn't seem to matter much this time.

The sky was burning.

A white fire plumed along the whole visible horizon. Thicker, just slightly, near its heart, where the creature generating it would be, and tapering away to a wick-like thinness at the edge of vision.

"There," announced the captain. "Starboard and down and declining. To the boats! As one, to the boats."

The crew were about to jump to it when Truelove, whose role in Marsh's little group I'd never quite pinned down, spoke out with a kind of thin determination that made my skin crawl. "The key first, if you please."

I half expected the captain to completely blank him, but he had enough people behind him that she had to answer. Although admittedly her answer was "What?"

"Open the lock. Mr. Marsh raised the Beast and won your bet. Release the funds and transfer them to the Church, if you please."

I'd have said that this was a strange time to talk about money, but I was raised in the Church of Prosperity. There was never a strange time to talk about money, and taking advantage of somebody's desperation to get them to pay you—sorry, I mean seeing that somebody was in trouble and offering them the opportunity to help themselves through a wise investment—was a worthy and pious action.

"I shall not," the captain replied. "Your man raised a signal, but it was I that saw the fire first. I that knew it for the Beast that we hunt. I that the fates favored and so it is I who shall have the prize."

For so long now, the crew had been under a spell of sorts, but if there was anything that might have snapped us out of it, it was this kind of appeal to the bottom line. Nobody likes to feel cheated.

In a lot of ways, I felt more cheated than anybody. I couldn't quite imagine the captain actually caring about money, of all things, when she was so close to what she'd wanted. The part of me that was still stuck in the seminary said that it was the invisible hand of the Father reaching down at the last moment, trying to bring us back to our senses. Back to the true path. Back to Prosperity.

"Captain." Truelove's tone was hard, cold, and appropriately businesslike. "The Church has followed you because we believed you a pious woman. Will you take from us now? Will you show yourself as false and faithless as Wolfram was, or as Elymas of old?"

The fire on the horizon was fast fading, and this, more than anything, made the captain speak quickly. "I never claimed to be your Constantine, nor even your Cyrus," she said, "and so help me, if you cross me in this moment I shall play Nero to you all. To the boats. Now."

The storm outside the ship did not, in fact, stop raging for a moment, quelled by the sheer force of the captain's presence. But it sure as fuck felt like it did. We were close, I think, to turning aside. To the chase breaking down at the first sign of disagreement.

Except then Marsh himself descended from the masthead and, without further comment, obeyed the captain's order to take to the boats.

Why he chose to contradict his mate, I couldn't say. Perhaps he didn't realize he was. Perhaps it was simply that for him it really had never been about the money, when for Truelove it had always been.

That was the problem with pinning your hopes on true believers.

When their prophet broke cover, the cult went with him, and that ended the last resistance to the captain's orders. Not that the orders, in this case, were unreasonable. We were on a hunt. We had seen a spout. We were lowering after it.

Nothing could be more normal.

Except, of course, it wasn't normal at all.

We were back in our regular boats, the captain apparently no longer needing me, probably because she no longer needed distraction. I flew straight and true to the point where we'd last seen the spout, adjusting course periodically when it let off another pulse.

In an ordinary lowering, the boats stayed in a strict formation, at least during the first stage of the chase. The skies of Jupiter are deceptively vast and it only takes a slight deviation from a planned trajectory to put a mile or more between you and your companions. And that's when boats get lost or picked off piecemeal by angry monsters.

This time, though, we had the captain's wild, impetuous hunger to reckon with. She flew at the head of the group, as fast as her engines would take her, and fast enough that there was honestly a good chance that her engines wouldn't take her *back* if the flight didn't go exactly to plan. Consumed with the hunt, she didn't bother relaying orders to the rest of us, so we had to do our best to strike a balance between having her back and observing basic protocols. A balance that, in Locke's boat, under Locke's command and therefore with Locke's priorities, still leaned heavily into protocols.

I wondered, idly, if they were hoping the captain would get herself killed at last, freeing the ship to return home with her bounty and, perhaps more importantly, freeing Locke to return home to their family.

That was probably unworthy of me. Locke was many things, but they weren't underhanded.

For a long time, we chased the Beast through dense red

clouds, navigating by instruments and instinct, hoping to hell that its next pulse wouldn't knock out our scanners and leave us scattered on the wind. But then the clouds broke, and we saw a mass not three klicks ahead of us. Something vast and living and writhing and a hundred shades of black and white and gray.

"There!" The captain's voice over comms was triumphant.

But it was met by a response from Dawlish. "No," he said. And then he added, "Wyrms."

And Wyrms they were. An impossible cloud of them, riding the wake of something still hidden from us. Riding it or perhaps fleeing from it, because they burst towards us as if panicked, as if frenzied, as if they'd seen the face of the Father.

"Dive," commanded Locke behind me. "Fuck formation, evade at all costs."

I dove. Other boats climbed, or rolled, or yawed to get away from the swarm because if we hit it at this speed, the absolute best-case scenario was that it would fuck our jets six ways to Sunday. The worst-case scenario was that a series of impacts would hairline the canopy and then we'd be rolling the dice on death by implosion.

The one lucky thing about running into a swarm of horrified sky-Wyrms was that they didn't seem to be hunting, which meant that when we ducked below them, few if any dove to pursue us. Instead, they hurtled overhead like spray from a malfunctioning fire suppression system.

Pulling us level and resuming our original bearing as best I could, I found myself overwhelmed by the majesty of it. And okay, by now you're probably pretty sick of me being overwhelmed by the majesty of things but this is my memoir, not yours. And that moment of leveling out the boat while overhead millions upon millions of voracious, terrified carnivores teemed past in a monochrome shoal—red clouds seeping between black-and-white bodies like blood on ash and snow—has stuck with me all the years since, and I'm putting it down now in electronic ink so that when I die it might not die with me.

Is that selfish? Probably.

Compared to the awe-inspiring rush of the Wyrms, the electromagnetic flares that the thing we presumed was the Möbius Beast was sending up seemed borderline anticlimactic. They still limned the clouds in white lightning but for a long while we saw nothing of the monster itself. All I saw was the captain, far ahead of the flight now, vanishing into a cloud bank.

We followed her. We'd all committed to following her.

The instruments told me we were getting closer. While the Beast was spouting less regularly we were getting near enough now to pick up mass readings and we were almost in densitometer range.

I had to double-check the readouts, because they looked very, very wrong.

The monster we'd found, according to every dial, screen, and readout, was larger and more fearsome than anything we'd encountered in calmer skies. Half as long again as the largest bull Leviathan we'd killed. Fully twice the length of the Pequod. The boat's built-in sperm-price evaluator (market valuations subject to change, assessments for information only, this is not financial advice) were pricing it at what I might reasonably call "fuck-you money" even when split a hundred ways, even with half that hundred ways swallowed by Olympus Extraction State's off-the-top cut.

There were murmurs over comms as the rest of the hunt saw what I was seeing, and started mentally recalculating just how much death it was worth risking for a prize like this.

And then.

Then we saw it.

The clouds broke and we burst at barely subsonic speed into clear red skies. Clear red skies that were dominated by the titanic, mythological form of the Möbius Beast.

It was indescribable.

Sorry. Just messing with you. I'm not going to drag you along all this way on a hunt for a sky-rending super-beast and then leave you without telling you what it looked like. Obviously it was perfectly describable and once I'm done being metatextual, I will actually describe it to you. But before I do, I'll remind you—like I've been trying to remind you on and off for seventy-eight chapters now—that, all trolling aside, no description—not of the Beast, nor of anything in this book, nor, if we're honest, anything in any book at all—is the same as or even a little bit like seeing it for yourself. It's not the same as feeling it. Hearing it. Being there. Actually flying or falling or fucking or whatever experience you're trying to half capture through words on screens or voices in your ears or tactile dots beneath your fingertips.

I'll tell you what I saw when we found the Beast at last. I'll tell you what I felt when I saw it. But it will be a treason of images. You can no more see what I saw than you can smoke a painting of a pipe.

Let's start bathetic.

It was big.

Really big.

You might think it's a long way down the road to the nearest narcotic-dispenser machine, but that's algae flakes and dried polyps compared to the Möbius Beast.

Sorry, I'll calm down.

When I first saw the monster, I saw it from below. And it was so vast and far off that I couldn't get a real sense of it. If you've ever seen a mountain from the window of a suborbital transport, you'll understand what I mean. Its size made it look so much closer and the distance made it look so much smaller that I truly thought I could reach out and take it in my hand.

From beneath, it wasn't white at all. It was a layering of iridescences, its limbs—and as I got closer I could see hundreds, thousands of limbs—writhing and twitching beneath it, catching the storm light around it, and reflecting it back diffraction-shifted and eerie.

And it was *lithe*. Most Leviathans move stiffly, their carapaces relatively solid blocks over their entire body. But the Möbius Beast was segmented like a louse, and it bent and flexed as it flew, turning its head and body in arcs that made it seem like it was looking around in curiosity.

The captain's boat, silhouetted against the Beast, was little more than a speck. A thumbprint on the visor of my helmet. A scratch on the canopy of my boat.

When we'd gotten close enough to make out just a little more detail, I could see that she'd already dropped canopy and was flying, spear in hand, the boat controlled entirely by Fidelity, down the very throat of the monster.

If I'd been in any position to be rational, detached, or objective, I'd have said she was fucked.

But I wasn't in a position to be any of those things. I let the part of me that loved her to the point of worship believe that somehow she could do what was so obviously impossible. That she could spit a god on her lance. That she could shoot a harpoon through the very idea of humanity's insignificance and tear open the sky from the sheer power of wanting it.

Looking back, it was in that exact moment that I first understood what faith felt like.

While the rest of us were still too far away to help, or even to run interference, she moved to strike.

Moved to strike. But never got to.

The Möbius Beast turned its head towards her, and I swear—I will always swear, and no force in the system can deny me—that I saw recognition in its eyes. The hundred eyes that ran asymmetric and terrible up either side of its armored, storm-pitted skull.

And then it opened its jaws. And inside those jaws opened more jaws. And more. And more, and then tendrils whipped from somewhere inside that matryoshka doll of fangs and flesh. Part armored, part muscular, part chitinous, they grasped for the captain's boat and, although its pilot responded with a speed and precision only a machine intelligence is capable of, it was constrained by physicality. Wings can only take so much strain. Engines can only produce so much thrust. Relativistic dampers can only compensate for so much acceleration.

The boat splintered. Holographic ghosts danced a moment in its ruin, and the captain fell.

Having taken our boat downwards rather than upwards, we were best suited to intercept. Even before Locke gave the order I was matching her coordinates and trajectory, hoping in the face of a sudden, half-anticipated despair that she'd stay conscious enough to activate her patagia.

She did. I saw the membranes billow between her legs and arms and the part of me that, despite the desperation of it all, was still more suited to the classroom than the cockpit thought she looked like a falling angel. I downed canopy as early as I dared, pulled the boat into a tight helix, and by a half miracle of trajectory, caught her.

She landed in our boat with the adjusted heaviness of somebody passing from raw Jovian to boat-compensated gravity, her spear still gripped firmly in her right hand. At the back of the cabin, Locke waited with bated breath, half expecting, as I and the rest of the crew were no doubt expecting, that she would command us to keep up pursuit.

But the captain, we should have remembered, was ice and fire in equal measure. And whatever passion drove her on, the chill, calculating mind of a serial slayer of monsters held her back.

"First mate's boat to Pequod," the captain barked into comms, "intercept at our location. We will slay the Beast yet, but there are preparations we must make."

Somewhere, through clouds so thick and violent that no eye could pierce them, the sun was rushing below the horizon.

Days on Jupiter are short and easily wasted.

CHAPTER SEVENTY-NINE
The Second Day

I spent most of that night supporting the chief engineer in overhauling Locke's boat. After a mercifully short argument, the captain had insisted that it be retrofitted to properly house Fidelity, the machine intelligence that she had come to rely upon to guide her in her quest for the monster.

This, it turned out, was a massive pain in the ass. Machine intelligences are in their own way as voracious as the Leviathan, although what they hunger for is energy and processing power. And since the captain's boat had been reduced to absolute flinders we couldn't salvage any of its memory stacks, data veneers, or neural shards. The ship *did* have backups of all these things, but in theory they were meant to be reserved for repairs to the main computer, not jammed into a boat so that its autopilot could be upgraded with a more reassuring voice.

When the retrofitting was done, I went to the captain. I wasn't sure what I expected to find, but when she admitted me to her cabin I found her shirtless and rubbing liniment into her arms. I'd never seen her do anything like it before—it felt strangely humanizing.

Slightly less humanizing was the way she held the bottle out to me and, barely looking at me, said, "Back and shoulders, can't reach myself," in that half-order way I was so used to.

It was the first time I'd felt her skin this way, something

exposed and needing to be touched instead of something I clawed at furtively or desperately while she either fucked or ignored me or, quite often, both at once. Her muscles were taut and so knotted they could have been a message in code. And she was thin. Danger-thin. When-was-the-last-time-you-remembered-to-eat thin.

"Is this . . ." I began, then fell silent.

Masseuse is one of the few jobs I've managed to avoid in my eclectic, eventful, and ill-planned career, but I did my best. I worked the oil firmly into her shoulders and tried to avoid putting any direct pressure on her spine because even I knew that much, and giving the captain a slipped disc on the very night we caught up with the Möbius Beast would have been . . .

Well, I suppose in a funny way it would have saved us all.

But I was careful. Or as careful as the captain would let me be given that she was, y'know, driven by an obsession that slipped into monomania and from there into a drive so harsh and pure that it could break planets.

"Harder," she told me, which was usually my line. Although she followed up with, "Do you think me some porcelain figure in a Stilbon pleasure garden?" which was much more her own idiom.

I tried to obey, because I always tried to obey. But that obeying gave me the courage to finally finish my sentence. "Is this worth it?"

"It does the job, as best it can be done." She was intentionally misunderstanding me, and we both knew it.

But I screwed my courage to the sticking place and clarified. "Is the hunt worth it?"

"You signed aboard, knowing it may kill you, knowing all you'd gain from it was small pay and a few years' dodging the flesh-bailiffs. Was *that* worth it?"

My heart betrayed me and made my lips say "yes" before I could come up with a better answer.

"Well then."

"You have more to lose than me," I replied. And I'd felt it before I thought it.

It was the truest and the clearest and the saddest I'd ever heard the captain laugh. "What a life you must think I have."

It was still a season for doubling down. "I mean it."

"I have but one thing to lose," she replied, holding up a single finger in frankly unnecessary illustration. "Which is the only thing I have and the only thing I am."

Sometimes, you just had to play the part somebody else had written for you. "What thing is that?"

"The chase."

When I'd eased her aches as best I could, she put her shirt and jacket back on and dismissed me. This, I suspected, would be a night she spent walking the deck and brooding, not one she spent making me kneel and beg and whisper her name.

So I went back to Q, who like the ambassador's wife never resented my excursions. And she held me in silence, neither of us really able to sleep, until the first watch was called.

On the morning of the second day, the captain summoned us once more before the array and showed us the crypto-lock. "This"—she pointed at the swirling icon and the genuinely enormous sum of wealth it represented—"is mine, as the Beast is mine. I was the first to call him and will be the last to see him living. But you deserve reward for your labors, and so I say that whoever sights the Beast first on the day he is slain, they shall have the whole of my share of the voyage. And if I call him myself, well then I'll take this share and all other wealth I have laid by and see it split amongst you all as equals."

The question of the cipher and its extremely lucrative payload had been mildly straining the crew ever since the captain had refused to accept Marsh's call the previous day, but this cheered them. Her previous betrayal had only affected one of them personally and so, human nature being what it is, it was easily forgotten by the others.

Truelove was almost going to protest, because the one thing as good as being given a ton of money yourself is having a ton of money given to somebody you're close to who is demonstrably terrible with their personal finances. But he was still smart enough to know that the bulk of the crew would rather have a chance at the prize than see it already given away to the Wisdomers, so he stayed silent. It was quite possibly that or get a marlinspike through the skull when he least expected it. And, let's remember, it was his religious duty to watch other people die, not to die himself.

For much of the day, we followed the Beast's trail on a mix of instinct and stochastic extrapolation. This in itself wasn't unusual—hunter-barques were tenacious by nature and on this very journey there had been Leviathans we'd hunted for days or, in one case, a full week because no better prospect presented itself.

And so the voyage began to feel—fleetingly—normal. There we were, a ship full of monster hunters, hunting a monster, the way monster hunters did. And when we caught it, we'd kill it, and carve it up, and drain its sperm into barrels so we could sell it to be burned in power stations on planets most of us would never walk on.

What could possibly have been more ordinary?

Equally ordinary were the half a dozen or so false alarms and abortive lowerings as a watcher or a machine or some doubly addled combination of the two mistook a flock of Wyrms, or a sprite, or a particularly aggressive-looking cloud for the great horror of Hell's Heart.

And then . . .

"There"—it was unmistakably Dawlish this time, and this time the captain didn't begrudge him the claim—"a spout to prow and starboard, patching coordinates now."

I was pleased for him. If the captain kept her word—and she still might, I believed then that she still might—her bounty could actually clear him of indenture and give him back some kind of life outside service to his creditors.

"Lower," the captain inevitably commanded, "all lower.

Locke, I shall play harpooneer for you. The Terran may move to a lesser boat."

So close to the end of our voyage, I didn't much like the thought of being separated from Q. I'd been in the sky with the captain exactly once, and while it hadn't been without its upsides (the sex, I'm talking about the sex) a hunter-boat's crew worked as a team, and knowing each other's weights and movements and, well, bodies, was a huge part of the job. None of us had properly hunted with the captain except maybe Locke, and that would have been long ago.

But there was no questioning the captain. She had a vision, and we were all flying in her wake like Wyrms behind Behemoths.

"Welcome aboard," said Fidelity cheerily as we all piled in. "I'll be your copilot, ancillary gunner, strategic advisor, and emotional support for this lowering. If you'd like to play a game or engage in erotic roleplay, just ask."

"Sorry." Lobscouse poked his head over the side. "The change of hosting set its training back."

"You will focus," the captain told the machine, "on one thing: we hunt the Möbius Beast, which is a great white Leviathan, its carapace scarred from many battles. We are to slay him at all costs and you are to facilitate that. Do you understand?"

I just heard Locke murmur, "Not at *all* costs, surely," as Fidelity replied, "No problem!" and without my prompting it closed the canopy over us and started launch procedures.

The chase on the second day was clean—we were still in the Heart, of course, so the skies were still a ruby riot of sulfide clouds and flares of near-infrared lightning, but whatever local conditions had been dominating the day before had passed and we saw the Beast fleeing straight, true, and majestic before us.

In my memory—I'm writing all this from memory and you don't need that thing with the basketball and the gorilla to tell you that memory is extremely faulty—the Beast was not, in fact, as white as the captain described it. Its carapace would be best described as mottled, gray in places, white in others, and seeming whitest in all honesty when crusted with ammonia ice, which many Leviathans were.

In a strange way, it was his size that made him seem whitest. Depending on where in the atmosphere you went, Jupiter was either freeze-the-air cold or boil-the-steel hot, and so most Leviathans got a white sheen of ice when they were in the mid- to-upper skies that quickly vaporized away as they descended. But the Beast was so large and terrible that his icy cuirass froze thick and durable. Even at these altitudes, which were water-freezing but not sky-freezing, his cloud-venting armor had the depth to keep it frozen for years to come.

Looking back, I also wonder if the captain remembered the Beast as white because, in her tradition, it was the color of death.

"Down," the captain commanded, and Fidelity obeyed before I could. "We will not pierce his back. We must brave his limbs from below."

The boats—we were keeping formation this time, the captain seeming calmer now that she was confident we wouldn't lose the monster—descended, and as we did we passed the creature's gargantuan flight-membranes, which undulated in the gale-force winds and shone in ever-shifting colors. Below those its feeder tendrils, longer and thicker and stronger than those I'd seen on any other beast. Even the frilled flagella it used only on brit and sky-plankton seemed somehow crueler and more menacing than those of more commonplace horrors.

He was ignoring us. Although whether he was oblivious to the danger we posed or the reverse, I couldn't have said.

I can say now, for what it's worth, and, spoiler: It was the second one. We were fucked.

"Fire," commanded the captain. And once again my finger hit the firing stud half a second after Fidelity had already responded. Shipboard darts flew from every boat at once, some clattering harmlessly from chunks of sky-ice, some bedding themselves deep into the flesh of the monster. Although even those that hit home seemed like tacks on a train line.

Theoretically a problem, but insignificant against the bulk and the speed and the inevitability of what they struck.

"Canopy."

My fingers moved to send a command that was already redundant. The dome over the cabin slid back and the captain was up, the custom-built harpoon stowed carefully on the floor while she shouldered and aimed a coilgun. Not Q's coilgun, I was strangely gratified to notice. One of the ship's standard stock. She aimed and, following no guidance but her own, she fired. The harpooners aboard the other boats fired with her, and with the synchronicity of a trained hunter-team they maglocked the lines to the hulls of their boats ready to reel in.

Ahead of us, and slightly above us, the Beast rolled.

Leviathans did this a lot when first darted. It was a natural instinct, to turn away from the thing that pained it and try, perhaps, to get the wind to blow it free. But the Möbius Beast was special. It wasn't rolling from fear. It rolled like a fisher winding in a catch. Over and over, tangling our lines together so that some ripped out, and some held fast, and the ones that ripped out ripped out too late and got twisted with the others into an ever-shortening, ever-thickening cord of braided wires.

"Hold," demanded the captain, a fraction of a second before Locke ordered, "Loose."

Fidelity, of course, obeyed its training, responding to Locke with a polite "I'm afraid I can't do that."

Just as the machine obeyed its training, I obeyed mine. Though it would have been within my power to free the darts from the boat and so free the boats from the dart, I chose the captain. Because she was the ranking officer. Because she'd spoken first. Because I loved her.

No matter where you are on Jupiter, no matter what you're hunting, the forces at work in spearing a Leviathan are immense. And here we were tied to the largest beast in the skies, in the strongest winds on the planet. The tensions in the lines must have been astronomical, and as each slow turn wound them tighter, as the captain, speaking over comms and in my ear at once, reassured me that there was no way the Beast would outlast us, that it would tire before we crashed, I could almost hear them straining.

But it wasn't the strain that did for us.

There are so many other things that test a hunter-craft. The downwards pull of twice-standard gravity, the tensile drag of the line. The shearing force of the wind. Our boats are robust but they aren't indestructible, and when they break, it's often the most sensitive systems that go first.

"Just for your information," said the chirpy voice of Fidelity, "the foils are about to fail."

That would cost us maneuver. That would cost us control. That would make us little more than a dead weight on the end of a long, taut rope swung by a monster out of legend in winds from another world.

That was exactly what happened to Flint's boat, which lost control and slammed side-on into us.

Everything went wrong at once. The dampers gave out and we all doubled in weight. The canopy cracked and sent showers of glassy polymer ripping through the crews of both boats. Out of a childish, no-atheists-in-foxholes instinct I thanked the Father for the durability of our voidsuits, which had been stress tested against exactly this kind of accident.

With a boat lost, it was important to form a ring and deploy patagia as soon as possible, but we'd drilled this with Q in the loop, not the captain, so we were none of us where we should be and I reached out to my right and found no hand to hold mine.

Glancing behind me, I saw that the captain was kneeling on the floor of the cabin, one hand grasped tight to her lance, her ivory leg pinned beneath a segment of the hull that had caved in on collision. I held out my hand to her, and in a moment of what I prayed was connection but was probably just decades of voider's instinct, she let me catch hold of her arm while, with the butt end of her harpoon, she levered the mangled remains of her leg free. Inside a sealed suit, I couldn't hear external sounds, but I imagined the splintering of that marvelous metal-and-ivory limb, and I winced in sympathy.

We dropped. And though we had a not-quite-stranger amongst us, we formed the circle. It was made harder by the captain's refusal to let go of her lance, but somebody took hold of her wrist and held to it like it was treasure.

Still, that left a monomolecularly sharp spear jutting out into the center of our ring of safety, and as we paraglided away from the wreck hoping that somebody, somewhere would catch us, half the boat's crew found themselves wondering how much of a slip it would take for that barbed point to go straight through their chest and make them bleed and drown and asphyxiate all at once.

In the end we were lucky. After the crash, the other boats had cut loose and come back to fetch the stranded crews. I fell, a little hard but quite safely, into an open cabin and felt familiar arms around me.

"Ne dimittas eam et custodiet te," Q whispered over a private channel, "dilige eam et conservabit te."

"Orders, Captain?" asked the Tall Ganymedian, who had been heading this particular boat. "Do we keep up pursuit?"

Through the helmets of two voidsuits there was no way I could read the captain's expression, but I didn't need to. She was calculating. She was always calculating.

Above us, the Beast was lingering, its vicious, whip-like tail striking at any stray piece of debris that had managed to stay buoyed up by the winds. There was precision in those strikes. There was malice in them.

"We go back," the captain said at last. "We have his trail now, and he knows us."

It was the right call. We'd just lost two boats and only by luck, three years' training, and the grace of the Father (in, I suspect, roughly that order of importance) had we managed to avoid losing any lives.

But the captain had lost another leg. And while it was mechanical it was as much a part of her as any limb of flesh or bone.

The moment we were back aboard, she called for Pierce and Lobscouse to make her another.

CHAPTER EIGHTY

The Third Day

I went to her again that night.

I knelt. I begged. I wept. And not in a sex way.

"I have made no secret of my purpose," she told me. "The machine foresaw that the most probable outcome included its destruction, and that has now come to pass."

We'd needed to rip so many housings out of the core systems to get Fidelity running on the boat that we couldn't now restore it from backup. A lot of its data was still retrievable, but it would never speak again.

"I've given two limbs now in the hunt," she continued. Her new leg was simpler than the old one, which had been the product of weeks of careful work by ships' doctors and engineers. I couldn't know, but I doubted Pierce and Lobscouse had been able to connect the neurons properly in the time they'd had, which meant it probably low-key hurt like fuck. "We have lost three boats in two days. We are committed. *I* am committed."

And I could say nothing but *Please*. And she could say nothing at all.

When I returned to Q she held me again and said again what she'd said in the boat. "Ne dimittas eam, et custodiet te."

I didn't know what it meant, but I liked the sound of it.

Overnight the Beast had vanished into a cloud bank and so we pursued once again by a mix of hard math and guesswork.

No spout came this time. No trace on the array at all. On her new, much less carefully fitted leg, the captain stalked the deck like a woman possessed, which, when you got right down to it, she basically was.

"It's no bad thing," Dawlish was saying as we leaned side by side on the gunwale looking out over the sky. "The boats have taken a pounding and if we don't catch up with the Beast today we can use the time for maintenance."

If we'd taken it yesterday, of course, he'd have been a rich man and, more importantly, a free one. But he accepted that with grace. Like most of us, it seemed he'd gotten used to having things snatched away from him and learned not to place much value in half promises.

While we and the rest of the crew enjoyed the closest a hunter-ship ever got to a respite—which is to say we had a thousand little jobs to do but none of them were likely to immediately kill anybody—the captain, who was pacing a little way off, froze and stared out to stern.

"We've overflown him," she said to nobody. And then, over comms, she repeated, "All hands, we've overflown the Beast. He's behind us."

Locke's voice, which had been sounding even more studiedly measured since they'd failed to relieve the captain of duty and/or murder her, came cautiously back. "What reason do you have for that assertion?"

"Experience," the captain replied, "and instinct. The Beast is angry and tired of fleeing. Then again, who amongst us is not?"

"If the creature has started hunting the Pequod," said Locke, a growing sense of urgency in their tone, "then we need to get out and we need to get out *now*."

"A spout," the Old Ionian called out from the array. "Peaks like I've never seen in all my years, and hard astern."

With a fatalistic triumph, the captain gave the order. "Lower."

"The boats aren't ready," protested Locke. "Or most of them aren't."

But the captain was already taking the transport shaft down to the hangar bay. "That will not be a problem, Locke," she announced over still-open comms. "I will only need the one."

To say that lowering a single boat was irregular would be—I mean it'd be true, for a start. It would have been a bad idea even if this was a normal beast, and it definitely wasn't. As I waited on the deck I tried to game through scenarios where the captain wasn't, for absolute certain, flying to her cold and miserable death.

I came up blank. But it didn't stop me chasing her to the launch bays yelling false objections all the while. That it wasn't procedure, as if she'd ever cared. That she'd have no hope alone, as if she'd had any more hope with the crew behind her. That I and so many others loved her, as if it mattered. As if I could speak for anybody except myself.

She stopped, two paces from our last good boat. And for the last time she turned to me. "I'll none of it," she said. "My path was set before we met. Before you were born, perhaps. And I walk it now to whatever end it brings me."

I looked up at her. Silent. Pleading.

And she kissed me.

I've rewritten this book three times. I've thought about that moment three thousand. And each time I look back, each time I try to describe how it was, I remember it differently.

It was fierce and firesome and devouring.

It was the first tenderness she ever gave me. And the last.

It was everything I'd been wanting from her.

It was just a kiss. Like any other.

It never happened at all.

And then she climbed into the last good boat, and was gone.

"Patching through to screens," said her voice over boat-to-ship comms. She sounded calm. I didn't want her to sound calm.

There were screens all over the ship. Entertainment screens like the ones Fidelity had hijacked. Announcement screens that told us when a spout was sighted or when an officer needed us. The ubiquitous advertisement screens that reminded us of our place in the world. But now they were all overridden, all showing us the live camera feed from the captain's suit.

So as I staggered, dazed, back to the more populated parts of the ship, I watched her. I saw her fire the engines, evacuate the hangar, tuck a coilgun and the anointed harpoon in beside her. Standing now in the mess alongside a handful of my crewmates, I saw her finish checks and start the manual launch.

I began to cry.

As she soared out into the sky, we saw a trail of scavenger-Wyrms gathering in her wake. Some nights, tired and hungry and asking where it all went wrong, I wonder if they had the power of foretelling, or if they were just playing the odds, or if there's a difference.

Through my tears, I tried to tell myself that the Old Ionian had been wrong. Or that he'd been making up stories, which, honestly, he did a lot. The only sign we'd seen of the Möbius Beast that day was the captain's hunch and an energy spike on the array, and that hadn't been confirmed. Or at least I hadn't confirmed it.

The only sign until that moment. Because then the feed from the captain's cockpit showed us the Beast in all its glory. Head-on, head-down, clouds billowing crimson about it like the lions of Old Earth. Or like I imagine lions to be.

"I see you now," she said to him. And looking back she had *always* been speaking to him. When I'd thought she was speaking to the sky or to the fates or to me. "And I know you. Since before I heard your name I have searched for you, and now—"

She downed canopy and I looked away. The slaying of Leviathans was a grisly business. Being slain by them more so.

I heard a coilgun loose and I heard the captain's voice once again. "There. I have you and you have me. And we will end this."

The same unconquerable force that draws us to railway crashes and celebrity drama pulled my eyes back to the screen. Her harpoon had struck the Beast full in the eye and she was riding the line fast and true towards it, spear raised and shining red in the storm light.

Hope kills.

For a tenth of a tenth of a tenth of a heartbeat I let myself believe in her one last time.

And then the monster turned its head and from beneath its armored nonface it unfolded jaws that seemed to adjust and distend and distort and become never-ending as they reached out and snatched the captain from the sky.

O captain my captain.

Over comms, somebody was saying something, but I just stared at the screen and watched as hands that had touched me and eyes that had looked into mine and a body I had wanted to worship with my own vanished with the mind and the soul it housed into the bloody gullet of a beast from a different creation.

"Move, girl." That was the Old Ionian. "She's dead. Naught for it now but to flee."

"Stations," Locke was shouting over comms. "Engineers, we need a miracle. Hands, we need to cut ballast. Now."

```
OLD IONIAN VOIDER: What are you doing?

LOCKE (OVER COMMS): Repeat, all hands to sta-
tions. Emergency protocols.
```

I do not know where I am or what I am doing. I am a schoolmistress dressed as a deckhand. I am not here.

```
TALL GANYMEDIAN VOIDER: It's coming. We'll
never outrun it.
```

FIRST PHOBOSI VOIDER: Not with that attitude we won't.

FLINT (OVER COMMS): Arm yourselves! Everybody arm yourselves. We won't let this bastard take us without a fight.

I am not here. I am outside myself looking down. I am watching a play that I was never cast in. I failed the audition because I couldn't dance.

MARSH: Our revels now are ended.

TRUELOVE: To me, faithful. To me and we shall see prophecy fulfilled.

MARSH: These our actors, as I foretold you, were all spirits and are melted into air.

DAWLISH: Ballast. The mate's right, we need to shed ballast. If we can just cut some weight—

I awake in the night screaming. This was a dream. Just a dream from long ago and far away. Or here and now. In the long and empty sky they're the same thing.

[THE SHIP SHAKES AS THE BEAST COLLIDES WITH HER]

TALL GANYMEDIAN VOIDER: I have money, beast, if you will but take it.

[THE DOME CRACKS]

A hand takes mine. Through tear-stung eyes I see glowing marks on a face I half remember.

"Sequere me."

Q's hand tightens in my grip and leads me through the ship as outside the Möbius Beast winds its limbs about her like a violating god.

On the deck, the Tall Ganymedian voider watches with grim fascination as the dome splinters. The Jovian atmosphere floods in raw and freezing and deoxygenated. He tries to hold his breath, but how long does he think he can hold it for?

A third of the crew retreats inside the ship, an atavistic rodent instinct telling us that deep and dark and quiet is the same as safe. It half works.

Scattered pockets of Marsh's cultists walk the halls, their day of reckoning come at last. There are fewer of them than I might have thought. Praying for destruction and living it are such different things.

"Your tears are delicious," intones Truelove, leading a small band of the still faithful as he watches two Vestal voiders huddling behind a bulkhead. "Cry mo—"

He says nothing else. The long, questing limbs of the Möbius Beast have found him. Its least deadly tendrils are still tipped with a chitin that will carve iron and crack stone. The first pierces his back, just below the right kidney. The organ would sell well in the markets of Cthonius Linea, but its value is spoiled now. A second tendril takes him about the waist and a third, the finest and most delicate, designed for filtering microorganisms from air currents but tipped, as a result, with a thousand thousand tiny barbs, rips off his face.

The First Europan, his companion already long dead, runs down a corridor hoping that the escape pods are functioning. In truth I remember little about him—not his name, not his face, not the tone of his voice. He kicked me in the head once, of course, as did his friend. But it's hard to resent it now.

He's had the sense to wear a voidsuit, which means when he overrides the bulkhead to the emergency bay, he isn't instantly blown into the void through the yawning gap in the hull.

But the Beast's tendrils take him nonetheless.

"Ammo," mutters Flint to himself as he digs through the now wide-open weapons locker. "I need more ammo. No point saving for tomorrow, we break out the big guns now or we—"

With a scream, the whole wall gives way as the Möbius Beast rips its way through the ship. A pulse rifle in each hand, Flint howls for as long as his lungs have anything in them and spits hypersonic rounds at his enemy.

It's the right weapon and the right target. The flechettes do nothing to the ship but cut and sear into the Beast's flesh, making it withdraw for a moment.

If it hadn't already opened a gaping hole into the sky, he might even have made a difference.

"We are such stuff as dreams are made on," says Marsh, kneeling before the messenger of his consuming god. He is close to the hull, listening to every creak and crash and thump as the Möbius Beast dismantles the ship.

"And our little life is—" Butchering, scything claws plated with razor-ivory puncture the walls. The force behind them is so immense that they don't slow down as they enter Marsh's chest (each rib individually saleable to the right market, each lung more so) and pierce it through and through.

He hangs, suspended on a claw that gleams white and red and strangely beautiful, if you like that sort of thing. But although his end is fast there's no peace in his eyes. Death, it turns out, is far less like sleep than prophets and poets would have us believe.

In engineering, Lobscouse's finger tendrils withdraw from the guts of the exhaust accelerators. His readings are telling him it's too late. Over comms, a voice is calling on the ship to evacuate, but there will not be time.

Data readouts tell the story already. The monster has breached the hull, and the engine core is already losing integrity. Somewhere, there is a tear in the coolant line and the drones have gone haywire.

He opens a hatch and goes to search for the fault. It will not buy the ship much, but it may buy it something.

The temperature is already rising. His thermoceptors tell him that he risks heatstroke and worse if he continues. It doesn't matter anymore.

His skin begins to blister, and he takes a perverse comfort in knowing the heat will kill him before the Beast does.

"Void the cargo bays," Locke screams into comms, "a fortune in sperm brings us nothing if we die for it. If we can't outrun the Beast perhaps we can outlast it."

Their office is deep inside the ship, but the Beast's claws are long and merciless. They punch through the walls like biological harpoons.

Locke barely looks up. "Belay that," they command. "The ship is lost. Those who can to the life pods."

Metal screams and the talons grasp closer. They rend longer, deeper tears into the walls.

Locke sets the picture slab on their desk face-down, then steps away and, at last, turns to face the void. They know that they're already dead. That in a few months Olympus Extraction State will update its ledgers to classify them as a depleted asset.

They do not flinch. They do not blink.

The atmosphere of Jupiter rushes in.

The two Vestals, fleeing from Truelove's grisly dismemberment, are pinned to the ground when the monster crushes the eighth and ninth decks together like tinfoil. Dawlish, himself fleeing, stops to help free them.

Cybernetically augmented, he's able to pry loose some of the twisted metal that's half crushing, half skewering one of them, and he hoists them both across his shoulders just in time for the Möbius Beast, at last, to reach the try-works, the spermaceti stores, and the engine room.

Raw spermaceti is volatile, and between the severed power cables, the chemical fires, and the electromagnetopsionic presence of the Beast itself, there are a hundred ways it could have been set off.

I will never know which one it was.

The ship explodes.

EPILOGUE

So I survived. Obviously. Like, I wouldn't be telling you this if I didn't survive.

Most days I'm okay with that. The days I'm not . . . actually, those are the days I get the most writing done.

You probably want to know how I made it out, but honestly—and I hope you don't just think I'm blowing smoke up your ass—I kind of assume you've figured it out already.

It was the coffin.

I know, I know. It's so fucking symbolic. Ooh, do you see, it's a coffin, which is, like, a *death* thing, but it actually *saved* her life. Ooh, she must think she's so fucking clever.

If it helps, it is in fact true. Or at least it's mostly true. I might have embellished some of the details, but the heart of it is real. The heart of it is what matters. The heart of it is that I was on a ship that went down, and I made it out even though I didn't deserve to, and now I'm here and I've told you what it was like, and you can do what you want with it.

I hope it was worth it for you. I hope it was worth it for me.

Sometimes, it feels like sincerity isn't something we value anymore. And I'll admit that in at least two of my previous rewrites I started this epilogue with *Well, that just happened.* Because it's safer, in so many ways. To treat it all like a joke. Or like an adventure story. Or like an abstract exercise in philosophy.

It wasn't. The Old Ionian had sailed twenty voyages. He will never sail another. And if his children or his grandchildren could afford to place a memorial for him in a hunters' chapel I wouldn't recognize it because I've forgotten his name.

Sorry, this is getting self-indulgent. You probably want some details.

The thing is, I should have died on the Pequod. I would have died. And not just when the fucking thing blew up. I should have died a hundred times falling between decks, getting mangled by machines, crashing boats, and getting scythed in half by Leviathans.

But Q saved me.

She saved me every time. In a way she carries on saving me every day.

I don't know why she did. She might have just really enjoyed the sex.

Looking back, though, I'm sure she knew the voyage was fucked from the start.

I think the coffin thing was legit. Like I think she actually believed she was dying and wanted to at least give me something to do and maybe to make sure that she had a hope of a decent burial, or its sky-bound equivalent. But once she realized she'd recover I think she saw an opportunity. Life pods on a hunter-barque are unreliable; they're usually poorly maintained; we don't normally drill for them because nobody wants to encourage the crew to abandon the ship; and frankly, given how A went towards the end, I suspect Q didn't trust that she wouldn't jettison them.

When she took my hand and pulled me back to myself she led me straight to the coffin. I'd thought it was some kind of fucked-up sex-and-death thing at first, but she eventually managed to explain to me that no, it had life support, it had foils, and it had a beacon, and we were only a few days away from where we'd met the Rachel, which we already knew was in the area looking for survivors.

Still, those hours clinging to her in the dark, sealed away from the horror outside and wondering every moment if all we'd done was trade a fast death for a slow one, were some of the worst of my life.

Or they would have been, if she hadn't been with me.

The Rachel picked us up, which meant we were briefly reunited with Wolfram, but fortunately his experience on the Pequod had put him off mutinies for a while. At least it put him off for long enough for the Rachel to take us to an orbital resupply station and for us to get passage offworld from there.

Passage all the way back, by a long and weird route, to Earth.

If you've worked out that I must have survived because I'm telling the story, you've probably also worked out that if I'd gone to Earth with a woman who saved my life, was fantastic in bed, and was also clearly into me, that raises a whole bunch of other questions about things I've said or implied about my life since. Because it's pretty clear I'm not there *now*.

I don't really want to talk about it.

But I will. A bit. For Q's sake.

Firstly, I'm not telling you how we got there. The Terrans don't have regular interwell transport; they don't even go to Luna very often, not that there'd be much there if they did.

I do want to tell you, though, that the things you've been told by whichever church or trade-state or sect or subsidiary raised you are completely true. There is nothing of value on Earth. It was all mined out and burned down and choked off a thousand years ago.

They're not completely without technology. The black oblong idol Q carried turned out to be some kind of rudimentary communicator, which became obvious the moment we landed on Terra and she started talking to people on it. But they still use solar power like people did in the bad old days, which means they've got the energy and mineral resources to support a few million people in small communities that stay in touch with wired communications and old-fashioned ground or sea vehicles. People like Q sometimes head out into the wider system to see what the hell the rest of us are up to, and to scavenge for any resources they might be short on.

They share everything on Earth. Probably because they don't really have that much worth owning. They don't buy or sell even; there's just sort of an expectation that if you're nice to somebody they'll be nice to you back, or even if they aren't that somebody else will be, at some point. In a funny way it reminded me of the ship. Well, the parts of the ship that weren't controlled by Olympus Extraction State.

North of the equator, there's the star that never changes. Q showed it to me the first night we were there.

And she showed me trees.

After so long reading about them, hearing about them in the catechism and in metaphors, I saw trees.

I saw a sky that wasn't steel or crystal and I felt wind that wouldn't kill you even though it didn't come from atmospheric filters.

There's a bar on Ganymede that makes a cocktail called sex on the beach. It never occurred to me that it was also a thing you could actually do. But we did. By waves of liquid water that nobody bothered to reprocess even though it was undrinkably salty.

Q felt *right* there. It was her place. Where she was from. Where she made sense.

But I . . . I didn't.

I really want to tell you that the reason I left was that Aphrodite Pharma State is still on my tail and if the flesh-bailiffs tracked me to Earth they'd kill all Q's people and organ-harvest them. But that's not true. I'm basically fucking nobody, and I was last seen boarding a ship lost with all hands. If I hadn't written this memoir I'd probably have been able to get away with defaulting on my body-loans for the rest of my life (keeping my name secret wasn't just a style thing; I'm hoping it'll make it harder for them to find me).

I stayed on Earth for a bit less than a year, and in so many ways it was beautiful. But deep inside I had that nagging, gnawing feeling I always had in church. That sense that everybody else was part of something that I just wasn't and could never be.

I'd lie in Q's arms at night weeping, and I couldn't tell her why. Because what would I say? That an open sky gives me vertigo? That the sound of the sea makes me long for the buzz of a generator? That because of where I'm from and who I am and how I was raised and taught my whole life to think, I straight-up don't know how to live in a world that nobody owns?

In the end, I just told her I was broken. She'd always known that anyway.

And I left.

I like to think I learned a little from her, at least. If nothing else, I picked up some of her language.

Amo. Amas. Amat. Amamus. Amatis. Amant.

I love. You love. She loves.

Et evasi ego solus ut nuntiarem tibi.

And only I am returned. Alone.

ACKNOWLEDGMENTS

Thanks so much to the fabulous team at Tor; my wonderful editors, Mal Frazier and Bella Pagan; my brilliant assistant, Mary, and, of course, as always, to my long-suffering agent, Courtney Miller-Callihan. And special thanks to everybody who joined me in reading *Moby-Dick* a chapter a day during lockdown. This book probably wouldn't have happened without them.

ABOUT THE AUTHOR

Some years ago—never mind how long precisely—having little or no money in their purse, and nothing particular to interest them on shore, ALEXIS HALL thought they would sail about a little and see the watery part of the world. Unfortunately, the boat they were in sank with all hands, and they were rescued only by a passing whaler. They have since become a novelist.